The Chalky White Substance [1980]—Tv of a vast canyon, overlooking a dried-o from unnamed and uncountable nucl air. It is the chalky white substance scramble in darkness and fear, fighti. sources of water, food, shelter and human warmth. Ma... gled in this apocalyptic world together, but the primal instinct for survival will lead to betrayal. "What a huge creature, what an immense beast [God] must have been to have left such enormous white bones when He died. . . . Endlessly long ago, the bones of Him now turned to powder that blows and blows about His broken creation. . . ."

The Day on Which a Man Dies (an Occidental Noh play) [1960]—"Does life have room for death?" asks the Japanese narrator of this play about an American artist and his mistress ending their volatile relationship in a Japanese hotel. The artist (inspired by Jackson Pollack, whom Williams first met in the summer of 1940) is doomed, and how he takes his own life is viewed from both Eastern and Western points of view. Their story is told in scenes that include traditional techniques from Noh, Kabuki, and Gutai, and utilize elements of performance art, including—much ahead of it's time in American theater—art created on stage with a spray gun. Williams dedicated this play to his friend, the writer Yukio Mishima.

A Cavalier for Milady [c. 1976]—One of several plays Williams' designated as "for the lyric theater," *A Cavalier for Milady* is a psychological and sexual fantasy in which two late-middle-aged women go off for an evening in New York City with male escorts from agencies such as "Companions for Madam" and "Cavaliers for Milady," leaving behind an adult daughter in the care of a hostile "babysitter." The adult daughter, Nance, who is dressed in the clothes of a Victorian child, quickly drives off the unhappy babysitter and spends the evening with a Greek statue that has "come to life" as an apparition of the great Russian dancer Vaslav Nijinsky. Free from the control of Diaghilev, the dance world, and demands of the flesh, Nijinksy's apparition keeps Nance company, but cannot alleviate her loneliness or satisfy her desire which forced celibacy have made almost unbearable.

The Pronoun 'I' (a short work for the lyric theatre) [c. 1975]—A parody of classical forms and contemporary mores, this "short work for the lyric theatre" concerns the reign of haggard old "Mad Queen May" of England—disguised behind a mask, the hag is actually the young and beautiful "Fair Queen May." Her narcissistic and nearly naked young lover, the poet Dominique, can only begin his terrible poems with the pronoun 'I.' Queen May can only watch as revolt and anarchy bring her reign to an end, but she is energized by the arrival of a "Handsome Young Revolutionary" who steals into the castle to murder her. A campy frolic with touches of absurdity, *The Pronoun 'I'* ends with a mob scene and a lover's embrace.

The Remarkable Rooming-House of Mme Le Monde [1982]—In the attic of a rooming-house in London (a "rectangle with hooks") lives Mint. Unable to use his legs, Mint is forced to grab onto giant hooks which hang from the ceiling, and swing from hook to hook to get around; he is sexually abused on a regular basis by one of Mme. Le Monde's many male "children"; he is taunted with food that is withheld by his landlady or doled out in stingy amounts; and on this day he is visited by an old friend, Hall, from their private childhood boarding school, Scrotom-on-Swansea, who shows no interest in relieving Mint's suffering. The play is filled with images that resonate from the work of Beckett and Genet; then with the arrival of Mme. Le Monde herself—*"a large and rather globular woman with a fiery red mop of hair that suggests a nuclear explosion, as does her voice"*—Williams' sinister vision of cruelty gets only darker.

Kirche, Küche, Kinder (An Outrage for the Stage) [1979]—Three giant turning screens in primary colors allow the stage to become the *Kirche* (church) or the *Küche* (kitchen) while the gigantic "daisy of daytime" and "moon-vines" mark the hour. Miss Rose, an organist; the First Lutheran Minister of the Island of Staten, known as "Papa;" the ninety-year-old and pregnant Fräulein Haussmit-zenschlogger; the adult *"Kinder"* lewdly dressed as children; and "The Man" (a blond young hustler in leather pants, and self-proclaimed descendant of "the old kings of Ireland") populate this bizarre and bawdy play written in the style of the theater of the ridiculous. With its vaudevillian humor, cartoon sets and characters, ribald takes on religion and marriage, and sentimental Irish ballads, this is one of Williams more chaotic mixtures of the comic and the dreadful—slapstick and brutality are interwoven to create a breakthrough piece of performance art.

Green Eyes, or No Sight Would Be Worth Seeing [1970]—A young couple are spending their honeymoon in a hotel in New Orleans' French Quarter when they wake up one morning to find the "girl's" body covered with mysterious bruises. The "boy," on a short leave from serving in Vietnam, is enraged and blinded with jealously. As they fight—over her evasiveness, his courage or cowardice in war, their fears and expectations for a life together—it becomes clear that the bruises are no mystery at all. Reminiscent of *Talk to Me Like the Rain and Let Me Listen* and *27 Wagons Full of Cotton*, *Green Eyes* raises the stakes much higher. In his most candid and intense exploration of sexual extremes, Williams builds anger and fear to a communion of total emotional exposure.

The Parade, or Approaching the End of a Summer [1962]—"Love makes some people charming but it makes me dull." In the summer of 1940 Williams lived in Provincetown, Mass., where he fell in love for the first time—the man was Kip Kiernan, a dancer and Canadian draft dodger. Their affair lasted most of the summer, until Kip broke it off and left with a woman. Williams immediately drafted *The Parade*, which he finished in the 1960s. This play, which is related to the full-length *Something Cloudy, Something Clear,* not only presents a completely unguarded story about gay men, but also a portrait of passions unrequited and passions denied, that reveals the depth of compassion which can be found in friendship. "Williams' words poignantly call forth the passion, and heartbreak of a long-lost summer." —*Cape Cod Times*

The One Exception [1983] —An artist named Kyra has had a complete emotional breakdown from which she shows barely any signs of recovery. Now taken care of by a friendly nurse, Kyra's greatest terror is to be sent to a mental institution. Just days before she is to be committed, Kyra is visited by Viola, an old friend from the art world who has come looking for a loan. Viola offers only "hilarious" updates and gossip about the successes of all the people who abandoned Kyra to her madness, those who left her alone and now judge her the only one from their group to be a failure—the one exception. "*The One Exception* betrays the playwright's desperation in his old age, a terrible fear of loneliness and the cruel isolation of despair." —Bruce Weber, *The New York Times*

Sunburst [c. 1980]—Miss Sylvia Sails, a famed actress of the American stage who long, long ago chose retirement at the peak of her career ("not willing to decline from it") is awakened at 3:00 in the morning by Giuseppe, a handsome and felonious night clerk at her live-in hotel. It becomes clear soon enough that Giuseppe is after Miss Sails' extremely valuable sunburst diamond ring, but Miss Sails' knuckle is so swollen that the diamond ring cannot be removed from her finger unless her finger is removed from her hand. Held hostage, Miss Sails resists her captors, Giuseppe and his boyfriend Luigi, by reciting Shakespeare, by drinking with them, and most of all by endurance, outlasting them until daybreak when help arrives and the sun finally comes up.

Will Mr. Merriwether Return from Memphis? [1969]—Women are waiting for their lovers to return, widows are longing for their husbands who will never return, and young ladies are just discovering the fires of early love—sounds almost like a parody of a Tennessee Williams play, and in a strange way it is. With ragtime cakewalk dancers, séances and ghosts, hags called "the Eumenides" who weave the fate of the characters, a "Romantically Handsome Youth," a gay French instructor, a banjo player in every scene, and the triumph of love found, love returned, and love forgiven, Williams wrote a comedy as full of poetry as of pleasure. "Pensive and muted, a violin to *Camino Real's* trumpet, *Mr. Merriwether* laces together reality and fantasy, the romantic spirit and the appearance of actual cultural heroes of the past, such as Van Gogh and Rimbaud." —*Time* magazine

The Traveling Companion [1981]—It not incidental that Williams was seventy when he wrote a short play about the relationship between a younger and an older man—an inexperienced hustler full of sexual potency named Beau, and an older, insecure writer named Vieux. Emotional and personal compromise can be assumed in a relationship in which one person is a paid "assistant," "secretary," or "companion," but here the questions of who is being used or who is using are not so simply decided. With an underlying wit, Williams reveals the common needs that keep traveling companions together. "*The Traveling Companion* offers subtle humor and the affecting story of two people demanding something concrete from each other, along with something more elusive." —David Cuthbert, *The Times-Picayune*

BY TENNESSEE WILLIAMS

PLAYS

Baby Doll & Tiger Tail

Camino Real

Candles to the Sun

Cat on a Hot Tin Roof

Clothes for a Summer Hotel

Fugitive Kind

A House Not Meant to Stand

The Glass Menagerie

A Lovely Sunday for Creve Coeur

Mister Paradise and Other One-Act Plays:
> *These Are the Stairs You Got to Watch, Mister Paradise, The Palooka, Escape, Why Do You Smoke So Much, Lily?, Summer At The Lake, The Big Game, The Pink Bedroom, The Fat Man's Wife, Thank You Kind Spirit, The Municipal Abattoir, Adam and Eve on a Ferry, And Tell Sad Stories of The Deaths of Queens...*

Not About Nightingales

The Notebook of Trigorin

Something Cloudy, Something Clear

Spring Storm

Stairs to the Roof

Stopped Rocking and Other Screen Plays:
> *All Gaul is Divided, The Loss of a Teardrop Diamond, One Arm, Stopped Rocking*

A Streetcar Named Desire

Sweet Bird of Youth

The Traveling Companion and Other Plays:
> *The Chalky White Substance, The Day on Which a Man Dies, A Cavalier for Milady, The Pronoun 'I', The Remarkable Rooming-House of Mme. Le Monde, Kirche Küche Kinder, Green Eyes, The Parade, The One Exception, Sunburst, Will Mr. Merriwether Return from Memphis?, The Traveling Companion*

27 Wagons Full of Cotton and Other Plays:
> *27 Wagons Full of Cotton, The Purification, The Lady of Larkspur Lotion, The Last of My Solid Gold Watches, Portrait of a Madonna, Auto-Da-Fé, Lord Byron's Love Letter, The Strangest Kind of Romance, The Long Goodbye, Hello From Bertha, This Property is Condemned, Talk to Me Like the Rain and Let Me Listen, Something Unspoken*

The Two-Character Play

Vieux Carré

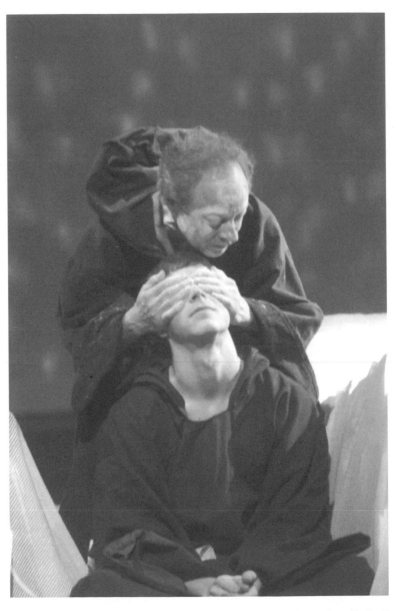

Jeremy Lawrence as Mark and Ben Greissmeyer as Luke in *The Chalky White Substance*, directed by David Kaplan at the Tennessee Williams/New Orleans Literary Festival. *Photograph courtesy of Earl Perry.*

THE
TRAVELING
COMPANION
AND OTHER
PLAYS

TENNESSEE WILLIAMS

EDITED, WITH AN INTRODUCTION, BY
ANNETTE J. SADDIK

A NEW DIRECTIONS BOOK

The Traveling Companion and Other Plays is published by special arrangement with The University of the South, Sewanee, Tennessee.

The epigraph for *Will Mr. Merriwether Return from Memphis?* from "To Brooklyn Bridge" by
Hart Crane copyright © 1972 by Liveright Publishing Corporation.

The Chalky White Substance was originally published in issue 66 of *Antaeus* in 1991; *The Remarkable Rooming House of Mme. Le Monde* was originally published in a limited edition in 1984 by
the Albondocani Press, New York; *The One Exception* was originally edited by Robert Bray and
published in *The Tennessee Williams Annual Review,* Volume 3, in 2000; *Will Mr. Merriwether
Return from Memphis?* was originally published in *The Missouri Review,* Volume XX, Number 2,
1997; *The Traveling Companion* was originally published in 1981 in *Christopher Street* magazine.

Cover and front matter design by Rodrigo Corral.
Text design by Sylvia Frezzolini Severance.
Manufactured in the United States of America
New Directions Books are printed on acid-free paper.
First published as New Directions Paperbook 1106 in 2008
Published simultaneously in Canada by Penguin Canada Books, Ltd.

Library of Congress Cataloging-in-Publication Data

Williams, Tennessee, 1911-1983.
    The traveling companion and other plays / Tennessee Williams ; edited with
an introduction by Annette J. Saddik.
        p. cm.
    "A New Directions Book."
    Includes bibliographical references.
    ISBN 978-0-8112-1708-8 (alk. paper)
    I. Saddik, Annette J., II. Title.
PS3545.I5365T73 2008
812'.54—dc22
                                2007049520

New Directions Books are published for James Laughlin
by New Directions Publishing Corporation
80 Eighth Avenue, New York, New York 10011

CONTENTS

INTRODUCTION:
TRANSMUTING MADNESS
INTO MEANING

"A new, plastic theatre . . .must take the place of the exhausted theatre of realistic conventions if the theatre is to resume vitality as a part of our culture."
                    —Tennessee Williams, Production Notes to
                                    The Glass Menagerie (1945)

"Man: I'm working with absolute freedom for the first time."
—Tennessee Williams, *The Day on Which a Man Dies* (1960)

"The future accepts more readily what the present rejects."
                    —Tennessee Williams, 1963

In a 1979 interview, Tennessee Williams condemned the use of violence as a means of political resistance, prompting his interviewer to remind us that Williams' form of social protest had always been peaceful, using art to resist injustice, challenge the status quo, and promote understanding. In this way, he concluded, Williams' "life effort" has been "transmuting madness into meaning." Williams' vision of "madness"—this chaos of life that surrounds us—and its expression into artistic forms evolved from his earlier plays of the 1940s and '50s—*The Glass Menagerie* (1945), *A Streetcar Named Desire* (1947), *Summer and Smoke* (1948), *Cat on a Hot Tin Roof* (1955), *Suddenly Last Summer* (1958), and *Sweet Bird of Youth* (1959), for example—to what he called in 1972 "freer" forms that "fit people and societies going a bit mad," the forms that would dominate his work of the 1960s, '70s, and '80s. While Williams expressed his dissatisfaction with dramatic realism as early as 1945, introducing anti-realistic dramatic conventions into much of his early work, it is with the later plays presented in this volume that he finally achieved the "new, plastic theatre which must take the place of the exhausted theatre of realistic conventions" that he called for in his Production Notes to *The Glass Menagerie*.

Williams' later plays responded to the changing social climate of the 1960s and '70s, as well as to his own personal growth and artistic development. During the 1960s, Williams claimed to be moving deliberately away from what the critical establishment saw as the essentially realistic dramatic forms that dominated his early career to a more anti-realistic, fragmented, and playful type of drama characteristic of new theater movements of the time. The critics, however, failed to evaluate these works on their own terms and often dismissed them altogether. They did so either because they didn't expect this sort of avant-garde style from Tennessee Williams, because they didn't fully understand the plays and weren't willing to look at them through a different lens, or because of personal biases. Williams insisted that the deliberate changes in style and presentation since his early plays disturbed the majority of critics, and that their nostalgia for plays such as *The Glass Menagerie* prevented them from accepting his later experiments with language and dramatic form. He was so prolific during these later years that not every play he wrote was completely successful. But most of these plays represent conscious *and* successful departures from his earlier work, and deserve a central place in American experimental drama.

Between 1945 and 1961 Williams had a total of eleven plays produced on Broadway, and virtually all were successful with critics and audiences, winning major awards—Pulitzer Prizes for *A Streetcar Named Desire* and *Cat on a Hot Tin Roof*, as well as four Drama Critics Circle Awards, a Tony Award, and dozens of other accolades and prize nominations. Commercially successful Hollywood films were made of almost all of Williams' plays from the same period, starring major names such as Elizabeth Taylor, Marlon Brando, Vivian Leigh, Katharine Hepburn, Montgomery Clift, Paul Newman, and Geraldine Page. After *The Night of the Iguana* in 1961, however, no Williams play was to win any major award or experience any significant measure of critical success or popular acclaim. Yet he kept writing diligently every morning, no matter where he was, often getting up as early as 5 A.M., and continued to oversee productions of new plays until his death in 1983. These plays opened primarily off-Broadway or regionally, and in a 1975 interview Williams told Charles Ruas that his "great happiness in the theatre" was now "off-Broadway and off-off-Broadway."

Most of Williams' later plays have been published by New Directions, and a partial list of them suggests how prolific he was after 1961: *The Milk Train Doesn't Stop Here Anymore* (1963), *The Gnädiges Fräulein* (1966), *I Can't Imagine Tomorrow* (1966), *Kingdom of Earth* (1968), *The Two-Character Play* (*Out Cry*) (1973), *In the Bar of a Tokyo Hotel* (1969), *Small Craft Warnings* (1972), *The Red Devil Battery Sign* (1975), *Vieux Carré* (1977), *A Lovely Sunday for Creve Coeur* (1978), *Clothes for a Summer Hotel* (1980), *The Notebook of Trigorin* (1980), *Something Cloudy, Something Clear* (1981), and *A House Not Meant to Stand* (1982). The two films that were made of Williams' later plays—*The Last of the Mobile Hot Shots* (1970), a version of *Kingdom of Earth* with Lynn Redgrave and James Coburn, and *Boom!* (1968), a version of *The Milk Train Doesn't Stop Here Anymore* starring Elizabeth Taylor and Richard Burton—were not successful, yet John Waters, always a connoisseur of the outrageous, has asserted that he loves *Boom!*, calling it "The Best Failed Art Film

Ever." Legend has it that Joseph Losey used to brag that he was the first director to ever lose money with Taylor and Burton.

The twelve late plays included in this volume are available here for the first time in a definitive edition. Manuscripts of these plays exist as multiple drafts in archives at The Harry Ransom Humanities Research Center at the University of Texas at Austin, The Harvard Theatre Collection, The New Orleans Historic Collection, The Department of Special Collections at the University Research Library at the University of California, Los Angeles, Columbia University Library, and in the private papers of Williams' friends, agents, publisher, and former secretaries. Most of these plays have never before been published, have received only limited productions, are just now being produced, or have never been produced at all.

While the plays that Williams was writing during the 1960s, '70s, and '80s retained many of his earlier concerns with the ravages of time, the predatory nature of human beings, and the inevitable struggle to survive and endure, these late works express these concerns in a much more direct and brutal manner. The subtlety of symbolism and metaphor in the early plays is replaced with an irreverent representation of the human tragicomedy (to use Samuel Beckett's term), as a new social permissiveness allowed Williams to turn to a sense of the outrageous, the "camp," and the extreme in dealing with intersections of the personal and the political. The outrageous comic elements in several of the late plays, such as *Kirche, Küche, Kinder* or *The Remarkable Rooming-House of Mme. Le Monde*, for example, are countered with a sense of the brutality of human nature stripped of cultural artifice, reminiscent of the work that was being done in France by Antonin Artaud and Jean Genet from the 1930s to the 1960s.

Artaud's theories can best be seen in practice in the plays of Jean Genet who, although he had read little of Artaud's work, shared his goals for a primarily ritualistic theater that focused on accessing pre-logical consciousness and primitive existence through the symbolic, where action is separated from function. Both writers sought to invert the conventional moral code of good and evil, and, therefore, what was deemed "good" in traditional society (culture, repression, self-control, obedience to the law) became universally evil, and what was considered "evil" (nature, sexuality, violence, power) was encouraged as good. Like Nietzsche, both Artaud and Genet wanted characters to be judged outside of good and evil, and Artaud's "theater of cruelty" (outlined in his 1938 treatise, *The Theatre and Its Double*, translated into English in 1958) forces the spectator to confront the harsh facts of a cruel world and his or her own isolation. These writers explored the contradictions and hypocrisies of bourgeois society and often championed the "primitive" impulses of the socially marginalized.

Williams may not have been directly familiar with Artaud's work, though it is likely he encountered Artaud's theories during his studies at the New School for Social Research in New York City in the 1940s, and he certainly knew Genet's work. In fact, in a 1960 essay in *New York Magazine*, Williams cited Camus, Genet, Brecht, Beckett, Anouilh, Ionesco, Durrenmatt, and Albee as his "fellow defendants" in writing honestly about life. The ending of *Kirche, Küche, Kinder* is unmistakenly Brechtian, as the Man "crosses right through that fourth 'invisible' wall" to exit through the theater, and the Wife directly addresses the audience, leaving it to "ponder those questions" that she poses "for a while. . . ." *Kirche, Küche, Kinder* contains moments remarkably similar to Artaud and Genet's work as well. For example, a scene in the play, where the Minister throws a paper bag over the character Hotsy's head, "plops a huge Bible under [her] derriere and mounts her [as] members of the press" burst in, is reminiscent of the same dismissal of good taste in Count Cenci's violent pursuit of his daughter as he seeks to rape her in Artaud's *The Cenci* (1935), an adaptation of the texts by Shelley and Stendhal. There are similar scenes of brutal rape and incest in *The Remarkable Rooming-House of Mme. Le Monde*, where "a delicate little man with a childlike face" named Mint, whose "legs are mysteriously paralyzed," is repeatedly raped by his landlady's son, a "muscular" boy "hung like a dray horse" who is "kept on the place for . . . incestuous relations with the lady." In Williams' *THIS IS (An Entertainment)* (1976), the role-playing of the Count and Countess that opens the play is strikingly similar to Genet's *The Maids* (1947), and the invasion of the hotel by the mob outside, with the Countess's lover, General Eros, leading the way, echoes the ending of Genet's *The Balcony* (1956), as does the ending of *The Pronoun 'I,'* wherein a young revolutionary steals into the Queen's chamber to assassinate her as the revolution escalates.

Many of Williams' later plays in this volume focus less on elaborate language and character psychology, and more on the physical and visual aspects of theater, which was in keeping with the new dramatic styles in the theater that emerged during the 1960s. These included not only the work done by Samuel Beckett, Harold Pinter, and Edward Albee, for example, that was often influenced by the theories of Artaud and Bertolt Brecht, but also avant-garde theater troupes such as The Living Theatre, The Open Theatre, The Ridiculous Theatrical Company, and the Performance Group, which all did away with realism—the style that had dominated the American theater in the 1940s and 50s—and experimented with theater conventions from all over the world. In fact, in 1959 Williams went to Japan to visit the writer Yukio Mishima and was introduced to Kabuki theater, which very much influenced his later work. Williams had first met Mishima in 1957, and dedicated *The Day on Which a Man Dies* to him. The earliest complete version, published here, was begun in 1957, and is dated in Williams' handwriting as finished in 1960. *The Day on Which a Man Dies, The Milk Train Doesn't Stop Here Anymore*, and even *The Night of the Iguana* and *I Can't Imagine Tomorrow* all exhibit the influences of Japanese Kabuki and Noh theater—a style of theater initiated in the fourteenth-century that combines dance, music, and story-telling. Mishima wrote a series of modern Noh plays that were published in English in 1957, and two years later New Directions published Ezra Pound and Ernest Fenollosa's *The Noh Theatre of Japan*. It is this spelling of "Noh," rather than the equally common spelling "Nō," that Williams uses. As director David Kaplan notes, Williams seems to also have been aware of the Japanese art movement known as Gutai, since *The Day on Which a Man Dies* appropriates aspects of Gutai performance art, particularly the death of the painter and the eccentric means by which paintings are created and destroyed on stage.

These later plays were often anti-realistic in their treatment of language, character, and action. Like Japanese Noh and the avant-garde European plays of the time, meaning is found not through language, but in the pauses and silences, in what is not said. Instead of the long, poetic passages for which he had become famous, Williams' later plays often contain truncated and unfinished sentences. In *The Two-Character Play*, for example, the broken dialogue exists mostly for diversion, as in the plays of Samuel Beckett, to subdue the characters' sense of panic, and the play expresses a contemporary sense of dread. Instead of characters with elaborate psychological and social backgrounds in the style of realism, the characters are generically named "One" and "Two" (*I Can't Imagine Tomorrow*), "Boy" and "Girl" (*Green Eyes*), or "Man" and "Woman" (*The Day on Which a Man Dies*). Instead of conventional plot development, themes are explored, often along with a collage of images. For example, a later draft of *The Day on Which a Man Dies* ends with an explosion of political and cultural images, much in the style of the artist Robert Rauschenberg.

Throughout his career, Williams was aware of evolving contemporary art and culture, and his own style changed with the times and reflected these new developments. Yet critics did not know how to evaluate these later works of Williams, and so they often judged them via the standards of realistic theater, dismissing them as failures and complaining, for instance, that Williams' characters weren't well-developed and that they didn't finish their sentences, which of course misses the entire significance of theater that challenges realistic conventions. In the same way abstract painting by artists such as Pablo Picasso or Jackson Pollack (whose acquaintance with Williams dates back to 1940) challenges realistic painting that reproduces what an object looks like on the surface—a bowl of fruit or a landscape, for instance—Williams' later plays often eschew realistic representation in order to access those truths beyond reality's surface.

Williams' exploration of freer dramatic forms later in his career was a direct reaction to changes in society, in the theater, in television and popular culture, and in his personal views of life. He continued to write about the cruelty of the world as he did in the earlier plays, but he depicted this cruelty more graphically and literally, rather than veiling it in symbolism. He admitted in 1975 that his work had become "darker" and that "people find it painful." Politically and socially, American society was changing, and Williams' late plays respond to and address these issues. His plays were becoming more directly political and more overt in terms of sexuality in general, and homosexuality in particular. In the 1960s and 70s there was no longer a need to downplay homosexual themes as subtext or subplot, as Williams had done in *The Glass Menagerie*, *A Streetcar Named Desire*, or *Cat on a Hot Tin Roof*, for example. In 1968, laws forbidding the depiction of "sex perversion" in the theater, including homosexuality as it was classified at the time, were repealed in the United States (and similar laws were repealed in Britain), allowing for greater freedom in the theater. In 1969, the "Stonewall rebellion" in New York City—in which gay and transgendered patrons of the Stonewall Inn on Christopher Street fought back against police oppression—brought attention to gay rights, and marked a watershed moment for social and political recognition, sparking the national Gay Liberation Movement. The new freedoms that American society increasingly embraced also led Williams to finally come out publicly as a gay man on national television in 1970, which he could not have done safely, either professionally or personally, in 1950.

On an even larger political scale, the Vietnam War had absorbed the nation by the late 1960s, and by the 1970s America was also struggling with difficult economic times and tumultuous social revolutions: Gay Liberation, the Women's Liberation Movement, the Black Power and Civil Rights Movements, as well as race riots throughout major U.S. cities. With the threat of nuclear war still looming during the 1980s, Williams' plays often focused on the national paranoia fused with his own personal paranoia. *The Chalky White Substance*, written in 1980, is set in a post-apocalyptic world where there is little human tenderness, and the earth is covered with a mysterious chalky white powder that continually blows through the sky and envelopes everything and everyone. Although the names of the two characters, Luke and Mark, evoke the Apostles, they live in a post-apocalyptic wasteland where cruelty and survival of the fittest dominate. In *The Remarkable Rooming-House of Mme. Le Monde*, which was written in the early 1980s (probably completed in 1982), Mme. Le Monde has "a fiery red mop of hair that suggests a nuclear explosion, as does her voice." In *A House Not Meant to Stand* (1982), the collapsing house serves as a metaphor for a disintegrating society, which the father of the family, Cornelius, describes as imminently threatened by nuclear devastation. In both *The Chalky White Substance* and *The Remarkable Rooming-House of Mme. Le Monde*, a world of instability and meager resources is marked by the cruelty and ruthlessness of individuals in their fight for self-preservation.

The themes of fundamental human selfishness and the predatory aspect of nature that appeared in plays such as *Suddenly Last Summer*, *The Gnädiges Fräulein*, and *Kingdom of Earth*, for example, are intrinsic to the later plays published here, particularly *The Chalky White Substance*, *The Remarkable Rooming-House of Mme. Le Monde*, *Kirche, Küche, Kinder*, and even *The Traveling Companion*. In *The Chalky White Substance*, Luke's "protector," Mark, threatens to turn him in to the authorities in order to claim the reward for cooperating with a totalitarian regime. Mark claims that he is capable of such action to save himself, since self-preservation has become the way in a world which "can't support its shrinking population . . . a man will use a woman a while and then, when she's no longer desirable to him, not as she was before, he's likely to destroy her." In *The Remarkable Rooming-House of Mme. Le Monde*, natural law dominates and the characters are reduced to their bestial origins, as Mint can now "get about only by swinging from hook to hook, like that historical ape man swinging from branch to branch in the jungle." Mint is used for violent sexual gratification throughout the play: raped, neglected, mocked, and starved. Mme. Le Monde distributes meager rations for Mint's consumption, and eventually these disappear as Hall greedily devours the tea and biscuits without regard for Mint's suffering, even as Mint begs him to "Have pity on a broken and desperate soul, subsisting on diminishing bits of—charities. . . ." In *Kirche, Küche, Kinder*, the Wife preempts any request of hospitality from her father, the Lutheran Minister, saying that she would like to offer him some coffee and crullers, but "I got to preserve it all for myself."

This sort of desperate self-concern is described by Williams in both *Kirche, Küche, Kinder* and *The Traveling Companion* as the "give-me's." In *Kirche, Küche, Kinder* the Wife suspects that her father has thrown her mother off the Staten Island Ferry because "Mama, she had the gimme's, huh Papa? And in dis world, die gimmes ain't often die getters." And in *The Traveling Companion* Vieux proclaims that "New traveling companions reflect the indifferent times we live in, neglect everything but themselves and their own concerns. Got the 'give-me's.' Give me, give me, give me. But the give-me's don't always get. Unquestionably there is some intellectual as well as moral delinquency in your new type of traveling companion."

The withholding of comfort and sustenance in these Williams plays is also strongly reminiscent of Beckett's work, particularly *Endgame* (1958), and both playwrights depict a world of frustration, degeneration, decay, and lack, coupled with the cruelty of self-preservation. The sadistic hoarding of resources in *The Remarkable Rooming-House of Mme. Le Monde* and *Kirche, Küche, Kinder*, for example, can be compared to Hamm's cruel manipulations in *Endgame*, as he uses the promise of food and its withholding to get what he wants. He keeps his parents, Nagg and Nell, in ashbins like animals, and agrees to give Nagg a sugarplum only if he will listen to his story, exhibiting a generosity based primarily on a system of exchange. When Nagg requests his payment, however, Hamm replies that "There are no more sugarplums!" Similarly, Clov keeps Hamm from his "painkillers," stating that there are "no more painkillers." When Hamm threatens Clov with starvation if he does not serve him efficiently, Clov replies that he will therefore die. Hamm's retort is the ultimate cruelty, prolonging suffering and denying satisfaction: "I'll give you just enough to keep you from dying. You'll be hungry all the time."

This sense of frustration can be seen from the beginning of *Endgame* in the stage tableau, described with "two small windows" set so high up that Clov needs to climb a ladder to look out of them. In *Kirche, Küche, Kinder*, the Man's description of his room is strikingly similar: "Soon the room, this box square as a block, containing a single window, set so high in the wall that it could only be reached by a wall-painter on a ladder. . . ." The frustration that opens *Endgame* moves to a sense of degeneration that is evident throughout the play, as Hamm has lost both his eyesight and the use of his legs, while Nell complains to Nagg that they "don't laugh anymore," and Clov laments the fact that beauty inevitably wanes: "We too were bonny—once. It's a rare thing not to have been bonny—once." This Beckettian sense of loss and decay weighed heavily on Williams' mind when writing *The Remarkable Rooming-House of Mme. Le Monde*. Like Hamm, Mint's legs are "mysteriously paralyzed," and his misery appalling, as he must use his hands to swing from metal hooks set high above, often just out of his reach. In an earlier draft of the play titled *A Rectangle With Hooks*, there is another exchange reminiscent of Beckett that was cut from the final version: when Mint asks if the tea is still warm, Hall replies that "It has a faint recollection of having been warm once."

Yet survival in the face of ultimate decay—"going on"—is inevitable for both Williams' and Beckett's characters, who persevere until they no longer can. In both *Kirche, Küche, Kinder* and

Beckett's narrative trilogy—the three novels *Malloy, Malone Dies, The Unnamable* (1955, 1956, 1958)—desire stubbornly remains in a perversely comic guise well after youth and beauty wane. In *Kirche, Küche, Kinder*, a decrepit ninety-nine-year-old woman is not only presented as grotesquely sexual, but she is also pregnant. Similarly in *Malone Dies*, Malone narrates the "love affair" between Moll, an ancient, foul-smelling, decaying woman, and Macmann, whose "desire to take her, all stinking, yellow, bald and vomiting, in his arms" is not at all diminished by her degenerated state. Beckett's famous ending to his trilogy, the acknowledgment that "you must go on, I can't go on, I'll go on," echoes Williams' famous battle-cry—"En Avant!"— which appears throughout his letters, journals, and interviews.

Williams' suspicions about human motives and his loss of faith in good will may have been natural in a world threatened by economic crises and nuclear catastrophes, but he was, after all, also now viewing life through a different lens, as an older man. Yet his characters in these later plays are not simply jaded; they are decidedly stronger. His heroines are no longer defeated by life and left at the mercy of a cruel world—Williams said there would be "no more Southern belles" in his later work. These women survive on their own terms and are no longer victims. Both *The One Exception* and *Sunburst* are marked by moments of tragicomic dark humor and the stubborn strength of survival that characterizes the later plays. *The One Exception*, dated by Williams as January 1983, is apparently the last play that Williams completed before his death a month later. The play's main characters, Kyra and Viola, are both artists who cling to creative work for meaning, but Kyra has lost touch with the most recent artistic trends and fears the isolation that awaits her, while Viola approaches her in her moment of crisis only to secure a loan to promote her own career. Institutional confinement, loneliness, and the un-kindness of predatory "friends" were fears that plagued Williams throughout his life. Kyra and Viola symbolize his internal struggle for survival and his insistence on always moving forward, as he, like Kyra, faced a "Paralysis of—decision." While the play recalls both the final scene of *A Streetcar Named Desire* and Williams' own three-month confinement to the psychiatric ward of Barnes Hospital in St. Louis in 1969, it most directly echoes the institutionalization of his sister Rose, with its looming threat of "The Lodge"— a likely reference to Stony Lodge in upstate New York where Rose spent much of her life. Kyra's outcome, however, is less certain than Rose's, and a possibility of survival remains at the end.

In *Sunburst*, Miss Sails, "a lady of somewhat advanced years" who is "in retirement from a long career as an actress," foils the plot of two scheming young men who want to steal her priceless sunburst diamond. *Sunburst* was probably completed sometime between 1978 and 1980 (cultural references that belong to the late 1970s, such as the thinly disguised Club 54 and the popularity of cocaine use, support that dating of the play). The play's humor surfaces as Luigi and Giuseppe try to manipulate and subdue Miss Sails, who resists her captors by stalling them and even by reciting quotations from Shakespeare. Like Miss Sails, Williams' later characters find the strength to survive on their own terms and mirror Williams' own struggle in his later years. In *The Pronoun 'I,'* Mad Queen May, a young woman masquerading as old, fools her pursuers and escapes, through secret stairs and underground passageways, the revolution raging outside, while she has her young lover, who tried to betray her, captured before he gets away—so the "old Queen" wins. Similarly, in *The Traveling Companion*, Vieux, the older writer who is accompanied by Beau, the lovely young man he met in a gay bar, takes control of the situation and refuses to be conned by Beau. And in *Will Mr. Merriwether Return from Memphis?* the aging Southern belle, Louise, waits on the front porch for her lover, Mr. Merriwether, who has promised to return for her, and he *does* return.

Will Mr. Merriwether Return from Memphis? is a fantasy with a quasi-realistic structure, as the plot is interrupted with visits from historical apparitions, some of whom have gone mad, such as Vincent Van Gogh. Louise resigns herself to waiting for her lover, claiming that "There's nothing to do but wait, with fox-teeth in the heart." We see this reference to "fox-teeth in the heart" again in *The Traveling Companion* ("Cypress woods are demon dark—boys are fox-teeth in the heart") as well as in Williams' novel *Moise and the World of Reason* (1975), and in his poem "Winter Smoke is Blue and Bitter," which also contains nearly the same line. The looming madness of frustrated desire—"fox-teeth in the heart"—is a theme repeated in both *A Cavalier for Milady* and *The Parade*, along with the mysteries of desire, a topic that occupied Williams until the day he died. In *A Cavalier for Milady*, as in *Will Mr. Merriwether Return from Memphis?*, an apparition is conjured to ward off loneliness, and in *The Parade* Don questions the very nature of desire, asking "What makes desire? Desire for a face or a body? Why does flesh in certain forms become an obsession with you? Why does it darken your mind?" *The Parade* was begun in Provincetown in the summer of 1940, where Williams fell in love with a dancer named Kip Kiernan, who ultimately disappointed him. The play, based on the events of that summer, was revised and finished in 1962, and submitted to his publisher in 1979 in a collection of odds and ends titled *Pieces of My Youth*. Don explains his obsession with the object of his desire as fulfilling "an erotic image which must have been lurking secretly in some closet in my mind." The events that led Williams to write *The Parade* are revisited with a different focus in his later play, *Something Cloudy, Something Clear*, which is seen through the shifting perceptions of both the younger and the older Williams as a writer struggling to reconcile the past and the present.

A *Cavalier for Milady* was one of the *Three Plays for the Lyric Theater,* including *Now the Cats with Jeweled Claws* and *The Youthfully Departed*, written during the mid-1970s. *A Cavalier for Milady* addresses the nature of desire in its various incarnations: sexual innocence, the sublimation of sexual desire into artistic creation (which *The Parade* touches upon as well), the predatory and consumptive aspects of desire, and the compromises we make as we age or, in some cases, go mad. Nance, a young woman who is dressed like "a child going to a party," is obsessed with her erotic fantasies. She is "visited" by the apparition of the dancer Vaslav Nijinsky, and eventually wants him to satisfy her carnal desires. She is left with a sitter as her mother and her mother's friend, Mrs. Aid, go off to nightly encounters with expensive paid escorts, even as they also try to neutralize Nance's sexuality by forcing her into the costume of a child. Like Williams' sister Rose, who was punished for her "inappropriate" sexual desire, Nance is threatened with institutionalization for expressing her sexuality. From the beginning of his career, most famously in *The Glass Menagerie*, Williams used Rose as an inspiration in his work, and the specter of Rose haunts his late plays as well. The organist in *Kirche, Küche, Kinder*, for example, is named "Miss Rose." *A Cavalier for Milady* (much like *Suddenly Last Summer*, a play which referenced both Rose's institutional confinement and her eventual lobotomy) is about power, language, and desire: the role of money and power in deciding one's fate and the need to "shut up" the truth of human desire. Nance's "morbid derangement" is sexual frustration, and her mother wants to commit her for the same "depravity" in which she herself indulges. In fact, Nance is competition for her mother and Mrs. Aid (as Catherine is for Violet Venable in *Suddenly Last Summer*), and Mother insists that she did not let Nance seduce the chauffeur because she herself had "priority there till his wife made him quit."

In *Green Eyes*, desire is seen as central to one's "life story," as the Girl narrates for her new husband the story of her life-altering sexual experience with a man who had "enawmus green eyes." An erotic moment that defines one's life also comes up in *Vieux Carré*. Nightingale, the tubercular painter who denies that he is dying, validates the Writer's claim that he fell in love with a paratrooper after a casual sexual encounter, insisting that "Love can happen like that. For one night only." In *Sweet Bird of Youth*, the Princess asks her paid "companion," Chance Wayne, to tell her his "life story." And Williams' poem "Life Story," which begins "After you've been to bed together for the first time," ends "and that's how people burn to death in hotel rooms." For Williams' characters, life often begins and ends with desire.

Many of Williams' later plays were clearly influenced by cultural and artistic developments such as pop art, vaudeville, camp, and a sense of the outrageous in the style, for example, of The Ridiculous Theatrical Company, which Charles Ludlum founded in 1969. Williams mentions the Theatre of the Ridiculous in *Moise and the World of Reason*, so he was certainly aware of Ludlum's developments by the time of the novel's publication in 1975. The Theater of the Ridiculous resists conventional, formalized notions of "art," preferring instead to allude to icons of popular culture and current events alongside classical literary texts. In erasing the distinction between "high" and "low" art and indulging an ironic sensibility typical of postmodern aesthetics—that is, making a statement and simultaneously mocking and denying it—the performer/author "winks" at the audience members as co-conspirators in some kind of cultural joke. These plays combine serious social critique with a highly self-conscious and playful style. Similarly, in *Kirche, Küche, Kinder*, for example, there are numerous nods to popular culture and current events alongside self-conscious references to classics such as *Medea*, *The Sea Gull*, "Dover Beach," and "Danny Boy." Ludlum's plays combine parody, pop culture, drag performance, and high camp theatricality. He describes camp as a kind of excess, or "overdoing," in order to make a point, and also recalls Proust's discussion of camp as "an outsider's view of things other people take for granted," a "reverse image" incorporating a sly sense of humor because of its inversions that speak to a particular, usually marginalized, social group. Susan Sontag, in her 1964 essay, "Notes on Camp," writes that "the essence of Camp is its love of the unnatural: of artifice and exaggeration," and that it is a "sensibility that, among other things, converts the serious into the frivolous." Williams embraces a camp sensibility in many of these late plays, which spring from the 1970s, a time of new languages for cultural expression.

In *Kirche, Küche, Kinder*, directed by Eve Adamson in 1979, the ninety-nine-year-old woman known as "Hotsy," who is hypersexed and pregnant, was played by a man in drag. The history of the play's title is significant in terms of its camp reversal. The title of an earlier version of the play is *Kitche, Kutchen, und Kinder,* which Williams later revised to *Kitche, Kutche, Kinder.* He finally settled on *Kirche, Kutchen, und Kinder* for the play's performance at the Jean Cocteau Repertory Theatre during their 1979-80 season. "Kitche," presumably an invented word that refers to "kitchen," was eventually replaced with "Kirche," the German word for "church," and "Kutchen," the German word for "cook," was restored in lieu of the earlier "Kutche," a misspelling of "Küche," the German word for "kitchen." Williams is consistent with "Kinder," the German word for "children." Of the three variations on the title, this last one, *Kirche, Kutchen, und Kinder*, is closest to the old German expression that designates the proper role of women, "Kinder, Küche, Kirche"— "Children, Kitchen, and Church"—functionally equivalent to "barefoot and pregnant." Not fluent in German, Williams probably confused "kitchen" (*küche*) with "cook" (*kutchen*) in wanting to reference the original expression, but initially wasn't sure if an "and" was included. I corrected his German spelling, adding the umlaut mark, and removed the "und" to conform more closely to the German saying. Significantly, Williams' reworking of the title and the reversal of the word order (from "Kinder, Küche, Kirche" to "Kirche, Küche, Kinder") corresponds to the play's scenes: we are first introduced to the action in the Kirche, then the Küche, and finally the Kinder appear. Symbolically, the reversal of the expression—reading it backwards—is highly relevant for this particular play, as *Kirche, Küche, Kinder* is a comic reversal, turning everything upside-down. Like *Camino Real*—which the Gypsy in the play insists is "a funny paper read backward!"—*Kirche, Küche, Kinder* is, in scholar Linda Dorff's estimation, a "theatricalist cartoon," complete with invisible canaries that sing as the Wife "turns slowly and dizzily about" after getting hit over the head with the Minister's umbrella. In fact, Germans often appear as darkly comic figures in Williams' work, from his portrayal of the sinister Nazi tourists at the Costa Verde Hotel in *The Night of the Iguana*—whom Shannon describes as a "little animated cartoon by Hieronymus Bosch" when they emerge "trooping up from the beach like an animated canvas by Rubens," always cackling with "Rabelaisian laughter"—to similar portrayals of Germans in *The Gnädiges Fräulein* and *A Lovely Sunday for Creve Coeur*. Read as "camp," *Kirche, Küche, Kinder* fits in perfectly with Ludlum's assertion that camp "turns values upside down."

During the 1960s, '70s, and '80s, Williams traveled to the outskirts with his plays—both literally and figuratively. His anti-realistic, "outrageous" plays often take place in the outer boroughs of New York City, or in the more marginal neighborhoods: *Kirche, Küche, Kinder* is set in SoHo—now a fashionable neighborhood, but during the 1970s a seedy warehouse district of bohemian creativity and free behavioral license—and the play's Lutheran Minister lives and works on Staten Island. Williams' 1980 play *This is the Peaceable Kingdom (or Good Luck God)* is set "in a nursing home in one of the drearier sections of Queens during the 'nursing home strike' in New York City in the spring of 1978." And in *The One Exception*, Viola refers to her apartment on Ludlow Street in Manhattan's Lower East Side, another bohemian enclave that served as a refuge for artists. In *Kirche, Küche, Kinder*, the play's protagonist is a retired gay hustler who is writing his *Memoirs*, and the artist in the theater is seen as a prostitute vying for prizes and "patrons" such as Professor Emeritus "Hotlicker," so that he can "endure . . .and survive."

Williams' later plays in this volume often employ highly theatrical, or stylized, forms and use exaggeration and distortion of reality, humor, and satire as social critique, going even beyond theatrical absurdism. Even though Williams once said that he "could never make a joke out of human existence," many of these late plays do face life's tragic elements and laugh at them, which can certainly be very liberating. These highly irreverent plays employ humor for the purpose of social commentary, highlighting the tragicomic elements of life's struggles. In a 1978 letter to Truman Capote, Williams identified with what he called Capote's "period of disequilibrium" during a very difficult personal and professional time, and ended his letter with the advice not to despair, and to "never, never stop laughing." The later plays in this volume often present an ironic world view that is simultaneously comic and bleak, embracing a lack of romanticism, blurring high and low culture, and playing indulgently with exaggeration. In his 1996 essay, "The War Against the Kitchen Sink," John Guare mentions Williams' double bill of *The Gnädiges Fräulein* and *The Mutilated* that was performed under the title *Slapstick Tragedy*, pointing out that Williams "showed one way to that part of our brain or our souls. The part of theater that's vaudeville." Indeed, Williams' later plays embrace the spirit of vaudeville, as well as the liberating transgressions of what Mikhail Bakhtin, discussing the work of François Rabelais, termed "the carnivalesque"—the spirit of carnival as social resistance that included comic violence, bawdy language, exaggeration, inversion, and an irreverent mockery of what is held by society to be sacrosanct. In his own *Memoirs* (1975), Williams insisted that his place was always "in Bohemia," and in these later plays he is rejecting the bourgeois and the conventional, and indulging the taboo, the outrageous, and the unacceptable in order to write more "honestly about life" through a new lens.

Annette J. Saddik
January 2008

ACKNOWLEDGMENTS

First and foremost, this collection of later plays would not have been possible without the inspired initiative of New Directions, particularly president, Peggy L. Fox, and my editor, Thomas Keith, and I thank them for the honor of entrusting me with this volume. Thomas Keith worked tirelessly alongside me at every stage to bring these plays to light, offering his insight and expertise—he was a driving force in the completion of this project, and it could not have been done without him. Special thanks also to the staff at New Directions for their invaluable suggestions and support, particularly Barbara Epler, Laurie Callahan, and Michael Barron.

For assistance with manuscripts, productions, and general Williams matters, much gratitude to: Mark Cave, Curator of Tennessee Williams Manuscripts at the Historic New Orleans Collection; Genie Guerard, Head of the Manuscripts Division at the UCLA Library, Department of Special Collections; Richard Workman, Research Librarian at the Harry Ransom Research Center, The University of Texas at Austin; George Bixby of Ampersand Books;

everyone at the Tennessee Williams New Orleans Literary Festival, especially Paul J. Willis, Patricia Brady, Doug Brantley, Earl Perry, and David Hoover; everyone at the Provincetown Tennessee Williams Theater Festival, especially David Kaplan, Curator, and Jef Hall-Flavin, Producing Director. Special thanks are due to John Uecker, Cameron Folmar, Arnie Burton, Jeremy Lawrence, John Waters, Craig Smith, Fred Todd, Andreas Brown, Erma Duricko, Randy Gener, Ben Greissmeyer, Judy Boals, the late Eve Adamson, and to David Kaplan for his research and insights into the text of *The Day on Which a Man Dies*. My heartfelt thanks also goes out to John Guare for his support and his enthusiasm for Williams' late plays.

Al Devlin, John S. Bak, Robert Bray, Allean Hale, Kenneth Holditch, Philip C. Kolin, Nick Moschovakis, Michael Paller, Barton Palmer, Brian Parker, David Roessel, Nancy Tischler, and the late Linda Dorff, along with others in the warm and supportive community of Williams scholars have impacted this book with their knowledge, both formally and informally, over the years. Particular thanks to Nick Moschovakis, John S. Bak, and Allean Hale for many helpful suggestions and corrections. For assistance with foreign language consultation, I owe much gratitude: for the French in *A Cavalier for Milady* and *Will Mr. Merriwether Return From Memphis?*, John S. Bak; for the Italian in *Sunburst*, Leila Javitch; for the Japanese in *The Day on Which a Man Dies*, Matthew Keith; for the German in *Kirche, Küche, Kinder*, Kurt Beals; for the Russian in *A Cavalier for Milady*, Jelena Zurilo and Svetlana Patlar.

My work on this volume was supported by a PSC-CUNY Research Grant, and I wish to thank CUNY as well as my colleagues and students at New York City College of Technology for their support. On a more personal note, special thanks and much love to my parents, Dr. Meir Saddik and Gila G. Saddik, whose spirits continue to inspire and comfort me; my sister, Orly Saddik, who made sure I grew up with Tennessee Williams' plays; my aunt and uncle, Aaron and Tikva Murad; and my cousins, Morry Murad,

Renee Murad, and especially Eileen Murad for her thoughtful gift; much thanks to Kathleen and Michael Formosa, Shari and Harris Punyon, Peter and Julia Swales, Fitz Holloway, Mark Noonan, Charles Hirsch, Michael Page, Colin Attwood, Patti Yaghmaei, Walid Younes, Timothy Stostad, and my housemates in Kismet, especially Diana Frame and Clare McKeen.

THE

TRAVELING
COMPANION
AND OTHER
PLAYS

THE CHALKY WHITE SUBSTANCE

For James Purdy

The Chalky White Substance was first performed by the Running Sun Theatre Company on May 3, 1996 at Center Stage in New York City on a double bill with *The Traveling Companion,* collectively titled *Williams' Guignol.* It was directed by John Uecker; the set design was by Myrna Duarie, the costume design was by Robert Guy, and the lighting design was by Zdenek Kriz. The cast, in order of appearance, was as follows:

LUKE   Sam Trammel
MARK   Greg Cornell

Time and place: a century or two after our time and possibly an almost equal time after a great thermonuclear war.

At rise: against a cyclorama of sky, which is cloudless and yet faintly blurred by tiny granules of something like old powered bones, a youth of about twenty years of age, Luke, sits upon the precipitous verge of a chasm over what is presumably a dried-up riverbed (it is called, now, Arroyo Seco) with an air of perplexed and anxious waiting. He has a pure and luminous quality in his face when the hood of his monk-like robe is thrown back. Upstage and to the left of Luke, an older man, Mark, is seated watching him with an enigmatic fixity of expression. After some moments, Mark rises and slides stealthily off his upstage perch, disappearing from sight for a minute. He reappears silently behind Luke and stoops to clasp his large, powerful hands over Luke's eyes.

Throughout the brief play there is a wind that rises and falls, always infinitely sad in its implication as much as in its actual sound, for this is the wind that constantly blows about an earth shrivelled and desiccated as a terminally sick being.

MARK [*in a prolonged, deep growl*]: Whoooo?

LUKE: Youuuuuuu! —You can disguise your voice but not your hands. What makes you so late?

MARK: Boys are inquisitive, aren't they? What, why? I wasn't late. If you'd turned around you'd have seen me sitting back there on that boulder behind you.

LUKE: Why?

MARK: I thought to myself, "It could be the last time I'll observe him, sitting here, waiting for me?"

LUKE: You're planning to go away? Somewhere? Without me?

MARK: Make a departure? From you? From this precipice over the Arroyo Seco, this desolation, so beautiful through the continual screen provided by the—chalky white substance? No, I'm making no departure. But how I do know that you're not?

LUKE: A secret departure? One I'd not mentioned to you?

MARK: Don't you know departures can be made without warning? You don't say you're going, you don't even know you're going, then— [*He snaps his fingers.*] —you're gone. —Life's full of sudden departures; what a pity death isn't.

[*Mark removes his hands Luke's eyes.*]

MARK: Don't pull that cowl over your face.

LUKE: It protects my eyes from the dust always blowing, blowing constantly—from where?

MARK: The shrinking earth's a desert and barren mountains: in our part of it, the vicinity here, most of the chalky white stuff is provided by the Arroyo Seco, down there. I've heard that once, a few hundred years ago, there was a river in it—there's nothing drier and dustier than an arroyo in which there was once a river that's now dried up.

[*Luke lowers the cowl over Mark's head. Mark draws it back up.*]

LUKE: I thought you admired my eyes for being so clear, not inflamed?

MARK: This evening let me have a long look at your face, memorize it, as if I might never be seeing it again.

LUKE: You said you weren't going away and I told you I wasn't either. —I still don't understand why you kept me waiting here while you were right back there all that time?

MARK: You learn a great deal about someone you care for by observing him without him knowing you are. You notice whether he waits indifferently, or with increasing concern as it gets later, oh, you learn many things you'd never know otherwise.

LUKE: What did you observe you didn't already know?

MARK: More and more tension in you as the sky started to fade.

LUKE: You know I'm afraid of the dark when I'm alone at night. If it had gotten a bit darker I would have started home and missed our meeting.

MARK: —Fear, that's a bad thing to feel.

LUKE: A natural thing to feel. Now that women are so much fewer than men, there are bands of nomads that will seize a boy after dark and—

MARK: I know. Ravage him. And when their lusts are satiated, they leave no witness, just the lifeless body. —Lean back.

[*Luke leans into his embrace.*]

MARK: It always amazes me, the smoothness of your skin under the robe, not granulated at all by the chalky white substance.

LUKE: I know you like the touch of smooth skin so I keep mine smooth for your pleasure.

MARK: How do you do that?

LUKE: Before I go to meet you here, I bathe myself and then immediately I put on my robe.

MARK: You bathe once a day, before you come here to meet me, not just at night as we're ordered to do?

LUKE: I bathe twice, once for you and again at night, Mark.

MARK: Bathe twice? Did you say twice? But that would mean that you disregard the water restrictions as if they didn't exist. —You know, this confirms my suspicion that you have another protector, one in a high position in the regime, you little—cheater, yes, you get by with violating the restrictions because you give yourself at night to someone of great power among the—

LUKE: I've never had more than one protector at a time. That one protector now is you.

MARK: Before me, you had others.

LUKE: They were necessary. I hardly remember my parents. I'll tell you something that'll amuse you. On the wall at my place, I have a colored picture of the lady that was called the Madonna.

MARK: Those old mythological pictures are a rarity now and could be sold to the Center for special privileges, you know.

LUKE: I'd rather keep the picture on my wall.

MARK: What were you going to tell me that will amuse me. Something about the picture of the Madonna?

LUKE: Once I had a protector. When I woke up one morning, he was standing there staring at the picture. He said, "Is this your mother?"

MARK: Thought that the Madonna was your mother . . .

LUKE: The funny thing is that I said, "Yes, that is, that was my mother." —Women were a comfort. —Why are they disappearing? Do they succumb more quickly to the chalk all about us now?

MARK: The earth's not able to support its shrinking population. There's little food, and even less water. I've heard that a man will use a woman a while and then, when she's no longer desirable to him, not as she was before, he's likely to destroy her. You see, Luke, the battle between people that happened so long ago that it's barely recorded, I understand that it had a brutalizing effect. Do you understand me?

LUKE: Brutalizing—?

MARK: Opposite effect from the care of a Madonna.

LUKE: So that now we have only each other.

MARK: Have I told you that I have a woman at home?

LUKE: A mother? A Madonna?

[*Mark laughs harshly.*]

MARK: No, what remains of a girl, the remnant of her, used too much, not able now to excite me nor even to—serve . . . only to stagger about, looking more and more frightened. I suspect she knows.

LUKE: You suspect she knows what?

MARK: That her withering, frightened look, her choking sounds at night—

LUKE: From the disease? She has it?

MARK: She's breathed too much of the chalk. I think she knows that soon it will be necessary to relieve myself of her presence in my place.

LUKE: I don't think you'll do that. No, you couldn't do that.

MARK: You haven't sat for an hour observing me waiting for you and so you know me less.

LUKE: Since I know you completely—

MARK: Are you sure that you do?

LUKE: I feel secure with you, Mark. And as for the woman you've never mentioned before, have you told her about us?

MARK: I say nothing to her now but, "Oh, are you still here? Go lie down in that corner over there and don't cough and don't crawl toward me."

LUKE: You're making all this up, I know it's not true.

MARK: You know so little, boy. You know dangerously little. You don't know enough to distrust.

LUKE: Oh, I distrust them all except you, Mark.

MARK: That might be a mistake. The worn-out girl at my place, she—trusted me once as you do. But when I go home tonight, if she's still there—out she'll go, I'll throw the door open, and kick her living or dead body into the wind she can't stand against, that will sweep her away and bury her in white dust. No, don't trust. So. —You said you bathe twice a day, before you come here to meet me and again at night, violating the water restrictions?

LUKE: When I was very young—

MARK: Younger than now?

LUKE: Little more than a child, I had a protector, my first, who was very clever, very wise, at secret, mechanical things. Did I say that right?

MARK: Perfectly. Go on.

LUKE: One day he put his ear to the earth.

MARK: In or out of the house?

LUKE: Both in and out, and he discovered that not far under the earth running under the house there was water, he said a stream of it, not wide, not deep, but—

MARK: Ohhh . . . .

LUKE: He was a strong man, he dug and dug down to it and built steps down with stones.

MARK: But when the house is inspected by the—

LUKE: Inspectors, no. You see, the opening to the steps is covered over with an old, dry animal skin, and even if the inspectors looked under this ragged leather—you know their eyes are bad, half-blinded by the chalk—they wouldn't notice the width of the cracks

MARK: By which you can lift the cover to the underground spring of water? —How very foolish of you!

LUKE: He did it all, not I.

MARK: But he's gone, now, and you have it all to yourself for your own private and—illegal—use. You are not at all wise.

LUKE [*shrugging*]: I must live, and to live I must please.

MARK: But you mustn't talk about it.

LUKE: Of course not. To no one but you.

MARK: No, not even to me, because by talking about it to me, you make me a conspirator with you, as criminal as you are.

LUKE: Oh, but—you—

MARK: Would bear the same penalty you would, knowing what you've told me and not—informing.

LUKE: Whom would you—

MARK: Inform? The ones you inform to. The rulers, the authorities of the regime.

[*There is a pause.*]

LUKE: You believed that story? You didn't know that it was all made up? Just an invention, like yours about the woman and what you'll do to her tonight?

MARK: That was no invention. And neither was what you told me about the underground spring.

LUKE: You're holding me so tight it's hard to breathe.

MARK: You're a light-footed boy. You might suddenly spring up and take to your heels.

LUKE: From you?

MARK: Of course, now that you realize that you've made such a dangerous mistake. I suspected something. And now I know.

LUKE: But I know something, too.

MARK: What?

LUKE: You've told me how completely you love me.

MARK: A thing that I also told the woman when she was desirable to me.

LUKE: She doesn't still attract you. I do. Don't I? Mark?

MARK: You've put in my possession a secret that to keep from the authorities would expose me to the same penalty you're exposed to. You know what such penalties are?

LUKE: A term of imprisonment, but—

MARK: A long, long term, and even if you're alive when it expires, you'd be—unrecognizable, Luke.

LUKE: I'd be disfigured, you mean?

MARK: By more than time, by more than the terminal effect of the chalky white substance.

[*He clamps his arms tighter about Luke.*]

LUKE: What are you, why are you—!

MARK: I must deliver you to them and repeat your confession and—receive the bounty. Did you know there's a bounty offered for turning in a person who violates the laws, the restrictions? The authorities regard him with more respect, he's given a title, sometimes, and his licenses are extended. The inspectors pay his house a—respectful visit, they smile at him and say, "The place needs some improvements in keeping with your new position. We'll see to that right away."

LUKE: The authorities are vicious.

MARK: I understand that's always been their nature, even before the people of the earth divided into two or three hostile parts that

battled for ownership and rule with the great explosive devices.
—Who won? —Nobody. NOBODY!

[*The word "nobody" is echoed, after a couple of moments, from the opposite side of the chasm.*]

MARK: —Hear that? Know what that was? As if somebody called back? That was an echo. So many of the old words have dropped out of use and aren't known anymore.

[*Pause.*]

LUKE: The authorities are corrupt but we don't have to imitate them.

MARK: To save our skins we do.

LUKE: Would they still be worth saving?

MARK: I understand that there used to be considerations called moral. And for these considerations, morality, a thing such as the betrayal of someone you love, would be held in contempt. But that was once, long before I remember. Stop struggling. I'm hard and strong. What's the use? You can't escape. Light's faded. We must get going.

LUKE: Where? The cave? Or my place?

MARK: Neither this evening, Luke. We're going to the cabildo where you will stay confined till long out-used, to the end of your time. —TIME!

[*Pause. Then an echo of the word "time."*]

LUKE: Then kill me. Kill me, Mark!

MARK: And sacrifice the reward?

[*The wind rises. Luke thrashes impotently in the grasp of Mark.*]

MARK: Call him, the great protector called God. No breath? I'll call Him for you. PRO-TEC-TOR!

[*Pause. Then an echo of the word "pro-tec-tor."*]

MARK: What a huge creature, what an immense beast He must have been to have left such enormous white bones when He died . . . Endlessly long ago, the bones of Him now turned to powder that blows and blows about His broken—creation . . .

[*Mark bears Luke futilely struggling down the upstage declivity. The stage darkens.*]

THE END

THE DAY ON WHICH A MAN DIES

(AN OCCIDENTAL *NOH* PLAY)

For Yukio Mishima,
in token of long friendship
and much admiration.

The Day on Which a Man Dies, (an Occidental *Noh* Play), was first performed on February 1, 2008 at Links Hall in Chicago, produced by the SummerNITE, Christopher J. Markle, artistic director. It was directed and designed by David Kaplan; paintings were by Megan Tracy. The cast in order of appearance, was as follows:

THE ORIENTAL	Gerson Ducanay
MAN	Steve Key
WOMAN	Jennie Moreau
SECOND STAGE ASSISTANT	Faith Streng

SCENE ONE

An Oriental who performs as the First Stage Assistant, Chorus, and Supporting Player, appears in a spot of light on the otherwise lightless stage.

The Oriental bows slightly, then draws a string to release a large sheet of rice paper, nearly the size of the stage opening. He snaps his fingers: on the paper is projected in large crimson letters the Japanese title of the play, "The Oriental," in Japanese characters. He reads it aloud.

ORIENTAL: *Tōyōjin**

[*He then moves several paces aside and beneath the title in Japanese appears the title in English, projected in a vividly contrasting color.*]

ORIENTAL [*as Chorus*]: The day on which a man dies begins at the midnight which closes the day before his death-day.

[*He snaps his fingers: the projected titles in both languages disappear and the spot of light blacks out.*

A few notes of Japanese music on a reed instrument are heard. Then the stage is lighted fully and we see two rooms identical in form but quite different in all other respects. On stage right is the woman's room, a bed-sitting room in a Tokyo hotel, sparely furnished and well ordered. On stage left is the room in which the man, an artist, works at his painting: it is a room whose effect of violence and disorder, fearfully subjective, is expressed by great stretched canvasses stacked about the walls, all painted in primary colors in abstractions that seem to utter panicky cries.

The man, the artist, stands over a canvas stretched at his feet. He is holding a spray-gun with which the paint is applied

---

* pronounced: toe-yó-geen (ed.)

to the canvas. He is breathing as heavily as if he had been in fierce physical combat with the demon inhabiting the canvas beneath. He wears flesh-colored tights on which are painted in color his anatomical details: pink nipples, blue outlines of skeletal prominences, arteries and musculature, blond hair at armpits. A vivid green silk fig leaf covers his groin. He is still young, his physique muscled and tendoned as if his work were a laborer's. His face is ravaged by the rage apparent in the canvasses.

After a few moments of staring down at the canvas, he sprays it with more red paint, then hurls the spray-gun away and falls to his knees, smearing the paint about the canvas with his fingers: the image fails him. He falls back on his haunches with a sick gasp in his throat.

The woman enters the adjoining, well-ordered room, followed by the Oriental, now performing the part of a law student at the Imperial University of Tokyo.]

WOMAN: Sit down, please. I'll bring him in. Excuse me.

[*The Oriental bows slightly. As the woman crosses to the partition between the two rooms, he sits on a stool downstage, briefcase over his lap. He is decorous, detached.*]

WOMAN [*opens the sliding door in the partition*]: Ha!

MAN [*staring straight ahead of him fiercely*]: *You still don't know that—?*

WOMAN: The hotel-manager told me—

MAN [*his face quivering with rage*]: *I can't be interrupted when I'm—*

WOMAN: That you were destroying your—

MAN: At *WORK!*

WOMAN: —Room!

MAN: I have always locked my studio against you.

WOMAN: This is not—

MAN: GET THE—

WOMAN: A studio, this is—

MAN: FUCK *OUT!*

WOMAN: A room in a hotel.

MAN: Where I work is my—

WOMAN: You've had the furniture removed?

MAN: Studio!

WOMAN: This isn't work, this is—

MAN [*fists clenching*]: OUT. NOW! OUT!

WOMAN: Lunacy, utter—

MAN: OUT! [*His eyes and lips clench tight on an inner violence about to erupt.*]

WOMAN: Lunacy! I knew from the sounds that something—

MAN: Just once, my first year with you—

WOMAN: Mad was happening in here when—

MAN: You interrupted my work with a supper tray and I—

WOMAN: I heard you shout last night: "Now I've got you, you bitch!"

MAN: Threw it all on the floor and the tray at you!

WOMAN: I thought: "Is he screaming through the wall at me or—

MAN: I thought that had taught you—

WOMAN: Has he got a Japanese hooker in there?"

MAN: The possible—consequences of—

WOMAN: But now I see—

MAN: Intruding upon and shattering an image at the point of— [*He stalks, on this line, to the far side of the room and aims the spray-gun at her.*]

WOMAN: You'd reached the stage of shouting at—

MAN: *Coming!*

WOMAN: Your work the sort of insults you shout at—

MAN: See what I'm pointing at you?

WOMAN: Me! Oh, yes, a spray-gun!

MAN: Want it?

WOMAN: And two empty bottles.

MAN: *Okay, you get it!*

[*The man advances and sprays red paint all over her dress. The woman screams furiously. The Oriental sets his briefcase down and rises from his chair, facing the adjoining room. The man's rage is suddenly satisfied. He makes a sound of choked laughter.*]

WOMAN: Mr. Kuniyoshi, will you please call downstairs and have an ambulance sent here to remove this madman.

MAN: Red paint on purple sequins! *Marrrrr*—velous! [*He throws back his head and laughs so hard that he staggers.*]

WOMAN: At this point you know it's no use to continue. It's time to stop, to rest. You could go to Kyoto with a doctor and nurse or to the Izu peninsula where they have pacifying hot springs and little Japanese girls to bathe you like a baby till your nerves are calmed by their tender ministrations.

[*Smiling in sweet triumph, she is suddenly quite beautiful: her skin is flawlessly smooth and deep olive, her figure superbly lithe and perfectly molded under the purple-sequined silk sheath splashed with crimson.*]

WOMAN [*removing a little bottle from her evening purse*]: Put this little round white bit of dynamite under your tongue. [*She advances fiercely toward him.*] —Before you drop dead. I can see your heart through your ribs. Open, open, mouth open!

[*He complies.*]

WOMAN: Pop! In it goes! Mr. Kuniyoshi, have you called downstairs?

ORIENTAL [*as law student*]: I think it is better if you—

MAN [*to the woman*]: *You* go to Kyoto or the hot springs till I—

WOMAN: I'm not an artist in a state of collapse. I am just your whore.

MAN: Mine? Only? With a Jap in your bedroom?

WOMAN: A bilingual young Japanese who has studied—

MAN: Christ!

WOMAN: Law at the Imperial—

MAN: You used to—

WOMAN: University and spent years in the States, his—

MAN: Pay me the compliment of—

WOMAN: Father's a consul.

MAN: Not bringing them home under my—

WOMAN: He's made a comparative study of—

MAN: Nose!

WOMAN: Eastern and Western law. I told him what you told me,

19

that I am a woman without any legal position in your life, lived with you eleven years without one!

MAN: I reminded you you were free, that I had no chains or claims on you.

WOMAN: This young man is of the opinion that I have a claim on you that American courts would uphold.

[*They stare at each other in silence for a few moments.*]

WOMAN: So! I didn't know you were painting with spray-guns now!

MAN: You see now that I am.

WOMAN: Yes, now I see, and I see why the gallery has refused to exhibit this new work.

MAN: What makes you—?

WOMAN: Think so? This! [*She produces an opened cablegram from her purse.*] Since I was aware that something extraordinary was happening in here, I took the liberty of opening this cablegram to you from Frelich's Gallery. [*She reads.*] "What in hell's going on, you must be sick or kidding? We value your reputation too much to consider the exhibition of these canvasses photographed for us. Come home, baby. We love you, want to help you, could only harm you by exhibiting work done in obvious state of confusion. All our love, Sarah."

MAN: Cable her back: "You know what to do with your love, all of it. Put my new work in storage while I make arrangements with another gallery for the exhibition of my most important new work."

WOMAN: You don't believe that, do you?

MAN: I'm working with absolute freedom for the first time.

WOMAN: So's a child making mud-pies.

MAN: Get out. I'm going back to work now.

WOMAN: Nobody can help you, you have gone beyond human help.

MAN: I've never been given any, I've never been offered any and have never asked for any. Now will you please get out? You've got somebody in your bedroom, go in and go to bed with him.

WOMAN: What's my bottle of Lysol doing here, are you painting with Lysol now, too?

[*She goes into adjoining room which is lighted. The Oriental rises.*]

WOMAN: It's horrible.

ORIENTAL [*as law student*]: What?

WOMAN: Lock that door, he'll come in here.

ORIENTAL [*rising*]: I think perhaps I should go now.

WOMAN: No. Why should you? This is a serious business appointment. Sit back down. Would you like some whiskey?

ORIENTAL: Thank you.

WOMAN: I'll have to get it from him. [*She enters the other room.*]

MAN: What the fuck do you want now? Besides that man in there with you?

WOMAN [*seizing bottle*]: The whiskey. The man has come here to discuss my legal position, he's a young Japanese law student at the Imperial University, and a graduate of Harvard: brilliant. We'll have a drink in there till you pull yourself together, then come in. And we'll all have a quiet, plain discussion of my legal position.

[*She returns to adjoining room with whiskey bottle. A Second Stage Assistant rushes on with small table and glasses. The woman and the Oriental drink together as she talks.*]

WOMAN: I found a bottle of Lysol in his room.

ORIENTAL: What is Lysol?

WOMAN: A powerful disinfectant: American women use it, diluted, as a douche, but undiluted, it's poison; I mean if you drink it.

ORIENTAL: —Did he drink it?

WOMAN: No, of course he didn't. He just put it in there to scare me. He's ridiculously childish, infantile, and—perverse!

[*The man enters.*]

MAN: What's this Jap doing here, I didn't think you liked them, I thought you considered them sexually inadequate.

WOMAN: He understands and speaks perfect English.

ORIENTAL: Excuse me, shall I go now? Yes, I think I'll go now.

WOMAN: No. Wait. I want you to tell him what you told me about my legal position.

MAN: What does this Jap know about your legal position, and what do you mean by your legal position I'd like to know anyhow?

WOMAN: My legal position with you after eleven years of unlicensed co-habitation with a dangerous psychopath, continually proposing a double suicide pact.

ORIENTAL: Please, I think I should go now.

MAN: No, don't go now. Tell me what you told her about her legal position? [*To the woman.*] How in hell could a young Jap know about what you call your goddamn legal position in the States when you have none and even a Jap would know it.

ORIENTAL: Excuse me, I'm going to go now.

MAN [*restraining him forcibly*]: NO, YOU ARE GOING TO STAY, NOW.

ORIENTAL: I will come back later after the—

MAN: —After the *what*?

ORIENTAL: Discussion between you and the lady. It's after midnight, I will come back tomorrow.

MAN: Hell, tomorrow begins at midnight, this is already tomorrow. Stay here and tell me right now about her legal position after her years with a madman she's driven mad and now she wants to get rid of.

WOMAN [*lifting a phone brought to her by the Second Stage Assistant*]: —I have the phone. I'm going to call for help downstairs if you don't let this young man alone. He is a graduate of Harvard, and now a post-graduate student at the Imperial University here in Tokyo. He says that I have a very strong legal position.

ORIENTAL: I said a very strong *moral* position.

WOMAN: A very strong moral position that would—

MAN: Moral position, you've brutalized my nature, you've driven me out of my mind and brutalized me completely, systematically, for eleven years, what moral position does that give you? You've destroyed me as a man and destroyed me as an artist, both, equally, both! How does that give you a moral or legal position? HEY!

[*The "HEY!" is shouted at the Oriental, who has picked up his briefcase and gone out.*]

WOMAN: How about my nature? Being your whore for eleven years hasn't brutalized my nature in your opinion, or don't I count in your opinion? Artist you, whore me! Artist is a dirty word to me, now, a dirtier word than whore is! Artist, artist, a disgusting word to me now. Get out your spray-gun, you painter, spray, spray paint on the canvas, you artist, you spray-gun painter, you SHIT, you MOTHER GRABBER! I LOVED YOUUUU! Otherwise would I have lived as your whore, without a legal position except a whore's in your rotten life all these years if I didn't love you, damn you!?

[*He stares at her for a moment. Then lifts the spray-gun still in his hand and sprays paint in her face. She screams. The Second Stage Assistant enters with a can and a towel.*]

SECOND STAGE ASSISTANT: Turpentine, please.

WOMAN [*sobbing*]: Ahhh.

SECOND STAGE ASSISTANT: Permit please. [*He removes the paint with the turpentine and towel.*]

MAN [*in doorway*]: I can't work anymore, finished! An artist has got to have the support of some decent, dignified relationship with somebody in his life. [*He is painting, jerking his head violently at the audience.*]

[*The Second Stage Assistant bows slightly as if to efface himself more completely.*]

MAN: That is the spring of his talent. You've poisoned the spring: deliberately, systematically, out of God knows what twisted feelings. That's what I can't forgive. You have muddied, dirtied, poisoned the spring of my talent! My God how I've fallen since you! All dignity gone from my life, all pride gone out of my life! The will to live gone out of my life, completely. And brutalized life and work both, both! Yeah, yeah, equally, both life and work, you, you—horrible! Merciless! *Bitch!*

[*He makes a sobbing sound and rushes back into his room. She follows as far as the threshold. She is superbly in command of herself as she always is when he flips. She is beautiful, cool: a queen.*]

WOMAN: Blame me for your dead talent if that makes you feel better.

MAN: Oh. "Dead talent"?

WOMAN: You said it was and I'm afraid I agree. Yes, it's dead, and stinking. When you start putting your canvasses on the floor and painting with a spray-gun instead of a brush and then mess it around with your fingers like a kid making mud-pies. —Who wouldn't know it was dead? And yet you refuse to go into a clinic. And get psychiatric treatment, which is the only hope for you.

MAN: OUT, GET OUT, OUT, OUT, OUT, GET OUT!

[*This cry is accompanied by action: he thrusts her violently out the door. She offers no resistance. He snatches the whiskey bottle.*]

MAN: You know where to stick the knife in! —You're an artist at that. [*He retreats from the door. He picks his canvas up from the floor and puts it on the easel. He looks at it with a sick sound in his throat.*] You never knew what it meant to me. I never valued myself or my life in my life, my work was all I valued, just my work that used to, to—*purify* me! It rose above me and gave my life some meaning. [*He picks up the bottle from the floor and drinks.*]

WOMAN: I can see you in there: drinking out of the bottle—already drunk—and wallowing in self-pity.

[*The man sets the bottle down as noiselessly as possible on the stool before the easel.*]

WOMAN: I heard you putting the bottle down in there.

MAN: *Here's something else you can hear!* [*He hurls the bottle against the door locked between them.*] You can hear that too!

WOMAN: That means you'll come in here to get another bottle out of the case. But I'm locking the door on *my* side now. Artist! —Creep! —Phoney!

MAN: You're showing your hand plainly now. It's my work that you hate me for most.

WOMAN: Yes! Because it's sick, sensational crap!

MAN: And you? And you?

WOMAN: Me *WHAT*? Go on and say it.

MAN: —You make me attack you. I don't want to attack anybody—nobody. I just wanted some little decency in my life and some little bit of tranquility in my life so I could—

WOMAN: So you could *what*?

MAN: Try to be what I was. I used to have decent feelings. I had many friends before I latched on to you. I was liked, I was loved and respected.

WOMAN: For what! You were always the same as you are now. People like you never change, they just develop like cancers. Just grow in their sickness like a malignant growth grows. Oh, if I ever told you what you have done to me!

MAN: Tell me, tell me: —What have I done to you besides providing you with the means to be *utterly idle*?

WOMAN: How cheap you are! What a cheap idea you have of human relations.

MAN [*slamming door open again*]: What is your idea about human relations? After eleven years, I don't know!

WOMAN: You may have noticed that I have friends and you don't!

MAN: I don't have any because I took you! —In place of all friends, took you!

WOMAN: You had no friends, just leeches!

MAN: *You* are the big blood-sucker! [*He slams door and locks it again.*]

WOMAN: I won't forget you said that.

MAN: I hope you don't forget it: *Remember* it! —Not that you give a shit . . .

WOMAN: You are the leech, not me: You've sucked my blood, sucked my arteries dry, dry, dry, till I feel like the shell of a—locust! —And now you pity yourself and tell me that I have "brutalized your nature." You artist! You—pretender!

MAN: Let's cut this out, this is hell.

WOMAN: *Yes*, it's hell!

MAN: Well, then let's cut it out, it's the same old fight that we've been fighting eleven years, the longest war that's ever gone on!

WOMAN: How do you think it's been for me for eleven years, having no hold on you but the sexual act and knowing that that was the only hold I had on you?

MAN: How do you think it's been for me, wanting to be loved and just offered sex now and then?

WOMAN: Is that how you think I have "brutalized your nature?"

MAN: Yes, that's how, exactly!

WOMAN: Did you hear my question? I asked you how do you think it's been for me just being your whore, God damn you!?

MAN: That's all you wanted to be. You could have been—everything else, everything, anything else, you could have, you could have—at least deceived me, fooled me, made me believe that there was some love between us, not just the sexual thing and the eleven year power-struggle, battle of—

WOMAN: *You* got what you wanted! —I gave you all my young life and now I'm fading, I'm faded.

MAN: Oh, you still manage. You still make pick-ups in bars, continually, with no effort.

WOMAN: That's just one of your paranoiac delusions.

MAN: I'm going to pack up and check out.

WOMAN: You can't pack.

MAN: Oh, yes, I can. I packed plenty of suitcases in my time.

WOMAN: Before you turned into the feeble mess you are now.

[*Pause. He throws his hands to his face and cries into them for a moment.*]

MAN: Christ, what a monster you are: The cruelest, hardest person I've ever known in my life! —I've been castrated by you! —I knew it eight years ago but wouldn't face it, kept kidding myself that the act you put on in bed was true, sincere. I told my analyst that: I said you were so sweet in bed. You want to know what he said? He said, isn't that the business of a whore, to be sweet in bed?

WOMAN: You told him that, you said that to him about me?

MAN: Yes, I did, and that's what he said to *me!* About *you!*

WOMAN: You were paying him fifty dollars a day for telling you just what you wanted to hear about me. Now I'm going to tell you something about yourself and it won't cost you fifty dollars or fifty cents! —You are the meanest, lowest, and cheapest mothergrabber there ever was: no lie!

MAN: —Well, I'm packing up, now, and checking out of this hell. [*He moves forward and calls for the maid like a drowning man shouting for help.*]

MAN: *Otetsudai**

[*A little Japanese maid rushes in, bowing and uttering breathless little exclamations.*]

---

*   pronounced: ó-te-tsoo-dye (ed.)

MAN: Will you please help me pack? I am leaving, going! [*He has to repeat this several times before the maid understands.*]

WOMAN: How is she going to pack for you in there? Your luggage is in here and all your clothes. Send her in here. I'll give her your things and your luggage. Just write me out a check for my plane fare back to the States and stick in under the door. I don't want you back in this room, I don't want to see you ever again in my life.

MAN [*to the maid*]: Go next door for my things.

[*She doesn't understand: keeps ducking her head with frightened little gestures.*]

WOMAN: Let her in here, I'll explain, I'll give her your rotten things and your luggage.

[*The man unlocks the door and motions to the maid to enter.*]

WOMAN: Here! Here! Here! [*She is hurling his clothes from a closet to the floor, then kicks his suitcases toward them.*] —Now take all this stuff in there. IN THERE!

[*The frightened maid gathers up clothes and suitcases. The man has slammed the door. The maid raps timidly. He lets her in. She keeps murmuring little apologies. She starts folding and packing garments into luggage, crouching on the floor.*]

WOMAN [*through the door*]: That's what you need: a servant to live with, a slave! —A little crouching, whimpering, ducking and bowing little slave! —At your feet.

MAN: I needed love, understanding: the tenderness of a woman, not the tricks of a whore.

WOMAN: Why are you leaving? These women are perfect for you! —They'll kiss your feet when you kick them.

MAN: Because—

WOMAN: —Because of *what?*

MAN: —You were beautiful to me and I loved you. With all my heart I loved you.

WOMAN: You mean you enjoyed me in bed. That's all you mean.

MAN: I loved you. That much you know, you can't deny that you know it. That I did love you until you made me choose between you and—my last bit of self-respect, that much you must know, you can't deny that you know it . . .

WOMAN: You're in there drinking, getting slobbery drunk.

MAN: What are *you* doing in *there?*

WOMAN: Under the circumstances, I don't see how that concerns you!

[*On her side of the unlocked door, the woman is making up at a mirror with calmness and care. He is drinking. The little Japanese maid is bustling and murmuring as she packs with a tenderness and precision like a mother caring for a sick child.*]

MAN: I wish you could see the sweetness of this little Japanese girl: She packs my clothes like she was dressing a child.

WOMAN: Yeah. Talk about tricks, *they* know them! [*She picks up a phone.*] May I have some tea, please? Strong tea, not the green tea, the strong tea. Do you understand me? Strong tea, I want the strong tea. [*She says the Japanese word for it and hangs up.*] Koi kōcha* [*Then she comes downstage and speaks to the audience.*] Packing up, is he? Shit! Where is he going? He's going nowhere without me: I have him, I've always had him where the hair's short and he knows it. Not as well as I know it but he knows it. We've been together eleven years, nearly twelve. About him I know everything; about me, he knows nothing! —Except my body which

---

* pronounced: coy-kó-cha (ed.)

I can still hold him by. By which I've always held him. I belong to an old Mediterranean race and he's a sort of blond mongrel: a little Welsh wildness, a lot of Puritan English, and a big hunk of German sentiment, mostly self-pity. —A mess! —However he can still pass himself off as an artist, and sell it. [*She laughs conspiratorially to the audience.*] —At prices in four figures. Oh, his work was worth it till he pushed it too far and it turned on him like a tiger and started to tear him down. But that's his bag, mine's protecting my interests. I'll have to play my cards right. That I can do. That's the kind of knowledge I was born with. Sometimes I have to figure the next best move. This time I think the next best move is not to move at all. Just have my tea and—

[*The Oriental enters in the part of a waiter, bearing a china tea service.*]

WOMAN: —Thank you.

[*She signs the bill. The Oriental bows and withdraws.*]

WOMAN: You know what happened to him? When he was a little boy he practiced the little boy's vice: masturbation. His mother caught him at it. She said that it made God mad, that it made Mama mad and it made God mad and he didn't want to make God and Mama mad, did he? —That's how it started, like that . . . She said that God would punish him and Mama would punish him, too. He loved Mama and he loved God so he stopped it. He didn't want to be punished so he stopped it. But he wanted it. So he got mad at Mama and God, he began to hate Mama and God and disregard their wishes. The Puritan pattern! —Of guilt. And then atonement. Guilt and atonement, atonement and guilt. —It's inescapable, he will never escape it, and so he won't escape me. In a minute he's going to open that door and come in to beg my forgiveness. —I'll have to go to bed with him to express my forgiveness and Mama's and God's . . . —How would you like to live with something like that? Pretty messy, some drag! —Oh, well, that's life. The disgusting thing is that he can still think it's love.

[*The woman drinks her tea. The Japanese maid completes the packing and the man gives her a tip.*]

MAN: Sayonara!

WOMAN [*derisively*]: Sayonara! —Shit. —Been here six months and the only word he knows he got from a movie title . . . —When he started painting with a spray gun I knew he was finished. I don't know what I am but I'm glad I'm not an artist. —Started painting with a spray gun and has to get drunk to do it! —Sayonara! Shit! —Slobbery son of a—Spray gun . . .

[*The man starts slashing the canvas to pieces with his palette knife.*]

WOMAN: —Now what? Cutting up his canvas! —Doesn't have the guts to cut his throat. [*She turns to the door and shouts*]: WHY DON'T YOU CUT YOUR THROAT? [*Pause. She turns back again to the audience and says wryly*] —No answer. —I've got no legal position. Goddamn atheist but claims he can't get divorced from his wife because he's Catholic and she's insane. —I have no legal position after eleven years with him.

[*The man falls back from the slashed canvas. He cries convulsively into his hands, stumbling about drunkenly with crazed gestures. He falls, at last, to the floor.*]

WOMAN: —Now what?

[*After a moment, the man staggers to his feet again and moves toward the door in the partition. He tilts his head attentively for any sound in the adjoining room.*]

WOMAN [*in a whisper*]: Yes, here he comes, he's about to come in, now.

[*The woman takes a stool downstage and sits on it, waiting calmly for the man's surrender. He opens the door like a sneak-thief. He has put on his black Japanese kimono and slippers. Now he enters. In the room with her, he has the manner of an Oriental servant. Quietly, almost stealthily, he picks up the other stool, pads softly downstage with it, and sets it next to hers. They sit side by side in grave silence. The Second Stage Assistant enters the set. He opens a sliding glass panel in the upstage wall to reveal a formal painting of a tree in flower. There is soft Kabuki music. The Second Stage Assistant removes an artificial flower from his black sleeve and puts it in a delicate vase. Deferentially crouched, he places this pale, delicate, and sorrowful flower of reconciliation between and just before their two stools. Then he returns, walking backwards in the formal attitude of an Oriental servant. The man extends his hand toward the woman. She appears not to notice this gesture. He nudges her arm with his fingers. With a long sigh, she closes her eyes and extends her hand to the cup of his hand. Their hands clasp.*

Their facial expressions are almost the same: They are like two children in school, asked the same question that neither of them can answer.

And so the calcium glare dims out and . . .]

THE CURTAIN COMES DOWN

SCENE TWO

The Second Stage Assistant opens the panel in the back wall, this time exposing the round red disk of the risen sun. The hard white calcium glare floods the scene again. There is a distorted musical mimicry of morning sounds: birds waking and cocks crowing.

The woman suddenly springs out of the tumbled bed sheets. She wears flesh-colored tights with anatomical details painted on in colors. Her body is triumphantly alive: it proclaims how she took the man in the night and mastered his nerve-shattered body. She performs a kind of narcissistic dance before a tall narrow mirror that the Second Stage Assistant brings to her. She clasps her hands on her belly, her breasts, her buttocks, with total appreciation. Suitable music plays. Then she throws back the crumpled sheet that contains the man, exposing his body in skin-fitting tights. She grins triumphantly at the audience, pointing at his figleaf, her eyes as open and shining as the risen sun. Timpani is played. The man starts up and meets her merciless glare and pointing finger.

MAN: What?

WOMAN: What?

MAN: I thought you just said something. [*He draws the sheet up over his body with shame and sorrow.*]

WOMAN: What's there to say?

MAN: We mustn't fight anymore. It leaves me so exhausted I can't make love.

WOMAN: The last time we had sex you said to me afterwards, I don't know if that was love-making or hate-making.

MAN: Well, last night—

WOMAN: Let's don't talk about last night.

MAN: When the work goes better the sex will go better, too.

WOMAN: I think we'd better lay off the sex until the work goes better, if you are right about that. We'd better wait till the work starts going better, without the spray-gun.

[*The man sighs and crawls out of bed. The Oriental enters.*]

ORIENTAL: I am sure that you already understand what happened between them last night: this poor young middle-aged man doesn't understand about death of body and spirit and all he can do is to make these panicky, hopeless efforts to show himself he's not dying by trying to sleep with this woman. Lately these efforts have all been unsuccessful, just as lately his efforts to paint a new, powerful picture have all been abortive till finally, lately, he has started using a spray-gun on his canvas instead of paint brushes. He has turned Japanese very suddenly. I mean that he is prepared to kill himself now. He is going to do it; at least he's going to attempt it. The idea hasn't occurred to him yet, this morning, but this is possibly the last day of his life. They're dressing together in silence, absolute silence, and neither one of them is quite sure what they are thinking or feeling but certainly the woman is the one in power. She seems ruthless but let's regard her fairly. Objectively and fairly. She has a beautiful body and he has enjoyed it greatly —Till lately. And it's perfectly true that she has no legal position with this man. And this man is humanly selfish. So is she. And who knows which is more so? The only obvious thing is that she is in the ascendancy and he is bereft of all power. Look how he puts his clothes on, in comparison to the way she dresses. She dresses with assurance, knowing precisely what she wants to put on, and doing it with a quick, sure animal grace, while he wonders and fumbles. Yes, I think it's the last morning of his life. And see the way he looks at her, those wistful side-long glances. Looking at her, he gets a slight erection, even now, his last morning, remembering all the past pleasures of her submitting flesh and the young sweetness of it. Perhaps I was wrong in saying that he is Japanese. I think I should have said that his fate, his situation, is Japanese. Our suicide rate is the highest in the world. [*He gives some statistics.*] —It's particularly popular among our creative artists. We seem to have a gift for it. He doesn't have that gift. He will probably do it today but he won't do it respectably. He will not do it with dignity, but he will almost certainly do it unless the woman forgets that she has no legal position in his life enough to want to save him. I see no sign of that coming. No. Her face is unrelenting: a Mediterranean face. I suppose a Mediterranean body as perfect as hers must have that kind of face to sit like a stern chaperone, well, not so much a chaperone as a Madam. The body of a beautiful whore, the face of a relentlessly practical Madam, guardian of the body, procurer of its users, no, bargainer with the users, the face was combined somehow with the face of the frightened cashier facing the bandit's revolver. You see what I mean? — [*He rises from the straight chair, which is removed by the Second Stage Assistant.*] I could have explained things better if one of our suicidal young writers had been on the script. Good morning!

[*He bows and goes off. The man and the woman are now dressed.*]

MAN: Let's have lunch together. Where shall we have lunch together?

[*The woman doesn't answer; she is applying her make-up.*]

MAN: Shall we have lunch at the Imperial, in the new building of the Imperial?

WOMAN: You're not going to work today?

MAN: I'll stop for lunch, if I do.

WOMAN: I'm not going to have lunch today.

MAN: Why not?

WOMAN: You said I was putting on weight, so I'm cutting out lunches so I can take the weight off. —Having no legal position in your life, I have to please you, don't I?

MAN: I wish you'd forget about the legal position. You keep saying that to me, you've got no legal position.

WOMAN: Because I haven't. Have I?

MAN: We've been together for eleven years. I would have married you the first month if I'd been free to, Sweetheart. Can I change the law forbidding a man to divorce an insane wife? So he can marry the woman he loves and lives with?

WOMAN: I'm not and have never been anxious to be married to you. However I would like to have a legal position in return for the eleven years I've given you out of my life. In which I could have made a very good life of my own, with independence, with self-respect, with a little happiness, even.

MAN: We've had good years together. Eleven! We've given each other great freedom. It's only this last year when I've been under such strain as you can't imagine that things have gone wrong between us. Don't judge our life by this last awful year.

WOMAN: Have you ever considered the situation that I would find myself in if something happened to you?

MAN: If what happened to me?

WOMAN: If you killed yourself, for instance, like you keep threatening to?

MAN: I've —I'm —Perfectly willing —To leave you all my new work, I mean to make out a will leaving all my new work to you! Call a lawyer, get a lawyer up here, we'll make out a legal document, now, today! —Leaving you all my work, everything that's unsold.

WOMAN: Thank you. —Suppose it's worthless?

MAN: Do you think it's worthless?

WOMAN: How do *you* feel about it?

MAN: I think I'm— breaking new ground, I'm— breaking new ground, I'm—

WOMAN [*coolly*]: You're rationalizing.

[*He stares at her helplessly as she receives a phone message on a slip of paper, presented to her on a saucer, with a bow, by the Second Stage Assistant.*]

MAN: For me?

WOMAN: For me. [*She continues making up. A Stage Assistant trots up with another saucer of messages.*]

MAN: For me?

WOMAN: For me.

MAN: All three?

WOMAN: No, all four. [*She has completed her make-up. She starts out.*]

MAN: Where are you going?

WOMAN [*coolly calling back to him*]: I'm going to have my tea downstairs.

MAN: Then come back up, don't leave me alone all day!

WOMAN [*calling back*]: After my tea I'm going to The Ginzah.

MAN [*shouting after her*]: Meet me at the Imperial for lunch?

[*She is offstage. Her answer is indistinct but negative.*]

MAN: What? What?

[*He gets no answer. He shuffles back to where she has dropped the crumpled slips of paper. Picks them up, one by one, unfolds them, crumples them and drops them again. The Second Stage Assistant opens the upstage panel on a line-drawing of a grotesque Cothurnus. The Oriental, serving as Chorus, has entered discreetly and announces—*]

ORIENTAL: The Tragic Muse—of self-pity! The mask of masochism . . . . Hideous? Because ridiculous! To achieve anything respectable in our dark and oblique eyes, he will have to rise above this.

[*The man rises, brokenly.*]

ORIENTAL: He has risen, physically.

[*The man sobs.*]

ORIENTAL: But is still crouching in spirit. Our history, our culture, has given us a deeply inborn contempt of spiritual crouchers. Even as a defeated nation, with the highest suicide rate in the world, we have only appeared to crouch. Our art, our culture, is hard and erect and fiercely, proudly cruel. I suppose this play is really about the difference between the Oriental and Occidental forms of self-destruction. We consider ours more dignified. Committed for practical, not for romantic, reasons. The Kamikaze planes in World War Two? Proud, not masochistic! —and practical. Necessary. The Orient means rising, where the sun rises. Watch us, we will rise! Our flag asserts our faith in it . . . . Excuse me please. There is to be some more action.

[*The Oriental retreats to the wings. Light is brought up on the man.*]

MAN: Where are they, where did they go, the images, the visions?

[*A Stage Assistant opens the panel again to reveal an abstract design of birds in flight.*]

MAN: —They say if you wait for them, they'll come back. —Sometime, by something or someone, something was broken in me and to repair the break I used a—what? —imitation of—what? —a frantically and fiercely aggressive imitation of a pride I could only feel under liquor and drugs, and out of this I —created, attempted to—create. Consequently, what am I ? A painter, now, with a spray gun.

[*A Stage Assistant rushes up to him with the spray-gun.*]

MAN: The paid-for wisdom and kindness of a doctor that said rest, rest! —It will come back, meaning they would come back, the visions, the images, and the power to paint them on canvas with something more orderly than this— [*He accepts spray-gun from a Stage Assistant.*] —Spray-gun . . . [*He clasps violent hands to either side of his head.*] Images! —Come *Back!* [*He turns about, giggling crazily, and whistling for them (his lost visions) as if they were dogs.*] I think I could do it today, I think I could really do it!

[*On this line, a Stage Assistant rushes in to him with a small table; sets on it a large brown bottle and a tumbler. A toneless offstage voice says— "LYYY! —SOLLL!"*]

MAN: Luck fails and the light goes out: no candles, no matches. —What then? The steady going along with each morning and a day and night? —No, I think I really *can* do it, this time! But *now*, right *now*, or *never!*

[*He rushes to the table and drains the bottle of Lysol. It cuts him like a fire in his mouth, throat, and belly. He gags and crouches over. A Stage Assistant jerks a string that releases from the ceiling a paper transparency on which is a line-drawing of the woman's lovely nude body. It falls in front of the man. Percussive music. After a few moments, the man stumbles through the thin paper. Instantly the Stage Assistant lowers another paper transparency on which the woman's body is projected still larger. The man breaks through the second piece of paper. Then the Stage Assistant lowers another large tissue rectangle on which the woman's body is three times larger than life-size.*

The percussion is augmented by wind instruments, grotesquely lyrical and mocking.

It takes some moments longer for the man to crash through this third projection, and when he does, he's dying. He has his hand in his mouth to gag his cry, and his teeth have drawn blood. The percussion is still building. The man collapses onto his knees and now he tries to cry out but hasn't the breath. He crumples: dies.

An abrupt stillness.

A circle of light is focused on the forestage on a small table at which the woman is seated. She is incomparably cool and in command of herself and her ambiance at first appearance, but this impression is soon dissipated by the interior monologue which follows. It is accompanied by the soft sounds of a monsoon wind. She is in a bar on The Ginzah: the street is represented by vividly painted strips of ideographs which flutter in the keen wind with a rustling that comes and goes, serving as punctuation to her interior remarks.]

WOMAN: Restlessness! Irritable nerve-ends! Inflamed! Ha. The concave needs the convex like a famished mouth needs feeding.

[*The monsoon wind rises: there is a wild fluttering of rice-paper strips.*]

WOMAN: Hmmm. [*She crosses her legs tightly.*] Want, crave, *need*, deep in me! [*Turning down a white glove, she glances at her wrist.*] My lunatic keeper is late on The Ginzah today. By this hour he usually appears on the street, stumbling along it in panicky pursuit of me, his fierce eyes blazing blue-white as the center of flame, the eyes of a Goth, a Hun, a—broken Attila. —Did I break him? Maybe. As he broke me. Unable to save each other, we struck at each other with an equal fury . . . Bull! A woman of my breed can't be broken that easy. The blood of a people that sprang from volcanic islands, fiery as my unsatisfied— [*Pause. She places a gloved hand slowly over her groin.*] —holds me still intact while he crumbles to bits . . . [*She crosses her legs in the other direction. She touches her groin again.*] And yet I'm here alone in spite of the four calls from casual lovers whom I've used in place of "The Man" to pacify for a while my— [*She lifts her hand from her groin and drops it again with force.*] I almost seem to be considering—not surrender, but—cease-fire . . . Is he searching for me or am I waiting for him? Sitting on The Ginzah, alone, waiting till he finds me, or I, as if accidentally, come across him, with a fake look of displeased surprise? —If love is need, and what is it if it isn't, aren't I the one who loves more? He has his work, even if he's gone in his head and paints, now, with a spray-gun, and I, what do I have, what have I got from this man who asks, who demands, that I give him all of me in return for half of what's left of him? And with no legal position while he's living or after he dies? —But I'm not afraid *of* him but *for* him. It seems that I —*love* "The Man" . . .

[*Strips of painted posters flutter wildly again. The woman shuts her eyes tight, then opens them wide.*]

WOMAN: —These ideographs! A language printed in simplified picture-images . . . . If they put me into an ideograph, I'd be a thing hanging naked, yes, a line-drawing in colored ink of a naked thing, outlines in cool color but not color here—and here . . . [*Her gloved hands touch her breasts and groin.*] —Oh, this calls for—

[*She pours a cup of steaming tea. A Stage Assistant enters and stands beside the table with a large paper poppy as the woman opens a laquered box, removes from it an opium pellet and drops it in the tea.*]

WOMAN: —a pacifying pellet of the stuff they extract from the seeds of— [*She points to the large paper poppy suspended over her. The Second Stage Assistant exits with the poppy.*] —Hmm. They translate time into moons here. Everything is the moon of something or other. —And this is my moon of fertility. Oh, I keep up a cool front, but the barren emptiness of my— [*She curves her gloved hands over her abdomen; then, with shaking fingers, lights a cigarette and lifts her tea cup.*] —burns, burns hidden in me! My blood is hot with—my arteries burn with—volcanic lava-flow of—unseeded fertility! Not to be seeded and to bear by this mad-man who might discard me in favor of some cringing little Jap whore at any moment, in favor of her or of—*death*, at any time, such as now? Christ! No legal position because his wife's in a madhouse which he probably drove her into . . . What have I got but vacant hours in public places, phone calls from inconsequential bed-partners wanting to have me again. [*She crumples her phone messages and throws them away.*] And that bit of plastic inserted in my vagina to prevent conception. —Why don't I take it out of me and conceive a child by "The Man?" It might at least improve my legal position, and—I wouldn't be empty with his child in my body and then at my breast . . . Hmm, yaisss! I'll take it out of me, now, and this afternoon or tonight I'll give him back his male power which I skillfully confiscated and I'll let him seed in my body, in my womb which is ready to incubate the seed of the mad-man. —Waiter! Check! I'm leaving.

[*She rises, dark eyes blazing. The strips of vivid ideographs flutter in the monsoon wind as—the spot of light dims out and the posters are lifted. Behind the forestage area, another area is lighted. The Oriental stands over the man's lifeless body. Kabuki music plays.*]

ORIENTAL: The day on which a man dies is no different than any other day of the year's calendar. If it should be windy and gray, that's just the monsoon. If it should be the day of the most yellow butterflies, well, it's just that day, with no reference to the death of the man since, naturally, it is the day on which so many others are born and on which so many continue their existence. The death of a man and the formal tokens of mourning are incidents of a very localized nature. Don't they always, everywhere, seem to be rushed like an embarrassed farewell. WE know all about death: it's practically the *Specialité de la patrie* . . . And yet even we are able to ask seriously this: Does life have room for death? [*He utters a sharp, mirthless note of laughter and crosses upstage to open a panel which reveals a line-drawing of a formalized funeral wreath.*] Not much, is it? No cosmic disturbance? Just this? And yet we could even ask seriously this: Does death have room for life? Hmm. Each is too enormous and yet not enormous enough to— [*He frowns and his voice hesitates uncertainly over the words.*] —contain and be contained by—the other . . . Hmm. —This is not an Oriental preoccupation, concern, idea—or at any rate it is not an idea or concern that an Oriental would be likely to care to try to express. Familiarity breeds—familiarity . . . [*He shuts the panel over the wreath.*] —Why isn't there more? Why can't I open the panel on another image? The music has moved West, it isn't our kind of music. It seems to be trying to create the condition for another image behind the panel. It wouldn't be our image. It might be undignified, romantic. Shall we or shall we not run the risk of violating the truth which we think is a rock, not a flower? Or at least, a flower that grows out of rock? Yes? Or no? Yes? No? [*He has moved upstage to the panel and seems to wait for an answer. Then he bows as if an answer was given. He opens the panel on a pure morning sky.*] —A morning sky, a white cloud drifting across it. I was afraid—I'll tell you what I was afraid of, that it would be a lily for resurrection but it's truthfully just the sky of the day on which a man dies: serene as the face of God, indifferent to our passions; a mask, a fair sky, a light cloud drifting across it: majesty, greatness, purity. What's behind it? Look. [*He knocks politely at the sky image with his fist as if rapping at a door.*] No response: harder? All right, I will knock at it harder. [*He pounds harder and harder: it remains unchanged.*] —The *Occidental* touch, we *never pound* at this image . . .

[*The stage is darkening so that only the serene projection of the sky remains clearly seen.*]

ORIENTAL: We live and die under this image as if we understood it, we never paint with the spray-gun, we never write with it either. We live beneath this sky and surrounded by water: an island people, a quieter island people than the Mediterranean ones. But suicide is very familiar to us, not to them.

[*The woman comes into the lighted area. She has been informed of the man's suicide which she didn't really believe he'd ever perform. She's like a Mediterranean peasant in the presence of an awe-inspiring religious phenomenon. It's more fear than any*

Protestant, Northern idea of love-in-grief for a loved one, but it is moving and there is dignity in it. She delivers a token wail beside the dead body—a token gesture of mourning, and it should not be indicated whether she is still thinking about her legal position or not, since we'll never know.]

ORIENTAL: Look at her now. She is rising although still weeping from the dead lover's—dead artist's—body and making up her face before a mirror. The phone is ringing. The world is approaching her heart and her heart will not betray him. She will be simple and truthful, both, at this moment. But she will not bow before this image as I am about to bow to it.

[*He kneels formally before this image of the sky's ineffable, indifferent purity as everything dims out.*]

CURTAIN

A CAVALIER FOR MILADY

(A PLAY IN TWO SCENES)

CHARACTERS:

NANCE
THE MOTHER
MRS. AID
MRS. JOSIE FLATTERY
AN APPARITION OF VASLAV NIJINSKY

Author's note: The play contains brief quotations from Nijinsky's diary.

SCENE ONE

Scene: A parlor in an old house in a smart section of Manhattan. The furnishings are Victorian-chic, an interior that could be created by Johnny Nicholson. On a little period sofa in a three-windowed bay is seated Nance, a young woman dressed a child going to a party, the dress corresponding in period to the decor. The actress should be between twenty-five and thirty.

At rise Nance holds an open book on her lap and is staring dreamily at a dim arched doorway opposite her. What appears to be a piece of life-size statuary, a Greek Apollo with fig leaf, is dimly visible through the doorway.

MOTHER: And today I had a lunch catered by *Chanticleer* under the drier at Mme. Rubenstein's. Smoked brook trout. Salad Niçoise. Very low calorie lunch but—mm—*delicious*!

[*Mrs. Aid has rushed to the dim pier-glass in the parlor.*]

MRS. AID: Yes, these lunches at beauty salons are catching on at Elizabeth Arden's too. I had a cheese souffle to end all cheese souffles there today.

MOTHER: Bad as that? [*She calls out.*] Come in please, Miss Josie.

[*A stocky, fiftyish-looking woman enters glumly.*]

MOTHER: Heavens, don't glower like that! —This is my child. Nance, dear, this is Miss Josie.

JOSIE: The name is Missus. Flattery.

MRS. AID: Flattery will get her on the wrong side of the Queensborough Bridge. [*She pirouettes flirtatiously before herself in the pier-glass.*]

JOSIE: I think you better give me the cab fare to and from. There's something not natural here.

MOTHER: Now, Miss Josie.

JOSIE: I told you Missus Flattery is my name.

MOTHER: The child always calls her sitters Miss Something or other.

JOSIE: She better not call me Miss, I'm a married grandmother.

MOTHER: I suspect that she'll call you nothing at all unless you force her to. She seems not to notice your presence and maybe that's just as well. Now do get settled. Nance? Nance?

NANCE [*impatiently*]: Yes, Mummy?

MOTHER: This is your sitter tonight. She'll sit with you 'till Mummy returns from her social engagement. [*To Josie.*] If we're out till midnight, tell the child it's bedtime. The child's nursery is the second room to the right in the upstairs hall.

JOSIE: —How old is this "child"?

MOTHER: We don't discuss that in her presence.

JOSIE: I don't sit with mental patients.

MOTHER: Nance will give you absolutely no trouble.

JOSIE: I sit with infants and I sit with small children but not with nothing morbid, nothing unnatural, no.

MRS. AID [*at the mirror, gaily*]: How limiting.

MOTHER: Look at the child.

JOSIE: I see her, that's enough. I waited twenty minutes outside the door. My fee is five an hour so with cab fare from Queens and back—

MRS. AID: We have escorts waiting! This is intolerable!

MOTHER: Mrs. Flattery, please don't invent complications. Nance has the breeding and manners of a sweet little girl well-brought-up. Now my friend is right. We have gentlemen waiting for us, and so we must go.

NANCE [*clasping her hands ecstatically*]: Oh, Vaslav!

JOSIE: Who'd she speak to, why's she sitting like that with her eyes bugging out?

MOTHER: Because you've disturbed her. The child is sensitive, she's led a very sheltered life. Please don't disrupt it at a single sitting. Now everything's at your disposal but the little Regency chairs, they're delicate antiques, you wouldn't be comfortable in them and they'd collapse, so compose yourself on the big leather chair by the table. You'll find soft drinks in the cooler of the little bar over there, there's ice in the silver bucket. If you prefer beer, there's beer. I see you've brought your sewing, so just settle down and sew, and if Nance appears restless, give her a valium tablet from this little pill-box.

JOSIE: Oh, drugs, is it?

MOTHER. Heavens, no, a prescription medication. She likes a card-game sometimes. And is quite good at rummy or double-solitaire or even Black-jack. Of course if she wants to go out, divert her from the idea, oh, and she hates TV unless it's something artistic on the educational network.

JOSIE: I always watch *Cannon*, *Cannon* is on tonight.

MOTHER: The child detests such unrefined things on the tube, you mustn't expose her to them.

JOSIE: I never been on a job of this type in my life.

MRS. AID: She's inventing problems to over-charge you.

MOTHER: That I know. Josie, you can see she's reading a book, not restless and won't be restless unless you're unpleasant. We've never had trouble with sitters that weren't unpleasant. Now just enjoy a few hours in charming surroundings including the child.

JOSIE: She ain't readin' no book, she's starin' at a naked man's statue in the hall there.

MRS. AID: This is a woman with a dirty mind.

MOTHER: *Tais-toi. Je peux faire la paix. Tu peux appeler un taxi.*

JOSIE: Talkin' in some secret foreign langwidge, something secret?

MRS. AID: Oh, *mon Dieu! Les hommes attendent: dépêche-toi!*

MOTHER: Miss, excuse me, Mrs. Slattery? Is it?

MRS. AID: Call her Madam and kiss her goddam ass, we've got to go.

JOSIE: Flattery and no madam.

MOTHER: The child looks into space when she's meditating.

NANCE [*behind her hand*]: Wait, wait, don't go!

JOSIE: Who's she tellin' to wait? The naked man's statue? She's staring direckly at it.

MOTHER: What a disgusting suggestion! I think you had better not talk to the child if you have such depraved ideas. If we had time, I'd engage another sitter . . .

JOSIE: You wan' me to go, I'll be happy to go. I wasn't told that I was engaged to sit with a grown woman disguised as a little girl. I noticed at once she wasn't readin' no book but was starin' at that naked man's statue in the hall and her hand is—look at her fingers, she's—

[*Mrs. Aid chuckles while preening at the pier-glass.*]

MOTHER: You are going too far. Sit down and stop expressing these disgusting and ignorant ideas. Classic statues are called nude, not naked. And it's wearing a fig leaf.

JOSIE: If they're naked I call 'em naked and I expect a special price for a special job like this one.

MRS. AID [*turning from mirror impatiently*]: Oh, will you stop haggling with that biddy, we're going to be late at the Plaza and find ourselves without escorts.

MOTHER: I was waiting for you to stop admiring yourself in the mirror, dear. Are you satisfied with your appearance now?

MRS. AID: Quite!

MOTHER: Now, Aida, on this occasion.

MRS. AID: Which?

MOTHER: Our adventure tonight.

MRS. AID: Ah?

MOTHER: Don't be so aggressive. Permit the young man to make the first advances.

MRS. AID [*realistically*]: What if he doesn't?

MOTHER: He will if you don't grab at him practically on sight.

MRS. AID: You plan a date like an old general does a military campaign.

MOTHER: Yes, wisely and well.

MRS. AID: My advice to you is don't pay in advance.

MOTHER: I wouldn't dream of it.

MRS. AID: You wouldn't dream of it but you did it, I haven't forgotten if you have. It was at the Pavillon. We'd wined and dined them and you said, "Dear, would you mind paying the check?", slipping a couple of hundred to him under the table. He smiled with delight, and said, "Why, yes, of course, but excuse me a moment while I drop by the boys' room." Well, he dropped by it forever, not a sign of him since.

MOTHER: Aida, shall we?

MRS. AID: Shall we what?

MOTHER: Dispense with reminiscence and get on the go?

[*The cab honks.*]

MRS. AID: If I were you, I'd remove some of those rings.

MOTHER: This escort service assured me the young men had excellent character references.

MRS. AID: I hope that's not all they've got.

NANCE [*to the statue in the hall*]: They're leaving: then you can enter!

MOTHER: Nighty-night, Nance, darling, be a good little girl. Oh, my gloves and purse.

MRS. AID: In opposite importance.

MOTHER: *Au contraire! En avant!*

[*They go out. Josie stares suspiciously at Nance.*]

JOSIE: —What're you lookin' at, Miss?

NANCE: The moon-vines are open.

JOSIE: There's no moon-vines in that hall.

NANCE: They open around the windows.

JOSIE: The windows are behind you. —What's your age, why are you dressed like a child?

NANCE: I don't reply to impertinent questions.

JOSIE: Oh, impertinent, huh?

NANCE: I'm not obliged to answer personal questions of any kind from sitters.

JOSIE: Oh. So. Why don't you look at your book instead of that naked statue?

NANCE: I look wherever I wish. Why don't you do your sewing?

JOSIE: —Where's the phone, I want to phone my husband in Queens.

NANCE: The phone is on the table, right beside you, behind the jar of peppermint stick candy.

JOSIE: Aw. Hmm. [*She dials a number on the phone.*] —What're you doing, Pat? —Ice-Hockey fight on the tube? Hmm. How many beers you had? Look, watch it tonight. I want you to pick me up so I can keep my cab-fare. I'm sitting here with a loony. A grown young woman dressed up like a kid in party clothes, this is a real bummer. She's got her eyes on a naked male statue in the hall and her hand is in her lap with the fingers movin'. Get the pitcher? If she starts being indecent I'll call you back so stay by the phone, this job is a weirdie. *Don't git drunk now, Pat!*

SCENE DIMS OUT

A while later. Josie is sewing, but looking up repeatedly at Nance.

NANCE: —It rained last night. The dead come down with the rain.

JOSIE: I don't know about this. [*A slight pause.*] What's that book you got there? [*She crosses to Nance and seizes the book.*] Photographs of a boy dancer in tights. Give it here.

NANCE: NO! He isn't yours!

JOSIE: He ain't yours neither. You got indecent thoughts, it makes me sick.

[*Nance hold the books tight to her breasts.*]

NANCE: Please return to your chair, he won't come in till you do. [*She looks back at the shadowy life-size stature in the hall, and speaks in a cultivated adult fashion.*] I recognize you from your photographs. Never mind the old woman, she's employed to sit with me while Mother is out. I know if I were alone, you'd come in and sit here with me and we'd have an intimate—conversation . . .

[*Chimes ring.*]

NANCE: That's just the clock, don't mind it . Being a dancer, perhaps you'd like some music to make an entrance? There's a music-box. I'll turn it on. Do come in! You're beautiful as the chauffeur.

JOSIE: That does it! I'm going to call my husband again to pick me up, crazies I won't sit with! [*She dials phone.*] —Pat, you come right over and pick me up here, I can't take no more of this creature I'm sitting with. She's still acting indecent with her hands in her lap and staring at that naked man's statue and you come here, this is no place for a clean-living woman. Know how long I sit here? Till midnight, probably later, while the Mother and her friend are out with pick-ups. Now you come right over. Or I'm going to walk out without pay. I left you the address, Fifty-fifth and Park, come quick, before I—You heard me! [*She hangs up.*]

[*The statue becomes the apparition of Vaslav Nijinsky. He advances to the parlor door.*]

NANCE: Oh, how do you do!

JOSIE: How's who do?

[*Vaslav assumes a dancer's first position with grave concentration.*]

JOSIE: Answer me, you disgusting idiot!

[*Josie shakes Nance. Nance pushes her away rather violently.*]

NANCE: You are not allowed to touch me!

VASLAV: You have an unpleasant companion. I understand what that's like. To be stupid is worse than to be mad, but probably more comfortable to be.

NANCE: Pay no attention to her, she's employed to sit with me.

VASLAV: I can't perform if she creates a disturbance.

JOSIE: Here's your pill.

NANCE: I've had one already.

JOSIE: Then go up to bed.

NANCE: Not till midnight. Please return to your chair and go on sewing.

JOSIE: If I was your mum I'd lock you up and throw the key away. [*She returns to the chair and her sewing.*]

VASLAV: You would like me to dance.

NANCE: Yes, please.

VASLAV: It's been so long and there isn't much space.

NANCE: But you can leap, I've read you spring like a bird.

VASLAV: I had great levitation.

[*He leaps over a small table. Nance gasps and applauds.*]

VASLAV: Don't applaud 'till I bow.

JOSIE: This makes me sick, I'm going to the bathroom. [*She exits.*]

VASLAV: The harpie's out. [*He dances for a few minutes.*] —The music's stopped.

NANCE: Shall I start it again or will you? I wish you'd sit by me here and talk.

VASLAV: I went mad, you know, and when I talk it's madness.

NANCE: Just sit beside me a while.

VASLAV [*on sofa*]: Are you a lunatic too?

NANCE: Mother says I'm a child.

VASLAV: But you're not.

NANCE: No. I'm very different, though.

VASLAV: —Yes, very—different, though.

NANCE: I wish that you would embrace me.

VASLAV: Impossible. You wouldn't feel it at all, it would be nothing.

NANCE: Well, may I touch you?

VASLAV: Physical touches—dissolve me.

NANCE: They make you—

VASLAV: Disappear, go away.

NANCE: No, no, don't!

VASLAV: Then no touches between us, just—

NANCE: It's—unbearable—to just sit here beside you without any contact.

VASLAV: But you know, I'm an apparition.

NANCE: A fantasy?

VASLAV: Something—similar, yes, it's like a vision, or a shadow or a figure in a dream.

NANCE: —I—don't dream.

VASLAV [*with a sad smile*]: You mean you don't distinguish between waking and sleeping.

NANCE: Just that the room is darker when I sleep.

VASLAV: Otherwise, no difference?

[*Nance shakes her head. Pause.*]

NANCE: I don't understand apparitions.

VASLAV: They're contradictory, paradoxical things: maybe only possible on a stage, in a play written by a madman.

NANCE: I want to touch and be touched.

VASLAV [*touching her hand*]: This is my touch. Do you feel it?

NANCE: If you say so.

VASLAV: You'll believe so?

[*Nance smiles.*]

VASLAV: The licenses of madness are almost unlimited. I know, since I've explored them too.

NANCE: You're—beautiful.

VASLAV: Well, I created the illusion. *Et ça va.* Actually, I was short. Slant-eyed, my hair receded early. My legs were so muscular that my upper torso, while hairless and well-formed, seemed inadequate to them. However, costumes and light and the creations of Bakst and my passion for my art, and, I must admit it, the possessive care that Diaghelev gave me 'till I defected to matrimony and madness, made me appear to have beauty. And I had an arrogant way. Well. The apparition of a dancer leaps without effort, nothing to make him breathless. —You seemed to be dressed for a little girls' party.

NANCE: Mother prefers me to. [*Pause.*]

VASLAV: Little frosted cakes: *petit fours.*

NANCE: Won't you have one?

VASLAV: Oh, I don't eat, apparitions can't, no digestive tract.

NANCE: Well, sit down with me on the sofa again, and—

VASLAV: Embrace you? I thought I'd shown you that apparitions can be seen but not touched and not touch. I understand erotic impulses, was taught them early in life and was a good pupil. But, finally, found them inadequate as my torso to my abnormally muscular legs. To be disembodied is a release from passions. But music haunts me still.

NANCE: Music. Arensky's "Vals a Deux Pianos"? [*She returns to the music box.*]

VASLAV: You want me to dance again?

NANCE: Please.

[*He dances. She stands ecstatic. He stops and bows.*]

VASLAV: Applaud, applaud, shout Bravo and I will take bows.

NANCE [*applauding*]: Bravo, bravo!

[*He takes repeated bows.*]

NANCE: Isn't that enough?

VASLAV: I would take fifteen, twenty, in a storm of flowers.

NANCE: Do you still care about that, I mean does your— apparition?

VASLAV [*imperiously*]: Hand me those roses! [*He indicates flowers in a vase on incidental table.*]

NANCE: Oh, but—that mean old woman will notice!

VASLAV: *Vite, vite,* do as I say, the house is thundering with applause!

[*She rushes to hand him the roses; they fall from his hands to the carpet. Josie enters from the hall.*]

JOSIE: Oh, throwin' things about, are you! [*She kicks viciously at the roses.*]

NANCE: I can't imagine a person kicking roses! Can you imagine anyone kicking roses?

VASLAV [*ecstatic*]: I don't imagine, I bow with Karsavina! Now with Pavlova! Now with the *corps de ballet* and the ovation continues, now Stravinsky joins us, and now— [*His face darkens.*] That demon Diaghelev. [*He swears in Russian and spits.*] *Chort s nem* * —Now Bakst . . . [*He takes a final bow.*] —Nothing afterward ever really existed! —Madness and death are unbearably lonely . . . [*He averts his head in torment.*]

NANCE: So are madness and life.

JOSIE [*frightened*]: Too goddam much! I'll wait outside for my husband!

[*Josie exits through the hall. Vaslav returns to the sofa.*]

---

* Pronounced: chórts - n'yem. (ed.)

NANCE: She's gone now, we're alone. [*She touches his face and throat lingeringly.*]

VASLAV: I'm sorry I can't respond. —What is your name?

NANCE: My name is Nance.

VASLAV: *Enchanté.* —Why haven't you gone to the party?

NANCE: I wasn't invited to one.

VASLAV: You're dressed as a little girl for a *bal masque*, for a masquerade party.

NANCE: No. This is how I dress when alone every night.

VASLAV: Hmmm. —If I were still human, I would be—*sympathique* . . . Please remove your hand. —I suspect that you will have no love in your life outside of your fantasies, because when people go mad, they're usually, almost always, kept under close custody, and intimacies are forbidden.

NANCE: —There are diamonds of perspiration on your forehead and throat.

VASLAV: You do—imagine—well . . .

NANCE: I feel this blue vein pulsing in your throat and I feel—

[*He catches her hand.*]

VASLAV: No, no. No more, I'm sorry. I can't go back that way, not even in your fantasy. It was too much: it burned me up, it interfered with my art and finally blasted my mind. I know how sad it is, to be deprived of gratification of strong natural longings, but there are other things, there's a lifetime of dreaming before you in this elegant house, or at least till—you're abandoned.

[*She continues to caress him.*]

VASLAV: No, no, I said no. —Well, of course if you have to. —I'll—submit, I was—always passive permissive. —You do know where to touch to thrill the skin—if the skin of apparitions could be thrilled.

[*She continues her touches.*]

VASLAV: However —If you go on with this, I'll dissolve. You'll find your hands are empty, moving in air. —Of course I admit that's probably not much different from the caresses of those that caressed me and whom I caressed when I lived but there is a difference and that difference is a great one. —You've *defiled* me! I'm not yet entirely free from the memories of my body and the disgust of being exploited as a body when I existed as a great dancer and wanted only that. I told them and wrote in my diary that I am spiritual food.

NANCE: I know your diary. I have read that, too.

VASLAV: Begun in St. Moritz, a place of retreat from war.

NANCE: You devoted yourself to music and choreography and then your words to the world.

VASLAV: I informed the world that I am spiritual food. People go to the church in order to pray and there they are made to drink wine and are told that it is the blood of Christ. The blood of Christ does not intoxicate—on the contrary, it makes people sober. Catholics do not drink wine, but make use of it in a symbolic way. They swallow white wafers, thinking that they swallow the blood and flesh of Our Lord. I am the spirit in the flesh and flesh in the spirit.

NANCE: Yes, remember the flesh, it cries to be remembered.

VASLAV: In becoming an apparition, I rise, I rise, above flesh!

NANCE: Please, not completely! Not above my—desire!

VASLAV: Don't play Diaghelev with me. [*He retreats.*] He dyes his hair in order to look young. Diaghelev's hair is white. He buys black dyes and rubs them in. I have seen this dye on Diaghelev's cushions. His pillowcase is blackened by it. I hate dirty linen and therefore was disgusted by this sight.

NANCE: Not with me, please not disgusted with me!

VASLAV: Then control your hands, control your ravenous lips!

NANCE: I know my age is disguised by inappropriate clothes. Please be tolerant of my hungry flesh, my—my ravenous lips, they're human!

VASLAV: Accept me as I am.

NANCE: You are?

VASLAV: I am the Lord. I am Man. I am Christ.

NANCE: I know, I read, I remember, but for tonight—for me? Be man?

VASLAV: Woman disguised as child, false child, lonely woman.

NANCE: Loneliest woman, prisoner of child's clothes!

VASLAV: I consent no longer to the service of lechery, at the height of my ascent into purity as an artist. You know my words by heart but you don't understand me. No. You're a lunatic in their eyes, so was I. Led about, watched over, treated like a pet monkey on a chain!

NANCE: But there was Romala. You had flesh for her, were man, not apparition!

VASLAW: In her I bred Kyra, direct descendant of Christ. A difference, no?

NANCE: Let me be Romala for you; breed for you a descendant of Christ!

VASLAV: Watch what your hands reach for! I don't live there except in your madness and fever. *Stop it! —I am Spirit!* [*He retreats from her hands.*] Or I will leave you and not come back. You can stare your eyes out at my photographs in a book and I'll not enter the room . . .

NANCE [*extending her hand again*]: Please, it can't be wrong to—

VASLAV: Not just wrong but impossible. You must learn to accept. IT—WILL—NEVER—BE—REAL! You can only—dream!

NANCE: How long can you stay if I—don't touch.

VASLAV: Till you go up to bed or till the moon-vines close.

NANCE: But touches I just imagine, if they satisfy me, if they seem so real, why can't I, why won't you permit it?

VASLAV: I can't bear to be reminded of—being used for—don't make me repeat all that.

NANCE: But it's agony for me.

VASLAV: When Diaghelev took Massine and out of spite I married on that long Pacific voyage this woman who used me for ambition, to advance herself from the chorus to first ballerina, that was agony, too.

NANCE: But yours is past. Mine's now!

[*There is the sound of a door opening offstage.*]

VASLAV: Someone is coming in.

NANCE: It's Mummy and her friend.

MOTHER [*off*]: Dynamite, he said, and offered me a popper.

MRS. AID [*off*]: Mine, Bill, said "Wow!" He said, "Wow, Wow!"

[*Mother, Mrs. Aid, and Josie enter the room.*]

MOTHER: Aida, Bill was my date.

MRS. AID: Which was mine?

MOTHER: The Puerto Rican, Riccardo.

MRS. AID: No, no, no, Riccardo was night before last.

[*The spotlight on Vaslav dims.*]

NANCE: You're dimming out! You mustn't!

MOTHER [*noticing Nance*]: Mummy's precious Angel! Mummy's back!

NANCE [*closing her eyes*]: I see! And he's disappearing, oh, God, you're disappearing! Don't, please don't dissolve.

VASLAV: An apparition fades when your attention's distracted from it.

NANCE: I'll get them out somehow!

MRS. AID [*suspiciously*]: Who is "the child" talking to?

MOTHER: The child always has her imaginary companions.

MRS. AID: Then why get her a sitter?

MOTHER: Imaginary companions are no protection.

MRS. AID: Protection from what? The sitter? This one does look like a menace out of the silent films, a villain in drag!

MOTHER: Not even sitting, standing by the door.

MRS. AID: She's offering you her hand?

JOSIE: I'm offering nothing and will touch nothing here but cab fare to and from Queens and double pay plus compensation for insult to decency while you "ladies" was out.

MOTHER: What is she saying to me?

JOSIE: *Pay, pay!*

MRS. AID: Get her out of the house at any price. The "child's" much better with an imaginary companion than with this wretched old creature.

JOSIE: You're old yourself, maybe older.

MRS. AID: I am young as tomorrow! *L'esprit de la jeunesse* and Elizabeth Arden's and—nightly adventures with youth and romance!

MOTHER [*airily*]: "Romance, romance, may come with the Spring or the Fall!"

JOSIE: Shit.

MRS. AID: Did you hear that? The child could pick up vulgar expressions from this tenement drop out.

MOTHER: The child ignores all language and behavior beneath the purity of the dream world she lives in.

JOSIE: Shit.

MOTHER: Out, you insufferable thing! Not another word from you in the child's presence! [*She tosses a bill to the floor.*]

JOSIE: Pick that up and hand it properly to me.

MOTHER: Pick it up or leave it!

MRS. AID [*sprawling to the floor*]: Here, take it and shove it and get the fuck out of here!

MOTHER: Aida, your language, watch it in front of the child. [*To Josie.*] You are paid and dismissed, so be off with you at once!

[*Josie rushes out and slams the door.*]

MOTHER: Exit the Marchioness of Queensborough!

[*Pause. They admire themselves in the mirror.*]

MOTHER: Well, we had quite an evening of it, again. When an evening starts at the Plaza it usually goes well.

MRS. AID: It might have gone better is you hadn't insisted on a buggy ride that took us directly to the bushes at West Seventy-second.

MOTHER: I found it very romantic.

MRS. AID: With that old nag expelling gas in our faces every few steps?

MOTHER: I noticed only the moon, spring foliage, and my escort's importunate advances.

MRS. AID: Well, your olfactory sense has failed you, dear.

MOTHER: So impetuous that I had to restrain him as best I could. Eyes devouring, hands so busy about me, I lost my breath.

MRS. AID: Be that as it may, real or imaginary, a fantasy of your libido, I think it might have been well to have booked a suite at the Plaza. "Wow, wow, have a popper!" —more appropriate there.

NANCE [*in a whisper*]: Are you still near?

VASLAV: *Pour le moment. Pas maintenant* .

NANCE: I will die if you go! You know what loneliness is!

MOTHER: Aida, I sometimes wonder what's going on in their heads.

MRS. AID: Perhaps it's better not to.

MOTHER: Probably for the first time in their lives they're encountering ladies of taste and distinction.

MRS. AID [*dizzily*]: I quite agree that may be. Did you say taste and—?

MOTHER [*dizzily*]: Distinction, ladies of taste and distinction.

MRS. AID: Oh, yes, *that*, the widow of the late Stuyvesant Aid and the widow of the late, heavens, how depressing, widows of the late, we mustn't think of the late. It *is* getting late. Where is my—Goddamn it, my adorable little—!

MOTHER: What?

MRS. AID: Pendant Cartier watch, platinum, diamond and amethyst studded, gone. And you declared to me they had honest credentials?

MOTHER: Don't jump at conclusions, a pendant watch could easily be torn loose by accident in—

MRS. AID: Removed! By intention!

MOTHER: During all that wild activity in the forsythia bushes?

MRS. AID: Activity in the forsythia—no! "Wow, wow, have a popper!" —Broke it under my nostrils and detached the, oh, they're quick at detachments, ladies of distinction doesn't obliterate their monastery concerns.

MOTHER: Monas—?

MRS. AID: MONETARY! —detachments, calculations, concerns with! —Oh, well, less time than money.

MOTHER: Them?

MRS. AID: No, dear. Us.

MOTHER: —Aida?

MRS. AID: Did I tell you he said "Wow, wow, wow!"?

MOTHER: Yes, and "Dynamite, have a popper."

MRS. AID: But the "Wow, wow, wow," it reminded me of the old times in Havana where our party wound up one night at a private sex show.

MOTHER: Aida, please, the child.

MRS. AID: Finale of the performance! All the actors and actresses, so to speak, got down on all fours, hands and knees, and started barking "Wow, wow," to imitate dogs, you know, while indiscriminately mounting each other.

MOTHER: Aida, I said the child.

MRS. AID: Exactly, barking "Wow, wow," and one little performer in the show looked up and said very sweetly, "Dogs"—to explain the commotion, the action.

MOTHER: Aida, I think you should try to limit yourself to a single toddy at the Plaza, not several, before we sally forth, since otherwise you're inclined to follow not one but several trains of thought, which is confusing to me.

MRS. AID: Who's confused, you or me? I'm—you know, I do wish the young men were not so—narcissian, so self-infatuated . . .

MOTHER: You're never quite satisfied. After all, a hired escort is just that.

MRS. AID: That depends on the service that supplies them. I think we ought to switch to—I have the card. Oh, here, it's called "Companions for Madame."

MOTHER: I don't like the sound of that. We'd probably find ourselves with a pair of middle-aged, broken-down brokers getting paunchy.

MRS. AID: Not if we specified exactly what we like and refused compromises.

MOTHER: It was a nice evening in the park, moon nearly full. My young man knew exactly where to direct the driver. Of course, it's a little indiscreet outdoors.

MRS. AID: My dear, if we start to worry about discretion—

MOTHER: We should start at the Plaza and cross the park to a little apartment kept for such occasions.

MRS. AID: Yes. You mean a pad.

MOTHER: With a view of the reservoir. A powder room and kitchenette for making Welsh-rarebit or a crabmeat omelette with chilled wine.

MRS. AID: Speaking of wine.

MOTHER: Of course you'd like a night-cap.

MRS. AID: *Pourquoi pas?* It's nice to remember an evening over a night-cap.

MOTHER: *Crème de?*

MRS. AID: No, no, I think I'd prefer a mellow, reflective libation such as medium dry sherry.

MOTHER: You'll find a bottle of *Pedro Domcq* at the bar.

MRS. AID [*at the bar*]: And you? What would you like for a midnight libation?

MOTHER: The usual.

MRS. AID: Which is?

MOTHER [*turning slowly with a lascivious smile*]: —The warm, salty juice of a young lover's loins . . .

VASLAV: This is—abominable.

MRS. AID: That libation is kept in laboratory bottles, *chère.*

MOTHER: I've found it outside bottles. But, you know, I thought it a little presumptuous when he put my hand on his equipment so quickly. Not that I—but you know they shouldn't be quite so forward—so quickly.

MRS. AID: They have other assignments, I suppose.

MOTHER: Yes, before and after. One should demand escorts that aren't debilitated by previous engagements.

MRS. AID: I suppose it was a mistake going into the bushes. You came out looking a bit disheveled and your escort complained that his clothes were irreparably damaged.

MOTHER: They always pretend to have lost their cuff-links or torn their something or other, it's part of the game. And you. I noticed a great agitation among the forsythia bushes that you disappeared into with that suspiciously dark Lothario of yours.

MRS. AID: But all in all considered, we didn't have too disappointing a time.

MOTHER: No, but we ought to investigate other services. Such as, let's see, where's the, oh, here's a service with a superior sound: "Cavaliers for Milady." It's engraved which means it involves more expense. But we could be more specific about our requirements.

MRS. AID: Yes, why not, we're still attractive enough to settle for only the best.

NANCE: Mummy, please, please, leave us alone a while!

MOTHER: The child wants some privacy with her imaginary companion. Let's indulge her and take our drinks to the garden and plan tomorrow's adventure. [*She exits.*]

MRS. AID [*lingering at the mirror, a moment of candor*]: Into my sixties, and no relief in sight . . . Well, despair is no where! No where! [*She exits.*]

[*The light returns to Vaslav.*]

VASLAV: What strange women, quite shameless.

NANCE: Why don't they take me with them and their young men?

VASLAV: Be satisfied with your fantasies.

NANCE: They're not always as lovely as you are. [*She continues caressing him.*]

VASLAV: I wish you would sublimate these desires. What you caress is totally unresponsive, it's all your fancy, *rien de plus.*

NANCE: Oh, but it's so—real to me! [*She drops to her knees before him.*]

VASLAV: Stop it, I said stop, or I'll leave at once as I warned you before!

NANCE: *No, no please!*

MOTHER [*from offstage*]: Nance, was that you screaming?

NANCE: —No, Mummy—practicing—classic drama.

VASLAV: If you continue, I'll disappear again, and this time completely and not appear ever again.

NANCE: Oh, I'll—kill myself if you leave before morning.

VASLAV: Then don't go on with imaginary love-making.

NANCE: To me it's real.

VASLAV: To me it's a degrading memento of what I can't accept now. [*He springs up from the sofa.*] God loves the artist.

NANCE: I know, but—

VASLAV: God loves and protects the artist, even your fantasies of one. *Bonsoir, je pars!*

[*He rushes into the dark hall. Nance screams despairingly. Her Mother and Mrs. Aid rush into the hall.*]

NANCE: WHEN WILL YOU COME BACK? WHEN? WHEN? [*She collides with the antique sculpture in the dim hall.*]

MOTHER: Nance! What are you—? Child, what is it now? She's cut her forehead, it's bleeding.

MRS. AID: Yes, I see. She tried to embrace the statue in the hall, collided with it violently. And look! There's blood on the *fig-leaf*.

MOTHER: Gracious—yes!

MRS. AID: Obscene, salacious, face it, you're harboring a monster in your house, a travesty of a child in a ruffled white skirt and pink sash and Dotty Dimple curls!

MOTHER: —Are you reproaching me for it?

MRS. AID: Isn't it your idea to pass her off as a child in costumes like that?

MOTHER: No, it's Lucinda Blair's. That sentimental dressmaker regards her as a child. Says, "Oh, she's a child, just a precocious child, every night she should be in a little girl's party dress to receive her dream beaux!" You see, she was here one night when the child received Valentino after an old flick at the Modern Art cinema and performed an Argentine tango with his—apparition, I suppose you'd call it.

MRS. AID: Oh-ho-ho, then why didn't she dress her up like— Nita Naldi, was it?

MOTHER: Whoever, I don't remember.

NANCE: Must you discuss me so— [*She weeps a bit.*]

MOTHER: Oh, it's all so confusing. Who invented madness if not God?

MRS. AID: Show Lucinda the blood spot on the fig-leaf: she'll dress her differently then.

MOTHER: Yes, it is a little bit *de trop*, the blood of the fig-leaf bit. I had no idea she had such—embarrassing aberrations. [*She sighs dramatically.*] Tomorrow I'll simply have to find a place away for her. I suppose Riggs Institute or—

MRS. AID: They wouldn't accept her. She'd make disgusting advances to the attractive male patients and even young doctors. Where she belongs, if anywhere on earth, is in a segregated ward of a real asylum, that sort of institution is the only solution: face it!

NANCE: *Be still about me! Please!*

MOTHER: You see that she isn't retarded in the clinical sense.

MRS. AID: Fuck the clinical sense: obscene is what she is and it can only grow on her. Time'll make her hideous as the portrait of Dorian Gray.

NANCE: Deserted? —Put away?

MOTHER: The child has a morbid derangement that defies diagnosis. She reads adult fiction and she expresses herself in the language of a refined, grown-up young lady, except it's twisted, depraved, so shocking that I've stopped taking her out. Last time I did, she suddenly leaned forward in the car and said to the young chauffeur, with her hand on his neck, "Take me for a pilgrimage after dark."

MRS. AID: Pilgrimage?

MOTHER: After dark, meaning she wished to seduce him.

MRS. AID: Did she?

MOTHER: Indeed she didn't. I had priority there till his wife made him quit. —*Nance, go up to bed!* —Do you hear me? —*I said go up to bed!*

NANCE: He may return, after all . . . [*She picks up the book of photographs and opens it on her lap, as primly as if it were a book of scriptures.*]

MOTHER: What's she reading? [*She snatches the book.*] Why, it's a book of memories and photographs of Nijinsky, she's staring at him in costume for *L'Apres Midi d'un Faun!*

MRS. AID: And got him confused with the statue in the hall.

MOTHER: *Bed, I said go up!*

[*She tries to pull Nance off the sofa but the "child" clings desperately to it.*]

MRS. AID: Oh, leave her there, what does it matter if she stays there all night! —Let's finish our drinks and tomorrow's arrangements. My Fabergé case, where is it?

MOTHER [*leading Mrs. Aid off through the hall*]: In the garden with your hat and gloves.

[*They are off: we hear their indistinct voices and laughter until the curtain. Nance looks desperately about her: she abruptly notices the escort service cards on the table, reads them aloud.*]

NANCE: —"Cavaliers for Milady"—"Companions for Madam"— with phone numbers for both! Oh, I'll *call!*

[*Nance is dialing the phone.*]

MOTHER [*from the garden*]: —The secret is thinking young.

MRS. AID [*from the garden*]: —And feeling young. Yes. And a little cosmetic surgery after a while . . .

MOTHER [*from the garden*]: —We have a few years to make the most of . . .

[*Nance is dialing the phone.*]

NANCE: "Cavalier—Companions?" I, I—want one—tonight, no, it's *not* too late, I'll—pay—extra! [*Snatches her mother's evening-bag from the table.*] Whatever is charged! —You have the address, Park at Fifty-five, I'll be waiting outside on the stone steps, and, oh, please hurry. I'll be on the steps of stone with a—lighted candle, don't disappoint me, please don't keep me waiting and send me an escort cavalier that looks like him! —*Nijinsky!*

[*She turns about excitedly, snatches a candle from the cande labra on the table and rushes out to the entrance, which be comes visible as the interior is dimmed. Nance is lighted with her lighted candle and evening-bag.*]

NANCE: Oh, God, make him hurry, I don't have—a few years left me!

SLOW CURTAIN : VALS LENTE

THE PRONOUN 'I'

(A SHORT WORK FOR THE LYRIC THEATRE)

The Pronoun 'I' (a short work for the lyric theatre) was first performed at the Provincetown Tennessee Williams Theater Festival
on September 29, 2007. It was directed by Julie Atlas Muz; the set
and costumes were designed by Jerry Stacy and Jon Pacheco; the
lights were designed by Megan Tracey. The cast, in order of appearance, was as follows:

MAD QUEEN MAY	Julie Atlas Muz
DOMINQUE, her young lover and a poet	James Tigger! Ferguson
A YOUNG REVOLUTIONARY	Zachary Klause
A COURTIER	Daniel Nardicio
A NUMBER OF BEDRAGGLED MOBSTERS INTENT UPON THE QUEEN'S DESTRUCTION	a dozen members of the audience
LEADER OF THE MOB	Adam Berry

Time: some centuries past. Scene: minimal representation of a throne room, and a section of the Queen's bedchamber, upstage right, concealed at rise by a purple velvet curtain bearing the crest of her House.

Mad Queen May should be performed by a young actress, lovely of face and figure. Since she is required on all public occasions and most private ones to play a part old enough to be her grandmother, age must be simulated by an artfully designed mask over which is usually drawn a veil suspended from the tip of her medieval, cone-shaped hat, which is gleaming and glittering with pearls and jewels.

At rise she lolls in her throne chair, toying with the curls of a petulantly pretty youth named Dominique, sprawled indolently on cushions at her feet. He is her latest lover and an enormously vain poet who cannot begin a poem without the pronoun 'I'. Only his genitalia are clothed. Offstage there are sounds of a riot, reduced to a murmur by closed gates and curtained casements.

QUEEN: I am May of England, now known as Mad Queen May. —I wonder why?

DOMINIQUE: And I?

QUEEN: I doubt that you're more than partly why.

DOMINIQUE: I?

QUEEN: My ministers were supposed to report to me on the latest insurrection. The report was to be delivered hours ago. There's still not a peep out of them and I can hear the rabble louder than ever, as if it were—

[*A ragged young revolutionary steals into the room and conceals himself behind a tapestry beside the door, downstage right. The Queen is not unaware of his entrance, but seems unperturbed.*]

DOMINIQUE: I?

QUEEN: Yes, it's always "I".

DOMINIQUE: You call yourself "we", which is the plural of "I".

QUEEN: On public occasions only—privately I am "I." Once I was known—could you believe it, my dear? —as Fair Queen May.

DOMINIQUE: That I don't remember.

QUEEN: I'd hardly expect you to remember what I was called before you were born or conceived, but I was once known as Fair Queen May. Later, as Good Queen May. And now? As Mad Queen May.

DOMINIQUE: So you were once favorably regarded by your subjects?

QUEEN: Favorably, once, and tolerantly for quite a while. [*She moves downstage to address the audience.*] My ministers say that my failure, my refusal, to make important alliances with various foreign princes to whom I was neither sexually nor spiritually attracted has made it necessary for them and their successors to impose upon my subjects a series of deceits, passed off as miracles, which have replaced Fair Queen May and Good Queen May with this reproduction of Mad Queen May. —I trust none of you enough to disclose the unscrupulous methods by which this deception was practiced upon my subjects and the successors of my subjects. Well. Of course the kingdom, they tell me it's now an empire, has been visited by such distractions as the black plague, the pox, reverberations of the inquisition in Spain, attacking armadas from hither and yon, Irish wars, altered conceptions of the shape and movement of the planet: then more wars, always and always more wars that we've survived by grace of a surrounding sea—

[*She has, during this, revealed her fair young face, and there has been the music of a court dance. Dominique lolls in slumber beneath the throne. She dances a bit to the music.*]

QUEEN: —Now there seems to be a very, very serious insurrection among my subjects against whom they believe to be still Mad Queen May who is also Despised Queen May. I didn't despise my subjects, not in any of my earlier impostures and certainly not in the present. I was simply immured from them, I was permitted no contact after Fair Queen May the First could not be passed off any longer as young and fair.

DOMINIQUE [*rousing slightly from slumber*]: Did you say "fair"?

QUEEN: Did I? Why, Yes, I did—remembering times long past . . . [*She lowers her veil over her face and replaces the mask.*]

DOMINIQUE [*dreamily*]: Were you ever as young and fair as I?

QUEEN: Courtiers told me so but mirrors exposed their deceit. Still. —I had young lovers which is a considerable compensation . . . No? dear final boy . . . —my doom. May of England known as Mad Queen May declined to play the game demanded of her. Chose her own rejection of politically advantageous marriages to princes who repelled me, for—gifted young courtiers, lovely of face and figure, excellent dance partners, some of whom could sing sweetly into my ear in bed at night. It didn't matter to me that I had to apply my fingers and tongue to their privates to make them rise to the intimate occasion. I was young, once, and fair. [*She returns to throne steps.*] Kiss me, Dominique.

DOMINIQUE: Caress me. Play with my body.

QUEEN: Adorable little narcissus . . .

DOMINIQUE: Have you read my new poems?

QUEEN: Of course I did, as soon as you gave them to me.

DOMINIQUE: You haven't commented on them.

QUEEN: By commented, don't you mean praised?

DOMINIQUE: Naturally. Why not?

QUEEN: I thought them pretty as you. However—I have a suggestion to offer. —Delete from them all sentences that begin with the pronoun "I".

[*He shrugs. His eyes close again. Dominique snores softly. The Queen now addresses the intruder behind the tapestry.*]

QUEEN: He's fallen asleep, the subject of discussion not being himself. —Do you hear me? I mustn't raise my voice, it might wake him up, and I'd soon be obliged to comment on his latest dalliance with the art of verse. Pretty boys, pretty boys, if I didn't have them I would have to invent them but preferably none of the literary persuasion. —Come out from behind that arras, this isn't the chamber scene from Hamlet and you're much too young for the part of Polonius, Sir.

[*The Young Revolutionary, dagger held behind him, emerges from behind the wall-hanging.*]

QUEEN: —We offer you our compliments on your youth and beauty. We know your purpose, although the weapon's concealed behind your back, but we're not alarmed, somehow. It's our ancient sovereignty, I suppose, a thing that runs in our blood. A certain chill, almost a thrill, is aroused in us by the abrupt and still not spoken-out meaning of your presence. —Are you speechless because you confront a crowned witch on a throne?

DOMINIQUE [*rousing slightly*]: What?

QUEEN: Nothing concerning you is nothing and so go back to sleep. [*Queen May removes her slippers and descends from the raised level of the throne.*] Voluntarily we approach our possible assassin, old veins inflamed by the fearless approach to— [*She crosses to the Young Revolutionary with a candelabra.*] —challenge of insurrection. . . . [*Slowly she lifts the candelabra.*] Ravishing, your appearance . . . Look! Here's Fair Queen May. [*She removes the mask from her face.*] —Well? What say you, Sir?

YOUNG REVOLUTIONARY: I came to assassinate a demented old hag—not you. . . .

QUEEN: Then drop the weapon you're holding behind your back.

[*He stares at her a moment. The weapon falls to the floor.*]

DOMINIQUE [*dreaming*]: I.

QUEEN [*to the Young Revolutionary*]: Meanwhile I'll find a way to get rid of that pretty little obstruction. —A critical comment on his verse should do it.

DOMINIQUE [*eyes shut*]: You've made no comment on my latest poems.

[*The Queen points to her bedchamber entrance. With a slight nod, the Young Revolutionary picks up the weapon he dropped and enters the bedchamber, leaving the arched doorway uncurtained.*]

DOMINIQUE [*drowsily, eyes shut*]: Where are—why are—

QUEEN [*to the Young Revolutionary*]: Since the boy never looks at my face why should I bother with this uncomfortable mask. —The charade, the bal masque is nearly over now . . . Now I offer you the secret of my young body . . . [*She opens her padded robe.*] If your preference is for boys, well, there's Dominique, all but the genitalia exposed. A lovely-looking boy and his limitless narcissism—sadly amusing. —Victim, yes. We all are. —Victims . . . Our defects are not things chosen but things imposed. My defect—the eroticism that runs riot in my veins, an hereditary thing as common to my House as, say, the arrogance of the Hapsburgs and their pride . . . —collateral relatives. Name them, the Houses, I've got a bit of them all. But something entirely my own. [*She leans forward.*] *I am very, very clever*! —in that respect at least, allow me to say that I crown the lot of them. You'll see! —Centuries from now this thing I have in my fingertips, this sensual stroking compulsion—would classify me as a—"skin-freak"? —So what? [*She runs her fingertips over the body of her boy-beloved.*] Music! Dance—celebration of the flesh! [*She throws off her padded robe and whirls about the room in an ecstatically sensual dance.*] —While obscene drawings of one I'm supposed to be are carried about the streets and effigies burned—of one gone long ago.

DOMINIQUE: My new poems! Are you ready to discuss them?

QUEEN: I've advised you not to begin so many with the pronoun "I". [*She toys with his curls.*] Of course I realize that that would reduce their number quite drastically, yes, to a fraction of—

DOMINIQUE: *All* of my poems begin with the pronoun "I".

QUEEN: Oh, dear, I suspected as much, since I've yet to come across one not begun with a great gilded assertion of the first person singular, the largest and most brilliantly illuminated letter on the page, appearing not just at the beginning but scattered throughout with a truly staggering succession of the same without variation. Change the pronoun, change it at least to "we".

DOMINIQUE: Meaning include you in it?

QUEEN: No, no, I wish no part of it, dear boy. Collaboration between us? In a literary form? Disastrous, in view of the unpopularity that we both suffer equally at this time. The pronoun "we" could concern a common human condition, a confession of sharing the general human fate. This might disarm certain critics who find you unduly infatuated with the—what do they call it? Enormity of personal concern, disregard of all others on earth.

DOMINIQUE: Detractors are dishonest. —Life commences with the pronoun "I" and probably ends with it, too.

QUEEN: A passable aphorism, dear boy, but not an impregnable defense against your detractors who charge you with total self-concern, complete narcissism.

DOMINIQUE: My narcissism is true.

QUEEN: Unquestionably, sweet plaything, pretty toy of mine.

[*A trembling courtier enters. The Young Revolutionary retreats from view.*]

COURTIER: Madam, the enemy has entered the palace grounds.

QUEEN: Overcome my guards?

COURTIER: They've all deserted you, Madam.

QUEEN: So. That's how it is, that's how it goes. Well, if our defenders do nothing, what are we to do? What action would you advise, Sir?

COURTIER: Take flight at once.

QUEEN: Once there were secret stairs and passageways through which one could take flight, but the stairs have collapsed and where do the passageways go?

DOMINIQUE: What will happen to *me*?

QUEEN: —That's something best not considered. [*She rises.*] Why am I seated on this—mockery of what I now am? [*She stumbles down three steps from her throne, staggers to the casement windows—throws them open.*] Smoke blowing in. The capital's on fire. Gates battered, stormed. —I've no defenders. Have you? Poor shivering boy, you haven't even a voice to answer. Title and position meant little when I had them and mean even less when lost. —I'm going to retire to my bedchamber now. Hadn't you better come with me? —The relation between us is known. —We're condemned together.

DOMINIQUE: You made the mistake of—

QUEEN: What mistake did I make? [*To the Courtier.*] You're excused, Sir.

DOMINIQUE [*as the Courtier rapidly exits*]: —Using your ridiculously inappropriate position to indulge your lunacy.

QUEEN: As grave an error as beginning too many sentences with the pronoun "I"?

DOMINIQUE: The consequences appear to have been more fatal in your case.

QUEEN: Only *mine*, Dominique?

DOMINIQUE: I'm still young. I can escape in disguise. Throw on a monk's cloak and cowl—there are vestments in the chapel.

QUEEN: Which is across the courtyard.

DOMINIQUE: It's not yet daybreak. [*He runs to the opposite door.*] I'll race quickly across through the wall shadows.

QUEEN: Yes, do that, go quickly, quickly, quickly!

[*He dashes out. She seizes a candelabra and rushes to the windows and throws them open.*]

QUEEN [*crying out*]: THERE GOES MY LOVER! THERE GOES MY BELOVED DOMINIQUE!

[*She holds the candelabra out the windows. The mob howls wildly below and there is a shrill, despairing cry from the fugitive boy. She closes the windows and crosses slowly to her bedchamber.*]

QUEEN: —Poor treacherous young fool. He's done with the pronoun "I". —not just with me.

[*She enters bedchamber. The Young Revolutionary springs forward—tears her regal clothes off, strips her naked.*]

QUEEN: Now when they enter, they will ask "Where is she?" To that, what shall we say?

YOUNG REVOLUTIONARY: Say that she is dead.

QUEEN: Several times over.

YOUNG REVOLUTIONARY [*embracing her*]: How was that accomplished? By what magic?

QUEEN: Perhaps she had her own secret assassin in her heart.

[*A mob of revolutionaries burst into the thrown room.*]

LEADER OF THE MOB: Where is she?

YOUNG REVOLUTIONARY [*to Queen*]: Turn.

LEADER OF THE MOB: —Where is she?

QUEEN: Down secret stairs, to underground passageways, hurry, let's pursue her!

[*The candles blow out in the windy rush as the mob about them runs from the room. They are alone and resume their embrace.*]

YOUNG REVOLUTIONARY: You.

QUEEN: You . . .

CURTAIN

THE REMARKABLE ROOMING-
HOUSE OF MME. LE MONDE

CHARACTERS

MINT, a tenant
HALL, his visitor
MME. LE MONDE, the landlady
THE BOY, her son

A delicate little man with a childlike face, Mint, is spotted near the door to the "rectangle with hooks," which is actually the attic of Mme. Le Monde's residence in London. He is partially dressed in his old public school uniform, that is, he has on the short pants but the middy-jacket lies at his feet. The whole attic is equipped with curved metal hooks which provide the little man with a means of locomotion, as his legs are mysteriously paralyzed and his hands swing him from hook to hook. Stage left, there is an alcove with semi-transparent curtains to provide a retreat for certain occasions that require privacy. At rise a muscular, tow-headed young street-boy, son of Mme. Le Monde, appears in the doorless entrance, grinning lasciviously.

MINT: Oh, no, no, not now. I am expecting a visitor.

BOY: [*advancing toward Mint*]: We got time. He's downstairs in bed with Mom.

MINT: But he might surprise us!

BOY [*removing Mint from hook*]: Don't worry, it takes Mom a long time to come.

MINT: Oh, but can't we—

BOY: Shuddup!

[*The boy carries Mint into the alcove. A perverse sexual act occurs behind the semi-transparent curtains. Moans of masochistic pain-pleasure are heard from Mint. The act is quickly completed and the boy emerges, fastening his fly.*]

MINT [*off-stage*]: Put me back on a hook, please, please, put me back on a hook before my guest arrives for tea.

BOY: Aw, him, let him hook you back up if he ever hauls himself out of that ole buffalo waterin' hole of Mom's.

[*The boy exits. Pause. There is a rumble of thunder and sounds of gusty rain sweeping the attic roof. Mint's arm snakes out of the curtained alcove to haul into it an old chamber pot decorated with faded roses, and also some crumpled newspaper sheets. Sound of footsteps rapidly ascending the attic stairs are heard. Hall enters. He is a tall, sharp-featured young man in a flashy, tight-fitting plaid suit, obviously subjected to long wear.*]

HALL: Well, where are you, Mint? —Was told you occupied this untenable-looking attic.

MINT [*in a thin voice from the alcove*]:
> Scrotum-on-Swansea,
> Ever do or die!
> May the heavens bless thee
> Through eternity!

HALL [*glumly*]: Yes. If my recollection serves me correctly, the composer of that dear old school song was accidentally dropped off the chapel belfry soon after its composition. Now did you or didn't you ask me up here for tea?

MINT: Did, did, oh yes, certainly did, repeatedly—repeatedly, dear Hall . . . Care of your last known address, P.O. Box Sixty-six, was it? [*Mint crawls out of the alcove.*] What a happy reunion this is!

HALL [*dubiously*]: Hmmm. —What're you crawling for, Mint?

MINT: To extend greetings.

HALL: In that horizontal position, half in and half out of your pants?

MINT: Will explain later. Soon as I've fetched my box of old snapshots, mementos of our glorious days at Scrotum-on-Swansea.

HALL: No, no, no, no, no. I am gasping for a good hot cup of tea.

[*A mechanical piano fades in faintly with the old tune, "Tea for Two."*]

MINT: I may require of bit of assistance from you to conduct you to the tea table.

HALL: Seeing you in this condition, I must congratulate myself that I've never suffered an affliction.

MINT: None at all?

HALL: No, none ever.

MINT: Accidents?

HALL: Not since a bee stung me in Hyde Park at the age of eleven. No allergy, no ill effect.

MINT [*gasping*]: What—amazing—luck! Do hope—will continue.

HALL: Confident of it. My theory about afflictions and accidents is that they're self-induced.

MINT: By— [*He swings to another hook.*] —what?

HALL: Tendency. Susceptibility. As for you, Mint, there was never much question among us acquainted with you at Scrotum, really no question.

MINT: About?

HALL: Your inclination toward accident and affliction. In fact, I find it surprising that you've survived even to hang on a hook. No offense intended.

MINT: Oh, none taken— [*He swings to the next hook, and another.*] —none whatsoever, dear Hall. [*He loses his grasp of a hook and falls to the floor.*] Ow.

HALL: Took a bit of spill?

MINT: Would you please hook me back up?

HALL: Now how could I do that?

MINT: Just, just— [*Gasps.*] —lift me, please, I'm—not heavy.

HALL: Not at all sure I wish to take the risk.

MINT: Risk? Risk of?

HALL: Placing myself within range of your itchy fingers, Mint. You know what I mean, that old impulse of yours to take unsolicited liberties with the lower appendage of a schoolmate after lights out in the dorm. Must confess to you that I only accepted that flirtatiously phrased invitation to tea because I found myself in the vicinity of Mme. Le Monde's rooming-house, it was starting to rain and my expensive new bumbershoot was turned inside out by a fearful gust of wind that swept Piccadilly Circus about an hour ago. By the way, may have to borrow yours or Mme. Le Monde's when I brave the elements again after tea. Meanwhile let us remain at a respectful distance, you over there and me here.

MINT: Please be assured, dear Hall, that I, that I, that I—

HALL: Out with it, man, you *what*?

MINT: Entertain no such impulses, I swear by the blood of Our Blessed Saviour.

HALL: Remain unconvinced.

MINT: Also I've just experienced a sexual assault by one of the Madame's innumerable— [*Gasps.*] —children, a male one, hung like a dray horse, kept on the place for— [*Gasps.*] —incestuous relations with the lady.

HALL: All right, all right, I'll run the risk of hooking you back up if you'll quit this unappetizingly sordid chattering blather. [*He lifts Mint from the floor with pretense of terrible effort and holds him under the hook farthest removed from the tea.*] Grab hold before I drop you, you bloody sod! [*The intimidated Mint seizes a hook beside the entrance.*] There now, stay there, lemme get on with my tea.

MINT: Oh, dear, you've hooked me up hopelessly far away from—

HALL: Sorry. Too many hooks to distinguish one from another. Curious situation here, Mint, did you grope me when I picked you off the floor?

MINT: No, no, no— [*Gasps.*] —I assure you— [*Gasps.*] —I didn't.

HALL: I assure you you did. Perhaps the unconscious impulse overcame propriety for a second. Nevertheless however be that as it may. [*Pours himself more tea, slurps noisily.*] Need restoration after that strenuous workout with your landlady down there.

MINT: Do please wait till I— [*Gasps.*] —join you. I'm not complaining but I did, you did, well, give me a bit of a set-back to that hook by the door.

HALL: Yes, curious, very. [*He munches a biscuit.*] At Scrotum-on-Swansea you were a notorious fag and bed-wetter but reasonably mobile. Now you get about only by swinging from hook to hook, like that historical ape-man swinging from branch to branch in the jungle. [*He puts on broken spectacles to look about.*] Twilight descending with intemperate weather. [*He picks a crumb or two off the floor and pops them into his mouth.*] Haven't had time to stop by my bank today. Can you spare me a couple of quid?

MINT: Oh, dear, no. Haven't a shilling, not even a copper since— [*Gasps.*] —remittances stopped and lower paralysis— [*Gasps.*] —started.

HALL: Well, then. We won't pursue the financial subject further. When did this dependence on hooks begin, Mint?

MINT: Almost immediately after Mommy's commitment.

HALL: Did I understand you to say it's connected with a commitment?

MINT [*in a choked voice*]: Yes, Mommy's.

HALL: [*munching a biscuit*]: Commitment to what?

MINT: Asylum.

HALL: Mental?

MINT [*with a sob*]: Yes.

HALL: Events of this nature frequently occur. When the genes are a fuck-up.

MINT: No further allowance incoming—cut off completely since dear mother's commitment. However I don't wish to depress you with the misfortunes that have taken place in my life since Scrotum-on-Swansea.

HALL: This tea is restorative, a strong brew, but it's getting a little tepid.

MINT: I'd hoped you would arrive sooner.

HALL: Arrived punctually, but was detained downstairs. [*He pours himself another cup of tea and munches a second biscuit.*] The biscuits are a bit moldy, if you'll forgive my candor on the subject.

MINT: Sorry about that, Hall. The weather's been damp all week.

HALL: Mmm. That's a pretty accurate observation . . .

MINT [*approaching Hall gradually by swinging from hook to hook*]: My arms seem weaker today.

HALL: Don't over-exert yourself, Mint. No hurry, y'know.

MINT: You are drinking the tea so fast that, pardon me for this concern which may seem to be selfish, I—I fear that the pot will be empty before I am able to join you.

HALL: That amiable landlady of yours, Mme. Le Monde, will surely provide us with more. Perhaps another platter of biscuits as well, being the last of the present lot.

MINT: Could you, would you?

HALL: The usual request? Sorry. Having just done my bit of in-out with the Madam—would not be inclined to repeat the performance with you, certainly not in your somewhat off-putting state of disrepair, Mint.

MINT: Oh, I assure you, you misunderstood me. I meant could you reduce somewhat the speed with which you are—I mean not quite so rapid, the—consumption of biscuits and tea, since—

HALL: Not a chance, old boy. You see, I've had such an active day in the sale of shares in Amalgamated that this is actually my first chance to ingest a bit of restorative brew and—mmm, yes, there was a bit of misunderstanding, Mint. You see, I haven't forgotten how you were after me continually for sexual gratification at Scrotum-on-Swansea.

MINT: Coming, coming.

HALL: An orgasm at the mere recollection of it, well, well, hmmm, that's flattering. However—the pot is practically empty. How do you call Mme. Le Monde, vocally or by a buzzer or a bell or a hard knock on the woodwork? [*Mint falls from a hook to the floor.*] Took another spill, hah?

MINT: Was making fairly good progress, oh, this is—distressing.

HALL: Remember the fighting spirit of Scrotum-on-Swansea, hip, hip, hurrah, jolly good show and all that. Hmmm. How did the second verse go?

> Scrotum-on-Swansea,
> Long may ye thrive!
> Da-da-da-da-daaa,
> May fellowship survive.

MINT: Yes, yes, yes, but please put me back on a hook—by the tea!

HALL: All in good time. I am as you see engaged in brushing some crumbs off my trow. [*He eats the crumbs.*] Now, then, back on the hook with you, Mint. [*He goes to Mint and moves him back toward the doorway.*]

MINT: No, no, Hall, wrong direction.

HALL: Everlasting complaints, sour element of your nature. Now call the Madame and tell her we need some repletions.

[*Mint lets go of a hook by the door and starts crawling toward the box. Hall intercepts him and returns him to the hook.*]

MINT: Tea, biscuits! Biscuits, tea! Finished! Have pity on a broken and desperate soul, subsisting on diminishing bits of—charities—reluctance . . .

HALL [*shouting into stair-well*]: *Madame Le Monde, Madame Le Monde!*

MME. LE MONDE [*cheerily from below*]: What, ducks?

HALL: We could do with a fresh pot of tea and a few more biscuits up here.

MME. LE MONDE [*from below*]: Could ya now, whadaya know!

HALL: Rather ambiguous answer. Well—I do feel a bit restored. [*Big Ben tolls in the distance.*] Six or seven by my count. What by yours? [*Mint sobs quietly.*] Seems to me I have a later appointment, and not much later. Name? Rosie O'Toole. Address? Closer to Soho than Knightsbridge. Nevertheless it was an interesting encounter, as such things come and go. I mean after midnight in a torrent of rain just off Trafalgar Square. Ah, yes, the details of it remain quite fresh in my mind. [*The mechanical piano resumes; an old sentimental tune.*] Heard a screech of tires and this cabbie draws up beside me. The passenger was a youngish female of a predictable species. She leans her head out the window and enquires of me if she can give me a lift. "Why, yes," I reply, "that would be a Godsend in this type of weather." She swings the door open wide and a nearby lamp permits me to observe her more clearly. Her apparel was startling, even to me. Transparent summer frock, pale green with floral embroidery on it. —Not a stitch underneath. [*He has taken the box downstage and is seated on it as he delivers this account of his previous night's encounter.*] Well, it so happened I'd just been taking a leak. No impropriety about it since it was two A.M. or after and the streets deserted. So. I had not stopped pissing, the whang was still out. You remember its size? From experience, Mint? In the old days at Scrotum when you hounded me for it relentlessly in the dorm? Frankly, I think that's what gave Abbey and Sessions the notion that you were a bit of a fag, to put it politely. Well, she saw it and so the encounter with Miss O'Toole was not so coincidental as you might imagine at first. I get in the cab and start to zip up but she says, "Oh, no don't bother. I am a nurse's aide and am accustomed to male anatomy but rarely a member of that size has come my way." Distinguishing characteristics? Of Miss O'Toole? The expression is to deep throat. Well, she was a deep-throater, took it all the way in. However. She said, "Don't come in the oral preliminary. I want you to fuck me." I told her frankly that I was not so inclined as her general deportment had given rise to the speculation that she might be diseased. Not wishing to contract the clap or syph from her, I politely declined. She became somewhat annoyed. "Then remove your cock from my mouth, please." I did not comply with this bad-tempered request. On the contrary, I shot my load immediately down her esophagus. "Officer," she screamed to a bobby on a corner. The cab stopped. "This man has tried to force himself on me." "Aw, git along witcha, Rosie," said the copper. Apparently he had met the lady before and was acquainted with her character and her habits.

MINT: Hall, do please save me some tea. I haven't eaten a bit for days.

HALL: I guessed as much. Wouldn't you say it might be a gentlemanly gesture to pay Miss O'Toole a call? Sure I could placate her anger at the disappointment she suffered at that first encounter. Also her circumstances, from what I could surmise from the superficial observations possible at that time, were better than, maybe considerably better than those of your usual trollop. Could kill two birds with one stone, so to speak. Get her to invest in Amalgamated, Inc. after indulging once more in her exceptional talent. Oh, she might cry out rape again. Not the first time I have heard that cry, which is water off the back of a feathered fowl. Hmmm. Address . . . [*He flips through some tattered cards in his pocket.*] What's this? Ah. An amazing item culled from the tabloid press. [*He reads.*] "Before the unprovoked slaughter of his devoted parents, 'Slasher' Slymm, of Hampstead, performed ghastly experiments on dozens of chickens that ran through the house, their terrified squawks disturbing the slumber of neighbors." Yes, credible, very. "Tools of his trade included instruments of destruction and torture that ranged from hacksaw to meat grinder." Hmmm. No frolicsome child with a slingshot was he, what Mint?

[*Mint falls to the floor, totally immobilized with panic.*]

HALL: Hold it there, will hook you up later. Continues to say that Slymm was trying to breed a super-chicken. Excellent idea, haven't had much produce or poultry lately. "So he took the brains out of live chickens and transplanted them into eggs." Ingenious, huh? Yes, very. "Abandoned this relatively pleasant practice to turn his attention to aforesaid devoted Mom and Pop." Mmm. "While a domestic sat reading this very same tabloid." Previous issue of it, presumably, "Slymm dismembered his Pop with a hacksaw." [*Looks up.*] Who's to say this male parent did not have it coming to him? Goes on to say, "Mom was due." Probably long overdue, I'd suspect. "On her arrival the so-called sicko experimentist chopped her to mincemeat." Well, what of it? Obviously suffered child abuse in his youth: finally evened it out. Ahh, here's Rosie's address. [*Produces another card.*] "Number 15 Straw in Shoreditch Mews." What Mews is this here, Mint? [*Slurps dregs of tea.*]

MINT: Sh-sh Shoreditch.

HALL: Ah. Makes it convenient.

MINT: My dear Hall, do hear me. Mme. Le Monde has so cut down on my rations that this is the first tea she's brought me up in I forget how many days, oh, and when she brought it up, she said she'd deliver no more to such a loser; intends to have me transferred to home for destitute crips.

HALL: Final indignity, Mint, last straw.

MINT: For the sake of our blessed Saviour, save me one biscuit!

HALL: None left of this batch, old boy, must hope for seconds. Now tell me. Has there been, as I suspect, a recent decline in your relations with the lady of the land?

MINT: Regrettably, yes. She has the impression that I have engaged in sexual improprieties with her strapping young son.

HALL: Quite unjustly, dear Mint?

MINT: You know that I was never blessed with a particularly strong nature to resist the lustful advances.

HALL: Cannot recall an occasion on which you retreated from it, Mint. So much for the matter of that. [*He rises. A subtle spot of light, stronger than the somewhat crepuscular attic, falls upon him as he preens himself in his oddly-fashioned outfit: plaid jacket flaring at the waist and the pants adhering tightly to his long legs.*] I was paid a pretty compliment by a lady somewhat advanced in years whom I encountered in Shepherd's Market. Said I reminded her of a famous gentleman of the theatre whom she'd admired in her youth. Harrison, Mex, Tex? Something like that. Quite sincere she was, and why not? [*He turns about, raising the flair of his jacket to expose his hips. A patch is conspicuous over one buttock.*] My circumstances should be inspiring to you, Mint, if you don't have too jealous a nature.

MINT: Not a— [*Gasps.*] —jealous bone in my—body.

HALL: Not a bone in your body, more like it. Your attention appears to be concentrated on the frontal equatorial zone, so to speak. [*He pats his "basket."*] Tch, tch. Available at a price beyond your reach, old boy. Now as for other assets, if I may distract you from that which you can't afford—health is *Numero Uno*, including dental prophylaxis, even while serving a short term at Wormwood-Scrubs—a partner in a certain enterprise involving bonds of highly fluctuant value had the audacity to—we needn't dwell on that subject. As for my apparel. Have a distinct preference for the Roman cut, obtainable at the finest tailoring establishment on Bond Street, shirt accessories, well, you can see. I would show you my monogrammed silk underthings if you hadn't groped me when I hooked you back up there. Can't risk repetition of that. —Inspired? Yes? No room for desperation, dear boy, this side of the last gasp. So what do you do to get replenishments out of Mme. Le Monde?

MINT: You [*Gasps.*] don't.

HALL: Maybe you don't but I do. [*He stamps the floor repeatedly.*] Obstinate old bitch; will have to confront her downstairs. Might offer an opportunity to interest the lady in some remaining share of Amalgamated, Inc. Back in a flash. Will send her son up to comfort you during my absence . . . [*He exits, singing a lively music hall tune.*] Carry on, carry on, carry on, while you can!

[*Mint sprawls on the floor with piteous bleating cries until the strapping lad, Mme. Le Monde's resident son, enters the attic, grinning as he unscrews the cap of a jar.*]

MINT: Oh, no, no, no! Well, maybe, since you've come with— lubricant, is it?

BOY: Astringent.

[*Mint cries out in terror as the boy removes him from the floor and carries him into the curtained alcove.*]

MINT: Oh, no! Please, different position, wow, wow, wowww! [*Loud footsteps are heard on the stairs to the attic.*] Oh, dear, put me into my panties. Mme. Le Monde is approaching! Doesn't approve of the old public school practice.

[*Mme. Le Monde and Hall enter.*]

BOY: Hold still a mo! Willya?

[*Mme. Le Monde is a large and rather globular woman with a fiery red mop of hair that suggests a nuclear explosion, as does her voice.*]

MME. LE MONDE: *What's going on? Boy, are you back of the curtains with that morphodite gimp?*

MINT [*crawls gasping out of the alcove*]: I was pointing out to your son—various glories of London . . .

HALL: While you were at it, Mint, Mme. Le Monde and I have negotiated a deal the likes of which the queen herself would scarcely equal if the whole British empire at its old height of grandeur fell back into her lap. Guess what! She has just acquired a controlling interest in Amalgamated, Inc. Well, she deserves it, wouldn't you say.

MME. LE MONDE: Oh, I don't know about that, that might involve a wee bit of overstatement, Mr. Hall.

HALL: Wait'll the news of its hits the Exchange tomorrow!

MME. LE MONDE: Soon as that, eh?

HALL: You should feel totally secure about the value as soon as possible, dear. —This, uh, stack of greens, I hope you won't be offended if I go through it.

MME. LE MONDE: They're good as gold, if not better. I know a value. I respect the prudent negotiation.

HALL: You're a business lady after my heart and you've no idea how wisely you've invested your nest-egg, at what a spectacular bargain.

MME. LE MONDE: I am nobody's fool, Mr. Hall.

HALL: Neither am I. We're a good match for each other. Oh, you're not a married lady?

MME. LE MONDE: Oh, no. A widow for years.

HALL: My sympathy if desired. Do you realize what a fortune you have acquired, Ma'am?

MME. LE MONDE: I have an idea.

HALL: Well—wheels must be set in motion.

MME. LE MONDE: Unquestionably their purpose, Mr. Hall.

[*Her son emerges from the alcove, zipping his pants.*]

MINT: Hall, did you remind Mme. Le Monde of the, uh, depletion of the, uh, tea?

HALL: An empty teapot was scarcely a suitable topic on an occasion such as this.

[*Mme. Le Monde abruptly floors her son with a lethal karate chop. This action is startling even to Hall. He lifts the youth's wrist, which is pulseless.*]

HALL: Was this your only offspring, Mme. Le Monde?

MME. LE MONDE: Mr. Hall, my fecundity is equal to the queen bee's. I am constantly reproducing drones such as that one.

HALL: Ah, yes, I see, and being the only mobile witness, you may rest assured that should my testimony be required, I will describe the incident as purely accidental. So let us dismiss it as such. And may I say that you strike me as a lady of highly judicious as well as precipitate action. Wouldn't you say so, Mint? [*Mme. Le Monde seizes Mint and throws him onto his cot which flattens to the floor. Mint evidences no sign of survival.*] Hmmm, yes. This sort of thing is what we need in the world now. Removal of the redundant. So—congratulations once more and my most obedient respects in all matters. *Adieu*, ta ta, *à demain*. There will be banner headlines in every financial center of the world when the staggering word is given.

[*He exits jauntily. Mme. Le Monde pulls a lever by the door. This act is followed by sounds mechanical and human as the stairs flatten out, becoming a long deep slide to the pits. Silence. Then the mechanical piano picks up again its sentimental and nostalgic refrain. Mme. Le Monde crosses in a grand but leisurely fashion downstage center.*]

MME. LE MONDE [*to audience*]: The world is accident prone, no use attempting correction. After all, the loss of one fool makes room for another. A superabundance of them must be somehow avoided if at all possible now. —Well. He threw me a good one before he descended to set the wheels in motion, as he quaintly put it. [*She turns majestically to pull the lever again. Mechanical sound of stairs resuming natural position.*] That's how it goes in a rectangle with hooks, Galileo be damned. Now evening descends. The moon is out, serenely. It goes, it goes. There's nothing more to be asked for that will ever be given.

SLOW CURTAIN

KIRCHE, KÜCHE, KINDER

(AN OUTRAGE FOR THE STAGE)

Kirche, Küche, Kinder was first performed by The Jean Cocteau Repertory Company as a work in progress under the title *Kirche, Kutchen, und Kinder,* in September 1979 at the Bouwerie Lane Theatre in New York City where it ran in repertory until January, 1980. It was directed by Eve Adamson; the set, lights and costumes were designed by Douglas McKeown; original music was composed by Robert Skilling; and the stage manager was John T. Bower. The cast, in order of appearance, was as follows:

THE MAN	Craig Smith
MISS ROSE	Karla Barker*
THE WIFE	Phylllis Deitschel
THE LUTHERAN MINISTER	Coral S. Potter
FRAÜLEIN HAUSSMITZENSCHLOGGER	Harris Berlinksy
THE KINDER	John T. Bower
	Christina Sluberski

later played by Amy K. Posner

ACT ONE

At rise: a suspiciously healthy, handsome, and powerful-looking man is seated in a wheelchair, stage center. The room, which he will describe in an opening monologue, contains certain elements suggestive of "High Church." The man is blond Irish, a self-proclaimed descendant of "the old kings of Ireland." His costume is the kind commonly worn by young male hustlers. His eyes are closed in light slumber, which is interrupted by the entrance of an elegant lady organist. I see her wearing a tall hat resembling a lady's riding hat of Victorian vintage, and a dress of dark purple silk of the same period. Her name is Miss Rose.

MISS ROSE: Sir?

MAN [*rousing*]: Ah.

MISS ROSE: I hope I am not intruding.

MAN: My dear Miss Rose, I'm sure you know that your entrances are always right on cue.

MISS ROSE: Then shall I go directly to the organ?

MAN: Directly and nimbly as a lark rises at daybreak.

[*She crosses directly and elegantly to the organ, removing her gloves.*]

MISS ROSE: And what would you like, Sir, in the way of background music to your opening remarks?

MAN: Hmm. Let me begin then, first, and then you favor us with a delicate accompaniment of whatever seems appropriate, Miss Rose.

[*He wheels his chair downstage center and addresses the audience.*]

MAN: —A man constructs about him his own world as the chambered nautilus constructs about it those delicately iridescent chambers which are its dwelling—its place of retreat and refuge.

[*He pauses. Miss Rose begins to play suitably delicate and evanescent music.*]

MAN: This dwelling is a product of his body, secreted from it and calcified about it for security from the hazards outside, the world external surrounding him near and far. Take a snail, the sort that restaurants of some class, and I have dined in such restaurants, oh, that I have, refer to as *escargots*. Well, even when sautéed in butter and Pernod, it pleases me not. I regard this creature, call it a snail or call it an escargot, even *immersed* in Pernod—I regard it as an insect, Miss Rose, and I do not eat insects—voluntarily, never!

[*Miss Rose plays an arpeggio on the organ.*]

MAN: Of course this may well be a deviation from the subject, which is how a man constructs about him, willy nilly, his own world and is then obliged to occupy it till he's evicted by— [*He smiles ruefully with a slight shrug*] —the expiration of his lease on personal—existence . . . The chambered nautilus, when its lease on existence has expired, leaves behind it those shimmering, iridescent chambers in which it once existed, as lovely as if its existence had been devoted to acts of charity, to saintliness and prayer . . . But I, when my time's run out, will leave behind me this single chamber now visible to you, ordered as best I'm able to my convenience and taste and protection, *pro tem.* —All is *pro tem*, and, my dear friends, if you get that into your ears, why, then, I say, your heads are not totally vacant.

[*Miss Rose performs another arpeggio on the organ and then segues into something a bit more allegro.*]

MAN: Now about me. Who am I? I am, God wot, a legitimate card-holding member of that union that's devoted to the care an' feedin' of actors of any gender. I trust mine's established as male. But more than that, what am I but the visionary projection of an old man's junk-heap of erotobilia, and if there be not such a word in *Webster's Unabridged*, then let us include it immediately in an appendix thereto. Why do I bother with 'im? Why does he bother with me? —Rhetorical is the question: an understandin' exists, never to be profaned in a penthouse Jacuzzi, East coast or West. As for this room, well, I call it the *Kirche*. You'll be introduced later to die *Küche* and die *Kinder*, not to mention the Lutheran Minister's daughter, whose appearance, when she appears, will provide y' with sufficient description of her, if not too much . . .

[*Miss Rose performs another arpeggio on the organ and then segues into a number such as "It's a Long Way to Tipperary."*]

MAN: Now about this *Kirche*, this room to which I'm confined by my state of invalidism, is in a section of lower Manhattan which is known as SoHo. You've doubtless observed that each wall is of a different color. That one, blue: I face it when I'm feeling sentimental. The opposite wall is red: a primary color all right. And stimulating, eh? Yesss—sometimes to violence. Over there is a red light that turns on when the door of the *Kirche* is approached from without. The wall behind me is yellow as the center of a giant daisy, yes—

[*A giant daisy begins unfolding upstage.*]

MAN: —as the center of the giant daisy of day that enters through the window quite high in the wall back there and which dominates the room throughout all daytime hours, all seasons of the year. As the sun begins to fade over SoHo, the giant daisy of day is mysteriously retracted, yes, it disappears through that window by which it entered and is shortly replaced by a fragrant night-blooming vine . . . Now this transparent wall which I face, the wall which is called, in theater, the fourth wall—is white, plain white, unadulterated, yes, unbesmirched by whatever good-natured vulgarities may occur in the course of this, uh—performance. It represents,

111

you see, the basic innocence of nature—not visible and therefore—invisible . . . SoHo? SoHo . . .

[*Miss Rose has risen rather abruptly from the organ.*]

MAN: Au 'voir, Miss Rose, à bientôt— Miss Rose . . .

[*She exits hastily but with elegance sustained. The man begins to grin, slowly, connivingly at the audience; and lascivious as the accompanying action may be, the grin is engaging. —Slowly he unclasps the brass-studded wide belt of his black leather pants. Then abruptly he whips the belt off and tosses it to the floor. His grin is replaced by a conspiratorial chuckle and wink.*]

MAN: SoHo. So! Ho! [*He sings as he starts to unzip his fly.*] Oh, blow ye winds, high ho, a-roving I will go! I'm off to my love with a boxing glove ten thousand miles away . . . Okay—a little bit more. And if you're not myopic, you'll observe the top of my blond pubic hair, ah, yes. I'm at least pubescent. Now what? All the way, exposin' me privates? Shame! I say shame without shame. This show is about as far out as the lingering bit of propriety in my nature will permit it to go. You'll see more of me later, but before then allow me the privilege, pleasure, and pride of presenting to ye my wife, a lady of the Protestant persuasion, in fact no more and no less than the daughter of the Lutheran Minister of the island known as Staten!

[*The man inclines his head with an engaging grin as the light dims on him in the Kirche. The three walls he described in his opening monologue all resemble huge Venetian blinds. The upstage Yellow and stage left Red Blinds flip sides to become flat black. The Blue Blind opens to reveal a dilapidated stove and chair, then it flies up as the lights come up on the Küche. The wife is discovered leaning over the stove. She is probably older than the man, and not so carefully preserved. She is inclined to slatternly ways of dress and behavior, and a certain roguery is apparent in her eyes and manner of speech. There are three knocks at the door.*]

WIFE: Who's knocking? [*There is no answer. The knocks are repeated.*] Maybe die rent man. Himself in die *Kirche*, lately he doesn't slip under die door the rent money as regular as he used to, which has provoked some strain of relations wit' die collector of it.

[*A tall and very dour-looking man all in black, bearing a Bible and an umbrella, enters.*]

WIFE: Oh, mein Papa! —Die Lut'eran Minister of the Island of Staten. Oh, mein Papa! To me you vas so vunderbar, etc. [*She sings a bar or two of the Eddie Fisher oldie, "Wunderbar."*]

[*The Lutheran Minister is not pleased and he expresses his displeasure.*]

WIFE: Ja! Die vedder attecks die voice-box, but setzen zie doon, mein Papa. How is things at die first, last, and only Lutheran Church on the Island of Staten? [*There is no answer.*] —Aw, bad as that! —Tch, tch. Who would've thought so unless he'd attended a service and stayed through die sermon, die offertory, and die collection. Well, here ye be where I never expected to see ye, under the roof of a Catholic household. Well. You're looking wonderful, Papa, I mean not much better or worse. How is attendance at the Lutheran Church on Sundays, overcrowded or empty? [*There is no response.*] Ja, Ja, I suspected. Sometimes I get intuitions. And the organist, you remember the talented organist, Papa, that led the choir before the choir disassembled, Fräulein Haussmitzenschlogger? Did I pernounce it correckly? Well, gossip travels fast, and a rumor has reached my ears and shattered my eardrums. Papa, is it true, Papa, that Fräulein Haussmitzenschlogger has took up residence in the rectory and that she moved in the night that Mama moved out and the two of you's livin' high on the hog there on Mama's accidental—bequest—without no formalities such as a ceremony with license? Huh, Papa? Well, a fairytale romance like that, Papa, it touches me too deep for expression of a nature suitable to a Catholic household, this close

113

to the *Kirche* of Himself. However, this I will say. If ever two human creatures deserved each other on earth it's you and Miss Haussmitzenschlogger. I mean something is better than nothing, and Haussmitzenschlogger is something. Oh, she's got her a few geriatric problems, a wood leg and a glass eye, but is otherwise well-preserved, ain't she? To look on the bright side of things at the Lutheran Church in Staten? Ja. And she knocked out a good hymn on the organ when I last heard her knock one out of the ballpark. Make yourself comfortable, Papa. [*There is no response or motion.*] I'd offer you to some coffee except I got to preserve it all for myself. But I tell you what. You finish up this cup 'n' I'll pour out a fresh one for me.

[*The wife turns to the stove. The Minister hits her over the head with his umbrella. Invisible canaries sing as she turns slowly and dizzily about. A sound effect has amplified the blow.*]

WIFE: —I don't know why I got this sudden dizzy sensation in *mein Kopf.* I got to set down till I recover from this little dizzy spell, Papa. —Lemme set your umbrella in a corner till it drips dry, while you do the honors mit die coffee. PAPA, LOOK THERE BEHIND YOU, QVICK!

[*She raises the umbrella, preparing to return the clout, but he turns back just in time to stop her with a stare.*]

WIFE: Well, Papa. —What a nice, long conversation we're having! —About Miss Haussmitzenschlogger, in my opinion you got you a good thing there. She maybe don't take the cake in the beauty contest department but Dame Gossip tells me she giffs wonderful head between hymns—while you're preachin' a sermon. I would offer you a cruller except I got to keep my energy up with all the crullers remaining in the oven. —You want to look in the oven? Why don't you look at the crullers in the oven?

[*She raises the umbrella again, taking several practice swings, but he remains standing and silent.*]

WIFE: —Papa, remember Mama? It breaks my heart to think how she jumped over the rail of the Staten Island Ferry. Now how did she do that, a woman that weighed 290 pounds on the hoof jumps over the rail of the ferry light as a flea? Poor Mama, she wasn't no beauty to win a contest in Atlantic, die boardwalk, you know, but she had *zwei Augen*, Ja, two eyes in her head and two legs, which is more than you could of said anybody could claim for die Fräulein Hausmitzenschlogger. Well, love is a mystery, huh? Remember the details, Papa, or are they too sad to remember? Too bad she craved a banana and mentioned to you die cravin'. I heard her say, gimme. Last thing I heard her say, as I went up to entertain die ferry boat pilot to Staten, I had dis sort of a school-girl crush on 'im, Papa. Well, Mama, she had the gimmes, huh, Papa? And in dis world, die gimmes ain't offen die getters. [*She sings.*] Gimme, gimme, gimme, a banana in Staten, ten cents a bunch— [*She speaks.*] —but Mama, she wanted just one. Maybe not much to die Rockerfellers, for instance, but to you, it was too much of a gimme. So vot did she get? Not a banana in Staten but ge-splash off die ferry. I heard the ge-splash while havin' polite conversation wit' die pilot. I thought nothin' of it till after die conversation w'en die ferry boat pulled into Staten. I come down die steps from die pilot. Vere iss Mama? Gone like she'd never existed. Vell, die past is die past and die future can only get better and I know vot heart-break you suffered, especially since you'd took out insurance on die life of Mama that week while she was still livin'. Double indemnity, was it? Well, she was an afflicted woman, poor Mama, afflicted with die gimmes and she must of had a poor balance since all she got was a little affectionate pat of die kopf und lost her balance, huh, Papa. Vell, die policy. That was some consolation. How much did you collect on it, Papa? Look, I got my hand out. Reach in your pocket and give me a piece of the bread. If you give me a piece of the bread, never will I remember how Miss Haussmitzenschlogger was waiting on the dock when the ferry pulled in to Staten with a big grin on her face. You got a good thing there. She wasn't a day over eighty in those days. No glass eye, no wood leg, and she had three teeth in her mouth. She was good at the organ and *also* good at the *organ*. —Hmm. So I get no piece of the bread. I am a girl that is used to such disappointments. Not that I don't appreciate this visit you give me and the long, lively conversation. Maybe you think it all over and drop by again with the bread before I take legal action. I hate to see you go. Give me a Lutheran blessing for old time's sake.

[*He grabs the umbrella and clouts her over the head.*]

WIFE: My God, what a wonderful Lutheran blessing you give me in a Catholic household! Ach, I forgot the banana. I been keepin' a vunderbar banana for you, Papa. Looky here, Papa, a great big ripe banana for just this occasion, your visit on me, God rest my soul. [*She hands him a large banana which has matured to the point of absolute blackness.*] I like a ripe banana, don't you, Papa? I showed this banana to a Nosey Parker next door, a Mrs. Molly Delaney of the SoHo Delaneys. "Have a banana," I said to Mrs. Delaney. "Why," she said, "this banana is been too long off the tree and the fruit stand." "Vot you mean?" I ask her. "Lookit die color! No vunder you offer me to it, dis banana is black." "A-course it's black," I says, "a ripe banana is black, not just in spots like a leopard skin, Mrs. Delaney, but black completely all over." So ve had this argument. Never mind. I still got this ripe banana. Take it, feel it, smell it. *Saftig*, huh? A nice ripe odor, huh Papa? Don't be bashful, take it , it is all yours, no hard feelings between us, a nice ripe black banana, nothing like it to dismiss— [*She thrusts the banana in his face.*]

LUTHERAN MINISTER: Blob, blob, blob, blob, blob!

WIFE: A girl should be so lucky as to receive such a visit from a Papa, the Lutheran minister even of Staten, the Island. Ven lightning strikes once, maybe twice. Ven you are dead maybe I visit your grave, so hurry back, Papa. [*She opens the door and shoves him out.*] Ha? Ja? All is understood, Papa? Perfect. Now I go tell die good news to Himself in die *Kirche* before die Vesper service commences. [*She starts out.*] Oh. Just in case. [*She returns to pick up the rubber axe.*] See what I got here? Maybe you think it ain't a genuine axe made out of metal? Maybe you think it is rubber? Well, so maybe you're right about something. But you know a good piece of rubber goods can be very effective in preventing the over-population growth mit if not in reducing already? Count your blessings, on with it—slowly, slowly, while he continues beatin' his gums about the wonders of that throne room he's set himself up in as a straight down the line descendant of the Old Kings of Ireland . . .

[*As she starts out, the Blue Blinds stage right descend abruptly and close, concealing the Küche. As the lights rise on the man in the Kirche, the Yellow and Red Blinds flip back to their original colors.*]

MAN: Something is impending.

[*There is a pause. The man then springs from the wheelchair, does some cartwheels, etc., to demonstrate an excellent state of health, then jumps back into the wheelchair.*]

MAN: The sham, the shameless sham and ham of the wheelchair is now established with an exhibition of the calisthenics befitting a descendant of the old Irish Kings, and I jumped back into the wheelchair to resume the sham for a party now approaching, this being a fact which I know because the reflection of the red light has intensified to the degree at which it flickers on the polished fake marble parquet of the floor, as distinguished from ceiling and walls. W-a-a-a-lls! —To me they've come to mean sanctuary such as once sought in places of worship. I like to think this is one. Pagan, in a way, being not alienated from the indispensable homage to Priapus, but Catholic, oh, yes, Catholic, and don't deceive ye'selves that there be much of a chasm between that they can't be reconciled. Worship. Put it not down! If there be nothing but mystery to worship, why, then worship that. And places of worship in which to sort out in the head those many, many variable ways in which to exist and to worship. A man must have his secrets and secrets must have their privacy, and that privacy is now about to be violated by the Lutheran Minister's daughter, herein before mentioned and adequately described to ye by her appearance. [*Very softly.*] "Wow," an expletive once popular and still appropriate among the Third World Culture.

[*The wife enters bearing the rubber axe. The man has turned the back of his wheelchair to her and picked up a copy of some such magazine as "Screw."*]

WIFE [*panting as if she'd been running*]: What are your plans for the future, if any?

MAN [*flips a page of the magazine, without looking at her*]: If any *plans* or any *future*?

WIFE: Either!

MAN: You mean, then, both, I take it.

WIFE: Yes! Both! [*She lifts the axe high over his unperturbed blond head, her expressive mouth stretched in a smile, her eyes very wide, a facial expression suggestive of the immortal Fanny Brice.*]

MAN [*serenely—though the axe now swings like a vertically mobile pendulum over his handsome, youthful head.*] My dear little *Dame, mein Leibchen,* you precious little *Hausfrau* given me by that force in nature called God—

WIFE [*impatiently*]: GIT IT ON, MEANING GIT ON WITH IT, YOU WORTHLESS EX— [*She stops for breath.*]

MAN: Oh, oh. You stopped just in time to save yourself the embarrassment of a suit for defamation of character there . . .

WIFE [*catching her breath*]: EX—*I'll say it, I'm going to say it!*

MAN: Then say it quietly, Miss Lutheran Minister's Daughter, say it very, very quietly lest the little ones should hear you. You know, certain matters, meaning subject matters, exist which are of too indelicate a nature for their, shall we say, tender years and sensitive ears. Yes, I believe that our little ones are barely, if yet, pubescent. Ah, such pretty ones too, especially the lad with the sky-blue eyes and the hair the color of mine, a chip off the old butcher-block, I'd call 'im, a true son of the ancient kings of Ireland, no less, Miss Lutheran Minister's Daughter, ah, but, the girl, well, the girl, takes a bit more after the distaff side, as it were. —Excuse me. You were saying?

WIFE: EX—

MAN: Don't put so much emphasis on EX. Remember that my retirement was premature and entirely of my own volition—as distinguished from yours . . .

WIFE: Are you implyin' that *I* was a hustler, *too?*

MAN: In the case of a female, the term is hooker, not hustler, *mein Herz.*

[*She swings the axe at him but he moves his wheelchair downstage with startling rapidity, thus escaping the blow.*]

MAN: Wow. Did you push my chair, dear?

WIFE [*raising the axe for another try*]: Put the brakes on the chair, dear.

MAN [*idly compositing a song of this line*]:
      Put the brakes on the chair, dear,
      Put the brakes on the chair.
      Put the brakes on the wheels of the chair
      And I won't need a comb to part my hair . . .

[*He takes out a pocket comb and mirror and smooths back his gleaming pompadour.*]

WIFE: Just you wait till I recover my breath . . . [*She draws up a straight back chair and sits behind him, breathing like an old hound-dog, the axe resting in her lap.*]

MAN: I was just looking through a page of recipes in this old issue of a ladies' mag called *Good Housekeeping*. This is a recipe for those who are called weight-watchers. Might be of some interest to you.

WIFE: Implyin' that I'm—?

MAN: To imply would be useless and the useless is virtually synonymous with the worthless.

WIFE: Now you're onto a subject that's relevant to yeself, Daddy-O, if ever a subject was.

MAN: Relevant? —Strange how I fail so consistently to follow your verbalized trains of thought . . .

WIFE: Man, have you made your peace with God?

MAN: —How do you spell that word?

WIFE: God is spelled just opposite to dog, and is capitalized, you shitzen!

MAN: It was the word peace I meant. A one-syllable noun in both cases. In one case it is virtually synonymous with accord or harmony. In the other case, it means part of, such as piece of, such as in the phrase "piece of ass" —I think the post-Vietnam kids sometimes say "piece of leg" —or is it "shot of leg," they say?

WIFE: DO IT QUICK, NOW, FALL ON YOUR KNEES AND ASK THE HEAVENLY FATHER'S MERCY ON YOUR BLACK SOUL!

[*She raises the axe in a final effort, but fails as the man wheels his chair suddenly about to face her.*]

MAN: —Why, how do you do today, Madam. Is that little touch of menstrual depression plaguing you slightly again?

[*She circles around, barking in frustration. Three loud knocks are heard.*]

MAN: Lass, be ye deaf, like a stone? Somebody is breaking the door down in die *Küche.*

[*The knocks are repeated, urgently.*]

WIFE: Ja, there is a bit of a rap at the door! Expect me back sooner than later!

[*The Man wheels his chair to a stack of gymnasium equipment. From beneath it, he removes a large sausage and takes a bite of it.*]

MAN [*facing the chair front*]: Aye, there's sorrow in a man's life but there's much of joy, too . . . Interpretation of experience never fails to discover elements of the beautiful as one discovers bits of a broken bottle catching sunlight in an otherwise sordid and ugly heap of rubbish. I do not deny that most of experience is a heap of rubbish, but I affirm, as I have always affirmed, there is somewhere hidden in this sordid heap of rubbish the translucent and hence lovely fragment of broken glass refracting the pure light of heaven as a mirror held to the eyes of Our Lady Immaculate. I have seen it with reverence and wonder in the eyes of the mad, innocent beings too fondly touched by the moon . . .

[*The walls go through their transformation again as the three knocks are repeated once more. The lights come up on the wife in the Küche. The man and the Kirche go dark.*]

WIFE [*shouting through door into alley*]: Catholic or Protestant?

FRÄULEIN [*off stage*]: Fräulein Haussmitzenschlogger!

WIFE: Fuck off. I don't have no time to discuss mit you die intentions toward you of die Lutheran Minister of Staten, *Verstehen Sie?*

FRÄULEIN [*off stage*]: I got terrific news for you.

WIFE: I giff you vun minute to deliver this news provided you keep your mitts off mein coffee and crullers.

[*A very old lady, the Fräulein—also known as "Hotsy"—enters. She is dressed like a groupie chick—short-cut Levis and a kind of sweat shirt decorated with cartoon characters and captions, etc.*]

WIFE: Ach, so. You make a disastrous appearance—a disgrace to Protestantism. Watch it! Don't reach for a cruller!

FRÄULEIN: Can't you see I'm eating for two?

WIFE: I can't see that you're eating for one in mein *Küche*.

[*The Fräulein sobs and wails, wringing her hands. The wife regards her without much interest. Pause.*]

WIFE: This disturbance has outlasted my patience. Now what in hell is it with you, dese lamentations, disturbing die peace of die *Küche*?

FRÄULEIN: Don't make out like you can't see I'm pregnant.

WIFE: All right. So you are pregnant. Tell it to the marines or any branch of the military service but not to me in mein *Küche* while I try to digest die crullers.

FRÄULEIN: Knocked up by your Papa who rapes me before and after church service and at choir practice back of the organ.

WIFE: Don't talk dirty in here! *Verstehen Sie?* Now repeat what you tell me giving me details such as how old you are, maybe?

FRÄULEIN: Ninety-nine.

WIFE: Don't admit it! You could pass for ninety-eight and three quarters with a few marbles missing in a dark room maybe. Here, have a cruller. [*She stuffs a cruller in the Fräulein's mouth. Pause.*] So the Lutheran Minister fucks you behind the organ. Well. I see what you mean now about the terrific news. What does he charge you for it, how much? And have you got witnesses? You took the rabbit test? —Positive? —Ja?! Maybe the rabbit was pregnant, Hotsy, not you. Ha. Imagine mein Papa, die Lutheran Minister of Staten die island still with a fuck left in him!

FRÄULEIN: At me continual. His motto in life is ficken ist gesund.

WIFE: Come on, Hotsy, look on die bright side of things. You got laid, Ja? Let's face it, Hotsy, a girl of your—I don't wanna get personal mit you, but, Hotsy, you got it better than Mama. Offen die ferry ge-splashen like a big piece a fish food offen die ferry to Staten. So? Not to get personal, Hotsy— *Hey, I didn't offer no seconds on die crullers!* Now mein husband he got a lot of time to sit and philosophize in die big room which diss descendant from die old kings of Ireland calls die *Kirche.* Now go in there for a vile und discussen diss piece of terrific news mit him. He is been waiting a long time for the sight and sound of you, Hotsy. Go on, don't be afraid. He sits in a wheelchair like a throne in Ireland. Come Sie mit me. I interduce you together.

[*The walls and lights switch back to the Kirche. The red warning light flashes. The man is doing various calisthenics. As the red light intensifies, he hops back into the wheelchair.*]

WIFE [*entering with the Fräulein*]: Okay, now, King of Ireland, diss is die organist from the first, last, and only Lutheran church on Staten.

MAN: She comes to make peace with the Pope, huh?

WIFE: She's got a non-secular problem, it looks like.

MAN: Name it, Babe.

[*Pause.*]

WIFE: —Vell, Hotsy, have you got lockjaw?

[*The Fräulein peers closely at the man, gives him a wink and a lascivious sneer.*]

MAN [*shuddering*]: —I am an invalid, Madam.

WIFE: Vell, nobody is perfeck, not even Hotsy, she's pregnant, rabbit test positive, by mein Papa, the Lutheran Minister of Staten.

Now talk that over together, philosophize on it while I go back to die *Küche* vere I expeck die young iceman to bring me some very hot ice.

[*The wife exits. Pause.*]

FRÄULEIN: Die pregnancy, is it noticeable, *mein Herr*?

MAN: —Noticable, yes. Credible, no. —However—

[*A pause.*]

FRÄULEIN: If the conversation is done with—I give you head, a good blow job, personal, private, no talk of?

[*The man smiles slowly and sadly.*]

—Ja?

[*Pause.*]

Madam, you are a lost soul in a lost world . . .

BLACKOUT.

ACT TWO

The same day—the Kirche.

MAN: I find that the hours of me voluntary retirement have begun to be tedious to me. Could it be the confinement, also voluntary, the better for undisturbed meditation and for concentration on me memoirs. [*He displays a notebook labeled "GREAT MEMOIRS."*]

WIFE [*entering Kirche*]: I see by the time-keeper daisy of day that it approaches the hour when die kinder return from die garten.

MAN: How delightful the prospect.

WIFE [*taking a swig from the large jug of sourmash she has carried on*]: Mmmmmm . . .

MAN: —An enigmatic remark.

[*Observing the man's inattention, the wife snatches up the jug of sour mash and takes such a giant swallow that it spills down her chops.*]

WIFE: Wow!

[*The wife staggers backwards against the organ, which resounds with a base chord.*]

MAN: Madam, if ye have to break wind, would ye be so good as not to break it in church.

WIFE: MARK! MY! WORD! [*On the loud "WORD" She sets the jug back down.*] Iffen die kinder bringen not home report cards from Yale.

MAN: —Yale, did ye say?

WIFE: That's what I said, nomenclature of Eli by which I mean not Wallach. Iffen, for emphasis I repeat, iffen die kinder return not this day from their seminar in physics—

MAN: Ah, laxatives they study.

WIFE: PHYSICS! Like Eisenstein's theory of rich and poor relations and curvature of die space age.

MAN: I still am confused about the academic pursuits of our loved ones, Madam. However—

[*There is a terrific clamor offstage and shrieks of childish frolicking.*]

MAN: —this familiar assault upon my eardrums informs me that our treasures may soon clear up my confusion and possibly even your own. HA! HARK! —the patter of little feet.

[*The children—die Kinder—approach like cattle stampeding. The red warning light flickers wildly. Two tall adolescents of opposite gender rush into the room. They are dressed as kindergarten students, a tiny sashed frock on the daughter, who has blonde pigtails, and a scanty sailor suit on the son.*]

MAN: Well, as I live and breathe, Madam, it does indeed appear that die kinder have rounded out another triumphant day at kindergarten. Does it not so appear to you, Madam?

WIFE: It don't appear to me as much as it sounds.

[*Die Kinder are frolicking noisily about.*]

MAN: High spirits, though natural in childhood, are not entirely suitable to this place of worship, die *Kirche*. [*He shouts*]: Cool it, a little Kool Aid with cyanide à la Jonesville, kinder!

[*They freeze in motion, but continue to grin and simper.*]

WIFE [*portentously*]: If I be not mistooked completely, dis vas die final day at die school on which on which is presented report cards. So? Vere iss die cards of report?

SON: She's got it.

DAUGHTER: He's got it.

WIFE: Neidder of youse got it, it's dropt on die floor. [*She snatches it up and removes paper from the envelope.*] —This is possible to see but not to believe!

MAN: Hold me not in suspense. What incredible bit of advisement was contained in the envelope, Madam?

WIFE: EXPELLED! —From kindergarten im himmel achtung mit!

MAN [*without apparent dismay*]: Expelled, did ye say, after fifteen years' attendance? Ah, well . . .

[*The Kinder continue to grin and simper.*]

It's wearing on toward supper-time and I would guess by the faint urinary aroma that waited in here with die kinder that the entree is kidneys sautéed in wine sauce. Ah-ha, there's a dish to salivate the chops of an Egyptian pharaoh turned to parchment and dust for a good ten thousand years. Kinder, your Mom is still reeling from the bit of school news. [*He smiles and shrugs.*] But my personal feeling is that a bit of a setback in the groves of Academe is no swooning matter, Madam. This is a world of many and varied vocations, not all of them best prepared for by such a protracted loitering in a room furnished with tiny chairs and tables all cluttered with alphabets and frames of colored beads on which you are first instructed the important business of counting. Well, now, you— [*He is addressing the daughter*] how many fingers is daddy holding up, huh? [*He elevates one finger.*]

DAUGHTER: One's no fun.

[*The Kinder giggle and exchange ribald whispers.*]

MAN [*raising two fingers*]: How many fingers now, boy?

SON: Two?

DAUGHTER: Three!

SON: Four!

DAUGHTER: FIVE!

MAN: Ha, that's me lass, always increase the number! But! — never less than a hundred an hour will do for the favors of such a flower as you! *Ach-ten-shun!* Line up and face your parents.

[*The Kinder line up and face the man and the wife.*]

WIFE: Make it singular.

MAN: Singular in die sense of unusual and bizarre?

WIFE: Singular in die sense of single: a single parent. I have just disowned them.

[*The Kinder return to frolicking.*]

MAN: This grave declaration doesn't appear to have depressed die kinder very noticeably, Madam. What are they up to, what is this antic behavior?

WIFE: Fidgeting, diddling, and whispering remarks that they've picked up in the alleys of SoHo.

MAN: Ah-ha, libidinous, be ye? Well, turn it to profit. —Which one of 'em is the boy?

SON: I, Sir.

MAN: Got any hair on you yet?

WIFE: Be ye blind? It's hangin' down to his shoulders.

MAN: And his apparel is boyish, but transvestisim's a common symptom of a society in an advanced state of decadence. However, Madam, I wasn't referring to the hair on his head but to the hair which is pubic, meant to be public only when professionally exposed. Now, boy. Retire to the vestry for divestment.

[*The man indicates an area upstage of the Red Blind. The son stares bewildered. The man hauls him behind the blinds. Then he backs the wheelchair into view.*]

MAN: Proceed with divestment! Get with it, drop your pants. —Hmmm. Not badly hung and just beginning to sprout a bit of blond fluff. SoHo, as it should be. Now make a half turn so I can assess the posterior attractions. —Ahh, there's your fortune, me laddie, waste it not in SoHo. Reserve it for uptown gentlemen who can afford to indulge the tastes of Tiberius without concern for the price.

[*The wife imitates the outcry of Dame Judith Anderson before she bursts out of the double-doors at the top of Medea. The son, half-dressed, runs to the man for protection.*]

MAN: Disregard your mother's interpolation. Heed only your Papa, the pro in your new profession. Head uptown, if ye know downtown from up. This world is geographic, and monetarily so. So. Get out of SoHo. Proceed with all possible haste to the public rooms of posh hotels overlooking the Central Park of Manhattan from the South or East side only. But into the park, wander not. Gang bangs in the bushes would reduce your price and prestige, not to mention your. . . .

[*The wife repeats the outcry of Medea.*]

MAN [*ignoring her*]: Lubricate well, but howl, howl, howl as if in insufferable pain. Shout out, I'm gonna tell Papa what you done to me UNLESS—

SON [*as he finishes dressing*]: Unless what, Papa?

MAN: He lavishes on you the whole contents of his wallet, and if this be not sufficient, advise him to draw out monies secured in the strong-box of the security vault in the lobby.

SON: Wow.

MAN: Yes, wow.

[*The son starts to rush off.*]

MAN: Hold your horses. You're not dismissed from the *Kirche*. I've yet to instruct your sister. Madam, what is the name of the female child?

WIFE: You must be jokin'. I hope to God he is jokin'.

MAN: Joking about a serious matter such as the given name of my daughter?

WIFE: Jokin' about not knowin' the name of the child.

DAUGHTER: Daddy, my name is—

WIFE: Don't tell him. If he don't know it, then leave him in blissful ignorance of it, Gretchen.

MAN: Ah, yes, Gretchen, Gretchen. Well, now, Gretchen. I'm drawing a little map for you. The geographical lay-out of the territory between this point in SoHo and a park in the Village called Washington Square, at which point you will get on a Fifth Avenue bus heading uptown.

WIFE: Die kinder understand nothing.

MAN [*drawing a map*]: Disregard the usual asperities and disparagements of you mother. Now. Like I say. Hop in this Fifth Avenue bus, enquire of the conductor if it be heading uptown. He will reply that it is. Now choose your seat carefully. Be sure that you share it with some gentlemen well-advanced in years. [*To the wife.*] Does she understand my instructions?

WIFE: Yeh, yeh, yeh, after fifteen years in kindygarten expelled, how could she fail to understand every syllable spoken!

MAN: I think this Gretchen has been provided with instinct and intuition that more than compensate for deficiencies in the department of intellect, Madam. Gretchen, what did Daddy just tell you to do?

DAUGHTER [*glibly*]: To follow the map to Washington Square where I will get onto a Fifth Avenue bus headed uptown and on which I will share a seat with a gentleman well along in years. And I will do what, then?

MAN: Absolutely perfect, see, Madam? —You will snuggle up closer and closer to the elderly gent, meanwhile applying to his left knee a bit of pressure with your right knee, and then this gent of advanced years, if he remains still living, will make some jocular observation such as, "What are you up to, Young Lady?"

DAUGHTER: What do I say to him, Daddy?

MAN: Speak not a word. —But smile. —He'll get the message. Now. Look here. I am producing a pair of greenbacks, paper currency, Gretchen. One is a century note and the other's a measly ten. Mark well the difference between them. When you retire to the gentleman's uptown quarters, do not dispense your favors until he has produced and dispensed to you a bill that corresponds in every detail exactly to this one called the century note. *Verstehen Sie* Gretchen?

DAUGHTER: Ja, ja, ha! [*She starts to rush out.*]

MAN: You hold your wild horses, too, I haven't dismissed ye. I must subject ye first to a bit of inspection, meaning show Daddy your dainties.

[*The daughter runs behind the Red Blind where the son had been.*]

MAN: Upzen ze mitzen die skirtsen. Well, now, how do ye do! [*To the wife.*] Madam I see no imminent time of privation about the place now.

[*Die Kinder start to leave.*]

MAN: Wait, Gretchen. Having seen what I've seen, accept not less than double what I advised ye before, not one century note but a couple. Not *eins* but *zwei*!

[*Die Kinder shriek together.*]

MAN: Wait, wait. Hereafter always remember that your daddy conveyed to ye all worldly knowledge he ever knew: limited, yes, but it will suffice. Dismissed! On with it, praise God!

[*Die Kinder gallop screaming ecstatically from the Kirche. There is an extended pause. The daisy of the day folds up and disappears.*]

MAN: A tear has moistened my eye, the left one, nearest my heart. I tell ye, Madam, the responsibilities of bringing up a pair of wee ones can age a man of profound moral scruples to such a point that— [*He takes out a pocket mirror.*] —he scarcely believes the youth which he still observes in the mirror . . . Yes, indeed, it truly boggles the mind. Oh are you still here, Madam?

[*The wife pivots slowly and retreats unsteadily, exiting almost in slow motion.*]

WIFE [*approaching the door*]: It's like a dream . . .

MAN: That exit line ye lifted from Chekhov's *Sea Gull*. Alas, is poor Anton now in the public domain? What's for supper, ducks?

WIFE [*as she exits from the Kirche*]: Kidneys sautéed in butter and vine sauce.

MAN: Margarine and the cheapest California Chablis which Madam pronounces in lower SoHo dialect as *Chab*-liss. An accomplished shop-lifter she is but with lower middle-class taste. Ah, well. She's not had the advantages of gourmets who shop at Gristede's and dine in the Oak Room of the Plaza.

[*The blinds sift again, and the lights cross-fade, revealing the Lutheran Minister and his Femme-à-Toute-Faire, Fräulein Hausmitzenschlogger. The Minister is spearing kidneys from the skillet on the stove. Whenever the Fräulein extends her hand, he utters a low growl, frightening her off. On her third attempt, he raps her on the head with his umbrella, accompanied by*] *the same sound effect as in Act One, when the Minister hit the wife with the umbrella. The Fräulein reels. The wife enters and stands transfixed for some moments after entering the Küche.*]

WIFE: —Ja, it's like a dream! Two return visits in one day by Papa and Hotsy.

FRÄULEIN: This time we make you a longer visit, provided the accommodations meets with our satisfaction.

WIFE: Longer the visit? What a piece of luck, Hotsy! And you come bearin' gifts by the sackful!

FRÄULEIN [*snatching up a clanking, fire-scorched sack*]: Household equipment and personal effects, all we could save from the explosion and fire!

WIFE: Let me get this, Hotsy, not so fast mit die tongue for me to absorb all at once! Did ye mention a fire?

FRÄULEIN: *Kirche* und haus, gone PFFT!

WIFE: PFFT? You sprechen of *Pfft?*

FRÄULEIN: Ja, PFFT!

[*The Minister interrupts his meal long enough to shove a sheaf of papers at the Fräulein and point at the wife.*]

FRÄULEIN [*reading from papers*]: Suit for damages, assault mit batteries, defamation of characters, blackmail, and suspect of arson! [*She breaks into sobs and wails.*]

WIFE: Wow! Just cool it a minute, huh, Hotsy? You got a hysterical nature and you are pregnant, advanced stage at advanced age! This miracle of nature could be affected, I mean not favorably, Hotsy!

[*Lightning quick, the wife seizes the handle of the skillet and removes it from the stove. The Minister growls and lifts his umbrella, crucifix-high above her, his eyes ablaze with Protestant rage.*]

WIFE: Advisable, now, under such circumstances, die SALT talks! You know die SALT talks, die opposite of die pepper? Like a quiet sitting down discussion, all smiling?

[*The Lutheran Minister's umbrella descends on the wife's head. Slowly, with a manic grin, She sinks to the floor, invisible canaries warbling about her. At this moment, Miss Rose, all Edwardian elegance of taffeta and gauze, passes through the Küche en route to the Kirche.*]

MISS ROSE [*stepping delicately over the wife's body*]: Good evening, I mean *Guten Abend*, excuse me. I'm expected for Vespers.

[*As she passes under them, the Blue Blind drops and closes. The walls and lights make their usual transformation from the Küche to the Kirche, revealing the man in his wheelchair. Miss Rose coughs decorously to rouse him.*]

MAN: Oh, Miss Rose, I was lost in reflection . . .

MISS ROSE: Undisturbed by the activities in the kitchen?

MAN: You entered by the—?

MISS ROSE: The evening being unusually fair, I came by the direct route down the alley, found the kitchen door opened and passed through very quickly, but not without observing some evidence of disorder.

MAN: There's been a bit of domestic trouble today, relative to the twins.

MISS ROSE: Ah, well, be that as it may. Your pleasure, Sir? [*She crosses to the organ, removing her gloves and sitting.*]

MAN: —Is yours . . .

[*Miss Rose begins to play.*]

MAN: The daisy of daytime, Miss Rose, has now completely folded—like many a good play in Boston . . . The night-blooming vine is now appearing in the daytime daisy's place. So time's passing's intruding even here, walled off from things external. But time is not a thing that can be walled off as external. It is within all places and organisms as well, be they of the animal or vegetable kingdom . . .

[*Over the following lines, a night-blooming vine slowly uncoils from where the daisy of daytime appeared and vanished.*]

MAN: The night-blooming vine trails delicately down the wall from the window. Should I have permitted that window to exist in my room? Otherwise as well but sparingly fitted to my needs and desires as the—shell of a crustacean such as the—chambered nautilus . . . —You needn't answer that question. You needn't ask that question, nor ask nor answer or even— [*Pause.*]

"Inevitably bringing the eternal note of sadness in."

Quote from "Dover Beach" that some people say is the first modern poem in the English language. Should remember more of it or forget it entirely.

[*Miss Rose finishes, rises, and slowly starts to exit.*]

MAN: Odd how tidbits of—incomplete recollection sometimes somewhat distorted—stab at the heart at—

[*Miss Rose turns back to look at the man.*]

MAN: —nightfall . . .

[*Miss Rose exits.*]

MAN: Anyhow, now, before the light expires—this I must say— Every man's life must be redeemed from the squalor which is inherent in human existence by some touch of beauty.

[*The man rises from the wheelchair and lounges by the organ to view the Küche. The lights fade out and the transformation to the Küche occurs again. The Fräulein, the wife, and the Minister are discovered in the same tableau as when their last scene ended. The Minister emits low growls and snorts like a bull in heat. The Fräulein reacts with apprehension. The wife slowly regains consciousness and rises. The Minister violently empties the sack of its contents and thrusts it over the Fräulein's head and throws her down, shedding his black garments with somewhat undignified haste. As the Fräulein pleads and whimpers in vain, and the wife looks on in shock, the Minister plops his huge bible under the Fräulein's derriere and mounts her. Members of the press burst in: there is a burst of flash-photos, shouts of ribaldry, etc., as the reporters shout questions at the Fräulein and the wife beats her way through them with the skillet. The Blue Blind crashes down, and the lights come up on the man sitting (not in his wheelchair) in the Kirche. He is softly singing "I want a girl just like the girl . . ." etc. The wife enters the Kirche, dizzily.]*

WIFE: All hell's broke loose in *mein Küche*. Die Pentecostals got wind of moral relations between mein Papa, die Lutheran Minister of Staten, and Fräulein Hausmitzenschlogger. PFFT, dey blew up die church and residence of it. PFFT, Ja, PFTT! —So into SoHo they migrate: specifically into mein Küche. Hot on the trail, the media. Ja, ja, they smell a newsworthy scandal and lickety-split die national networks pursue 'em to die door of mein Küche. Hotsy, oh, mein Gott, Hotsy, she's got her a Hollywood agent called Sifty, making deals for exposure world-over, competitive bidding between the Ringling und Barnum and Bailey, circuses, biggest existing. Now what? Mein Papa was throwing a good one into Hotsy when in the media crashes. So now? Hotsy is giving head to all comers, flash-bulbs popping, she is given' 'em head non-stop wit'out choppers: —Mein Gott in Himmel und in mein *Küche*.

MAN [*casually*]: A graphic description ye give me but not a surprise, for Protestantism, Madam, was ever the devil's pass-key to the Christian dominion.

WIFE [*after a slow take on the man*]: Und here in die *Kirche* somethin' seems not like usual to me, somehow. I vunder vot.

[*The man rises and performs a calisthenics display similar to that in Act One.*]

WIFE: —You, you, you FRAUD, you, you—IMPOSTER! [*She smacks him on the seat of his pants with the skillet, in the middle of his tow-to-chin exercise.*] Invalidism pretendin' all these years! I should of suspected as much when all dis gymnasium equipment was delivered to die *Kirche* by die late Abercrombie and Fitch, now retired from service like you! I am going to drop dead. [*She collapses into the wheelchair.*]

MAN: I'd better give her a quick Christening, before her soul quits her body.

[*The Man pours sour mash from the jug the wife carried on at the opening of Act One, into the wife's open mouth. She recovers with marvelous alacrity, seizing the neck of the jug as he starts to remove it.*]

MAN: She's an unrepentant and unregenerate Protestant, Miss Rose, but livin' she is. [*Then to the wife*]: You are excused from the *Kirche*. I said, you're excused from the *Kirche* meaning git back to the *Küche*, which has exposed itself now as a subtle symbol for show-biz on Broadway. —I am mentally occupied with reflections on beauty.

WIFE: Ah, yes, y'r own.

MAN: I know ye think me indolent both above and below, but, Madam, I'll have ye know—

WIFE: WHAT? —Not already known or suspected.

MAN: I've written a number of epic dramas since my second year in grade school, not all of which closed in Boston if opened. Let's say I have served my apprenticeship in the literary world, having composed a sequence of sonnets to spring, but most importantly, Madam, a three paragraph novella that won the Hotlicker Award at the age of fifteen.

WIFE: Die Hotlicker, vot iss die Hotlicker?

MAN: The Hotlicker Award's not one of those annual tributes of no more than annual significance but one that's awarded only on such rare occasions as it's *deserved*, even if that be no more than once in the life-time of an immortal.

WIFE: And who gives out this award?

MAN: It is named for the donor.

WIFE: Whose name is?

MAN: Hotlicker, Madam, Professor Emeritus Hotlicker.

WIFE: —Strange name. —Teutonic?

MAN: No. Descriptive.

WIFE: And this award of the Professor Hotlicker, is it a monetary award or just honorary?

MAN: It is axiomatic, Madam, it is axiomatic as the Pope is a Catholic and the bear shits in the woods, or vice versa, that an award is not honorary unless it is monetary as well.

WIFE: Substantial? The monetary part of it?

MAN: Substantial enough to sustain us for fifteen years in SoHo without deprivations of a practical nature, certainly none that I know of.

WIFE: I could mention one to yuh. It's been more than fifteen years since ye've thrown a good one in me. The screwing I get is not worth the screwing I got, if ye get what I mean.

MAN: Madam, at times I miss your point, and I swear I don't know if the miss is voluntary or not.

WIFE: What a fate for a Lutheran minister's daughter, to wind up the wife of a retired male hustler, contented entirely with his retirement.

MAN: Contented? Entirely? Soon the room, this box square as a block, containing a single window, set so high in the wall that it could only be reached by a wall-painter on a ladder, of which I believe we have neither, nor the pecuniary means by which to procure them . . . And due to the paralysis which afflicts me, how could I mount the ladder to take a look out at the—but soon the room. How very soon the room . . .

WIFE: Oh, but was you dozin' your life away while I sautéed the kidneys in wine sauce, leibchen, old ducks?

MAN: Entirely, entirely contented with this retirement? Am I? Is the light dimming on me? Time: relentless obsession. Only cure was the axe which you missed me with. "Wait for the next time," you said. I do not wait: I endure. Perhaps that's waiting. The verb to endure and the verb to survive are different, except in this instance.

[*There is a long pause.*]

WIFE: Balls!

MAN: That's better.

WIFE: What's better about it, reflector on beauty?

MAN: Spherical objects with life-generating power. Yes, balls are two parts of beauty.

WIFE: Outta your balls you give me a coupla cretins, expelled from kindergarten after fifteen years in it as not being up to snuff, not up to countin' the colored beads on the frames or puttin' the alphabet blocks in proper position, this is what your two parts of beauty produced. Words fail me! *Ficken mich*! —Words fail!

MAN: So let's get on with the action!

[*A trap door springs open alongside the organ, releasing a cloud of smoke. A devil with pitchfork appears, accompanied by peals of hollow, derisive laughter. The wife screams, turns about dizzily, and faints. The trap slams shut and the stage is immediately silent.*]

MAN [*calling right into the wife's ear*]: Help!

[*The wife snores.*]

MAN: That would be her response if wide awake. SoHo. Sleep doesn't become her as mourning did electric. Hmm. Well.

[*He sits and starts to work on his "GREAT MEMOIRS." Miss Rose enters.*]

MISS ROSE: Another selection, sir?

MAN: Yes, that would be suitable, yes.

MISS ROSE [*crossing to sit at the organ*]: Classical or what they call pop?

MAN: Miss Rose, in me very green days, I was not exposed to the great symphonic works that the uptown folk call classics. It was ever me practice to whistle the songs of the streets. Oh, not the vulgar songs, mind ye, but those that suited a lad strollin' innocently by the Plaza on his way to a bench that directly faced that grandest of grand ole wayside Inns, a bench beside a duck-pond. Quack, quack, quack, they quacked, merrily to me, for they knew me well as a lad without guile or craft but a smidgin of the old Celtic minstrels in 'im—and a sack of bread crumbs as well. So I would whistle, most early dusks, a song of the streets of Erin such as "Sweet Molly Malone" or "My Wild Irish Rose" or "Danny Boy!" Now having come, now, to a lyrical passage in me memoirs. . . .

MISS ROSE: Memoirs at your age, still green?

MAN: Oh, that old artificer, that charlatan called time, we've walled it out of the *Kirche*. As best we can. For a while, that much and no more. Our existence is magic devoutly believed in. The green of the heart withers not if ye defend it from seasons of corruption, and reflect upon beauty. Fifteen I was when a uniformed lad me

own age—a bellhop—crossed out of the Plaza to the duck pond
and blushingly delivered an invitation to visit a suite of four rooms,
illuminated by crystal chandeliers and with glistening tables heaped
not with crumb sacks for ducks but with the epicurrean delights of
the exceedingly privileged. Cordially was I received, first at the table
and then in a bed which befitted a monarch . . . a queen . . . When
the visit was over, and my host had rewarded me as was befitting
to a descendant of the kings of old Ireland . . . well, I was stunned
by the experiences. I excused meself from his presence and went
to another window facin' my humble bench in the park. I raised
it and heard the voices of my feathered friends on the pond. They
seemed to be agitated. Quack, quack, quack, they were quacking.
—But now their once joyful voices seemed rueful—reproachful . . .
And then me benefactor, propped on his pillows, said "Lower that
window, boy, a chill could take me away quite prematurely since I
do so anticipate your *future* visits." —which have yet to occur . . .

[*Miss Rose segues into "Danny Boy" and the man sings it.*]

MAN: Oh Danny Boy, the pipes, the pipes are calling
From glen to glen, and down the mountainside.
The summer's gone, and all the roses falling
'Tis you, 'tis you must go and I must bide.
But come ye back when summer's in the meadow
Or when the valley's hushed and white with snow,
It's I'll be here in sunshine or in shadow.
Oh Danny Boy, oh Danny Boy, I love you so.

And when ye come, and all the flowers are dying,
If I am dead, as dead I well may be,
You'll come and find the place where I am lying
And kneel and say an Ave there for me.
And I shall hear, though soft you tread, above me,
And o'er my grave shall warmer, sweeter be,
And you will bend and tell me that you love me,
Then I shall sleep in peace until you come to me.

[*When he is finished, Miss Rose rises and prepares to leave.*]

MAN: Could I ask for a more precise timekeeper than the giant daisy of day and the night-blooming vine, but time, time . . .

MISS ROSE: I know, Sir. It little concerns us when all's said and done. Eternity does not repel me. I sometimes wonder if I don't exist in it now.

MAN: Ah, Miss Rose—ye know ye've given me all of poetry that exists in my heart . . . Sorry if that sounds maudlin, but I thought ye should know . . .

MISS ROSE: Thank you, Sir—but I think that I *did* know . . .

[*Miss Rose starts to exit. The man rises and extends his arms to embrace her, but she fends off this intimacy with a delicate gesture. The wife's snoring becomes audible again.*]

MAN: Yes . . . Look above ye, Miss Rose, and tell me if the night-blooming vine has begun to abandon its vigil . . . my eyes seem to be a bit misty.

MISS ROSE [*looking up*]: Yes, Sir, I do believe that it's gradually, as if regretfully, retiring from the little window high in the wall. —Shall I accompany its retreat with the second ballad?

MAN: Ah, yes. "My Wild Irish Rose . . ."

[*She plays again and they sing the song.*]

THE MAN AND ROSE:
>   If you listen I'll sing you a sweet little song,
>   Of a flower that's now drooped and dead,
>   Yet dearer to me, yes than all of its mates,
>   Though each holds aloft its proud head.
>   'Twas given to me by a girl that I know,
>   Since we've met, faith I've known no repose.
>   She is dearer by far than the world's brightest star,
>   And I call her my wild Irish Rose.

My wild Irish Rose, the sweetest flower that grows.
You may search everywhere, but none can compare
With my wild Irish Rose.
My wild Irish Rose, the dearest flower that grows,
And some day for my sake, she may let me take
The bloom from my wild Irish Rose.

They may sing of their roses, which by other names,
Would smell just as sweetly, they say.
But I know that my Rose would never consent
To have that sweet name taken away.
Her glances are shy when e'er I pass by
The bower where my true love grows,
And my one wish has been that some day I may win
The heart of my wild Irish Rose.

MISS ROSE [*when the ballad is completed*]: I'm afraid I must be off now.

MAN [*recovering from sentiment*]: Nice to have three visible walls in three primary colors: yellow, blue, and red. Primary. SoHo. [*He does some exercises, runs in place, etc.*] Why does a man in his prime retire to a pretense of invalidism in a wheelchair in SoHo? Naturally as an expression of protest—social. Hmm. Was not my profession also a social protest?

[*He returns to the wheelchair, the wife awakens.*]

WIFE: Oh, it's you, you fuckin' *imposter*! Ow, such a nightmare I've had. The recollection escapes me, how long was I— LOOK! DIE CLOCK!

[*She is referring to the night-blooming vine, now receding snake-like back to where it came from.*]

MAN: So the night-bloomer is packing it up. A familiar phenomenon. It packs it up to make room for the brilliant giant daisy of day.

WIFE: Und die kinder still outzen! I tremble! —For die fates that could have detained 'em I tremble and pray.

MAN: Pray that they remembered the mathematical and geographical lessons the old pro give them before they made their first excursion into their—predestined vocation.

WIFE: Yep, die night-bloomer is out and now vill enter die king-size daisy of day.

[*Demented outcries of a euphoric nature, along with the clatter of racing feet, are heard from off-stage. Die Kinder crash into the Kirche, their clothing in obvious disarray. The wife attempts speech, but only opens and closes her mouth like a goldfish.*]

MAN: Ach, die kinder!

[*Slowly, as if cranked by a rusty machine, the wife turns about to regard her twin progeny. They stand stage center, weaving in unison with inebriate smiles and simpers.*]

MAN: Well, now, show daddy y'r profits on this first excursion into the world beyond *Kirche, Küche, und Kindergarten* from which ye've been so prematurely expelled.

WIFE [*in a choked, guttural voice*]: Vere iss die loot, die bread? Nein?!

[*Die Kinder laugh at her.*]

MAN: Now having gone forth on your first professional venture, my dears, your mother and me are naturally a bit concerned concerning the extent of your profits.

[*The simpering incomprehension of Die Kinder continues.*]

MAN: I mean the amount of the remuneration that you have received in the public rooms and the private suites of the great hotels uptown where you was directed.

WIFE: Ach shmitzen, address 'em in words of a single syllable only!

MAN: I never seen a more cock-simple look on human faces since I first removed my jeans before a Lutheran minister's daughter and also before a gentleman-patron of the arts at the Hotel Plaza!

WIFE [*with revived animation*]: Turn the boy's pocket's inside out, vile I look into die grab-all bag of die kleine Fräulein, mein Gretchen!

[*The examination is conducted rapidly; no profits are discovered. The man and the wife exchange glances.*]

WIFE: So!

MAN: Ho!

WIFE: NEIN, NADA, NIENTE? DIE PROFITS, DIE LOOT, DIE BREAD? Iss Diss die tragic outcome ye've delivered us mit, worsen die report card and die expellsion from kindergarten? — *Or have you concealed it privately somewhere about! Ja?*

DAUGHTER: WE

SON: GIVE IT

DAUGHTER: AWAY, LIKE FOR NOTHING, BUT *LOVE!*

SON [*sheepishly*]: —in SoHo . . .

MAN [*observing his wife's swaying motion*]: Put some pillows back of your mutter, I think she's about to drop dead.

[*The man tosses his wheelchair cusions to die Kinder, who place them under the wife just as she falls. She sits up immediately.*]

WIFE [*groggily, without inflection*]: —Hello.

[*On this cue, die Kinder burst into song, sweetly as songbirds at daybreak. The trap-door reopens and an angel appears for the duration of their song.*]

DAUGHTER AND SON [*singing*]:

Love came down from hea-venn
To dwell with us on earth!
L-O-V-E, LOVE, L-O-V-E, LOVE!
Love, Love—Love, Love,
L-O-V-E, LOVE!

MAN: *Miss Rose, Miss Rose!*

[*Miss Rose enters as the Angel disappears. The wife does not see or hear her. Die Kinder drift off into sleep after their song.*]

MAN: Miss Rose, I regret to say that there's been another bit of a domestic crisis here, desecrating the holiness of the *Kirche*. However, be that as it may, and indeed it *is*—Let us now get on with our much-delayed Vesper Service.

MISS ROSE: I am afraid, Sir, the delay has been too protracted for the service, if there is now to be one, to qualify time-wise with Evensong—or Vespers . . .

MAN: Nevertheless, would you please seat yourself at the organ.

MISS ROSE [*crossing to her seat at the organ*]: And what will be the opening selection?

MAN: Give me a few moments to gather me wits, Miss Rose; still somewhat shattered and scattered by the profitless return of die kinder from their first professional excursion into areas occupied by the *haute-bourgeoisie*.

MISS ROSE: Perhaps if I played very softly—

MAN: Ah, yes, softly, softly . . .

[*Miss Rose plays "Danny Boy."*]

MAN: The verb to endure . . . The verb to survive . . . I have endured—I have survived. It appears that I must now face and accept the old male responsibility and prerogative of providing a living for himself and household. [*Over his shoulder to the wife.*] Madam, hand me the brass-studded belt to fasten about my jeans.

WIFE: So you're up to it again, about to display your self once more on the park benches facing the grand Hotel Plaza, now owned and operated by the corporation Gulf-Western!

MAN: Ah, yes, the Plaza. Correct me if I don't remember correctly the telephone number.

WIFE: —What telephone? Ve got no telephone here, it's been removed for non-payment these past ten years.

MAN: Removed from your sight, only, but still here and in service. [*He produces the phone.*]

WIFE: What a fraud, veritably a fraud, a fraud of a fraud!

MAN: That's your good fortune, Madam, as well as mine. [*He dials.*] Seven, five, nine, three, oh, oh . . .oh. How do you do, Operator? —I wish to enquire if the esteemed Professor Emeritus Hotlicker, patron of the humanities and the arts, is still living and resident there. Oh. Ho. And still in the tenth floor suite that looks out by telescope onto the park? He was into duck-watching, you know, the ducks on the lakes of the park, as well as into the subsidy of great poets composing immortal odes upon the benches facing his way. Destiny, yes. It beckons artist to patron, immemorially so. —So? He is? Still living? And duck-watching by telescope? Oh? So? And now and then still dispensing the Hotlicker Prize for excellence in the art of rhyme? Ho. So. Destiny, the inscrutable, has provided it so. No, don't disturb him before he's up for roomservice. I shall be there to serve him, butter his toast, crack his three-minute eggs, and then, and then—contend once more for the great Hotlicker Award . . . [*He hangs up, the final notes of "Danny Boy" fading away. He puts on his brass-studded belt.*]

WIFE: And is it your intention, do you intend, to grace *us* once more with the abominations of your presence? Again?

[*The music segues into a rousing march.*]

MAN: Ah, love. Trust in habitude as you trust in the God of your Lutheran father.

WIFE: A piece of doubtfully brilliant advice, comin' after his visit to me this day . . .

MAN [*turning to her*]: And so, Madam, I leave ye now—*pro tem*—to the profligate progeny of your Protestant loins, and to your kidneys sautéed in margarine and *chab*-liss, yes, I go now and will not return empty-handed. I leave that simple but impractical practice to die kinder. Purity cannot be desecrated, if ever true . . .

[*As the music crescendos and ends, the man crosses right through that fourth "invisible" wall and exits through the house. The light narrows in the on the wife, who addresses the audience.*]

WIFE: And so? A happy ending? If it's not provided by life, what's wrong with so believing? That it was and it is, over a coffee mit cruller? Be our guests. Who is not the guest of life for a while? I said who isn't, I said the guest, I said of life, I said for a while. The punctuation mark was the mark of a question. I leave you to ponder those questions . . .

[*Die Kinder pop up and flank her.*]

WIFE: . . . *for a while.*

[*Die Kinder sing a soft, eerie reprise of their "Love Song," staring straight out and getting softer and softer, becoming inaudible as the lights fade.*]

CURTAIN

GREEN EYES

OR

NO SIGHT WOULD BE WORTH SEEING

CHARACTERS

BOY
GIRL
A WAITER

A boy and girl, about twenty years old, are rising from a double bed in a New Orleans hotel room. They are both from the rural South and are honeymooning in this French Quarter hotel. The room is silvery dim, as if the river mist had entered it. The boy has slept in his shorts but the girl is nude, and there are conspicuous abrasions on her body. Phonetic spelling of their speech is not invariably used after it has been established.

GIRL: I'm gittin' up.

BOY: So'm I.

GIRL: Call fo' breakfas'. [*He ignores the suggestion.*] Well, call for breakfas', will yuh.

BOY: You call fo' breakfas'.

GIRL: Ok. I'll call fo' breakfas'. You just sit there smokin' an'— [*She takes the phone off the hook.*] —Room service. This is Mrs. Claude Dunphy. We checked in here yestiddy an' we'd like some breakfas' now. I want two soft boiled eggs, not fried, soft boiled, coffee, two pieces of buttered toast. Claude? What do you want?

BOY: I want a explanation.

GIRL: Continental? What's that consist of? —Oh? What's a cwasong? —Ain't you got a colored boy on the place that could run out for a couple of eggs? We're goin' sight-seein' in New Awleuns t'day so I need a substantial breakfas' in me. Hmm. Well, send two of them continental breakfasts out here quick as you kin. [*She hangs up.*] That abnawmal boy, he told me they wouldn' send out fo' two eggs. —Git off my panties.

BOY: I want a explanation. You got tooth an' claw marks on yuh like yuh been t' bed with a wildcat.

GIRL: You squeezed an' bit me las' night in yuh sleep.

BOY: I didn' sleep. I stepped over you las' night an' turned my face to the wall.

GIRL: Thin how come I got all these bruises?

BOY: That's what I'd like explanation of.

GIRL: You come in drunk near mawnin', bit an' bruised me, that's the explanation.

BOY: That ain't the explanation. Lies ain't explanations.

GIRL: You're one of them people that do things in their sleep.

BOY: I tole you I didn' sleep.

GIRL: A man dead drunk is practicly asleep. At least his memory is. —Gimme a cigarette.

BOY: Take one. The pack's right by you.

[*She takes a cigarette from a pack on the night table.*]

GIRL: Light it fo' me.

BOY: Light it fo' you'self. Don't train you'self t' be helpless. Five days from now I'm flyin' back to Waakow*.

GIRL: You keep sayin' that to me. "I'm flyin' back to Waakow, I'm flyin' back to Waakow."

BOY: What's the explanation?

GIRL: Of you goin' back to Waakow?

BOY: No. Of the tooth an' claw marks on your body.

GIRL: Your sex-starvation, I reckon. I kep' sayin' ouch, ouch, but you wouldn't stop.

BOY: A fuckin' lie.

---

* Their slang for Vietnam—probably derived from "whacked out" or "whacko." (ed.)

GIRL: Well, if you're gonna call me a liar it's no good talkin' to you. Git into yuh clothes befo' they come out here with breakfas'.

BOY: I want a explanation of what wint on here las' night.

GIRL: I give you the explanation an' I'm not gonna repeat it since your memory's blank.

BOY: Um-hmm. No explanation.

[*The girl has gotten into a rayon wrapper. The boy remains in shorts on the edge of the bed, gloomily reflecting.*]

BOY: I don't see how you'd have the nerve to, not knowin' whin I'd come back.

GIRL: Claude, I don't know what you're talkin' about.

BOY: You know goddamn well what I'm talkin' about.

GIRL: I! Do! Not! Knowwwwww!

BOY: Well, I guess a fool has it comin' to him. [*He extinguishes one cigarette and lights another.*]

GIRL: Slow.

BOY: What?

GIRL: Room service.

BOY: Speed it up.

GIRL: You cain't speed up slow room service.

BOY: I got a mind to beat the shit out of you.

GIRL: I can take care of myself.

BOY: Some day a man is gonna beat the fuckin'—

GIRL: You ain't the man that'll do it. —I bet you run backward in Waakow.

BOY: What're you doin' at the window?

GIRL: I wish you would look at that!

BOY: Look at what?

GIRL: That ole middle-age couple out there in the yard.

BOY: That ain't a yard, that's a patio.

GIRL: Well, they're sittin' out there in the patio havin' breakfas' in the rain.

BOY: That ain't rain, that's mist off the river out there.

GIRL: Awright, it's not a yard, it's a patio, it's not rain, it's mist off the river, but you'd never catch me havin' rolls an' coffee out there.

BOY: What bus'ness is it of yours?

GIRL: You sure do seem to be in a contrary humor this mawnin'.

BOY: A middle-age couple like that, they make the best they can out of what's still possible fo' them. They'll send out postcards to their relations an' friends sayin' "This mawnin' we had breakfast in the patio of our New Awleuns French Quarter hotel."

GIRL: If that was the limit of what I could put on a postcard, I woulden bother to write it or to mail it.

BOY: I don't think you'd have any trouble thinkin' of more to put on a postcard but you'd have t' be careful who you mailed it to. In fack, I doubt that it would go through the mail unless you put that postcard in a mighty thick envelope. [*He reaches out and feels her buttocks.*]

GIRL: At least you still seem to appreciate my body.

BOY: It looks like I'm standin' in line to appreciate it.

GIRL: You jus' got up on the wrong side of the bed.

BOY: They's only one side to git up on.

GIRL: They got a ole dawg with 'em that's turned its back to 'em.

BOY: Soft.

GIRL: I only like a man to feel me at night.

BOY: The man you're married to can feel you whenever he wants to.

GIRL: Feel me but don't bruise me or bite me.

BOY: —Soft. Plushy. Made fo' the purpose of—

GIRL: Claude, you cain't have me anytime you want, day or night.

BOY: I didn' have you las' night.

GIRL: No, you preferred t' git drunk on Bourbon Street.

BOY: —I got things in my head I got to git out . . .

GIRL: A man's got to choose between gittin' drunk an'—

BOY: I been ordered to shoot down screamin' wimmen an' children, and I done it, I done it!

GIRL: —Well, you was ordered to, a soldier got to do what he's ordered, don't he? Besides—

BOY: Besides?

GIRL: —They're like animals, ain't they, those—those jungle people? Less'n human? Ain't they?

BOY: No, Christ, no, they're human, they're more human than you, and they're more human than me that shot 'em down!

GIRL: As ordered.

BOY: Could you have done it?

GIRL: If ordered.

BOY: Then you go back to Waakow in five days, you take my place there! Say I—

GIRL: I would if ordered.

BOY: You know you won't be ordered. —Git back in bed.

GIRL: Not with breakfas' ordered, wait'll t'night.

BOY: Come away from that window with your back to me like you hated t' see me.

GIRL: I don't hate to see you, Claude. Would I of married you, sweetheart, if I hated to see you?

BOY: Then why're you standin' there lookin' out th' window while I make love to you?

GIRL: Feelin' me like a melon t' see if I'm ripe is not makin' love t' me, Claude. Oh, oh. Huh. They gotten out of their chairs in th' mist off th' river in the patio, now.

BOY: Who? Done what?

GIRL: Them. Out there.

BOY: Cain't even wait five days for me t' be gone.

GIRL: Huh? —Hah! . . . The woman an' the old dawg are goin' into the office of the hotel. The old man's come a cropper*, fell down on the bricks an' the woman didn' look back to see if he had a stroke an' th' ole dawg jus' barked at him. —I hope we're never like that.

BOY: How we are is nothin' to brag about in my opinion.

GIRL: Not in mine either.

BOY: Le's go back to bed.

GIRL: We're waitin' fo' breakfas' an' after that we're goin' sight-seein', ain't we? At least that's my intention.

---

* Slang meaning "to fall on one's behind." (ed.)

BOY: That terrible headache that come on you last night, have you recovered from that or are you still sufferin' from it?

GIRL: I took two aspirin fo' it.

BOY: So you got over it. That's the explanation?

GIRL: What give me that awful headache was bein' took from one noisy, indecent place to another on Bourbon Street last night. By two A.M. I couldn't stand it no more and had to walk back here alone.

BOY: You were two blocks from here, and it's a well-lighted street.

GIRL: A girl alone on that street is mistaken fo' a whore.

BOY: Mistaken correckly sometimes.

GIRL: I don't like that remark.

BOY: If you don't like it, shove it.

GIRL: I don't like that remark neither.

BOY: Then shove it, too.

GIRL: T'day I think I'll go sight-seein' alone.

BOY: Ain't you afraid you'd be mistook for a whore?

GIRL: I'll go sight-seein' alone in th' Garden District an' no-body's gonna make the mistake you mentioned.

BOY: I got no objection to you sight-seein' alone.

GIRL: I'm goin' sight-seein' alone because of your insults to me an' you're gonna give me five bucks for expense.

BOY: I'll give you five bucks like shit.

GIRL: Don't talk to me in that langwidge, I don't let nobody talk to me in that langwidge, an' if you refuse t' give me five dollars t' go sight-seein', I'll go to th' desk in the office of this hotel an' say I need five dollars to go sight-seein' an' have it put on the bill.

BOY: I'll call the office of the hotel an' tell 'em t' give you one dime to see sights on.

GIRL: Yeah. I bet you would.

BOY: That's one bet you'd win.

GIRL: I think I'll call up my folks in River Bay an' tell 'em our marriage has already proved a mistake.

BOY: They won't say "Hurry back, honey."

GIRL: It was a whirl-wind marriage if ever there was one. You wanna know somethin'?

BOY: What?

GIRL: —Nothin'.

BOY: Go sight-seein'. I got a bottle here, I'll stay here with it. The weather ain't good and I might call up a fellow's on leave from Waakow, too.

GIRL: Any red-blooded boy ought to think of it as a priv'lege to serve his country in Waakow.

BOY: You've never seen the color of my blood and you've never been to Waakow.

GIRL: Don't lose my respeck by complainin' about Waakow to me all the time.

BOY: What respeck have you got fo' me which I could lose?

GIRL: Would I of married a boy I coulden respeck?

BOY: When I remind you I'm goin' back to Waakow it's not a complaint but a statement.

GIRL: It's easy fo' me to see your indifferent attitude toward it.

BOY: My attitude toward it is not indifferent at all.

GIRL: What is it, then?

BOY: Fed up and disgusted.

GIRL: —How do I git your Army paycheck, Claude?

BOY: You don't git it.

GIRL: Are you tellin' me that you don't intend t' support me?

BOY: Pracktilly all of my Army paycheck goes to my mother now that my father is in the hospital.

GIRL: That's a piece of shocking infawmation you should of give me befo' our marriage, not after.

BOY: Well, now you know, and I want to ask you a question.

GIRL: Ask it.

BOY: Who fucked you las' night?

GIRL: What a thing to ask a girl you're married to. I won't answer such a disgustin' question.

BOY: I found a rubber in the tawlet this mawnin' when I wint in there to pee.

GIRL: Are you suggestin' t' me that—

BOY: I don't suggest a thing I awready know is a fack.

GIRL: You're in no condition t' know a fack in th' world.

BOY: I recognize a rubber in a tawlet, Miss Newly-Wed.

GIRL: Mr. Newly-Wed, you wuh so drunk las' night you wuh seein' false sights, an' you blame it on me.

BOY: Just a minute.

GIRL: Just a minute you'self.

BOY: You had the goddamn nerve to—

GIRL: My feet still ache from—

BOY: You lef' me in that—

GIRL: Some honeymoon! Neither of us knowin' the other one from—

BOY: You lef' me in that—

GIRL: At two A.M. Worn out. You should thank your stars you married a decent girl.

[*The speeches overlap here.*]

BOY: I thank my stars for nothin'. "Claude," you said, "I got a terrible headache, I'm goin' home, good-night sweetheart." —You kissed me.

GIRL: Claude, if there was a rubber in that tawlet you put it in.

BOY: You wanna see it? It's still in the tawlet, I peed off the balcony so you could have a look at that condom. [*He seizes her wrist.*] Come on, have a look at it, an' try to explain how it got there.

GIRL: Don't pull at me.

BOY: I want you to have a look at it.

GIRL: Leggo my wrist befo' I hit you with somethin'.

BOY: Lissen, Miss Newly-wed, if you ever hit me with somethin', that would be a mistake that you would live to regret. [*He releases her.*]

GIRL: You torn th' sleeve of—I know what happened las' night. You had one of them strippers an' lef' the' rubber on yuh.

BOY: I never picked up no stripper.

GIRL: A rotten lie through your teeth. You picked up a stripper, you had relations with her, lef' the rubber on you and—

BOY: I never knowinly hooked up with no hooker, not even in Waakow.

GIRL: —The mystery of the rubber has been cleared up.

BOY: Shut up a minute. The waiter's comin'.

GIRL: My breakfas' had better include two soft-boiled eggs an' some buttered toast.

[*A colored waiter raps at the door.*]

BOY: Come on in.

GIRL: I'm goin' to the bathroom to fix my face for sight-seein'.

WAITER [*entering*]: Where do you want your breakfasts?

BOY: I don't see nowhere to put 'em but on that table.

GIRL [*sticking her head out of the bathroom*]: Does it?

WAITER: Good morning. [*He exits.*]

GIRL: Well, does it?

BOY: Does it what?

GIRL: Include my soft-boiled eggs.

BOY: The soft-boiled eggs rolled off the tray on the way.

GIRL: What's there to that continental breakfas'?

BOY: Come outa the bathroom an' see.

GIRL [*emerging from the bathroom*]: Coffee an' fruit juice. Is this piece of curved bread the cwasong?

BOY: Yais, I reckon it is.

GIRL: Well, maybe it'll provide me with strength to git out on the street.

BOY: That's a thought.

[*The girl dips her croissant in her coffee and eats it dreamily.*]

GIRL: Mmm. Not good, not bad. [*Pause.*] So I don't git your army paycheck?

BOY: Nope. It goes to mother like I tole you.

GIRL: Um-Hmm. Like you tole me. —You wanna know the truth about las' night?

BOY: Yeah, let's hear it.

GIRL: I'll tell you the truth about anything, now that I know you don't intend to support me. A man did follow me here and I never known or will know another man like him. We done it five times together. He had green eyes.

BOY: People with green eyes have nigguh blood in 'em.

GIRL: Nothin' nigger about him and he had enawmus green eyes. Said a hello to me when I turned off Bourbon to the hotel. Caught hold of my wrist, drug me between two buildings, befo' I could holler, put his hands on me. Then it was too late to holler. The hugest hands a man has ever put on me an' hot as blazes. They practicly burnt through my clothes before he got my clothes off me, and there was the first time we done it. And he wasn't ready to quit and neither was I, me neither. "Jesus," he ast me, "don't you stay somewhere?" I said, "Jesus, yais, I do, in a hotel two doors away." "Git me in there," he said, "and I'll ball you all night." "I cain't git you in the front entrance, but there's a back one," I told him, an' how to git in the back way.

BOY [*facing her with clenched fists*]: Go on with the story. You'll know it's finished when I knock your teeth in, you whore!

GIRL: Whores take money, I took no money off him.

BOY: You took disease off him to rot with!

GIRL: That green-eyed man had just got off a boat and was clean as the sea and worth twenty of you, thirty, fifty, a hundred.

Hurry, he said. He shoved me. I staggered into the hotel like I was drunk, fell down in the hall an' couldn't remember the number of this room. "I hope you didn' hurt you'self," said that abnawmal boy at the desk. "Never, never felt better in my existence. What's my room-number? Give me the key to it quick!" And it seemed forever to me before that enawmus green-eyed fire of a man come through the courtyard door. Here, up here, I called him and up he run and he burned the room runnin' in like it caught fire. I tell you it's a wonder I'm not burned black.

BOY: A whore fucked by a nigguh *is* burned black!

GIRL: Wait, now, lemme finish this life story of mine befo' you blow your haid. Lissen. He started to put a rubber on, it didn't fit him, it split, I said: "Don't mess with that." And he thrown it in the tawlet.

BOY: You didn't know I'd find it?

GIRL: Hell, you didn't exist in here last night, obliva, obliter, gone, gone back to Waakow! Lissen! To be in deeper, he put the flats of his feet on the wall and I swear that I bit the pillow not to scream!

BOY: I'm done with you.

[*The following speeches overlap.*]

GIRL: It's you that's been done with by me!

BOY [*overlapping, seizing her arm*]: A whore that brags to her husband—

GIRL: To a lyin' cheatin' jerk, go an' jerk off in a—

BOY: That she's been fucked by a—

GIRL: Foxhole!

BOY: Not in a fox's, in yours!

GIRL: In my nothing! [*She tears herself free.*] He had enawmus green eyes! But's in the Merchant Marine an' ships out t'day! [*Sob-*

bing and catching her breath.] "Ain't there no place fo' me on the boat?" I ast him, yaiss, *begged* him!

BOY: *Begged* this—?

GIRL: *Yais!*

BOY: *Nigguh?*

GIRL: That broke me in two with his—!

[*He seizes her.*]

GIRL: You lemme go, you goddamn nowhere—

BOY: Shit, baby, I'm somewhere an' you're—

GIRL: Where, where? I cain't see you!

BOY: Green eyes blinded you?

GIRL: Yais, blazed at an' blinded me, set me on fire that you will never put out!

BOY: Yeh, you're still hot with that fire!

GIRL: That's right, I am, by God, still blazing in it!

[*He slides down her body to his knees.*]

BOY [*frenzied*]: *Burn me in it, yeah, you're blazin' hot, burn me!*

GIRL [*sobbing*]: *No, no, I'm—goin'—sight! seein!* [*She is struggling to free herself from his grasp, which is now inescapable.*]

BOY: No sight would be worth seein'!

GIRL [*collapsing*]: *No, none! —After green eyes . . .*

[*He tears open her flimsy wrapper.*]

INSTANT BLACKOUT

THE PARADE

OR

APPROACHING THE END OF A SUMMER

The Parade, or *Approaching the End of a Summer,* was first performed by Shakespeare on the Cape on October 1, 2006 at the First Annual Provincetown Tennessee Williams Theater Festival. It was directed by Jef Hall-Flavin and Eric Powell Holm; the set design was by George Lloyd III; the costume design was by Clare Brauch and Scott Coffey; the lighting design was by Megan Tracy; the sound design was by Katharine Horowitz; and the production stage manager was Tessa K. Bry. The cast, in order of appearance, was as follows:

DICK	Elliott Yingling Eustis
DON	Ben Griessmeyer
MIRIAM	Vanessa Caye Wasche
WANDA	Megan Bartle
POSTMAN	David Landon

Provincetown, Massachusetts, August, 1940. Scene: a brilliant blue and gold expanse of sand dunes, sky, and sea on the New England coast. The white tower of a coast guard station rises to the left with several red and white pennants. In the foreground is a wooden platform, used to catch the airmail.

DICK [*indicating platform*]: —You see? A perfect dance floor, all it needs is mirrors.

DON: Are mirrors necessary?

DICK: For ballet practice, sure. Very necessary.

DON: What's this platform for, why's it out here on the dunes?

DICK: To catch the bag of airmail, the helicopter flies right over it and drops a canvas bag of mail on it. I noticed it yesterday and I thought to myself, there's my dance-floor.

DON: You'd better what out for the helicopter, son.

DICK: You watch out for it for me— Why do you call me 'son'?

DON: I feel fatherly toward you . . . sort of incestuously fatherly.

DICK: Don't say queer things like that.

[*Don grins and squints in the sun.*]

DICK: It's funny you call me son because when I was a child what everyone called me was Sonny.

DON: Sonny's even better than "son," I'll call you Sonny. OK?

DICK: My hair was yellow as butter.

DON: Now it's gold as your body.

DICK: Sun-bleached. In winter it's darker.

DON: Everything's darker in winter but winter's still far off.

DICK: That goddamn Wanda. She promised to meet me here with her portable Victrola.

DON: She will. People can't always be right where you want them at precisely the moment you want them, Sonny. You're grown up enough to know that.

DICK: Are they really going to do your play in New York or is that just a hopeful fantasy of yours?

DON: You saw the announcement of it in the Sunday *Times* drama section.

DICK: I saw it listed as a play that the Guild was considering for next season, but there's many a slip between considering doing and doing.

DON: Don't I know.

DICK: You ought to. I'm grown up enough to know that and I'm seven years younger than you. But if they really do it, and it's a hit, remember Sonny needs a wealthy patron. [*Pause.*]

DON: How would 'Sonny' reward this 'wealthy patron'?

DICK: That's the question.

DON: You've got the answer to it, nobody else.

DICK: I could have had five wealthy patrons last year in New York if I wanted somebody to keep me.

DON: You're very contradictory, just a minute ago you asked me to remember you needed a patron if my play was successful.

DICK: That was a joke, and the play won't be successful even if they produce it, which I doubt.

DON: But say they did and by some miracle, it turned out to be a hit—?

DICK: A penthouse apartment on the East River and a big room walled with mirrors and no demands that I wouldn't want to meet.

DON: What demands would you be willing to meet?

DICK: No demands at all. You don't listen to me, you look at me all the time with those crazy green eyes of yours but don't understand what I say.

DON: I could if you said what you mean.

DICK: I mean just what I say.

DON: But what you say makes no more sense than—than hieroglyphics make sense to a man that knows just English.

DICK: Well—like I said, I was joking. Even if they did do your play and it was wildly successful and you had the East River penthouse and a big room with mirrors, those crazy green eyes of yours would scare me away. They'd scare anybody away.

DON: My eyes would stop looking crazy, if I stopped being lonely.

DICK: Wanda, Wanda, where are you wandering, Wanda? Don, give me a little percussion: clap your hands together, I've got to work.

[*Don claps his hands together.*]

DICK: Faster, with some kind of rhythm. Oom-pah-pah, oom-pah-pah. Get it?

DON: What's it for?

DICK: I'm working out the choreography for my audition for Simon Godchaux's show.

DON: I don't understand what that is.

DICK: Simon Godshaux is casting a dance company for a coast-to-coast tour and it's my kind of dancing, savage, masculine dancing.

DON: Savage—masculine—dancing.

DICK: I'm going to audition for him soon's I get back to New York. I'm going to do an Indian warrior dance. That's what I'm working out now.

DON: Miriam says you auditioned for him last weekend in Boston.

DICK: I just had an interview with him. Told him what I was doing. He promised me an audition. Oh, he asked me to go sailing with him, but when I told him I wasn't that good a swimmer, I think he knew what I meant. —Where you going?

[*Don has started away; Dick continues his dancing, muttering oom-pah-pah to himself. Miriam, a girl about twenty-six, comes up to the platform.*]

MIRIAM: Where's Don?

DICK: He ran away.

MIRIAM: Why? What for?

DICK: I don't know.

MIRIAM: Did you hurt his feelings?

DICK: No. Why should I?

MIRIAM: He's sensitive.

DICK: I think he's nuts.

MIRIAM: Don't you like him?

DICK: When he's in a good humor. But lately he acts peculiar.

MIRIAM: With you?

DICK: Yes.

MIRIAM: I thought so.

DICK: What do you mean?

MIRIAM: He's in love.

DICK: With me?

MIRIAM: Apparently.

DICK: I didn't know he was queer. So that's it, huh?

MIRIAM: Yes.

DICK: These summer colonies are full of queers. It's kind of depressing. Seen Wanda?

MIRIAM: I passed her on the beach. She was hunting clams.

DICK: I need her portable. I'm working out the choreography for a warrior dance.

MIRIAM: Does she have suitable records?

DICK: I think I could use that thing of Bartok's for practice.

MIRIAM: Dick, be nice to Don.

DICK: I'm not queer.

MIRIAM: Maybe not, but you can be kind. It doesn't hurt to be kind.

DICK: How can a girl be sympathetic toward something like that?

MIRIAM: Love is love no matter what form it takes. And I've been in love. Hopelessly like he is with you.

DICK: You mean with another girl?

MIRIAM: No, of course not. With a boy.

DICK: Well, it's too messy. I can't be bothered with it. Oom-pah-pah, oom-pah-pah!

MIRIAM: I'm tired of this beach life. It doesn't seem real anymore. It's too removed from the world. I don't read papers. I don't listen in to the radio even.

DICK: That's what I like, being cut off from the world. Oom-pah-pah. Oom-pah-pah!

MIRIAM: I did like it here for a while. But now I'm fed up with it. Each day is too much like the others. They're like a string of gold beads. Monotonously bright. I want to break it and spill them all on the ground.

DICK: Oom-pah-pah!

MIRIAM: Do you think you have much talent as a dancer?

DICK: Of course. Or I wouldn't be working.

MIRIAM: I don't think you have. You're fairly good, you have a beautiful body. But I don't think you'll ever get anywhere. I think you'll go oom-pah-pah for a few more years and then go—*Blah!* Like that! You won't have anything left.

DICK: What have you got against me, Miriam?

MIRIAM: You're totally selfish and a terrible fool. I can't understand why he loves you. He has a great deal of talent. He has a future if he doesn't waste himself on something useless like you. [*Pause.*] You know what I think.

DICK: No. What?

MIRIAM: I think you're homosexual, too.

DICK: You're wrong.

MIRIAM: Wanda says you won't go to bed with her.

DICK: I don't go to bed with people.

MIRIAM: How old are you?

DICK: Twenty-two.

MIRIAM: Then you must have desires.

DICK: Not for copulation. I'm under-sexed I suppose.

MIRIAM: Then it couldn't possibly hurt you.

DICK: What?

MIRIAM: Being nice to Don.

DICK: My God. Do you go around procuring lovers for Don?

MIRIAM: I hate to see misery in people I like and admire. People with true possibilities.

DICK: Well, count me out. I can't be interested.

MIRIAM: I know that you're queer.

DICK: I'm not. I tell you I'm normal.

MIRIAM: So is a duck's egg. Don's your best bet. You're wasting your time with people like Libra and men like Godchaux. They aren't capable of caring for you enough to sacrifice anything for you. They'll want you, take you, use you and throw you back to the dogs. You know where you'll end up? On Forty-Second Street in pants like ballet tights.

DICK: I tell you I'm perfectly normal.

MIRIAM: Okay. Tell me. But I don't believe you, darling. [*She starts away.*]

DICK: Oom-pah-pah! Hey, Miriam! Tell Wanda to bring her portable up here.

MIRIAM: Go tell her yourself.

DICK: All right. Shit. Looks like I'll have to. [*He walks off.*]

MIRIAM [*moves off left calling*]: Don! Don!

[*Don returns.*]

MIRIAM: Dick says you ran away. What did you do that for?

DON: I don't know.

MIRIAM: He said something that hurt you?

DON: No.

MIRIAM: Why don't you transfer your interest to a more responsive object?

DON: You know better than to ask me that.

MIRIAM: This is my last afternoon on the beach.

DON: Leaving?

MIRIAM: On the Boston boat. Come away with me, Don. You'll find somebody in town.

DON: Do people of my kind have to be bitches, Miriam? Do we have to hop from one affair to another like slippery little rocks across a creek?

MIRIAM: Yes. Till you find the one that you don't slip on, and that gets you over the creek.

DON: I can't stand that any longer. It makes me feel cheap and disgusting.

MIRIAM: Your work could take you above it.

DON: No, I'm afraid it doesn't.

MIRIAM: Get away from him, Don.

DON: Oh, I will, when I have to. —Miriam?

MIRIAM: Yes?

DON: Am I alive? Do I appear to be living?

MIRIAM: Of course.

DON: The sun's so bright today it makes me feel like a shadow. All of my life begins to seem like a shadow. But I am alive, aren't I?

MIRIAM: Of course you're alive.

DON: Touch me! Do I feel solid?

MIRIAM: Perfectly solid, Don.

DON: Thanks. I didn't know.

MIRIAM: There is your shadow.

DON: It's reassuring. It should be reassuring. I thought perhaps the sun had begun to shine right through me. What makes desire? Desire for a face or a body? Why does flesh in certain forms become an obsession with you? Why does it darken your mind?

MIRIAM: Because you have passion. Put it into your work.

DON: I've put it into my work, but I'm still not satisfied.

MIRIAM: Then love someone who can love you. Transfer your longing to someone who could return it.

DON: Oh, it's too hard for me. I've given myself to people I don't care for but as soon as I love—then I lose all my character. I seem to dissolve. Love makes some people charming but it makes me dull. I haven't thought of anything to say for several hours. He was here dancing. I supplied the rhythm, we didn't have Wanda's portable. So I just sat here in the corner beating my hands together with a silly, squinting grin on my face while he danced. He danced and danced. Isn't the sunlight blinding? —Is there something about today that seems funny to you?

MIRIAM: It seems like yesterday or the day before.

DON: Yes. They're all alike here, all the days, but they have a cumulative effect, like equal blows on a rock, each alike but one finally cracking it open, making it fall to pieces.

MIRIAM: Who is the rock? You?

DON: I suppose I'm flattering myself. I'm dull as a rock but not as strong as a rock.

MIRIAM: You're probably stronger than you think. I don't think you're going to fall to pieces. Not unless you let yourself.

DON: Then what shall I do to prevent it?

MIRIAM: Get out from under whatever is striking against you.

DON: Not till I'm sure that it's useless. A miracle might happen. I might suddenly find my tongue in his presence and pour my heart out—and he might suddenly stop dancing for a minute.

MIRIAM: Do you think so?

DON: No. [*He turns with a slow tired smile.*] No, I don't.

MIRIAM: Then get away quick while you can, you little fool, don't stay any longer. Take the Boston boat this afternoon.

DON: Christ. I've been empty so long. I've got to have something to fill me.

MIRIAM: Your work.

DON: No, no, no, no! I want love.

MIRIAM: Then go where love can be given. Don't go for water to an empty well.

DON: I had to, I couldn't help it. How do you know that it's empty.

MIRIAM: You know it yourself. You said so.

DON: Today seems funny to me.

MIRIAM: How?

DON: I'm conscious of my whole life stretching behind me. I feel the weight of every single day. A weight and a vagueness, too. A tremendous vagueness. I think that I've been traveling through fog. But look how brilliant it is! Did you ever blow soap bubbles? No, I—I am looking back at everything. I remember single days, hours. None of them was ever complete in itself. They were all expectant. You know what I mean? They had their faces all turned one way, toward the future, as though— [*Pause.*]

MIRIAM: As though?

DON: As though a parade was coming, was going to pass. Well, I've stood here waiting so long that my neck's getting stiff from craning in one direction, toward the distant calliope's sound that doesn't get any closer. Is it imaginary? I see it all in my head.

MIRIAM: Then you don't have to actually see it, it's better in your head, a vision's less apt to be disappointing.

DON: No, no, I want to see the real thing, experience it in the flesh. I don't, I haven't, but I can describe it as if I did. The elephants are roped together with strings of pearls, the stately camels, they're ornamented, too, purple velvet trappings, brocaded, tasseled, the cleverly trained monkeys, they have on crimson silk jackets with golden bells. The bells clatter, there's a fanfare of trumpets. But it's all in my head, none of it's actually come by and my neck's getting stiffer. Fat people are moving in front of me, blocking my view. I squeeze between. They complain, they shove. One of them's stepped on my foot so hard it'll ache for hours.

MIRIAM: I'd give it up, then.

DON: Yes, I suspect you're right, it was just a false report, a rumor without foundation, a beautiful myth. Or maybe the route was changed. The elephants may have revolted against their drivers, possibly trampled them, even as they turned at some intersection not expected. See it? Slowly—ponderously with—beautiful, massive grace they've turned away from the route that was planned in advance, and the others have followed suit, they've all gone up a back street, just distant enough so I can't even be sure that I hear the music.

MIRIAM: You think the parade is love?

DON: What else is brilliant enough to make a parade?

MIRIAM: Perhaps your vision, your work.

DON: My work is a child's excitement.

MIRIAM: Don, I'm disappointed in you. I thought you had a—

[*The sea booms. Miriam looks squinting up at the racing blue-and-white sky, sun-dazzled.*]

MIRIAM: —a more distinguished kind of a mind than you're—

[*The sea booms.*]

MIRIAM: —something less ordinary than—

[*Don picks up the books that she carried out to the beach.*]

DON: I have a very ordinary mind, honey. I couldn't read this: Hegel. What is Hegel to me and what am I to Hegel? [*He tosses the book off the platform.*] Kant? Couldn't read the first sentence without washing down a couple of aspirins with a double shot of booze. Marx, hell, who wants to—Miriam, you're a—

MIRIAM: What am I, Don? In your opinion?

DON: Oh, you're *you*, whatever that is, and I'm me, whatever that is. . . .

MIRIAM: I'm more interested in what you *could* be than what you are at this moment.

DON: Don't you know that it can be unbearably dull to have people try to uplift you with inspirational claptrap about what you *could* be? Who is what he could be? I say fuck it, all that.

MIRIAM: You don't remember your first week here: I was the first person you met here and you were the first one I met here and we—

[*The sea booms.*]

MIRIAM: —We had such lovely, quiet evenings together, reading Rilke and— [*She looks squinting up again at the sky.*]

DON: Do you know what I like even better than Rilke? Movie fan magazines with pictures of young actors in them, actors that look like Dick because they're posing for pictures and are made up and flatteringly lighted. That's my choice literature, honey. Oh, I've read—

MIRIAM: You listened to me reading to you for hours, and weren't bored for a moment.

DON: Then, yes, then, but I've caught on fire since then, I have a belly full of burning sawdust in me now . . .

[*The sea booms. Don looks up squinting fiercely at the sky.*]

DON: —Honestly, Miriam, honey. Dick would be more interested in Kant, Hegel and Marx than I could be now, honey.

MIRIAM: Stop calling me, honey, it's—

DON: What you're angry about, what disturbs you, honey, is that we're now discussing something we didn't dare mention before, a thing that you think is rotten, decadent.

MIRIAM: I said stop calling me "honey"! I will not be patronized by you, now that I know you! I WON'T be!

DON: —Oh, Miriam—

[*The sea booms; they both squint up at the sky.*]

DON: —There is such a thing as great loneliness of the flesh and great longing to satisfy it, and the awful thing is that its satisfaction depends on the beautiful young Narcissans of the world such as—

MIRIAM: All right. But there's also such a thing as—

[*The sea booms.*]

MIRIAM: —the great white-plumed horses racing across the sky and the child's excitement of saying, doing, making . . .

DON: Love is something that's done and made too, and sometimes even said, too.

MIRIAM: But choose your object! The right one! —I'd been foolish enough to hope that— You see, I liked you.

DON: Until you found out I was "gay"?

MIRIAM: That doesn't bother me, hell, I knew that right away, well, almost right away, at least the first time I saw you looking at Dick which was the first day I met you. That's got nothing to do with the quality of your mind. I wanted you to have some rare, some—exceptional—something . . .

DON: Well, I do.

MIRIAM: You show no sign of it when you, you—you equate love! with—your lech for that gorgeous, graceful—moron that— [*She springs up and walks about kicking sand.*] —What do you think you've got that's exceptional? Rare?

DON: My capacity for making a sad, sorry sack of myself: publicly, interminably.

MIRIAM: Your self-pity is absolutely—boundless, you make me sick with it, damn you. You say "love"? About what you feel for—

DON: You admitted that he was gorgeous and graceful. Can't you admit that I am a sensual person?

MIRIAM: I thought I'd noticed something better about you.

DON: Stop kicking sand, the wind blows it in my face. Sit back down here with me. I wish I could love you. I wish that you could love me.

[*They both start to cry at the same instant, laughing an instant later.*]

MIRIAM [*suddenly springing up*]: Get up, the mail-plane, do you want to be brained by a mailsack?

DON: Yes.

[*She seizes his hand and pulls him off the platform.*]

MIRIAM: Stand back further, sometimes they miss.

[*The helicopter motor fades.*]

DON: It wasn't the mail plane, honey.

MIRIAM: Did you know it wasn't?

DON: The mail copter's rotors are red, white and blue.

MIRIAM: You weren't looking up so how'd you know?

[*Don shrugs.*]

MIRIAM: Indifferent, were you?

DON: There have been days when I've been more concerned with continuing my solitary struggle for survival.

MIRIAM: An orgy of masochism, that's you today, maybe always . . .

DON: Oh, you're full of psychiatric—clichés . . . how much did your folks pay that shrink you went to?

MIRIAM: A dollar a minute which made fifty dollars a session and they insisted on a Freudian. I wanted a Jungian, but Jung isn't Jewish.

DON: Universal unconscious. I like that. Isn't that Jung?

MIRIAM: Better for an artist.

DON: I think my work comes out of the universal unconscious and that's why it's so whatever the universal unconscious is, such as—what would you say it is? The universal unconscious? — Unconscious? And universal?

MIRIAM: Mind of God?

DON: I don't think my work comes out of the mind of God unless God is over-sexed, too.

MIRIAM: Be serious. And stop brushing sand off my legs, it—it tickles.

DON: Nicely?

MIRIAM: You know what I think you're thinking? I think you're thinking why don't I exploit this rich girl's interest in me: marry her. Be supported by her rich family: cultivate, or pretend to, a taste for the kosher cuisine, for lox and bagels, while I pursue my career without economic pressure and while I also indulge my lech for the silly Dicks of the world.

DON: —I'm not like that. I'm not like that at all. I may be a self-pitying masochistic shit or whatever you think of me, mistakenly, Mimi, but I'm not an exploiter, which is a thief. And a liar. When mother and me came north from Mississippi, Dad was already in St. Louis, he'd been so good a Mississippi drummer they'd made him sales manager of their St. Louie branch. Well, he met us at Union Station in Saint Louis. And just around the corner from the station was an outdoor fruit-stand. I picked a grape as we passed it. Dad slapped my hand so hard it burned for a good while, and he said, 'Don't ever let me catch you stealing again!' One goddamn grape was all! —And he taught me never to lie because he never lied. —Not lying, not stealing. . . .

MIRIAM: Gentlemanly virtues, of the old South.

DON: Old, but mountaineer: not elegant plantation.

MIRIAM: I'm afraid my race had to practice wiles and guiles to survive.

DON: What's necessary is necessary, no apologies for it.

MIRIAM [coolly]: No. —None.

DON: Sit back down.

[*She sits.*]

DON: —Closer—I'm cold. —That smooth skin of yours emanates—sun-warmth. —I've written a lot of verse this summer. I sent a batch of it off to my lady agent. She sent it back. "I'm sorry," she said, "but we don't handle verse." [*Pause.*]

> *Purity and passion are*
> *Things that differ but in name*
> *And as one metal will emerge*
> *When molten in a single flame.*

MIRIAM: —I wish that your poetry was a little bit better, Don.

DON [*grinning*]: So do I.

MIRIAM [*leaning her head on his shoulder*]: I don't mean I don't like it, I just wish it was a little bit better. I don't expect it to be as good as Keats or Rilke or Crane, but I do wish it—

DON: Was a little better. Don't you think that I wish it were, too? Miriam?

MIRIAM: I love you. I'm so sorry for you.

DON: That's patronizing as me calling you "honey".

MIRIAM: Okay, call me "honey".

DON: No. You've hurt my feelings again. Because it's all right for me to wish that my poetry was better but it isn't right for anyone else to and to say so. [*He grins up at the sky, then down at her. Then he strokes her long, dark hair that hangs loose about her ivory smooth shoulders.*] Let down the straps.

MIRIAM: What straps?

DON: Your bathing suit, I want to touch your breasts.

MIRIAM: I would if I thought you did want to, but I think you're just pretending.

DON: May I?

[*Miriam doesn't answer but lowers her head so that her hair falls in a dark, soft cascade over her face.*]

DON [*lowering the straps of her suit*]:
    Let down your hair, dream-dark at night,
    And I'll forget that fear was bright . . .'

[*He slips his hands over her breasts under the loosened jersey.*]

MIRIAM: —Do you think it's right to do what you're doing when you know—when you know?

DON: What do I know? I don't know . . .

MIRIAM: You know I'll go home and marry some nice young Jewish boy that my family approves of and will set up in business, and I'll bear children by him, and we'll both get plump and then stout and discuss his business together the way you and I read Rilke together, our first week here together?

DON: Maybe he'll like Rilke too.

MIRIAM: No, he'll object to Rilke because Rilke's German, you know that.

DON: Isn't that what you'll want later?

MIRIAM: Yes, but I won't forget our first week together. Will you?

DON: I won't forget today, either.

MIRIAM: I'm so frightened for you, I really am, Don, you know that.

DON: Yes. I know that you are. It's embarrassingly kind of you.

MIRIAM: Don, let people be kind to you.

DON: Will, they? Be kind to me?

MIRIAM: Some, a few, if you let them!

DON [*absently, indifferently*]: You're a beautiful person, I love you.

MIRIAM: Thank you so much for that sincere—declaration . . .

DON: Don't love; wait to be *loved*. You're lovely. Wait to be loved. Don't love till you're loved: have a studio in the Village with a skylight and entertain many people till the one comes that wants you, takes you under the skylight on the floor under the sky light, holds you, almost hurts you, yes, hurts you, he holds you so fiercely—bites your lips, your ears, your nipples, thrusts his head between your beautiful young thighs and devours—rapaciously. —Then you will know you are loved. Then you can love, not till then.

MIRIAM: —Oh? Go on

DON: All right. I will. Have music. Read Crane, Keats and Rilke. Chop away now and then on your heroic piece of sculpture of Man and Woman meeting like two rivers, passionately and serenely converging their separate waters like two rivers' waters. When he's tired from his post-orgasmic reaction, be womanly tender with him. Don't touch his sexual parts till they start to live again for you. Don't appear to be waiting for it but when you get up to get the cigarettes or the drinks, glance down at his naked body to see if his desire is reviving again. And even then, when you come back to lie down naked beside him, don't touch his "father of millions." Put your lips to his nipples, or whatever part of his upper body you've discovered is the erotically sensitive part, inside his ears, his mouth, his—well, you'll know, you'll know. . . . —Caress him all over with oil on your fingertip: keep the music going, of course, and don't let him get drunk. . . . All right, he'll make you a baby again and again and again with his father of millions and—there is a way to win, a way to play it. . . . —for you, not for me. I'll always bollix it up by being too quick and greedy . . . and scared!

MIRIAM: Don?

DON: Huh?

MIRIAM: Let's go back of the dunes and—

DON: No. No. Save yourself for somebody under that Village skylight.

MIRIAM: —Have you been making fun of me?

DON: No. You know I haven't. I'm not unkind to anybody that likes me and never could be, you know that. Don't you know that? Miriam? And how I wish I could be the right one for under the skylight? I'm the wrong one for in the dunes, honey. . . .

MIRIAM: —Well . . .

DON: Hmmm.

MIRIAM: Yes. . . . [*She sits back down beside him on the platform and leans her head on his shoulder.*]

DON [*absently stroking her long, loose, dark hair*]: It really is like sitting inside a soap-bubble out here today. All the colors of the—what time is it?

MIRIAM: Fifteen after six.

DON: The light will start fading in a few minutes now. —I'm all packed. I can catch a ride better at night.

MIRIAM: You're not going to hitchhike back. I'm going to lend you the money for the trip back on the Boston boat and on the—

DON: No, no, honey, no thank you.

MIRIAM: —And on the midnight special to New York, Pullman fare. I'm a Jew, you know, I'm a Jewish girl, and Jewish girls' folks have money and let their kids have it, you know. You can pay me back in New York. I'm going back in a week. I'm not sure I respect you much anymore but I still feel sorry for you, you're such a—what are you? —huh, Don?

DON: —I'm Fairy Glum from over the ravine.

MIRIAM: Shut up, stop making me sick. The Boston boat doesn't leave till half past eight so you've got plenty of time and even if you miss the Boston boat, I'll drive you to Boston.

DON: I'm going to hitchhike to New York, starting after dark, when all they'll see is what they think's a young boy with a— Oh, God, here they come back.

MIRIAM: Who?

DON: Him and Wanda, they've got her portable with them.

MIRIAM: You won't stay here?

DON: They've seen me. I can't run away. She's waving. Oh, God how I hate her. Do you think there's a chance she'll die? Won't something kill her?

MIRIAM: You don't mean that. You're an artist. You know she's a right to her life and her love as much as you have to yours. Don't fight against windmills, Don. You've got other uses for your force.

DON: Let me be brilliant, let me find words to say. Quick! Where's the bottle!

MIRIAM: No!

DON: Give me another drink, please, everything's going out, I feel dead inside.

MIRIAM: Look. There's the Boston boat, over there. It's coming around the Cape, Don.

DON: Let it come. She's all in white. Do you think she's beautiful?

MIRIAM: Very beautiful, yes.

DON: And it's hopeless?

MIRIAM: Yes. Go away. Don't stay here.

DON: I'm going to do something.

MIRIAM: What?

DON: I don't know but I'm going to do something.

MIRIAM: You'll make a fool of yourself?

DON: Go away, go on, go away!

MIRIAM: Okay. I'll see you off at the dock at 8:15.

[*Miriam walks away. The voices of Wanda and Dick are heard.*]

DICK: The choreography's very simple. Hi, Don. We worked it all out this morning.

WANDA: Hello, Don. What are you doing?

DON: Nothing.

DICK: It starts like this. See?

WANDA: Wonderful.

DICK: Then you do a *pliée*, a series of *pliées*. A *changement*!

WANDA: Ahhh!

DICK: Put the record on an' we'll run straight through it. Don't try to follow yet.

WANDA: No. I'll just watch you. Isn't he wonderful, Don? Don!

DON: Huh?

WANDA: Why aren't you looking at him?

DON: Sorry. I was distracted, Wanda.

WANDA: By what?

DON: As the summer approaches the end of the summer—have you noticed? —The sunsets from the dunes become more spectacular than ever. —Endings, approaches to endings, I guess they have a sort of special, theatrical interest for me which makes me suspect that I may write a good many bad or not so good plays but will probably always manage to come up with a pretty good ending for them. . . . um—hmmm . . . that's not enough but something . . . Well, it is unusually spectacular, this sunset. You ought to watch it, Wanda.

WANDA: I'm watching Dick.

DON: Is watching Dick better than watching the sun going down in such a spectacular fashion? Isn't there some difference in scale?

WANDA: I prefer watching Dick.

DON: You prefer watching a totally self-absorbed—definition of narcissism, do you? Oh, yes, he's beautiful this evening, young gold flesh, well-designed, but he's already at the zenith, the apex of his beauty. Wonderful? Now, yeah, not ordinary, just sort of oom-pah-pah . . .

DICK [oblivious to them]: Oom-pah-pah, oom-pah-pah.

WANDA: Don, I'm worried about you.

DON: Why, thanks, what a compliment, Wanda.

WANDA: What worries me about you is your change of character lately. You've started acting bitchy. Not like you were when I met you.

DON: What was I like then?

WANDA: Quiet. But agreeable, Don. You seemed to be nice. What's changed you?

DON: The bitterness of frustration.

WANDA: When did that begin?

DON: Almost as soon as I met him. —An erotic image which must have been lurking secretly in some closet of my mind.

DICK: Oom-pah-pah, oom-pah-pah. Wind up the Victrola, it's running down!

[*Wanda hastily obeys.*]

DON: A user of everyone he discovers to be possibly useful. No conscience about it, no sense of debt to—you, me, all others enchanted by the gob dazzle of him, here, now, at the height that he'll decline from.

WANDA: He's seven years younger than you.

DON: Time-wise. But in his heart?

WANDA: *Watch out! The helicopter!*

[*Wanda and Dick scramble off the platform as the sound of the helicopter zooms in. Don only moves to look up. A sack of mail drops on the platform. Don leaps onto the platform, fishes out some letters and tears them open, fiercely.*]

WANDA: Don! What are you doing?

DON: Opening letters not addressed to me: other people's mail.

WANDA: A criminal offense!

DON [*reading aloud*]: "Dearest—Marty?"—no, "Martha—how is everything there? Everything here is okay, as usual. Don't hurry back, we miss you but want you to have"—

DICK [*very quietly but ecstatically*]: Oom-pah-pah, oom-pah-pah.

DON [*leaning close to the letter*]: —"Want you to have the— peace and quiet that you need and— [*He leans closer to it.*] —you mustn't worry about us, all goes on pretty much the same as it was." —Hmm, I bet. —Oh, here's one for me, it's from my New York agent, maybe it contains a check.

[*He opens the letter slowly. Dick stops dancing.*]

DICK: It's gotten cold. Let's go have some chowder.

[*Dick doesn't help Wanda pick up the portable Victrola. They disappear over the dunes. Don is reading the letter. He rises slowly as its import strikes him, and he reads it aloud.*]

DON: "Dear Donald: I have just returned from a meeting with the Guild. They gave me the distressing news that every female star whom they had submitted your play to has rejected it with variations of the same criticism, that it is too negative, too sordid, although one or two have recognized its power. I am afraid this does not much surprise me as during war-years the public is drawn by light entertainment. I hope you will think about Burt's suggestion that you try your talented hand at writing the libretto for a musical. Burt has several ideas in his head if you have none in yours. There is a last option check waiting for you in the office. You change addresses so often we thought it best to hold it here till your return to New York now that—"

[*He crumples and drops the letter. He stares straight out. After a few moments the ancient postman appears and looks dully, hopelessly at the letters spilled about the platform.*]

POSTMAN: Hey, boy.

DON: Hi.

POSTMAN: How did the sack break open?

DON: Oh. The helly-bird dropped it from too high so it exploded on impact.

[*With difficulty, the old man stoops to gather the spilled mail, groaning and muttering.*]

DON: Sit down on the platform, Pop. I'll do that for you.

POSTMAN [*sinking onto platform*]: —Thanks. —My goddamn spine is going.

191

DON [*collecting letters from the sand*]: Oom-pah-pah, oom-pah-pah.

POSTMAN: Sight going.

DON: Maybe it's just the light going . . . [*He sits down beside the Postman as—*]

THE SCENE DIMS OUT

THE ONE EXCEPTION

The One Exception was first performed on October 2, 2003 by the Hartford Stage Company in Hartford, Connecticut. It was directed by Michael Wilson; the set design was by Jeff Cowie; the costume design was by David Woolard; the lighting design was by John Ambrosone; the original music and sound design were by Fitz Paton. The cast, in order of appearance, was as follows:

VIOLA	Annalee Jefferies
MAY	Jennifer Harmon
KYRA	Amanda Plummer

Scene: the front room of private home which looks as if it were not yet ready for occupancy. Women's voices are heard offstage.

MAY [*offstage*]: You are Miss—?

VIOLA [*offstage*]: Viola Shield, yesss. I'm sorry to have had to put you off till today but when a painter is preparing for an exhibition, in process of hanging—

MAY [*offstage*]: Oh?

VIOLA [*offstage*]: Yesss. There's very limited time for other matters.

MAY [*offstage*]: Your coat?

VIOLA [*offstage*]: No, thanks, the place is too chilly.

[*Viola Shield enters. She is an energetic woman of forty, followed by a distraught-looking woman in her fifties, May Svenson.*]

VIOLA: Why, it's so barely furnished, you must be just moving in.

MAY [*lowering her voice*]: Not staying but a few days. She has to be removed to an institution upstate and my leave of absence from Southern Baptist is up.

VIOLA: Evangelist, are you?

MAY: No, no, it's a Houston hospital. I work in the psychiatric ward.

VIOLA: Hmm.

[*The wind whines.*]

VIOLA: You'd better have your heating system adjusted. Hmmm. So she has to be put away?

MAY: Please. Quietly. The Lodge wants me to get as much of her past history, when old friends in the city knew her, I mean friends like you, as I can get for them.

VIOLA: Lodge?

MAY: Shhh—the private institution upstate. I see it as the only solution, at least till she's made some recovery. If she can, if she does.

VIOLA: You're whispering so I can barely hear you. Is everything top secret from the lady?

MAY: When speaking of the upstate institution. She's deathly afraid of institutions.

VIOLA: Private or public a mental institution is still a mental institution and scarcely preferable to a prison. I mean confinement is—oh, too loud? Forgive me, but I'm not accustomed to conversing in whispers.

MAY: She moves about so quietly I hardly know where she is even in this little place. Excuse me one moment, I'll see if her door is— [*She stealthily opens an upstage door.*] —still closed, yes. Everything's going to have to be managed without her knowing.

VIOLA: Who'll sign the papers?

MAY: Her nearest relative is just outside the city.

VIOLA: Could that be old Agatha?

MAY: Agatha Criswell, yes. She's said she'll commit her.

VIOLA: Agatha occasionally dropped by the little commune, as we called it, always trying to extort something from Kyra and Kyra would let her have it to get rid of her. None of us could stand that witch. Finally insisted that they meet outside the commune if the meetings continued.

MAY: I see. I haven't met Miss Criswell except by phone, a public pay phone. But that part's arranged. My part is most unpleasant. I have to see that she's under sedation and have her removed by ambulance.

VIOLA: Who'll pay the—

MAY: Someone's had power-of-attorney for a good while.

VIOLA: My God, not old Agatha!

MAY: No, a lawyer, no, no, her—accountant who pays my salary.

VIOLA: You certainly ought to be getting well paid for a job like this appears to be.

MAY: Yes, it's a frightfully painful situation for all concerned.

VIOLA: In such situations persons not paid to be concerned are naturally reluctant to become involved. [*She looks at her watch.*] My time here is running out.

MAY: Mine, too. You see, I'm on leave of absence. I had it extended once, but again—not possible.

VIOLA: People who have these collapses usually pull themselves together when they realize they must or surrender to the alternatives, which are one or two at best. —I thought I heard something. Has she emerged from her room?

MAY [*peeking out again*]: Not yet.

VIOLA: But she is expecting me, you did tell her I was coming?

MAY: I told her it was pointless being here if she didn't get in touch with old friends here. That it was necessary to, not *why* it was. She agreed. At first she agreed. Then said she wasn't ready to. "But if you're not ready now," I said, "When will you be ready?" She said "Let me think. Oh God! I just can't do it right now!"

VIOLA: Wanted to cancel the meeting with me? Make it later, when she was ready? Well, in that case, I might as well not be here. It wasn't convenient for me. Had to rearrange my schedule for the day. Gave up my morning's work, put off several appointments, including a very important one with a dealer who was quite annoyed. Actually, this is like her. I wonder how many of us would have bothered with her problems, her eccentricities, if in those times she hadn't been the one with—the one that was financially solvent. I know this sounds harsh but—just say I came by and regret she wasn't ready to see me.

MAY: Oh, no, don't go. There's no time to arrange another meeting.

VIOLA: No, there isn't, not with me. You've no idea, of course, about the disorder this cancelled meeting has caused in my plans today. Even in the art world, contrary to opinions outside it, there is a disciplined order of things. Oh, she never observed that, never had to, but I did, all of us did, the group you call her old friends in the city, we had to practice discipline, observe schedules. We still know the necessity of it, all of us survivors. One or two didn't. But the determined ones did, the dedicated ones did. I'm sorry about your disappointment, but— [*She starts off.*]

MAY: Please, please wait.

VIOLA: I tell you I have no time.

MAY: Fifteen minutes? Ten? It's so important. Please understand. When people aren't able to make decisions for themselves, you do have to make them for them.

VIOLA [*consulting her watch*]: Hmmm. —What a curious, what a very strange situation.

MAY: Strangest I've experienced, and most disturbing.

VIOLA: You're really concerned, aren't you?

MAY: Concerned as a friend would be.

VIOLA: Fortunately she has inherited money. I wonder just how much. Considerable, I imagine.

MAY: Enough to afford the expensive— [*She drops her voice.*] —institution.

VIOLA: Hmmm. I wonder if it wouldn't be better to put her in right away or there could be a repetition of the attempt to—

MAY: Hush. I heard a door open.

VIOLA: My God, but this is—spooky . . . she used to have periods of depression but pulled out of them. She had her work and us, her friends, to offer our moral support, in those days.

[*Sounds are heard from offstage.*]

MAY: She's up, out of her bedroom. I do hope she'll come in now. It will be a terrible effort for her. If you see she's tiring out, don't stay. I'll be in touch again. About the Lodge, not a word. She'd go into a panic. Probably run out of the room. Oh, I—

VIOLA: It seems so very unnatural to me. I honestly don't know how to deal with a thing like this. However, I'd do better to follow my instincts than instructions, I think.

MAY: Do be careful what your instincts are.

VIOLA: Oh, I shall. I shall. I've always trusted my instincts.

MAY [*in a whisper*]: She's hesitating to enter.

VIOLA: *Will* she?

MAY: Not so loud. She mustn't hear us talking. Oh, dear, she's retreated to her bedroom.

VIOLA: I think I'll go in and confront here there. Otherwise—

MAY: No, no, no. If she heard you approaching she'd bolt the door before you got to it.

VIOLA: Preposterous! Incredible!

[*There is the sound of hesitant footsteps.*]

KYRA [*offstage, in a shaky voice*]: May?

[*May places a finger to her lips, then returns the call.*]

MAY: Yes, dear?

KYRA [*same voice*]: Who is out there?

MAY: I told you, dear. Your old friend Viola Shield.

KYRA: Oh, I forgot, I'll—

[*Quick footsteps are heard, then a pause.*]

VIOLA: She'll *what*?

MAY: She'll either come out or she won't and I don't know which.

VIOLA: A sort of—paralyzed state?

MAY: Not physical. I mean she moves about, paces the room.

VIOLA: Which room?

MAY: Her bedroom mostly. I hear her at night, getting up, lying back down, then getting up again. I can hardly sleep, especially when I hear her moan "What shall I? Why?"—questions moaned to herself.

VIOLA: Mmm. Paralysis of—decision. —Miss Svenson, it's imperative that she be removed at once to the institution; no other action possible. Surely you see that. Don't you see that?

MAY: I keep hoping for some change, some improvement, but—

VIOLA: I hear the moaning. Sounds agonized.

MAY: "What" or "why" again?

VIOLA: Just a long "Ahhh." A long agonized "Ahhhh." Maybe this Lodge could give her some kind of medication. Something to relieve her. All that I can suggest.

MAY: The Lodge sent someone to try to interview her but got nowhere. She'd hardly speak so they do need this background, this earlier history that old friends can supply.

VIOLA: I'm willing to help all I can but I would like a chance to compare her condition now with when I last observed her, here in the city. [*She glances at her watch.*] I can't wait forever for her to emerge or not. At *most* ten or fifteen minutes. I have an active life. Frankly, I never quite understood her and what you tell me about her present state is definitely unnerving.

MAY: But you can imagine how it is for her?

VIOLA: I'm a reasonably imaginative person, being an artist myself, but this sort of willful retreat from, this sort of—whatever! —No, I'm not able to understand it at all. If one has life and a creative impulse—no, I've never, never, and I hope I will never *ever*—comprehend *giving up!* —that's just not what an artist's life is about as I can possibly conceive it. Creative work is the opposite as life is opposite to—

MAY: Please, not quite so loud.

KYRA [*off*]: What is—?

VIOLA: I hear her voice back there.

MAY: Did you?

VIOLA: Yes.

MAY: What did she say?

VIOLA: I heard "what," just "what." —Does she know you can't stay on? —She knows you're about to go? To leave her to the—

MAY: I can only refer to the matter indirectly. You see her dependence is total.

KYRA [*off, in a tremulous voice*]: May?

MAY: Yes, dear.

KYRA [*same voice*]: Someone's out there. Who is it, May?

VIOLA: An old friend of yours. Recognize my voice, dear?

KYRA: Oh, I don't think I—excuse me, I'll—

VIOLA: She'll what?

MAY: She dreads any encounter. Don't be offended. It's the same with everyone except me, now, and even sometimes with me.

VIOLA: I can't pretend to understand it at all.

MAY: She'll be out when she's worked up the courage. I think I'd better go back there and bring her in here with me. She'll need me with her.

VIOLA: Oh, but you must leave us alone together.

MAY: I'll just sit outside the door because, after all, if the meeting takes a wrong turn, I'll have to interrupt it. You see, you still don't quite understand her condition.

VIOLA: I want some chance to re-establish our old relationship and I can hardly do that with you in here or waiting just outside, eavesdropping, it would be impossibly difficult. Trust my instinct about this.

MAY: —Well—I think she's coming back out. I'll—open the door, now.

[*May opens the door upon an almost apparitional woman, Kyra, a woman in her middle-thirties with the look of a frightened child.*]

MAY: Kyra, this is—well, you know each other.

[*Viola rushes to embrace Kyra.*]

KYRA: Please, please, I—forgot something . . .

VIOLA: Kyra, you sit down. We have a lot to talk over.

KYRA: I—can't talk much. The past is—passed.

MAY: Do sit down, Kyra. Your old friend here has been waiting a long time to see you. I'll go to my room. Just call if you need anything. [*May leaves, closing the door partly.*]

VIOLA: You feel perfectly comfortable with me, don't you, Kyra?

[*Kyra sighs and looks away.*]

VIOLA: So much water has gone under the mill—or over—since the old days, dear, when you and Lola and Joan and I shared that charming apartment on Ludlow Street.

[*Kyra stares as if bewildered. There is a pause.*]

VIOLA: Your, your—companion? Miss Svenson? —she says I must ask no question but we've known each other so long. — I'm going to move my chair close and talk very quietly. There are things that I do have to know.

[*Viola moves her chair close to Kyra's. Kyra looks more frightened.*]

VIOLA: Lola and I are still in the Ludlow place but Lola has taken a loft to work in. She's really making it, Kyra. It all began with outdoor murals.

KYRA [*mechanically*]: Outdoor? Murals? —Are what?

VIOLA: Murals painted on the walls of buildings. They drew attention to her talent. And now she has a gallery exhibiting her work. All of our little group—remember we called it the commune? —all are prospering now, they had to and so they did. Joan, too. You might have thought Joan the least likely, stubbornly persisted in abstract realism long after it had gone out, abandoned it only when her idol, Geeko, looked at her work and simply shook his head at it. Now? George Shelton of Shelton and Shelton, one of the best on 57th Street, has taken her under his wing and is pushing her like mad. You see? You have to recognize inevitabilities and adjust positively. Change! No movement lasts in the city. Oh, and Carruthers, your young Wall Street admirer whom you gave such patronizing attention. Hear this! He's now vice-president of his own firm, draws down a smashing salary. Still unattached. Don't you want to see him? And Patricia, dear old Pat, she's discarded her Southern proprieties, my dear, is living openly with the Dutchman in Webly, openly and quite happily in the nicest part of Webly, the uptown fringe. Huge loft. We gather there once a week, they entertain wonderfully, oh, and finally, finally Bert has shuffled off Steve. To our universal astonishment and relief. Career-wise he shot up soon as he faced the realities of that attachment and cut it off at last. Constructive in every way, while Steve, he's even lost his looks, all he ever had, could never see them myself. Lives in bars, I understand, cadging drinks, I suppose. Now have you heard about Sally? We had a little scare about Sally. You know, a little mole appeared on her cheek, became more prominent and some doomsday dermatologist diagnosed it as a melanoma. You know melanoma? Heard of it? Invariably fatal. Well, it obviously was not. She's thriving! Lord, what a mercy! She's suing the dermatologist for those months of anxiety, desperation, his false diagnosis cost her. Sooo! All our little group's coming through with flying colors. Now about you, Kyra? You're the one exception. [*She consults her watch.*] Snap out of it, dear, it's just a little period of depression brought on by isolation after that irresponsible Canadian took you to Texas and—just walked out on you, did he? Canadian, Texas, impossible on the face of it as we all had warned you. Look. You're back in the city. If you don't care for this place, and I wouldn't blame you, have a real-estate person find you a nice loft, you can surely afford it, and what's past will fade into oblivion. Things do here in the city, rapidly. The rapidity of life in the city doesn't indulge one in time for morbid introspection. Oh, dear, I meant to—you know how my absorption in my work has always made me indifferent to externals such as clothes. Forgive my raffish appearance. My wardrobe is limited as ever. I *must* purchase and remember to wear some smart new outfits now that this important exhibition is about to open at the Baton Blanche. Kyra,

I'm at the brink of a break-through but right now—I do need a loan. Kyra, I need a temporary loan right now.

KYRA: Yes. Alone except for—

VIOLA: L-O-A-N, loan. A financial loan. You've always been so generous. Could you get your accountant, the one with your power-of-attorney, to arrange that for me?

KYRA: Alone.

VIOLA: Temporarily, only a month or two.

KYRA: Yes. Alone except for—

VIOLA: Externals concern me and this temporary loan will take care of it. The smart externals. Fur coat, a really smart outfit or two. Are you listening to me? You look so remote. Inattentive. Hmm. I've monopolized the talk and you show no sign of having listened at all. Why, you look a bit like Joan when she showed her work to Geeko and he just shook his head. —Kyra, tell me what happened, you know you can, anything, we all want to help, so. —What *has* happened, to plunge you into this practically bare ice-plant? [*She gestures about the room.*]

KYRA: Noth—nothing. Just—

VIOLA: Oh, but I know, we all know, just don't know why and there's always a reason. Things like this have reasons.

[*Kyra trembles and gasps.*]

KYRA: Excuse me! Not ready yet! Sorry, sorry . . .

[*She rises. Viola seizes her arm. Kyra calls out. May rushes into the room.*]

KYRA: Help me out, help me out!

[*Kyra stumbles and May catches her.*]

MAY [*to Viola*]: Instinct, what instincts, God knows what you've done!

VIOLA: Kyra, this woman is going to leave you. She's about to. You'll be alone, unless you let us help you. Or you enter a—

KYRA: NO, NO, please go!

[*May supports Kyra out of the room.*]

VIOLA: I made every effort but it's plainly impossible. And this complete day—wasted! [*She leaves the house.*]

[*The sound of Kyra's door slamming is heard.*]

MAY [*off*]: Kyra!

[*There is the sound of pounding at a door, then a pause. May comes back into the room and goes to the telephone.*]

MAY: Doctor, doctor, May Svenson, could you come over? She's locked herself in her room. Come quick as possible, please!

KYRA [*off*]: No, don't!

MAY: Kyra, come out here at once, unlock the door, come in here.

[*Kyra returns, panting.*]

KYRA: Phone the doctor, tell him not to come.

MAY: He will—

KYRA: No, no, can't help. Has that woman left? Is it time you're going away?

MAY: When you're—better. I do have to return to Southern Baptist but you won't be alone. The time has come for a—for a hospital, an—institution, till you've recovered.

KYRA: —When? How soon? Will you leave me? Alone here? [*Pause.*]

MAY: Kyra, you haven't eaten for two days. There's eggs in the fridge and fruit and cheese. I'll prepare you a little lunch. —Will you stay right here?

[*Kyra nods with a senseless look. May exits. Kyra takes a few hesitant steps in one direction, then another. Frightened by the sound of her slippers on the floor, she removes them. She then crosses to each door and bolts them stealthily. That done, she is again undecided of what to do next. At last, she seats herself rigidly in a chair, stage center, and closes her eyes.*]

THE SCENE DIMS OUT

SUNBURST

Sunburst was first performed at the Provincetown Tennessee Williams Theater Festival on September 29, 2007 in Provincetown, Massachusetts. It was directed by Patrick Falco; the lights were designed by Megan Tracy; the costumes were designed by Carol Sherry; the stage manager was Mary Jane Byrne; the offstage voices were supplied by Terrence Keene and Patti Hathaway. The cast, in order of appearance, was as follows:

MISS SYLVIA SAILS	Beverly Bentley
GIUSEPPE	Brian Patacca
LUIGI	Zachary Clause
WOMAN	Patti Hathaway
ATTENDANT	Terrence Keene

SCENE ONE

A lady of somewhat advanced years, in retirement from a long career as an actress, is seated with strange rigidity at a desk framed by the windows of an alcove, stage left or right, as the designer chooses. (I will leave the set description to the designer except to mention, at the appropriate time, pieces of furniture or props.) She occupies a suite in a small but distinguished hotel in the East Fifties or Sixties of Manhattan. Its half-opened bedroom shows that the room is unlighted. In the upstage wall is the entrance from the ninth floor corridor and someone is rapping at it. Miss Sails consults her watch: it is long past midnight. She is suspicious. She attempts unsuccessfully to rise from the desk chair.

MISS MISS SAILS [*to herself*]: Forgot that I couldn't get up— [*Then to an unknown person at the door.*] Who is there, please?

MALE VOICE: Dr. Santa Croce.

MISS MISS SAILS: You don't sound like the doctor. Have been expecting the doctor but unless my hearing's affected you are not Dr. Santa Croce.

MALE VOICE: Afraid your hearing's affected.

MISS MISS SAILS: Not in this way, no, your voice sounds false. If I could get to the phone I would call downstairs for someone to come up and identify you.

[*A young man of Italian descent enters. He is the night clerk, Giuseppe. He is handsome in the sensuous manner of young Southern Italians and wears a one-piece uniform tailored to accentuate his well-proportioned figure, bearing the insignia of the hotel. There is something malignly purring in his voice and it is evident that his entrance without permission has disturbed Miss Sails or, rather, increased her state of alarm.*]

MISS MISS SAILS: Why, Giuseppe, how dare you impersonate Dr. Santa Croce and enter my apartment without permission.

GIUSEPPE: You've had the "Don't Disturb" sign on your door for two days and finally I thought that I'd better have a look at you. You see, I studied medicine for a year before I went into business management. Don't have a stethoscope or the blood-pressure indicator but I can take your pulse.

MISS MISS SAILS: No. You will please leave at once and call Dr. Santa Croce.

GIUSEPPE: That would be very difficult. I can't summon the dead.

MISS MISS SAILS: Dead, did you say dead?

[*Giuseppe nods gravely.*]

MISS SAILS: —Ha! I would be terribly affected by this—this announcement if I believed it.

GIUSEPPE: You don't believe it?

MISS SAILS: Certainly not at all! I would've heard of it immediately since he's the house doctor, resident of the hotel and a close friend of mine for years.

GIUSEPPE: Miss Sails, events do occur in the world even when you're not quite with it, you know. A stroke called the doctor away immediately, well, just a few hours after you suffered yours in the restaurant of the hotel.

MISS SAILS: You give yourself away. I think you know very well that I did not dine in the restaurant last night.

GIUSEPPE: Night before last night.

MISS SAILS: I dined out that night with Mr. Virgil Peterson, retired president of the New York Stock Exchange.

GIUSEPPE: Dined at the stock exchange, did you?

MISS SAILS: I will not put up with your viciously— [*She attempts again to rise, unsuccessfully.*] —Mr. Peterson, *in-val-id,* bed-ridden, the table was set in his bedroom.

GIUSEPPE: How scandalous.

MISS SAILS: This is intolerable, stop it! Did not suffer my misfortune in the hotel dining room, but in the lobby crossing to elevators. Your credibility is—zero minus. —What is your motive, inventing this lie about the doctor?

GIUSEPPE: Regret to say it's the truth. Probably the shock of your "misfortune" brought on his. His death was not immediate. We were almost hopeful of his recovery, he put on such a good show. Lay propped up on three pillows. Wrote prescriptions for himself. Then, all at once, out like a light, permanently.

MISS SAILS: You've often betrayed this instinct to deceive me. Withheld urgent messages for me. Once I surprised you in here at midnight, sneaking about the suite for God or the Devil-knows-what!

GIUSEPPE: Miss Sails, this sort of agitation is not what a good doctor would order. He'd recommend this bottle of *Corvo Bianco,* that our charming young barman, Tony, told me to bring you. Says it's your favorite wine.

MISS SAILS: That bottle's half empty. I drink only *Pouilly Fumé.* And as for the charm of your barman, Tony, he had the impertinence once to brush my bare arm with his person while assuming the waiter's business of pouring wine.

GIUSEPPE: Brushed with what part of his "person"?

MISS SAILS: A part I prefer not to mention.

GIUSEPPE: Oh, back side or front?

MISS SAILS: Front!

GIUSEPPE: I see, I see. With the bulge of his crotch. Miss Sails, ladies of a certain age, especially in your agitated condition, are inclined to imagine little familiarities of that nature.

MISS SAILS: My certain age is seventy-five.

GIUSEPPE: You should never admit it since you don't look it at all. Had various lifts, I suppose.

MISS SAILS: None, ever. If I appear younger, it is due to a healthy regime—Gaylord Hauser's diet.

GIUSEPPE: Ah, *si*. Never mind. Wine for the lady.

MISS SAILS: Not from you or your barman and bottle half-empty, possibly containing poison.

GIUSEPPE: I've heard that you refer to me as that sneaky Wop on the desk at night.

MISS SAILS: Oh, that may be. Since I know the hotel owner, I could've had you discharged and obviously I should have.

GIUSEPPE: Take the wine!

MISS SAILS: You take it, the rest of it. Get good and drunk.

GIUSEPPE: Don't get drunk on wine.

MISS SAILS: On wine after how much hard liquor? Gin! You reek of it.

GIUSEPPE: Take it, I said take it. [*He presses the bottle to her mouth. She keeps it shut tight. He closes her nostrils. She is forced to open her mouth and he pours wine into it. She spits it into his face.*] That was naughty, that was terribly naughty. [*He rips the lace collar off her peignoir.*] You've forced me to damage your beautiful negligee. [*He wipes his face with the lace collar.*] One must have patience with a lady of your eminence in the theater, however long in retirement.

MISS SAILS: Retired at the peak of career, not willing to decline from it. Now what are you doing?

GIUSEPPE: Taking your pulse.

MISS SAILS: Oh, are you? A doctor looks at a watch when taking pulse, you're holding my hand and staring greedily at my sunburst diamond.

GIUSEPPE: I've heard it's a famous diamond.

MISS SAILS: From whom could you have heard this?

GIUSEPPE: Mr. Virgil Peterson's young companion, Luigi, told me about it.

MISS SAILS: That just might be the truth. I've never trusted that boy. Not since Virgil told me he slept beside him at night and, and intimacies—I don't wish to discuss it. Was rather taken aback that Virgil mentioned it to me. Must've been wandering in his mind a bit. Bed-ridden, you know. We must dine in his bedroom with that Luigi with us—smirking, why, sometimes whispering.

GIUSEPPE: Whispering what, Miss Sails? Little frivolous remarks about his ancient employer?

MISS SAILS: Little—whispered—obscenities! Warned Virgil about the boy but—useless! He'd change the subject. —Why are you tugging at the sunburst?

GIUSEPPE: Valuables such as this famous diamond should be kept in the hotel security vault.

MISS SAILS: It does not come off my finger. Having rheumatoid arthritis, the knuckle is so enlarged the sunburst cannot be removed from my finger.

GIUSEPPE: Unless your finger were removed from your hand?

[*Miss Sails gasps and attempts to rise but falls back into the desk chair.*]

GIUSEPPE: You don't appreciate my little joke?

MISS SAILS: For the last time, get out.

GIUSEPPE: Not before the nurse engaged for you comes to replace me.

[*A hypodermic needle falls to the floor as Miss Sails again attempts to rise from the desk chair.*]

GUISEPPE: Now what is this? You've been shooting up something?

MISS SAILS: Vials of Parentrovite, a mega-vitamin obtainable only in England. Mr. Peterson gets them for me through an English friend.

GIUSEPPE: This stuff is kept where?

MISS SAILS: Frigidaire in my kitchenette, of course.

GIUSEPPE: Excuse me while I see for myself.

[*He starts toward the bedroom door, the kitchenette being off the bedroom. Abruptly Miss Sails, with an amazing surge of energy, knocks the desk lamp from the floor and the room is plunged into darkness. We hear her fall to the floor. She crawls to the phone, and manages to lift the receiver.*]

MISS SAILS [*into the phone*]: Operator.

[*Giuseppe emerges from bedroom with a box of vitamins.*]

GIUSEPPE: Now what have we here? To get Miss Sophie on the phone you have to dial "O".

[*He dials "O." The room is faintly illuminated by traffic signals and blurred neon nine floors below.*]

GIUSEPPE: Sophie, baby? No outgoing calls from The Rose Garden Suite. Understand? Unless made by me.

[*There is a knock at door. Luigi enters. He has the same general type of sensuous appearance.*]

GIUSEPPE: *Ciao, caro.* [*He embraces Luigi.*]

LUIGI: Awful odor in here.

GUISEPPE: Yep. Vomit and urine and what we were taught as kids to call "Ca-ca." [*He switches on the overhead light.*]

MISS SAILS: What—vicious—remarks! Before this—partial recovery—used toilet—at that time still too confused to—

LUIGI [*to Guiseppe*]: Flush it, *Subito, prega.*

GIUSEPPE: You do that. Have to watch Miss Sails like a hawk. *Spit wine in my face!*

MALE VOICE AT DOOR: What's going on, what's this shouting about in there? [*Giuseppe covers the mouth of Miss Sails.*]

GIUSEPPE: Attending Miss Sylvia Sails till ambulance arrives.

FEMALE VOICE: Woke us up just now. Would you kindly transfer us to another suite?

MALE VOICE: Yes, fortunately we haven't unpacked, flying west tomorrow.

GIUSEPPE: Will arrange to have you transferred to The Mikado Suite on the twelfth floor at once.

FEMALE VOICE: Do, please, if the ambulance hasn't arrived.

MALE VOICE: Put your wrapper on, honey, we'll go right up.

FEMALE VOICE: Outrageous commotion!

[*The voices subside, grumbling.*]

SCENE BLACKS OUT

217

SCENE TWO

There is a short passage of time.

GIUSEPPE: Bitch bit my hand.

LUIGI: Thought you were going to clear this floor for the night.

GIUSEPPE: All cleared except for that couple.

MISS SAILS [*struggling, mouth still covered.*]: MMMM. MMMM.

LUIGI: What were they doing here?

GIUSEPPE: *Non lo so.* Charlie the night doorman probably put 'em up here.

MISS SAILS: MMMMM!

GIUSEPPE: Shuddup! [*He slaps her.*] Elevator just stopped. Look out.

LUIGI [*peering into the corridor*]: Yep, they took it. All clear now.

GIUSEPPE: Charlie's incorruptible, baby.

LUIGI: *Come tue balle.*

GIUSEPPE: She give him a five dollar tip to call her a cab. Now look here, Miss Sail Away, you've received no punishment like you're going to receive if you raise any more commotion. Just sit there. Remember your past triumphs.

LUIGI: Yes, in reverent silence. Or else.

GIUSEPPE: So watch it. —Come over here, Luigi.

[*They cross to the opposite side of the living room for consultation.*]

GIUSEPPE: You said that sunburst diamond is her most valuable gift from Peterson.

LUIGI: One of the most famous diamonds in world, catalogued in—

GIUSEPPE: Well, it don't come off her. Her goddam knuckles too swollen. Warned the bitch it could be removed by removing the finger. Question is would a missing finger be noticed if she accidentally or in a fit of despondency due to stroke managed to throw herself out the window.

LUIGI: This is just the ninth floor. Not high enough to dismember a tough old bitch like her. What's the top floor, never noticed?

GIUSEPPE: Twelve stories.

LUIGI: Should be higher.

GIUSEPPE: There's a water tower on the roof.

LUIGI: *Stupido!* Who'd think she jumped off a water tower on the roof of this old landmark hotel?

GIUSEPPE: We gotta work this out. Did you come here in Peterson's limo?

LUIGI: Sure.

GIUSEPPE: I'm thinking fast. [*Both are finishing the wine.*] Look. Maybe got the solution. We carry her down the service elevator and to your limo.

LUIGI: And then?

GIUSEPPE: How about you coming up with something, whiz-kiddo?

LUIGI: Gimme time.

GIUSEPPE: Precious commodity, running out fast. Five A.M. and sunup's when?

LUIGI: For me when Peterson rolls over slowly and starts the Bangkok massage mitt with me.

GIUSEPPE: Got it! Haul her to Peterson's. How many stories?

LUIGI: A high-rise, thirty-three stories, he's got a two-story penthouse.

GIUSEPPE: *Perfetto*, there's the solution.

LUIGI: Goddam jus' remembered, didn't come in the limo but a cab.

GIUSEPPE: Why'd you do a fool thing like that, *cretino*?

LUIGI: Car keys confiscated.

GIUSEPPE: By *Peterson?*

LUIGI: No. By female secretary that hates my guts.

[*There is a faint light appearing in the window.*]

GIUSEPPE: *Allora*, you could have taken Sail Away to Peterson's in a cab.

LUIGI: Will you try to think?

GIUSEPPE: You, too. *Anche tu!*

LUIGI: Cab driver would notice something wrong and report it.

GIUSEPPE: *Forse*! The sunburst is worth the risk.

LUIGI: *Da vero*. Think we'd better—think more.

MISS SAILS: "The rabbit—is pounding—the medicine in the moon . . ."

GIUSEPPE: Delirious.

[*The sky through the alcove windows lightens a little.*]

MISS SAILS [*quietly.*]: You have kept a long vigil, yes, the three of us have kept a long and tiring vigil. The options that you have discussed for my disposal, I've heard them and they all strike me as calling for—further—reflection . . . Sylvia Sails and her sunburst diamond have been so long together that separation of them now is difficult to imagine.

GIUSEPPE: Wha' she mimblin'?

MISS SAILS: —Memory test of lines, not for this occasion, or any occasion, just—memory test . . .

"Full fathom five thy father lies.
Those are the pearls that were his"
—no, no . . .
"Of his bones are coral made.
Those are the pearls that were his eyes"
—yes
"—clearing, without rest on three pillows . . .
Nothing of him that doth fade
But—doth suffer a sea change
Into—into something rich and strange . . ."

GIUSEPPE: Ch-rise . . .

[*He crosses to the love seat on which Luigi is resting. Luigi's eyes fall shut. Out of habit, Giuseppe drops a hand on Luigi's thigh.*]

GIUSEPPE [*his voice is liquor-slurred*]: How much did you drink before you came over here to provide ashistance?

[*Luigi breathes loudly in sleep.*]

GIUSEPPE: You pretty, you fuckin' dumb li'l *putana*. Prob'ly dropped off at Club 54— Will you wake up? Shaid wake up. [*He takes a packet of cocaine from a pocket.*] Sniff some a this.

LUIGI [*in his half sleep*]: Wha', Virgie?

[*Giuseppe attempts to sniff some himself, but the packet slips from his fingers.*]

MISS SAILS: Lady Macbeth had no memorable lines but even that ham Evans couldn't kill:

"Tomorrow and tomorrow and—
moves in its petty pace from day to day,
to the last—decibel —Digital? Syllable of recorded time.
And all our tomorrows—yesterdays—have lighted fools
the way to—dusty death . . ."

[*The sky brightens further.*]

MISS SAILS: Gentlemen, it is morning.

GIUSEPPE: Chrise, she's right.

MISS SAILS: Things are stirring, traffic and pedestrians on the street, elevators, chambermaids in the corridor. And the door remains unlocked.

GIUSEPPE [*staggering up*]: Better lock it.

[*A brisk woman enters with an empty suitcase.*]

GIUSEPPE: Luigi, for Chrissake, wake up! —We've had an all night vigil you know, watching over, you know.

WOMAN: Yes, I know. How are you, Miss Sails?

MISS SAILS: I have a friend, a lady of the theater, retired too early as I did. Now when we meet she puts things strangely, not "Good morning, how are you?" But seizes my arm with a wild look and says "How did the fortress of your heart endure?"

WOMAN: Tell me later. I'm packing your essentials right now, at Mr. Peterson's insistence.

GIUSEPPE: Luigi, we've been relieved.

WOMAN: Wouldn't put it that way.

[*Luigi staggers up out of sleep.*]

GIUSEPPE: Le's go, *andiamo.*

[*They start out.*]

WOMAN: Not far.

[*Guiseppi and Luigi exit.*]

WOMAN [*seizing the phone*]: Of course I know Luigi but who's the other?

MISS SAILS: Giuseppe—Yes.

WOMAN [*into the phone*]: Have the police here at once to intercept two young criminals who think they're getting out.

[*With amazing alacrity, the woman packs the "essentials", including a strong box concealed behind a painting. An attendant rolls a wheelchair into the room.*]

WOMAN: For the lady. Roll it to her, please.

MISS SAILS: I think I can make it unassisted, having survived such a night. [*She draws herself up heroically and with tottering steps goes to occupy the wheelchair.*] Morning! —Morning! Sunburst!

[*The stage dims out as she is wheeled out of the Rose Garden Suite by the attendant, and the woman dispatched by Virgil Peterson continues collecting "essentials."*]

CURTAIN

WILL MR. MERRIWETHER RETURN FROM MEMPHIS?

"And we have seen night lifted in thine arms"
—Hart Crane

Will Mr. Merriwether Return from Memphis? was first performed on January 24, 1980 at the Tennessee Williams Fine Arts Center of the Florida Keys Community College. It was directed by William Prosser; the set and costume designs were by Peggy Kellner; the lighting design was by Michael Orris Watson; the choreography was by Mimi McDonald; original music was composed by Ronald Maltai; and the production stage manager was Laura Balboni. The cast was as follows:

LOUISE	Roxana Stuart
NORA	Naomi Riseman
GLORIA	Melissa Leo
THE APPARITION OF VINCENT VAN GOGH	Jim Adams
MISS CALHOUN, a librarian	Jill McEnerney
A "ROMANTICALLY HANDSOME" YOUTH	Arnie Burton
MISS YORKE, an English teacher	Janice White
THE EUMENIDES ONE	Ruth Parker
TWO	Rona Paris
THREE	Barbara Robison
THE INSTRUCTOR AT LA CERCLE	George Gugleotti
MRS. BIDDLE	Tanya Duffy
THE APPARATION OF ARTHUR RIMBAUD	Sam Weman
THE APPARATION OF ISABELLE RIMBAUD, his sister	Cecelia Bierwirth
MRS. ELDRIDGE	Marion Stevens
MR. MERRIWETHER	David Williams
THE DANCERS	Mimi McDonald
	Kerry Garrett
	Gary Gonzalez
	Tony Barnes
	Bettye Harris
	Mercedes Valdez

THE BANJO PLAYER	Dennis Kellog
THE APPARITION OF	
CORNELIUS WADDLES	Barney Barnett
A VOICE FROM THE WINGS	Jeff Nacht

*   *   *

AUTHOR'S PRODUCTION NOTE:

At carefully spaced—not too frequent—intervals in the play a scrim should mask the white room and two or three Negro couples should dance out of the wings and perform a cakewalk to the ragtime music of the banjo. Of course, the banjo should be louder than during the dramatic scenes.

Perhaps a couple should sing, perhaps not. Underlying the gaiety of the dancing should be something of a different nature and I don't know how to define it except by saying it should correspond to Louise's comment—about the iridescent fan removed from her table— "The word for the fan is savage."

PROLOGUE

The principals, or perhaps the entire cast, are assembled on stage. A voice speaks to them.

VOICE: What is this?

PLAYERS: An entertainment.

VOICE: And what am I?

[*A whispered, argumentative conference takes place among the players.*]

VOICE: I ask you "What am I?"

GLORIA: A tiresome old man.

[*Her pretty young mother gives her a look of sharp reproval.*]

GLORIA: And probably dead.

LOUISE [*the mother*]: Gloria! You're being—

GLORIA: Impertinent? What of it? If he's dead he hears nothing and sees nothing and feels nothing.

LOUISE: He was living when he wrote the lines.

GLORIA: Yes, including mine. But isn't now. And I'm tired. We've been rehearsing all day and this is opening night. Face it, mother. He's just another one of your apparitions.

LOUISE: His.

GLORIA: Yours in the play which he calls an entertainment, and I would say the craziest, most improbable of the lot and, if this is an entertainment, why don't we get on with it?

LOUISE: I did not bring you up to be uppity like this, an uppity little—hussy!

GLORIA: A lovely example you set me with your "Mr. Merriwether."

[*Louise looks down, closing her eyes.*]

GLORIA: You have no answer to that.

VOICE: About one thing you were right: let's get on with the entertainment. Pick it up, keep it up. Remember: if it drags, I'll bring on the dancers and drown you out with music.

GLORIA: Who gives a damn, you dirty old—apparition! [*She has sprung up, staring defiantly into space.*] I think we're asked to excuse dead people too much!

[*Louise seizes her wrist. She wrenches free and starts off. Lights blink wildly, ragtime music strikes up, and the dancers sweep on.*]

ACT ONE

SCENE ONE

The action takes place in Bethesda, Maryland, early in the twentieth century. Scene: for all interior scenes of the play the setting is a white room with two enormous windows that look out upon clear evenings in spring. Illogically, between the two windows, is a curtained doorway. The curtain is purple-dark with little glints of silver and gold thread woven into it.

The set also includes a crescent-shaped runway or thrust, which can retract under the main stage when not in use, and it is outlined with light bulbs when in use. The actors sometimes walk or dance out on it. Globes of light above the runway should spell out "Tiger Town."

When the white room represents the home of Louise and her daughter, Gloria, there is a long table parallel to the proscenium. It has a cover which is delicately checkered in pastel colors, and it bears a collection of articles, selected and arranged as if for a painter's still-life. There are chairs at either end of the table, one pale yellow and the other pale blue.

Louise and Gloria sit as silent and motionless as figures in a tableau for several moments. Then a banjo begins to play a ragtime piece—as if at a distance. The banjo player remains on stage at all times, moving closer, or farther back, sometimes into the dark, as the stage directions indicate. Louise rises and carefully lifts from the arrangement of articles on the table a black lace fan which is sprinkled with bits of iridescent metal. Simultaneously the runway is projected from under the set. Along the runway are frosted globes that light up. Louise steps out upon the runway. Behind her, a scrim falls. The scrim is designed and colored with an abstraction of wild roses and clover.

Louise moves to the center of the runway. At the runway's center, she stops and inclines her head slightly to the audience. The banjo is softer. Louise begins to speak as if continuing a reverie.

LOUISE: Today I prepared his room for his return.

[*The banjo player plays "Waiting on the Levee."*]

LOUISE: And today an old Gypsy woman came to the door.

[*The banjo fades.*]

LOUISE: "Ask me the question most important to you," she said, and I said to the Gypsy: "Can I expect Mr. Merriwether to return from Memphis tonight or tomorrow or—?" The Gypsy said—it wasn't exactly an answer—

[*The distant banjo is heard playing a gypsy tune.*]

LOUISE: "He will never forget you." No, not an adequate answer. His life was mine, mine his. I bought some little sachets of dried flowers and herbs from the old Gypsy woman and put them in the back corners of Mr. Merriwether's chiffonier.

[*The scrim is lifted. Louise lifts the hem of her lace dress and returns to the room.*]

GLORIA: You're still dreaming that Mr. Merriwether is going to come back from Memphis?

LOUISE [*angry*]: Did I forget to tell you that he called me, telephoned me from Memphis, last night?

GLORIA: Has he given up his promotion?

LOUISE: There's no such thing as a promotion that takes you away from the woman you love.

GLORIA: Were you asleep when you received this telephone call?

LOUISE: What you mean is that I dreamed that he called me.

GLORIA: He seemed so pleased and proud of being made the sales manager of the—

LOUISE: Yes, at first, but—I won't discuss it with you. I suppose you're going to the library again tonight.

GLORIA: Yes, that's where I'm going. I'm going to the public library to write my theme for English.

LOUISE: Then dress yourself properly for a public place.

GLORIA: I'm properly dressed for a warm night.

LOUISE: For a warm night on the equator, that's what you're dressed for, and can you explain to me why—never mind! Never mind!

GLORIA: I need the big dictionary and the reference books at the—

LOUISE: I said never mind.

GLORIA: I always tell Mrs. Waddles that you'll be alone for a while and she comes right over.

LOUISE: Mrs. Waddles! A creature with a more appropriate name I've never encountered, and the scandal of your appearance in these, these—dresses for the equator, it's me that's blamed. Never mind. Go to the library or the, the—excursion steamer with ten or twelve boys to escort you to the dark upper deck.

[*Gloria picks up a notebook. There is a slight pause.*]

GLORIA: Mother, I think it's a little too late to pretend that we're conventional people.

[*There is a slight pause.*]

LOUISE: For some reason, when you're not well for some reason, you say things in a way you hadn't meant to say them. Of course I know that you're a girl whose feelings, whose sensibilities—you see, I know long words, too—and I know you're a beautiful girl, but Gloria, dear, watch out for early fire. You could—

GLORIA: I could?

LOUISE: Burn! In early fire! [*She descends the two steps from the stage apron.*] At a dance, once, the dance floor was outdoors—

a storm came up suddenly. A lantern, a paper lantern, was blown from—tumbled across the—flamed up as it touched my dress, burned the hem of my dress, burned my ankles. I screamed, started to run. A man caught hold of me. "Stop! Stand still!" —He put the fire out with a bowl of punch! [*She laughs.*] I still screamed. He picked me up in his arms and carried me into the house. There were slices of orange on my burned, wet dress. The room, I think it was dark. He picked the orange slices off my dress that I had been, oh, so proud of, and then he rubbed an ointment, a salve, on my ankles. The room, it was his bedroom. It was light, first. "Quiet, quiet!" he kept whispering. He locked the door of the room. He turned the lamp down. The man—dead, now—was your father. Be careful of early fire! [*She returns to the stage apron. Gloria has left the stage.*] Perhaps I—dreamed that Mr. Merriwether telephoned me last night . . . . [*She returns to the white room as her neighbor, Mrs. Nora Waddles, enters through the curtain.*]

NORA: Louise!

LOUISE: Nora.

[*Nora is a plump little woman of fifty. She wears a frilly apron over an equally frilly lemon-colored frock.*]

NORA: How're you feeling, your daughter let me in, looks more like your sister, I swear on the balls of himself—excuse me. I brought a bowl of strawberries and cream for you. Your weight's fallen off like you was disturbed over something. Here, now, eat 'em, there's powdered sugar on 'em. Delicious. I had two bowls so I know.

LOUISE: I'll save them for a bedtime treat. Excuse me while I put them in the icebox. [*She exits for a few moments through the dark door.*]

NORA: I guess I can't mention it to her, but she's grieving about that young Mr. Merriwether that boarded here. His company transferred him to the office in Memphis. If she misses him that much, why don't she go up to Memphis and—

[*Louise re-enters the room.*]

LOUISE: I had a scene that upset me this evening.

NORA: With who? Who with?

LOUISE: With Gloria. She doesn't dress properly and she walks half a mile through the dark before the gaslights begin. Oh, I—I'm very upset this evening. I suppose I should tell somebody, but who would I tell?

NORA [*softly*]: In late Spring—wildflowers.

LOUISE: Naturally, I am worried sick and—

NORA: Don't let it—

LOUISE: I'm not a competent mother. Do you know I've been told that high school boys wait on the steps of the library where she goes every night on the pretext of writing themes, they wait there for her and when she gets there, oh, it's disgraceful, they all get up and follow her inside like male dogs taggling after a female dog in heat. Since the death of Craig—I, I—just can't cope anymore with—And life does have to be handled or it gets out of hand.

NORA: Forget about it tonight. How about an apparition to distract you, honey? Last night I received one, an' what a one she was!

LOUISE: Anyone that I'd know?

NORA: I took down her name for my records. [*She produces a slip of paper.*]

LOUISE: Oh. Mme. du Barry. Could she speak in English?

NORA: A little but not clearly.

LOUISE: Mme. du Barry was a mistress of King Louis Fifteenth of France.

NORA: Ow. An apparition of importance.

LOUISE: Yes, some, Nora. Her head was chopped off in the French Revolution.

NORA: But it was back on her last night.

LOUISE: I've never exactly admired her. When she was carted to the guillotine, she said to the executioner, "Give me just one moment more."

NORA: Who could blame her for that? Havin' your head chopped off you is no agreeable thing.

LOUISE: One night I received the apparition of Marie Antoinette. When she went to the guillotine she tripped a little on the top step and she said to the executioner, "Sir, please excuse me."

NORA: Well, both of 'em had their heads chopped off 'em. Six of one and—

LOUISE: The queen had dignity.

NORA: That didn't keep her head on her. Tonight, ow, they're moving tonight. There's a fresh wind blowin' too. We'll receive one, huh?

LOUISE: Do you hear a banjo? It must be imagination but every night it seems to be playing a little bit closer and I—

NORA: And you what?

LOUISE: Sometimes I—it—makes me feel like—crying! For no reason at all. I'm almost desperate tonight. You see, since my husband was, was—taken away, I haven't seemed able to handle life anymore, oh, I know, I—excuse me, I'll talk no more about that.

NORA: No, dear, don't work yourself up. Let's turn the lamp down a moment and see if there's a sign of an apparition about. [*She turns down the lamp, the room is dusky blue. she peers out one of the large windows.*] Yep, tonight it's so gusty you'd think you was at the seashore. Hmmm. Yes. I see a patch of mist that's spinning about. That's how they solidify to make an appearance, y'know.

LOUISE: An apparition does not solidify for more than a moment or two before it makes an appearance.

NORA: I know their ways.

LOUISE: So do I.

NORA: You haven't been receiving 'em long as I have.

LOUISE: Well, be that as it may, I've observed their habits.

NORA': The wind is bending the wildflowers in the fields. That'll move 'em, give 'em some locomotion. Oh, this evening, by the balls of Himself—excuse me! —they'll be on the move. Clover's whisperin' as it bends in the wind, oh, and the moon vines have a, a—lumination! They're almost phosphorescent, and the ladies' handkerchiefs, they're unnaturally white, oh, the apparitions are moving tonight! This is a good night for them to wander about the world, we'll have at least one, maybe more.

LOUISE: They rarely appear in pairs.

NORA: Oh, no, not in pairs, in pairs very rarely, but one after the other.

LOUISE: One after the other tires me out and I'm already tired.

NORA: I think it's a pity the apparitions don't move about more in pairs. Now the little song of invitation?

LOUISE: Yes. The song.

[*They sit at opposite ends of the table and sing.*]

LOUISE AND NORA: TURN NOT BACK, GO ON, GO ON,
          ALL THE WORLD IS YOURS TO ROAM.

NORA: A little bit louder, dear. We'll sing it again from the start.

LOUISE AND NORA: TURN NOT BACK, GO ON, GO ON
ALL THE WORLD IS YOURS TO ROAM.
IT ISN'T STRANGE AND SINGULAR TO SEEK
AND FIND NO FINAL HOME.

LOUISE: Better?

NORA: Much.

[*The Apparition of Vincent Van Gogh enters through the curtains.*]

APPARITION OF VAN GOGH [*quietly, shyly*]: Ladies?

NORA: Well, now who is—

APPARITION OF VAN GOGH: I am the apparition of the painter Vincent Van Gogh. I am not alive, I have no existence at all in present time so don't be disturbed by my appearance . . .

LOUISE: We're not disturbed. Is there anything we can do for you?

APPARITION OF VAN GOGH: Thank you, but there's nothing a living person can do for an apparition except to receive him.

LOUISE: Would you like a bowl of strawberries and cream?

APPARITION OF VAN GOGH: Thank you for your kind offer but an apparition has no need to be fed.

NORA: I could have told you that. I've been visited by them so many times that I could have told you, Louise, that an apparition eats nothing and doesn't wish to. Never.

LOUISE: Who did he say he was?

NORA: He said a painter. The name sounded foreign to me.

APPARITION OF VAN GOGH: The only thing that I want is light again and paints and brushes.

LOUISE: Yes, he's the apparition of a painter.

APPARITION OF VAN GOGH: Yes. Even in my last few days in a madhouse, I went on with my painting, on, on, on, till something possessed me to hang myself from a tree. [*He touches his throat.*]

LOUISE [*rising*]: Won't you sit down and rest for a while, you look tired.

APPARITION OF VAN GOGH: Tired, I always looked tired. To be demented is tiring to the person demented and—all who know him—knew him. —Is there light in the room?

LOUISE: Yes.

NORA: Oh, yes.

APPARITION OF VAN GOGH: It's foolish of me to suppose that my apparition could see anything but dark, but—could you, would you hold the lamp directly in front of my eyes?

LOUISE: I am holding a lamp right in front of your eyes.

APPARITION OF VAN GOGH: Thank you.

LOUISE: Do you see light now?

APPARITION OF VAN GOGH: No. The usual dark of an apparition's—vision. Thank you for receiving me. Remember that light is a treasure of incalculable value. Whether you paint or not. Now I— [*He turns back to the curtains.*] Thank you. Good night . . . [*He exits.*]

LOUISE: It's turned cold in the room.

NORA: Doesn't it always after receiving an apparition? To receive an apparition always chills you a little. Always after I have received an apparition, I put on my little pink sweater.

LOUISE: Oh. I've always gone straight to bed.

NORA: No, no, that's the wrong thing to do after receiving an apparition. To go to bed makes your mind dwell on it so you might dream about it when you finally fall asleep. No. Put on a sweater, dear, and if you've got a light robe, I'll slip it on for a while, and we'll talk about other things than the apparition, yes, we'll chat a little with no reference to the apparition of that foreign painter, he did chill me worse than Mme. du Barry did. About to be executed and begging for one minute more.

LOUISE: I've got three light sweaters, excuse me while I— [*She exits though the dark door.*]

NORA: It's the suicides that chill me most. I don't know why. Yes, I do know why. Poor Louise. She's waiting hopelessly for that young drummer to come back for her. Attachments like that are dangerous for widows. Upsetting to the nerves and the system. What am I doing babbling away to myself till she gets back? Ow, the apparition of a lunatic is, yes, it does chill the bloodstream, gives you goose pimples. Brrrr. When she comes back with the sweaters—what's takin' her so long? I'll think of something to change the atmosphere. Ow, I wouldn't part with my apparitions. I know I could. I know I could keep them out by mental resistance to them, but I wouldn't do that, no, poor creatures, they feel nothing I guess and think nothing I know but sometimes they'll have a bit of a conversation with you and that I like since I live alone on a field of clover and wildflowers like dear Louise. Except that she does have her daughter that looks more like her sister. Up to no good at that library. Very hard on Louise. [*She rises.*] Louise? Louise, dear?

[*Louise returns with a pink and a blue sweater.*]

NORA: Oh, there you are.

LOUISE: Yes, here I am. Will you have the pink or blue sweater?

NORA: Either one that's looser, me being on the heavier side a bit.

LOUISE: Nora, I bet that you're a bedtime eater, I bet you eat snacks at bedtime.

[*They are getting into the sweaters.*]

NORA: Ow, that's true, I do that.

LOUISE: I—I had to cry a little over that apparition. It's the first one that we've received together. Isn't that right?

NORA: We're not going to talk about the apparition. Ow. I heard something today. You know there's a good deal of leprosy in this town?

LOUISE: Oh, yes, I've heard there was and still is and I'm still shivering, Nora.

NORA: Keep your mind off the lunatic's apparition, he likely feels nothing at all. Yes, dear, in Bethesda there's an unknown number of leprosy victims, mmm-hmm, hard to be known exactly how many there are, but by the balls of Himself, bless him, bless his heart and his soul, but, yes, it's estimated Louise, that there's at least twenty of 'em, the lepers, I mean, in the town of Bethesda. A doctor will change the subject if you bring it up, but there's about that many, mostly concentrated along Bella Street, y'know, between the white and black sections of town, y'know, and what I was told today is where the families of the lepers keep 'em hidden from daylight.

LOUISE: Attics and basements?

NORA: No, by the balls of Himself—excuse me! —I'm not talkin' proper tonight, it always makes me feel a little unbalanced. No, no, no, no, not in attics or basements, they keep the lepers in old empty cisterns.

LOUISE: Even in the sweater I feel chilly.

NORA: Listen to what I heard today and the chill will disappear, dear. [*She speaks loudly, almost shouting.*] The families afflicted with members afflicted by the disease of leprosy, keep the members IN OLD EMPTY CISTERNS, that's how they hide 'em from daylight, but at midnight, out they come from the old empty cisterns to receive their rations and congregate with each other. Oh, I haven't begun to tell you the shocking part of it, dear. The courthouse clock strikes midnight, out they come from the cisterns for the food their families've set out for them in the back yards. If you drive along Bella Street, you'll notice no dogs along there, just a quiet cat or two, is all you'll notice along there, because the dogs would bark when the lepers climbed out of the cisterns at midnight, no dogs on Bella Street, dear, oh, no, they don't want dogs, with lepers rising at midnight for the leftovers set out for them. There's hardly a sound to be heard, they talk in whispers together under the backyard trees and back of the moon vines on the fences along Bella Street at midnight. You're still shivering, dear. Are you sure you're listening to me? Listen to me, Louise. The lepers are out of the cisterns every night from midnight till just before daybreak. Somebody keeps watch on 'em from a dark window and calls "Lepers in!" just before daybreak, she told me. And back in the cisterns they go with their little packages of rations for the next day, by the balls of himself, excuse me, I'm still chilly myself, but the worst of it, dear, I'll tell you the worst of it, now. Now listen to me, forget the apparition received tonight. The backyards along Bella Street have all big trees, all big shadowy trees, and under the trees, in the shadows of 'em, the lepers not too far gone, they commit fornication together, by the balls of Himself, that they do, they retire to the shadows of the big pecan and oak trees an' there the young lepers, some, y'know, are comparatively not old, they fornicate together in the shadowy yards of Bella Street, and this, hear this, oh, this is a thing to be told, some of them bear children which are born in the cisterns without attendance by a doctor or midwife and not a cry from them in childbirth since everything must be quiet to keep the secret, y'see. Louise, are you feeling less chilly?

LOUISE: No, but, Nora, I have to tell you good night, now. I was expecting someone coming from Memphis but it doesn't seem like Mr. Merriwether—I mean, I mean somebody was going to get back here tonight, so I'd better go to bed.

NORA: I'll stay till you're safe in bed and throw an extra cover over you, dear.

LOUISE: I'd rather be alone, now, Nora, because it—I've heard a banjo all night. Have you heard it, too?

NORA: Yes, dear, playing away in a field, no harm in that, good night, sleep tight, I'll let meself out the door and close it behind me, now remember, no dreams— [*She exits through the curtains and a door is heard shutting.*]

LOUISE: Oh my lord, how she did go on and on, I wouldn't call her a person of very good social presence, but she's a good-natured creature under the skin, for all that. I'll not turn my lamp out tonight. No, no, what did he say? "Even in my madness I had a passion for light, the wonder and glory of light!" —I'll hurry to bed, since Mr. Merriwether isn't apparently going to— [*She has exited though the curtains and her voice dies out. The stage is dimmed out.*]

SCENE TWO

A scrim divides the white room from the forestage. It is delicately tinted violet and rose. Gloria wanders out moodily in front of it and speaks to the audience.

GLORIA: Yes, I wear light dresses. The school rooms have been so warm lately, and the boys—I suppose it's their age that makes their bodies fill the rooms with a sort of warm, heavy muskiness in late spring. It's not offensive to me. It's a natural thing, as natural as the pollination of plants and—flowers. It makes me feel half asleep, so drowsy, sometimes, that I don't hear a teacher's question or my name called to answer it. Questions, they seem to be coming from miles away. And the boys don't sit up straight in their chairs. They, they—loll in their chairs with their legs spread out or a leg thrown over the arm of the chair and—I think if I didn't wear light dresses to school I'd fall asleep and wouldn't hear the bell that ends the class. The teachers are irritated by the lolling and slouching of these older boys. Say to them things like this: "Will you boys kindly make an effort to sit up straight in this classroom, if your spines aren't broken?" [*She laughs a little.*] Sometimes they don't hear it the first time, the teachers have to repeat it, and the boys will sit up for a while, and then loll back again, fingers fiddling with pencils or—resting in their laps. Yesterday a teacher said to one of the boys "Stewart, where is the Bering Strait?" No answer from him. [*She smiles.*] His mind was where his— The teacher marched down the aisle that separates the boys from the girls, geographically speaking, and gave him a shaking and almost shouted at him: "Where is the Bering Strait?" [*Another light, languorous laugh.*] And then his answer was: "Stone Age." You see, he didn't know what class he was in. The air seems to hum. A piece of chalk seems almost too heavy to hold, yes, actually, I'm not exaggerating! Good night. I'd better go in, now.

The white room, altered slightly by lighting and the removal of the table, now represents a room in the public library. A big unabridged dictionary is on a metal stand.

The Librarian, a tense little woman in a pink linen dress, appears from the wings and calls out—.

LIBRARIAN: Oh, Miss McBride, may I speak to you for a moment?

[*Gloria enters the white room from the opposite wings.*]

GLORIA: What is it, Miss Calhoun?

LIBRARIAN: I'm afraid you're not using the library for the purposes it's meant for. And the way that you're dressed!

GLORIA: Is there something wrong about the way I'm dressed?

LIBRARIAN: You're dressed like a girl, like a dancer, playing a nymph in a ballet.

GLORIA [*turning away*]: I don't think the way I'm dressed is your concern, Miss Calhoun? [*She starts back to the wings.*]

LIBRARIAN: Hold on a minute!

GLORIA: Hold on to what?

LIBRARIAN: What I have to say to you.

GLORIA: What do you have to say to me?

LIBRARIAN: I've wanted to speak about this for several weeks now. And I think you know what it is. You come in the library every evening. Go into the reference room and sit at the big table and immediately afterwards all those boys that sit outside till you get here follow you in and sit about you at the big table and sometimes one and sometimes another sits in a chair touching yours, as close as he can get, and I have seen, I have seen! Now if this continues, I will forbid you to enter this library ever again at any time at all!

GLORIA: This is a public library open to everybody in Bethesda and you are just employed here and the reason I come here in the evenings is to write my English themes and if a bunch of boys come in, that is no fault of mine and no business of yours.

LIBRARIAN: Abuses of the library, the purposes of the library, are my business.

GLORIA: Miss Calhoun, the reason that I come here is to use the reference books and the *Webster's Unabridged Dictionary.*

LIBRARIAN: Oh, I've seen you go up to the big dictionary, and right away a boy comes up there beside you and you exchange whispers with him while you pretend to look something up, oh, I've seen and I know. And it will go on no longer!

[*A Romantically Handsome Youth, in white shirt and trousers, comes from the wings. He speaks with a stammer. His stuttering should only be suggested intermittently as indicated in the lines.*]

YOUTH: Gloria, let's go.

[*The Youth and Gloria leave.*]

LIBRARIAN: Yes! Go! And never come back here again!

GLORIA: [*Turning back to her.*] I will speak to the library superintendent!

LIBRARIAN: So will I!

GLORIA: I'll ask him if you have any right to tell me not to use the public library and to insult me as I have never been before in all my life!

YOUTH: Gloria, shhh, let's go. [*They exit.*]

LIBRARIAN: [*She gasps, presses a fist to her month, and turns distractedly this way and that way.*] Phone, yes, call! Immediately report it!

[*The scene dims out.*]

SCENE FOUR

There is a pin-spot on Louise as she holds a telephone of the period.

LOUISE [*in a hushed voice, almost a whisper*]: I want to speak to Mr. Merriwether.

VOICE [*off*]: Would you say that louder, please?

LOUISE [*still in a hushed voice*]: I want to speak to Mr. Merriwether.

VOICE [*off*]: I'm sorry but you'll have to speak louder than that.

LOUISE [*raising her voice a little*]: Mr. Merriwether.

VOICE [*off*]: Did you say Mr. Whether?

LOUISE [*now almost shouting*]: I said I wanted to speak to Mr. Merriwether.

VOICE [*off*]: Oh, Mr. Merriwether?

LOUISE: Yes!

VOICE [*off*]: Mr. Merriwether has asked not to be called after midnight.

LOUISE: He won't mind if I call him. Please, please, call him.

VOICE [*off*]: How do I know if he would mind or not?

LOUISE: It's not long after midnight, only half an hour. It's necessary!

VOICE [*off*]: Well, if— [*Ringing, off. —then a male Voice.*]

MERRIWETHER'S VOICE: Hello? Hello? Who is it? I said who is it, who's calling?

[*Louise draws in a loud breath and replaces the receiver of the phone on its hook as if it might cause an explosion.*]

LOUISE: Don't follow. Don't call. There's nothing to do but wait, with fox-teeth in my heart.

[*The pin spot goes out.*]

SCENE FIVE

The white room is now the English classroom at the library. The English teacher, Miss Yorke, sits at a small desk with a bunch of marigolds in it. The weather outside the window is fair.

MISS YORKE: All but one of you turned in a sorry lot of themes yesterday. As usual the one who turned in a good one was Gloria McBride. Gloria, will you come up here and read your theme to the class.

[*Gloria enters from the wings and goes up to the desk.*]

MISS YORKE: Oh, my, where is it? It was so good I may have left it home. [*She fumbles through a large bunch of themes at her desk.*]

GLORIA: Let me help you, Miss Yorke. I'll look through half and you look through the other half.

MISS YORKE: Thank you, yes. We'll do that.

GLORIA: This is it, here it is.

MISS YORKE: Oh. Good. Read it.

[*Gloria faces the audience and reads her theme to the class.*]

GLORIA: "Yesterday afternoon my geology class went on a field trip up Hinkson's Creek to look for fossils. We didn't expect to find any along the creek, of course, but our objective was the old, abandoned rock quarry. Almost as soon as we arrived there I discovered five or six fossils in the rock walls of the quarry and with my little chisel and hammer and the kind assistance of a boy in the class, I chipped them, or to be more accurate, he chipped them out of the rock. Two of them were fossils of ferns and three were fossils of very early and primitive kinds of organisms that existed in water millions and millions of years ago, you might say an incalculable time ago in the oceans and seas of the earth, which at that time were steaming like huge tea-kettles. I and the boy in the class that chipped the fossils out of the rock quarry for me were so absorbed in our five discoveries that the class went back down Hinkson's Creek without us, and we—"

[*At this point there is snickering by the boys in the classroom. Miss Yorke rises indignantly.*]

MISS YORKE: Stop that right this moment! What are you laughing over? The next one that laughs will go to the principal's office and explain why he did it. Gloria, go on.

GLORIA: I've lost my place. Where was I?

MISS YORKE: You were so excited over the five fossils that you became separated from the rest of the geology class.

GLORIA: Oh. Yes. There. —"We found ourselves alone with our five immeasurably old mementos of the earth's first vegetation and simple one-cell organic beings. The afternoon was fading but still so clear and lovely, and for some reason that I can't analyze and explain, I began to cry and tremble. No, I don't know why. The boy who had chipped the fossils out of the quarry wall for me was mystified by my trembling and crying. I was trembling so that he had to lead me, support me, back up Hinkson's Creek to Indian Road and help me onto a streetcar that took me home, and even when I entered the house and said hello to my mother, I was still trembling and crying a little. She noticed my condition and asked me what had happened. I said to her, "Oh, mother, look at these rocks, these little fossils on them! They give us evidence that there has been life on this earth for more time than we are able to estimate." But she wouldn't look at the rocks, she wasn't interested in them. Then the phone rang. She said, "Oh, that's for me!" She had been expecting a call from a friend in Memphis. But the call wasn't for her. The call was for me and it was a call from the boy who had chipped the fossils out of the quarry rock for me. "Are you all right?" he asked me, "Are you all right now?" I said, "I've almost stopped trembling and I will be at the public library tonight to write an English theme about the geology field trip and I hope by that time I'll know why I trembled and cried." [*She turns to the dark door.*] —I'm sorry, Miss Yorke.

MISS YORKE: I believe I can tell you why the fossils disturbed you. They made you think of how transitory things are. In their living state.

A VOICE FROM THE WINGS: What is "transitory"?

MISS YORKE: Things that pass, things of brief duration. Take these flowers, these marigolds, for instance. They're so lovely today, but tomorrow they'll begin to wither.

THE VOICE: And turn to fossils?

MISS YORKE: Possibly, during the passing of several million years.

THE VOICE: All of us will be fossils by that time.

MISS YORKE: If we have a rock quarry to record our—long— past existence.

[*Gloria, facing the dark door, makes a gasping sound and lifts her hands to her face, turning her head.*]

MISS YORKE: Miss McBride? [*She receives no answer. She rises and turns to the dark door.*] Miss McBride!

[*Gloria's only answer is another gasp.*]

MISS YORKE [*gently*]: Gloria? Gloria?

GLORIA: I'm all trembling again, I—

MISS YORKE: You've only got one more class.

GLORIA: —It's—geology!

MISS YORKE: Would you rather go home now?

[*Gloria nods.*]

MISS YORKE: I think someone in the class should take Miss Mc-Bride to the streetcar.

[*The Romantically Handsome Youth steps out of the wings.*]

YOUTH: I'm the, the, the, the boy—that helped her get the fossils out of rock, and put, put, put—her on the streetcar.

MISS YORKE: Then would you please do it again.

YOUTH: Gloria? [*He takes her hand and leads her into the wings.*]

MISS YORKE: The lesson— [*She takes a sip from a glass of water on her desk.*] The lesson to be learned from Miss McBride's theme is simple in a way and difficult in a way. I think it is that we must dare to experience deep emotion even though it may make us cry and tremble. Will the monitor for this week please erase the blackboard. [*A bell rings.*] The class is dismissed. Not for several million years, just till tomorrow. Good night. Good night . . . [*The white room is dimmed out.*]

Gloria and the Romantically Handsome Youth are sitting on a bench on the projected area of the stage. There is a silence between them.

GLORIA: I hoped you'd say something first.

YOUTH: —I—stutter.

GLORIA: I know that.

YOUTH: —Sometimes it makes me speechless.

GLORIA: It makes no difference to me except that I know it seems important to you.

YOUTH: —To speak is an agony to me.

GLORIA: Even with me? Richard?

YOUTH: —Not as much with you. —At school when I'm asked a question, any question, no matter how well I know the answer—to answer's an agony to me.

GLORIA: I remember one day you were asked to read something aloud in our Spanish class, you said, "I stutter," and old Mr. Quinn said to you "My dear boy, we all know that."

YOUTH: —Yes, I—remember that—day.

GLORIA: I thought it was kind of Mr. Quinn to try to reassure you that way.

YOUTH: —Sometimes you—feel humiliated—by kindness like that, it seems like—condescension.

GLORIA: But it wasn't. It wasn't condescension. It was sympathy.

YOUTH: —Sympathy—is condescension sometimes, and—you don't want it.

GLORIA: It was the kind of kindness that's not at all condescending.

YOUTH: —It didn't help. —I think it—made it—worse.

GLORIA: Do you feel that my feeling for you is condescending sympathy or kindness?

YOUTH: —No.

GLORIA: What you should do, before you speak in school or anywhere else, you should say to yourself, "There's no boy in the school or in the town of Bethesda that's handsome as I am."

YOUTH: —Would you—you wouldn't want me—I'm sure you wouldn't want me—to be—vain enough to—think such a thing as—

GLORIA: I want you to feel confidence in yourself. There's no light in the house. We're sitting in the middle of a field of wildflowers. There's no one to see us. Would it shock you if I took off my dress so it wouldn't be stained by the clover if we lay down in the clover?

YOUTH: —No. —No, it wouldn't. I—don't think it would, but—

GLORIA [*rising from the bench*]: You're sure it wouldn't disturb you or embarrass you at all?

YOUTH: I've had no experience at—what you're—suggesting.

GLORIA: I didn't think you'd had any but I think you ought to have some.

[*There is a pause.*]

YOUTH: Maybe I—

GLORIA: —No?

YOUTH: —It's—

GLORIA: What?

YOUTH: —Something I've—had no experience at, and—

GLORIA: And feel you wouldn't enjoy?

YOUTH: —I—

GLORIA: If I said that I loved you?

YOUTH: —I—

GLORIA: The worst that could happen to you is getting clover stains on your white shirt and trousers, and even that could be avoided, you know. [*Pause.*] Close your eyes for a minute or look the other way.

[*He follows her instruction. She unfastens and steps out of her dress, places it over the bench, and crosses into the wings. After a pause he turns cautiously toward the wings. There is the sound of the distant banjo for a minute.*]

YOUTH: Gloria?

GLORIA [*from the wings*]: Look for me. Find me. I'll be invisible to everyone in the world except to you. I mean if you want to find me.

YOUTH: I want to—find you, but—I don't know a thing.

GLORIA [*offstage*]: Can you tell where my voice comes from?

YOUTH: —Yes.

GLORIA [*offstage*]: Then if you want to find me, come the way that you hear my voice coming from. I'm not far away. The expedition won't be the least bit exhausting . . .

[*As he starts toward her—the scene dims out.*]

SCENE SEVEN

The white room: outside, night. Three crones bearing wooden stools, sewing equipment and a large hourglass, enter through the dark door. Their speech is in Irish brogue.

ONE: I like it not. I suppose we will have to identify ourselves as The Fatal Sisters—which sounds like three hook-nosed spinsters with barely a tooth among 'em.

THREE: An assignment is an assignment.

TWO: And a philosophical attitude is a sign of age advancing.

THREE: Be that as it may, we'll set here for a spell. Set down the hourglass where we can watch it without twisting our heads off our necks.

[*One sets the hourglass downstage. The crones sit behind it. The one called Two is munching at a sausage. Three snatches it from her and tosses it into the orchestra pit.*]

TWO: Ow, I wasn't done with it.

THREE: Wipe the grease off your mouth before I make the announcement.

[*Two swipes at her mouth with her sleeve. Three has remained standing before her stool.*]

THREE [*announcing*]: We are The Fatal Sisters, dispatched to this location to stitch on our fabrics the outcome of a certain initiation occurring in a field of wildflowers.

ONE: Be more specific about it.

THREE: It involves a romantically handsome youth with a stammer and a girl of no less beauty. The Fatal Sisters are not unconcerned with the always precarious matter of—

TWO: Why say more? Ow, let's get on with it.

[*A woman, with the voice of a wildcat, howls off.*]

ONE [*unsurprised*]: That sounds to me like her man has fetched her a clout.

TWO: That he did, and not a light one, aither.

THREE: She interferes with his drinking, she hides his bottle.

ONE: Little good does it do to hide a drinking man's bottle, and she's been long enough in this world to 'ave discovered that fact.

TWO: That she has, t' be sure, and for her trouble the woman is fetched a clout by her man, and howls about it so the neighborhood, knows and the social prestige of the couple is graded not up but down.

ONE: Ow, but ye see, the woman is lacking more than a little up here. [*She taps her forehead.*] And her man would receive no ribbon of honor for a thing but his thing, which rarely he's sober enough t' do more with than piss off his pints in a ditch when he comes staggering home.

THREE: Sisters, heed your talk an' watch your stitching.

ONE: Ow, but I doubt we're more than a vaudeville turn, and not much of that.

THREE: Sisters, stitch, the sooner to be transported to places that suit us better.

TWO: Once upon a time a poet spoke of us. "The Eumenides," he said, "are disclosed in a window embrasure."

ONE: We stitched his death with regret.

TWO: I hope their notion up there— [*She points up.*] —is less than temporary.

THREE: I have them both undressed now in the field of wildflowers.

ONE: A boy that stammers might not get a ready erection, or ejaculate too quick.

TWO: Well, I ever, I never!

THREE: No premature hints, stitch away.

TWO: The hourglass hints, stitch away.

THREE: Turn it, sisters, one of you or the aither. It can't be disregarded.

TWO: It's not my turn to turn it.

ONE: Then let it go unturned till the end of time.

[*Three rises, muttering, and turns the hourglass. Then she turns a disdainful look on One and Two.*]

THREE: She's got his belt off him.

TWO: She's unbuttoned his fly.

ONE: Progress. Ow, he's a broth of a boy!

THREE: It comes but once in a lifetime: the first, frightening rapture.

ONE: Her young-looking mother is half demented over a light-hearted man.

TWO: Will Mr. Merriwether return from Memphis?

THREE: Tell no secrets, sisters. Just stitch away.

ONE: Sometimes I wonder if we know what we do.

THREE: Know it or not we do it, it's our assignment on earth.

TWO: Ow, but she's gone philosophical on us this night here. Know what I'd like?

THREE: What ye'd like ye're not very likely to get.

TWO: I can weave the desire for it into the fabric, sister.

ONE: Ow!

THREE: What's the matter now with ye?

ONE: Stuck meself with me needle.

THREE: Because ye stitch with no mind.

TWO: Why don't we put down our needles and our fabrics for tea or a drap o' the creature?

ONE: Aye, fetch 'em both from the dark room back of ye, sisters, and faster we'll stitch with 'em, in our old, cold bellies.

[*Two goes into the dark door.*]

THREE: How her bones do creak!

TWO: Immortality has she if she likes it or not.

THREE: Assignment, that we have. All with creakin' knee joints that'll support the next thing to forever, all of stitching our fabrics always all the universe over, till the hourglass breaks and I never have seen an object more permanent-looking. Forever pleases me not. It's a condemnation.

[*One returns to the white room bearing on a tray a bottle, kettle and mugs.*]

ONE: Out of the peat bogs she creaks, bearing her pewter kettle, her cups, unscoured, and her bottle of rye.

THREE: Hush a minute, sister. Yes. In a field of wildflowers, the lovely young girl has imparted a tender knowledge to the boy and he'll stammer no more.

[*The white room dims out.*]

SCENE EIGHT

Louise comes out of the purple-dark curtains. Carefully she removes an iridescent fan from the arrangement of fantastic articles on the table. She stands holding it a moment against the bosom of her white dress, as if waiting for a signal to move. The crescent-shaped extension of the stage is projected, its white bulbs are lighted, the distant banjo begins to play a ragtime piece.

Louise nods as if the signal had been given and steps out on the stage right end of the extension and begins to move along it. Her crossing of the extension should be choreographed: it is dance-like. There are several pauses in which she turns to the audience with a gesture of the fan and a smile that has a slight touch of defiance in it. Each time she pauses, she lifts her summer-white dress above her white slippers. When she arrives at the stage left end of the stage extension, or runway, she stops as two stage-hands remove her table and replace it with a desk and several wicker chairs. They set two female dummies on the stage left side of the desk.

Nora enters the white room, finishing a candy bar. The banjo stops. Then Louise steps onto the stage, the lights go out on the extension or runway and the runway draws back. Louise seats herself in a chair beside Nora, who is licking chocolate from her fingers.

NORA: Oh. Louise. Hello.

LOUISE: Good evening, Nora.

NORA: Did you receive one last night?

LOUISE: What? Oh. No, not a one.

NORA: What time did you go to bed?

LOUISE: I think about nine-thirty.

NORA: A little too early for this one. I received this one at eleven-thirty.

LOUISE: I didn't want to receive one.

NORA: Oh, you never receive one if you don't want to, dear.

LOUISE: It's just as well I didn't receive one last night. I wasn't feeling up to it.

NORA: It's just as well you didn't.

LOUISE: Was it a tragic one that you received?

NORA: Yes. Very. And it appeared to me naked.

LOUISE: I've never received an apparition that appeared to me naked.

NORA: I don't think I've received a naked one more than two or three times before and I refused to look at them.

LOUISE: Yes, of course, they don't know it, but it's presumptuous of them to appear to you naked.

NORA: Yes, very presumptuous of them, even though they don't know it.

LOUISE: Perhaps it was an ancient one.

NORA: You mean from ancient times?

LOUISE: Yes, from ancient times.

NORA: Oh, the ancient ones, misty, dear, very misty. They don't solidify well, not well at all, and if they speak, it's a whisper in some ancient language so if they identify themselves to you, it's useless. In your record book you just put down apparition number whatever the number is. They're really not worth receiving. Once I received an ancient one with a spear, with a spear or a club, and it was so filmy I thought at first it was a puff of smoke.

LOUISE [*indifferently*]: Oh, now, no.

NORA: Oh, now, yes, not no. I was baking biscuits and I thought the biscuits were burning until I heard this whisper soft as the buzz of a fly in the next room. Um-hmm. Another ancient one dissolved in the house, right before my eyes, gold helmet and all.

LOUISE: I didn't know that apparitions wore out.

NORA: Oh, yes, dear, they wear out like everything else under the sun and I guess over it, too.

LOUISE: This one you received last night, whose apparition was it?

NORA: How would I know? It whispered in Greek or Latin or Egyptian or something. All I could do was list it in my book as apparition number eight hundred and fifty-six, unidentified, dissolved in my kitchen.

LOUISE: Didn't it seem sort of tragic?

NORA: I hate to say it Louise, but if I received a cheerful apparition it would be for the first time.

LOUISE: I've never received a cheerful apparition. In fact all the ones I've received have been more or less tragic.

NORA: I know they don't feel anything but sometimes I suspect that they know they don't feel anything. No. They don't know anything so how could they know that they don't feel anything.

LOUISE: I have a feeling that sooner or later I'll receive the apparition of a Saint and I hope it's Saint Francis.

NORA: I hope you will if you want to, but they're tragic, you know. I mean they've mostly been martyred. In fact the two saints I've received had both been martyred and I slept not a wink after their appearance and almost shivered the bed down.

LOUISE: The one I want to receive is Saint Francis of the Flowers.

NORA: Even him—not likely to be too cheerful.

[*The French Club Instructor enters through the dark doorway, bearing a suitcase. He is a brisk little man, but is disconcerted to find only four members in the room.*]

INSTRUCTOR: *Mon dieu, seulement quatre ce soir.* Translate. What did I say?

LOUISE: You said, "My God, only four this evening."

NORA: Mrs. Biddle asked me to tell you she was taking her little boy to the movies and would be a bit late.

INSTRUCTOR: Hmmm. Be that as it may. Mrs. Biddle should know that competing with the movies isn't our *raison d'être.* What was the phrase that I spoke in French, ladies?

NORA: I didn't catch it, I'm sorry.

LOUISE: You said, "reason for existence."

INSTRUCTOR: *Bon. C'est vrai.* What did I say in French, ladies?

NORA AND LOUISE [*together*]: *You* said, "Fine. It's true."

INSTRUCTOR: Mrs. Biddle and all of us should know that our club existed for two things, the study of the French language and the confession and purgation of what is troubling our hearts.

[*Mrs. Biddle, a mousy little woman, enters from the dark door.*]

MRS. BIDDLE: *Bonsoir, maître et mesdames du cercle.*

INSTRUCTOR: *Merci, Madame Biddle. Vous êtes un peu en retard.* What did I say in French?

MRS. BIDDLE: You, uh, *maître*, you said I was late—a little . . .

INSTRUCTOR: I'm glad that you understood me. Now, then. *Maintenant.* Who has something in her heart to speak tonight? Behind us is a dark doorway. It represents *l'élément du mystère de la vie.* What did I say? [*There is silence during a pause.*] Mrs. McBride, translate what I said into English.

LOUISE: It doesn't need translation. We've always known it.

INSTRUCTOR: *Oui, mais quelque fois, la plupart des fois—sans pensées, sans paroles.* What did I say? Translate, please, ladies.

THE LADIES: Yes, but sometimes, the greater part of the time, without thoughts or words about it.

INSTRUCTOR: An incorrect translation. Mrs. McBride?

LOUISE: Monsieur?

INSTRUCTOR: Regardless of your realization that it is too familiar, too cliché, would you please oblige me by translating the remark that I made in French about what the dark doorway behind us represents in our lives.

LOUISE: The dark doorway behind us represents the element of mystery in our lives.

INSTRUCTOR: *Assez bien.* Translate. *Tout le cercle.*

THE LADIES: You said good enough.

INSTRUCTOR: *Exactement cette fois.* Now. Who has something to confess. Something in the *belle langue de la française.*

[*There is a pause. Louise starts to rise, then sits back down.*]

NORA: Go ahead, dear. It'll help you.

INSTRUCTOR: Mrs. McBride, you were about to speak?

[*Louise is pressing a little white handkerchief to her nose.*]

NORA: I think she'll speak in a minute.

INSTRUCTOR: In the circle we mustn't repress our emotions and the confession of them.

NORA: She's crying a little but I think she'll speak up in a minute. Won't you, dear?

[*Louise shakes her head.*]

NORA: Shall I speak, dear, till you're ready to speak?

[*Louise nods, sniffling audibly.*]

NORA [*rises*]: Louise and I, we both live—

INSTRUCTOR: *En Français.*

NORA: *Excusez-moi, monsieur—hier soir j'ai préparé un dîner pour deux.*

INSTRUCTOR: Will the other ladies repeat the statement of Mrs. Waddles.

MRS. BIDDLE: Yesterday evening she prepared a dinner for two.

INSTRUCTOR: *Correct. Continuez, s'il vous plaît.*

NORA: *J'avais oublié que mon mari est mort, oh, depuis longtemps, depuis vingt ans.*

INSTRUCTOR: Will the other ladies please repeat this statement of Mrs. Waddles.

MRS. BIDDLE: She started on one subject and switched to another.

INSTRUCTOR: Be that as it may, please speak the statement that Mrs. Waddles just made.

MRS. BIDDLE: She said her husband had been dead for twenty years but yesterday evening she prepared a dinner for two.

INSTRUCTOR: *Continuez, s'il vous plait.*

NORA: *Je crois que j'étais peut-être un peu dérangée. Hier soir.* [*She sits back down.*]

INSTRUCTOR: *Pas du tout*. I think we all know it was a natural error.

[*Louise rises again.*]

LOUISE: *Même dans un rêve—* [*Pause. she touches her nostrils with a small white handkerchief.*]

INSTRUCTOR: *Ce n'est pas tout, j'espère.*

[*Louise shakes her head.*]

INSTRUCTOR: *Il faut continuer.* What did I say?

THE LADIES: You said it is necessary to continue.

INSTRUCTOR: *Oui. Bien.* It is necessary to continue and to complete the confession, Mme. McBride—*s'il vous plaît.* Obviously it is a distressing confession but it will be less distressing if it is delivered completely.

LOUISE: *Même dans un rêve—* [*She is overcome by tears again.*]

INSTRUCTOR: Translate, Mrs. Waddles.

NORA: —Even in a dream.

INSTRUCTOR: Yes, "even in a dream." Mme. McBride, *continuez, s'il vous plaît.*

LOUISE [*composing herself somewhat*]: *Même dans un rêve on peut souffrir—*

INSTRUCTOR: Translate, Mrs. Biddle.

MRS. BIDDLE: "Even in a dream one can suffer."

INSTRUCTOR: *C'est correct. Merci. Mais je pense que c'est n'est pas tout.* What did I say in French?

NORA: You said you thought there was more to the confession.

INSTRUCTOR: Yes. In essence, correct.

NORA [*to Louise*]: Speak out the rest of it, dear, and you'll feel better.

LOUISE: *Je sais.* I know. *Mais c'est difficile.*

INSTRUCTOR: All important confessions are difficult to speak out. Would you like to walk around the table and then complete the confession?

LOUISE: *Non, je peux le faire maintenant.*

INSTRUCTOR: Translate, ladies.

THE LADIES: "I can do it now."

INSTRUCTOR: *Très bien. Continuez, s'il vous plaît.*

LOUISE: *Même dans un rêve on peut souffrir l'angoisse d'une séparation.*

INSTRUCTOR: *Bien, bien, bien, très bien et complètement vrai et très à propos.* Translate, ladies.

THE LADIES: Very good and completely true and—appropriate.

INSTRUCTOR: Now will you please translate the confession of Mrs. McBride.

NORA: *En français?*

INSTRUCTOR: When I say translate I mean translate into English. Will you translate, Mrs. Waddles?

NORA: "Even in a dream you can suffer the agony of a separation." [*She touches her nostrils with a small white handkerchief, too.*]

INSTRUCTOR: Now, Ladies of Le Cercle, I have an equally difficult confession to make. [*He touches his nostrils with his pocket handkerchief.*] In the town of Bethesda I have had the indiscreet habit of going two nights a week, after midnight, to the Greyhound bus station for the purpose of making the acquaintance— [*He rises*

and circles the table to compose himself somewhat.] —for the purpose of making the acquaintance of, of—some youth in the military services of the country who are so often in transit. This habit
has drawn the unfavorable attention of civil authorities who called
upon me today and informed me that I must remove myself from
Bethesda before midnight.

NORA: Ow. What a pity. What a dreadful shame.

INSTRUCTOR: A pity and a disgrace but an order that it would
be very unwise not to accept, so I have come here tonight with my
suitcase and a bus ticket to Memphis. I have not spoken in French
but I have made a confession.

LOUISE: —Memphis is—

INSTRUCTOR: Memphis is what?

LOUISE: As far away as—a memory of—a dream . . .

INSTRUCTOR: *Mesdames, bonsoir—adieu—*the shortest farewell
is the best. (*As he lifts his suitcase and exits. . . .*]

[*The scene dims out.*]

ACT TWO

SCENE ONE

Louise and Nora are seated at opposite ends of the table in Louise's house. They are prepared to receive an apparition.

LOUISE AND NORA: TURN NOT BACK, GO ON, GO ON.
ALL THE WORLD IS YOURS TO ROAM.
IT ISN'T STRANGE AND SINGULAR
TO SEEK AND FIND NO FINAL HOME.

LOUISE: How are their traveling conditions this evening?

NORA: Not bad at all. Comin' across the meadow, I noticed a fair bit of breeze. One's approachin'. The air's gettin' chilly, yes, by the—excuse me. I never known temperature to drop this quick, by the balls of—ow! Excuse me. I, uh.

LOUISE: Yes, it's all right, Nora. I've had some acquaintance with that part of the male anatomy and so I can understand your excited references to it. I mean to them. But perhaps the references could be less frequent, Nora.

NORA: Cornelius, when he was sober, could—

LOUISE: Let's concentrate on receiving an apparition.

NORA: Yes. Let's.

[*An apparition of the poet Arthur Rimbaud, seated in a wheelchair, enters through the curtains. The chair is pushed by an apparition of his sister, Isabelle.*]

NORA: Ow, a pair of 'em, two of 'em at once!

LOUISE: How do you do. Please make yourselves at home. I'm Louise McBride, a widow, and the other, uh, lady is a widow, too.

NORA: I'm afraid these are tragic apparitions, Louise.

APPARITION OF ISABELLE: The wandering has been long.

APPARITION OF RIMBAUD: Interminable, I'd call it. Come through La Mystere, Isabelle.

APPARITION OF ISABELLE: I've come through it, Arthur. I'm directly behind you.

NORA: Identify yourselves, please.

APPARITION OF ISABELLE: My brother is the poet Arthur Rimbaud. I am just his sister. We are speaking English since we know you are English.

NORA: American. How does he spell his name?

LOUISE: Nora, will you be still?

NORA: I need to know for my records. I got three volumes of 'em, and the names of the apparitions all spelled out, exceptin' the ones that spoke Latin. Them that spoke Latin I didn't encourage to linger much in my house.

LOUISE: I'm not familiar with but acquainted by reputation with the gentleman's work.

APPARITION OF ISABELLE: At sixteen my brother became a poet. At twenty he gave it up.

APPARITION OF RIMBAUD: Poetry—*merde*! A thing for café degenerates! Identify me as a man who traded in ivory and firearms in Aden on the Red Sea. Made enough at it to impress my mother who had a farm in the North of France. Then, for no reason, then, my knee turned to cancer. My mother was sufficiently concerned to visit the hospital in Marseilles where my leg was amputated, but not to stay more than the day of the amputation. And resented my sister Isabelle caring for me in the hospital when she, my mother, had gone back to care for the crops.

APPARITION OF ISABELLE: Forget your bitterness, Arthur. These ladies who have received us out of the mist may be oppressed by it. Oh, but what joy he gave me when he consented to receive the last rites of the church!

APPARITION OF RIMBAUD: Yes, to please you. Have we ascended to heaven?

APPARITION OF ISABELLE: It seems there's a time of—

APPARITION OF RIMBAUD: Mist! Wandering mist!

LOUISE: Would he be so kind as to recite a bit of his verse?

[*There is a pause.*]

APPARITION OF RIMBAUD: Yes. I will be so kind. The last verse of *Le Bateau Ivre.*

NORA: Meaning? Please?

LOUISE: *The Drunken Boat.*

APPARITION OF RIMBAUD:

"Of Europe's waters I want now only
the cold and muddy stream where a lonely boy crouches at dusk
to release from his hands a paper boat,
as frail as a butterfly's wing."

LOUISE: Thank you.

NORA: Yeah. Thanks.

LOUISE: I'll read the whole poem at the public library. Is there, isn't there, something I can do for you?

APPARITION OF RIMBAUD: There's something she could do. She could provide you, Isabelle, with a sheet of white paper and a pen and some ink. I want to dictate to you.

APPARITION OF ISABELLE: What do you want to dictate to me, Arthur?

271

APPARITION OF RIMBAUD: I'm determined to return to Aden and get back at my job as a trader and I must write immediately to the head of my firm there.

LOUISE: I don't know where Aden is.

NORA: I never heard of the place.

APPARITION OF RIMBAUD: I have. I know the man's name. The situation is desperate. The letter must go at once. Some paper and ink and a pen.

LOUISE: Yes, of course, here you are.

[*She hands him the articles requested but he can't lift a hand to receive them.*]

APPARITION OF RIMBAUD: Give them to my sister. I'll dictate the letter to her and she'll get it off post express. [*He begins to dictate the letter.*] *Cher Monsieur Le Directeur*: Please let me know at once when my stretcher can be carried aboard a vessel in the morning. We are at the port of Marseilles and any dog in the street can tell you that I am completely paralyzed.

APPARITION OF ISABELLE: Oh, but Arthur, that's no way to apply for a position.

APPARITION OF RIMBAUD: They know me. Trust me. I was excellent as a trader in ivory and—

APPARITION OF ISABELLE: He's closed his eyes now. We will go on. Good night . . .

[*She wheels her brother back through the curtained door.*]

LOUISE: Nora, your teeth are chattering with the cold.

NORA: That they are. I couldn't feel colder if I was a plucked hen on ice.

LOUISE: Go home and put a comforter on your bed. What I'll do is put on a coat and make a few changes in the arrangement of articles on the table. Good night, Nora, sleep tight.

NORA [*starting toward the door*]: I'll drop in tomorrow evening.

LOUISE: You're always welcome, Nora. But give me a call on the telephone first because it's possible that tomorrow a friend of mine who's staying a while in Memphis might return to—what's the name of this town?

NORA: Louise, go straight to bed and forget everything but the comfort of sleep. [*She exits.*]

LOUISE: The possibilities of the possibilities are *sans fin*. Translate. Endless. [*During this line the stage is dimmed out.*]

SCENE TWO

The white room as it appears in the home of Louise. Louise is seated at an end of the table: beside her is a pitcher of iced tea and some glasses. Absently, she pours herself a glass of the tea, then absently dumps the tea back in the pitcher. Nora enters through the dark door.

NORA: Louise?

LOUISE: Nora.

NORA: I was planning to come over but I waited till I saw your daughter, who looks more like your sister, come out of the house, on her way to the public library, I suppose, so she, uh, could let me in, and I, uh, wouldn't disturb you.

LOUISE: I see. Would you like some ice tea?

NORA: No, thanks, dear. Ice tea and me don't agree.

LOUISE: I have nothing else to offer.

NORA: Your company's more than enough.

LOUISE: You're easily pleased.

NORA: I wouldn't say that at all. I invited an apparition but the air's not stirring enough to give 'em locomotion.

[*The conversation comes to a halt that lasts for half a minute. Nora is holding a napkin-covered plate in her lap.*]

NORA: Oh! I almost forgot it! I brought you over an upside-down cake, baked two of 'em, one for you and the other for myself!

LOUISE: What was that? I didn't hear what you said.

NORA: —Just that *I*— [*She puts on glasses and peers anxiously at Louise from her end of the table. she decides to leave the speech unfinished. Soundlessly, with a stealthy expression, she sets the cake on the table.*]

LOUISE: Did you set something on the table?

NORA: I just set down the upside-down cake on a vacant spot on the table.

LOUISE: There is no such thing as a vacant spot on the table.

NORA: Ow, but there was a space with nothing on it, I didn't move anything, not a thing, not an inch!

LOUISE: The spaces on the table are just as important as the articles on the table. Is that over your head?

NORA: I've seen your pitcher of ice tea on the table and glasses for it.

LOUISE: The pitcher of ice tea and the glasses for it are part of the composition.

NORA: The what of the what did you say?

LOUISE: In painting there's such a thing as plastic space.

NORA: Now that's way over my head.

LOUISE: It's very simple.

NORA: I must be too simple for it.

LOUISE: You can be sly as a fly when pretending to be simple.

NORA: Maybe the language was too literal for me, y'know.

LOUISE: If you've ever looked at a painting in your life you must have observed some spaces in the painting that seem to be vacant.

NORA: I've looked at paintings in the museum, dear, and I've seen vacant spaces between the objects painted.

LOUISE: The vacant spaces are called plastic space.

NORA: Ow?

LOUISE: What would a painting be without spaces between the objects being painted? *Rien*. Translate. Nothing. And so the spaces are what a painter calls plastic.

NORA: Plastic, y'mean, like a plastic bottle or—

LOUISE: No. Plastic like the spaces between the objects in a painting. They give to the painting its composition like the vacant spaces on my table give to the articles on the table its arrangement. D'you understand what I'm saying or is it going through one ear and out the other?

NORA: Well, it's less than—totally—clairvoyant, but I do know I'll never set another thing down on the table.

LOUISE: The articles on the table, including the spaces between them, make up a composition that's been admired by important apparitions such as Eleanor of Aquitaine.

NORA: That's one not in my records.

LOUISE: A queen of the Middle Ages, stately, and not much faded.

NORA: Ow . . .

[*There is a pause during which the volume of banjo playing goes up a little.*]

NORA: Is that a banjo playing?

LOUISE: Yes, it's a banjo being played or a—what did you say?

NORA: I just remarked that it's—another evening.

LOUISE: An accurate observation. Time continues according to its habit. Sometimes I pick up this fan which is a white lace fan with bits of mother-of-pearl that give it a hit of a glitter. [*She fans herself with it.*] "I see that you have a starfish on your table." That's what Eleanor of Aquitaine said to me when I received her apparition. Her voice was a little faint. I said, "I beg your pardon?" And she repeated the observation not quite so faintly. I said, "Yes, Madam, there is a starfish among the articles on the table, and there is a conch shell and a rosary and a tinted photograph of a young man named Henry Merriwether and many other articles. Pick out one you'd like, any one that you care for except the tinted photograph of Mr. Merriwether." "How kind of you," she answered, "but I am an apparition and an apparition is unable to carry anything where it goes. Good night, my child. I must go while the wind provides me with a means of going—going . . ." [*She abruptly rises.*]

NORA: Why did you jump up, Louise?

LOUISE: REST-LESS-NESS!

NORA: Oh. —Restlessness, yes, it's a condition that's sometimes called The Widow's Complaint. There's mild forms of it and forms that are aggravated. Sometimes a widow, especially one still young and I think it's excusable of 'em, will, uh, take in a young man as a boarder, and, uh, things, I mean feelings, may develop between 'em, emotionally, y'know, possibly even leading to a re-marriage, but himself, ah, himself— [*She blows her nose.*] Run down by a beer truck on a business trip to Milwaukee while still in his thirties, bless him, after himself I felt never the possibility of a future love in my life, that devoted I was, but what I've been meaning to suggest to you, dear, is that you take more interest in, uh,—civic— enterprises, you know, in, uh, community activities, such as— [*She can't think of any.*]

[*Louise stands motionless with tight shut eyes.*]

NORA: —Well, there must be many, such as— [*She still can't think of any.*] Of course, in our case, in fields of wildflowers on the outskirts of town, we receive apparitions and it gives us a good deal of unusual, uh, distraction, but maybe your being still young and energetic calls for, if you'll excuse me, the first suggestion, if you heard it, and—Oh, my blessed Savior, I left the front door open and someone's come in!

LOUISE [*breathlessly*]: I didn't hear his car but the sound of it may have been lost in the sound of your voice. Excuse me. Go out a window. [*She gasps, sweeps back the purple-dark curtain of the doorway, and exits.*]

NORA: [*Indignantly, to herself.*] Did she say "go out a window"? That I'll not do, not by the balls of Himself, I'll go out nobody's window, and me intendin' t' draw her into discussion of what's eating at her heart like a possum at a persimmon, oh, no, I'll go out a window's not likely in any whirl of the world! —Even if it whirled backwards.

[*A fantastic female creature, Mrs. Eldridge, enters the white room. Her sleeveless gown is Oriental, or pseudo-Oriental. Her arms, hands, face appear to be lacquered, to be covered with a glittering wax. Little silver bells are attached to all her fingers and her jeweled arm-bracelets so that her motions make a musical sound. Sometimes, to emphasize a point, she raises her arms and makes the bells tinkle louder.*

Louise, impressed to the point of forgetting her state of depression, enters behind the lady, Mrs. Eldridge.]

LOUISE: Mrs. Eldridge, this is my neighbor, Mrs. —

MRS. ELDRIDGE [*giving Louise no time to complete the introduction*]: My Phaeton has stopped on the road in front of your house not because of any mechanical difficulties but because the chauffeur had some kind of a seizure. I cracked him over the head with my cane and there was no response so I suspect he—oh! Your house has a fortunate location. Through the right window I can see Tiger Town and the lights of the Bar Apache where I'm expected. But I can't drive the Phaeton myself.

LOUISE: Oh.

NORA: Ho!

LOUISE: Would you like me to call you a taxi?

MRS. ELDRIDGE: Yes, that, exactly, a taxicab with two drivers, one to drive my Phaeton to Tiger Town and the other to return the taxicab to its—

LOUISE: I'll make the call. Sit down, please, I'll— [*She exits through the dark door.*]

NORA: Far be it from me to criticize or comment on your behavior or your outfit, Emerald Eldridge. [*Mrs. Eldridge makes a hissing sound, lifts her arms and sets the little bells ringing.*] A black man with a razor is what you're out for and in for, surely.

[*Mrs. Eldridge repeats the hissing sound and the elevation of her arms and ringing of bells. Louise returns through the dark door.*]

LOUISE: The taxicab with the two drivers is on its way here.

MRS. ELDRIDGE: Thank you, child. I'll wait outside in the field of wildflowers, to lift my heart to the sky with expectations that have never once failed me. [*She raises her arms once more to make the bells ring, pausing at the threshold of the dark door.*]

> "I walk in beauty like the night
> Of cloudless climes and starry skies,
> And all that's best of dark and bright
> Meet in my aspect and my eyes."

[*Mrs. Eldridge exits.*]

LOUISE: Was she an apparition that came uninvited?

NORA: That she should be but isn't, she's a creature still living.

LOUISE: A very strange living creature.

NORA: That she is, to be sure. Sit down, dear, and I'll tell you about her.

[*Louise sits in her chair at the table.*]

NORA: Emerald Eldridge she is, and the richest woman in the town she disgraces.

LOUISE: Her face appeared to be—lacquered.

NORA: That it is. Covered with glittering wax. She had it lifted five times. Am I speaking distinctly?

LOUISE: Yes.

NORA: After five times the face can be lifted no more, five times is the limit, so then she resorted to foreign cosmeticians, oh, by the balls of Himself—excuse me! —she had a slew, a crew of 'em, but after a short while of it, she gave up on 'em, shipped 'em back where they came from. Then the wax-works! Now for her nightly appearances in Tiger Town she has herself covered with glittering wax and from her fingers and arms are suspended these silver bells. And they say—

LOUISE: Who are they?

NORA: Everyone that knows of her, they say she sits motionless in a Tiger Town saloon till she spots a black man that attracts her. Then rises, with difficulty, hisses between her teeth like a serpent, raises her arms and sets the silver bells ringing. Out she goes then. The unfortunate young man follows. She whisks him away to her mansion, and he's never the same after that. His youth is confiscated, his youth is drawn out of him like blood drawn out by leeches or vampire bats, and there I've told you her story and I know it, I know her story.

LOUISE: Perhaps the story, Nora, is less than complete.

NORA: How would you complete it, dear?

LOUISE: It might, it could be, that she is waiting for someone to return from Memphis, or—somewhere . . .

[*The banjo plays louder as the white room is dimmed out.*]

SCENE THREE

Louise is seated at one end of the delicately checkered table. The banjo ragtime is slightly, very slightly, more distinct than in the previous scenes in Louise's white room. She is holding a glass of iced tea, the pitcher beside her. The moon appears serenely through one of the huge windows. Then—after a few moments—Nora comes bustling through the dark door with a bowl of something.

NORA: Louise.

LOUISE [*indifferently, almost with distaste and scarcely turning to look at the habitual visitor—*]: Nora. . . .

NORA [*taken aback somewhat*]: I, uh, I—made some *blancmange* for supper and I brought a bowl of it over.

LOUISE: *Blancmange*. Translate. White magic.

NORA: Won't you eat it right now?

LOUISE: Thank you, Nora, but would you mind putting it in the icebox for me?

[*Nora bustles back into the dark doorway. After a few moments she returns, disconcerted.*]

NORA: Louise, everything I've brought over to you is still in the icebox, untouched.

LOUISE: You shouldn't bother to bring me anything, Nora. I have no appetite, I have no sense of taste.

NORA: Louise, it's possible for a person to get in a state of depression where they won't eat, y'know. [*She sits in the chair at the other end of the table.*] It's possible for them even to get in a state of depression where they won't get out of bed. Of course I know that isn't true in your case. You get out of bed, and not just that, you dress as if you were going to a party. That white lace dress is lovely. All that I'm saying is—

LOUISE [*sharply*]: What is all you're saying?

NORA: —I, uh, shouldn't presume to—intrude, but . . . [*She sits there like a little dog, rejected. After a couple of moments Louise speaks to her, condescendingly.*]

LOUISE: Would you like some ice tea?

NORA: I'd love to, dear, thanks, but I don't dare to. Tea always gives me heartburn. You know, a little bit of gastritis, so I— [*She has begun to cry a little, dabbing her nostrils with a little white handkerchief in her apron pocket.*]

LOUISE: How are the lepers in the cisterns doing, what are they up to lately?

NORA: I have a feeling that you would rather I didn't come over, and it—

LOUISE [*relenting*]: If you didn't come over, nobody would come over.

NORA: —I, uh, brought a deck of cards with me. Would you like a game of double solitaire?

LOUISE: No, I wouldn't, no, thank you, the name of the game is depressing.

NORA: Oh. Sorry. —Casino?

LOUISE: I couldn't play cards tonight.

[*The cards spill to the floor. Nora crouches about picking them up. Louise seems not to have noticed.*]

NORA [*huffing a bit*]: I wonder if maybe you shouldn't take in a new boarder, a, uh, lively young traveling salesman to, uh, be, uh, to, uh—provide some lively company for you.

LOUISE: I am not a promiscuous woman.

NORA: Ow, by the balls of Himself—excuse me! —I meant to suggest nothing of that kind to you, I—

LOUISE: I am not a conventional woman but I am not a promiscuous woman.

NORA: Please, Louise, you know I meant not a thing of that kind, I—

[*There is a slight pause.*]

LOUISE: Among the articles on the table, this evening I noticed this.

[*She lifts and opens an iridescent fan.*]

NORA: Isn't that—I'm trying to think of the right word for it. —Exquisite! That's the word for it.

LOUISE: No, that's not the word for it.

NORA: —Wh-what is the word for it, then?

LOUISE: Savage! —After the nights between us, how could he accept a position to separate us! Oh, I could kill him! The word for the fan is savage! [*She rises with a stricken cry and throws the fan to her feet like a challenging gauntlet. A moment later—the sound of a car approaching and stopping. Louise leans back against the table.*] —Was that a car stopping?

NORA: Don't let it stop your heart, dear.

[*She has also risen: they both clutch the table. Mr. Merriwether steps through a window with a daisy between his teeth. He is an immoderately handsome man in his unusual size. Louise falls into her chair in a fainting condition.*]

NORA: Oh, by the balls of Himself, it looks like she's had a seizure.

LOUISE: You've returned from Memphis?

MR. MERRIWETHER: Don't you see that I'm here?

LOUISE: For just a visit or for a—longer—time?

MR. MERRIWETHER: I've come back to stay. That is, if my old room's vacant.

LOUISE: All the house was vacant till you returned.

MR. MERRIWETHER: I would have returned from Memphis if I'd had to crawl on my belly over brimstone. I wasn't cut out for a sales manager at a desk in an office. I was made for the road.

LOUISE: Because of the wild blood in you.

MR. MERRIWETHER: And the wild blood in you.

NORA: I'd better see what she has in her medicine cabinet.

LOUISE [*fiercely*]: No! Go!

[*Mr. Merriwether rushes up to Louise's chair and crouches by it. She touches his throat, his hair, his face as if she were blind. He draws her up in a rapturous embrace.*]

NORA: It's brandy she needs. I'll fetch it from my house and hurry back. [*She rushes through the dark door.*]

LOUISE: And I was about to follow you to Memphis.

MR. MERRIWETHER: Isn't it better this way? Me returning from Memphis?

LOUISE: Yes, it's better. It's a mistake, a useless mistake, for a woman to follow a man. He's a bird, the shadow of a bird, his home's in the sky, he rests on you for a moment. Then he's gone and after that, look for him in the sky. Try to follow him there. In his wings' hurry, the hurry of his wings, he takes your body but scarcely speaks your name. Oh, did I tell you—?

MR. MERRIWETHER: What?

LOUISE: I found one of your gold collar buttons under the chiffonier.

MR. MERRIWETHER: That's not what I've returned for. My old room's waiting for me?

LOUISE: My life is waiting for you.

[*The Banjo Player springs through one of the enormous windows and strikes up a ragtime piece.*]

LOUISE [*rising and whirling about*]: No more words between us until we're alone and then just whispers! I want to sing, I want to dance! Let's do a fantastic cakewalk to celebrate your return from Memphis.

[*Invisible suspension wires lift the table. Gloria and the Romantically Handsome Youth enter. The two couples do a fantastic cakewalk about the room. Fantastic it is, and rhapsodic, but there is a barely perceptible touch of sadness in it. They suddenly leap out one of the windows, followed by the Banjo Player. Nora returns to find the room empty and the music distant. She puts the little bottle of brandy in her apron pocket.*]

NORA: *Maintenant je suis seule.* Translate. I am alone, now. —*Il faut inviter une apparition.* Translate. It is necessary to invite an apparition. [*She comes downstage.*]

TURN NOT BACK, GO ON, GO ON,
ALL THE WORLD IS YOURS TO ROAM.
IT ISN'T STRANGE AND SINGULAR
TO SEEK BUT FIND NO FINAL HOME.

[*Through the dark door enters a male apparition in a stick-candy-striped silk shirt and pale gray trousers of a dandified cut.*]

APPARITION OF CORNELIUS WADDLES: Nora? [*She gasps—turns about slowly to face the apparition.*] I am the apparition of Cornelius Waddles.

NORA: —Of course I—recognized you.

APPARITION OF CORNELIUS WADDLES: You cooked very well, Nora, and you were always cheerful or pretended to be. You showed no sign of knowing what you must have known: that I was not just sometimes unfaithful, but unfaithful all the time.

NORA: Cornelius, your apparition has made it a little cold in the room. I will—get into this sweater. [*She removes a sweater from the back of a chair and struggles clumsily into it.*] Cornelius, why were you unfaithful to me so much?

[*Ignoring her question, the apparition of Cornelius begins to whistle the ragtime tune played by the Banjo Player. Slowly, a rakish smile appears on his face. The banjo is suddenly much louder. The two couples from the top of the play return through a window, followed by the Banjo Player. Delicate rainbow colors flood the white room and the almost-formalized cakewalk continues. Nora and the apparition of her late husband dance behind the others. The scene dims out.*]

CURTAIN

THE TRAVELING COMPANION

The Traveling Companion was first performed by the Running Sun Theatre Company on May 3, 1996 at Center Stage in New York City on a double bill with *The Chalky White Substance*, collectively titled *Williams' Guignol*. It was directed by John Uecker; the set design was by Myrna Duarie, the costume design was by Robert Guy, and the lighting design was by Zdenek Kriz. The cast, in order of speaking, was as follows:

VIEUX	Bill Rice
BEAU	Michael Harrigan
HOTEL EMPLOYEES	Jack Wernick

SCENE ONE

Lights come up on a bedroom of a New York hotel facing Central Park. The traveling companion, Beau, is standing at the foot of a double bed, his dingy, frayed canvas roll-pack still on his shoulders. He is a blond youth, about twenty-five, gracefully formed, dressed in a manner characteristic of the new youth with a vagrant lifestyle.

His employer, Vieux, is not so much an old man—the actor should probably be considerably younger than the character performed—as one of chronic infirmities such as defective vision, damaged liver, and somewhat mysterious disorders of the digestive system for which his doctors may have prescribed more medications than necessary. His manner is either nervously apologetic or nervously assertive. For the part to be "camped" would be so disastrous that to warn a professional actor against it seems quite unnecessary. The bedroom walls are transparencies: behind them is a cyclorama that later shows a blue-dark sky which includes a full moon through mist.

VIEUX: Having arrived here so dreadfully unnerved.

[*Beau grunts disparagingly without shifting his gaze from the double bed.*]

VIEUX: Should order wine, at once, two bottles and go straight to bed. Oh, God, my medicine kit, don't see the pill-pouch in the carry-on bag. [*He opens and roots through it frantically.*] Ah, *hère,* under manuscripts, what a fright that gave me! Beau, in the future, leave everything that goes in the carry-on bag to me, please.

BEAU [*ominously*]: Future?

VIEUX: You pack only the Val-pack. Naturally, I don't expect you to learn such things so quickly: just remember hereafter that only I take care of the carry-on bag.

BEAU: Hereafter?

VIEUX: This medicine kit would be a disastrous loss, always stuff it into the outside slit to be accessible at any moment— [*He gasps for breath*] —in the event of a coronary heart attack, first two or three minutes are decisive, and planes do strain a heart that's already defective—yes. . . . [*He touches the left side of his chest.*] That flight was well over five hours. I'm not supposed to fly more than four at a time.

BEAU [*still staring at bed as at an armed adversary*]: No shit.

VIEUX: Nerves go. Get short of breath. Used always to carry my own oxygen with me on long hops, transatlantic, small tank called Life-O-Gen, practice I've discontinued since the supersonic came in—unnecessary encumberance. Travel light with all, but all early drafts, only copies self-typed. Trolley deliberately broken by Tyler. Very funny scene. Oh, Lord, poor Tyler—took limit of double rums, when served no more of them, stormed into lavatory, smoked pot with angel dust, ignored the stewardess' calls and line of passengers waiting. When he emerged, was mad as ten hatters. Shouted out "This plane is full of Jews." Of course, this was true, being out of Miami. Shouting, near riot resulted. I quickly moved to other side of plane with carry-on bag, closed my eyes, faking sleep. Personally have no racial prejudice in me, no belief in the individual nor the collective guilt. Appalled by Holocaust, World War Two. But God, do you know when the Holocaust was shown on TV, poor sick Tyler applauded as Jews lined up for death chamber. Have had to send him home to West Virginia, with checks continuing reduced to amount insufficient for self-destruct drugs. He seems to understand this, and I get a letter a week from him now which is like a prose poem. Still love him, but he was as much too much as I am.

BEAU: That's for sure. You are too much.

VIEUX: Better much too much than insufficient, I'd say.

BEAU: Oh, insufficient, am I?

VIEUX: All references aren't to you, Beau. You know. That long flight to Dallas had to be made to check on Andrew's condition before leaving States. Imagine, years younger than me, once my lover, now fallen, so fallen. That Dallas nursing home, appalling beyond belief. His sister abandoned him to it. The odors! —of the incontinent ones unattended, strapped into chairs, comatose but groaning, the nightmare of mumblings, incoherent, of their pain and despair. Well. I did improve matters for Andrew, arranging his transfer to the Catholic home in suburbs with a down-payment. Poor man so touchingly grateful for restoration to life. Experience left me shaken, a person of such sensibility and professional stature, dumped in a place like that by his heartless sister. You never know, you never know . . . whether you'll live to see your old friends again.

[*The sound of a guitar fades in faintly.*]

BEAU: Excuse interruption: will you shuddup? I wanta ask you a question, I wanta know if you expected me to share this double bed with you?

VIEUX: Oh dear, yes, it's a double and I had wired for twins.

BEAU: I thought it was understood I would have a separate single.

VIEUX: Son, you know the hotel situation during Wimbledon, don't you?

BEAU: Ain't this New York and Wimbledon in—?

VIEUX: —Right! —When I'm so exhausted, could be anywhere and not know it. But obviously something must be going on here.

BEAU: That's right, something's going on here that's not connected with tennis.

VIEUX: Political convention or candidate's visit, that's it!

BEAU: That is not it for me.

VIEUX: You know we're lucky to have four walls under a roof here. Oh! The wine, room service till midnight. [*He lifts the bedside phone, changing glasses to peer at the dial. He dials.*] —Bellcaptain, no, no, a mistake, thought I had dialed room service.

BEAU: Dial the desk for my single.

VIEUX: Hello, room service, good night. I would like a bottle of good California Burgundy or the white that's called Eye of the Swan, a *Pinot Noir* called Swan's Eye, *Sebastiani*. No? Then *Salapurata* by Corvo.

BEAU: I said the desk for my separate single.

VIEUX [*to Beau*]: My favorite wine while working, a strongbodied wine is like a strong-bodied boy while I'm working. No more than three glasses of it or I strike the wrong keys. Oh, God, *portable*! —Oh, the other two pieces are not up yet.

BEAU: Mine's on my back till I've got my separate single, tell 'em you're with a strong-bodied boy that must have a single with bath or there is going to be trouble.

VIEUX [*slight pause*]: Trouble, what trouble?

BEAU: Very loud trouble in lobby. Want me to tell 'em about the Dallas misunderstanding and the one on the plane from Dallas when you spread that goddamn blanket over us both?

VIEUX: Cold as it was in that plane, I—

BEAU: I didn't feel cold, I felt your hand on me here! [*He slaps his upper thigh.*] Creeping higher! Want me to talk about that, downstairs at the desk, loud and plain, having been twice molested by a dirty ole man, huh?

VIEUX [*seriously*]: This is not any way for you to behave or talk to me, Beau. Misunderstanding, there's been no misunderstandings. Have you forgotten the night I made your acquaintance at that gay bar, The Wild Mission, in San Francisco when you sat at my table, I couldn't have been more outspoken about my little requirements of a traveling companion, and you understood and you expressed no objections.

BEAU: You were pissed, you were drunk, talkin' loud like an old whore so everyone at the bar was entertained by it and if that bar was gay, it was not to my knowledge.

VIEUX: Beau, you're amusing, a card.

[*The phone rings.*]

VIEUX: Oh, sorry. [*Into phone.*] What wine? All right, then a *Corvo Bianco*, but iced, iced, please, two glasses and two salads, green, with a plate of cold meats for two. [*He cradles the phone.*] Now.

[*Slowly, majestically, Vieux pivots to face the youth. His sovereign expression does not intimidate Beau.*]

VIEUX: —Beau? Why don't you put down that dirty sack still on your shoulders, have yourself a shower and we will watch an old movie, Bette Davis or Crawford on TV, there's usually one of them showing.

BEAU [*crossing to phone*]: You watch those fag hags, not me.

VIEUX: What are you—

BEAU: Gimme the desk, the reception, to correct a serious misunderstanding in room twelve-o-six. [*He pops a Quaalude in his mouth as he waits.*] —Desk, it looks like there's been a mix-up about the accommodations we've got here, not at all as expected, need two separate rooms. —None? Shit. Then how about twin beds with a barbed wire fence between, you know what I mean, I don't share a bed with nobody except my chick, I am this ole man's traveling companion, just that, nothing else but. Come off it. Essex, Essex, what Essex, no diff'rent to me than a bench in Union Square. Want me to come downstairs, straighten things out in the lobby? No? Then call me back when another room is ready and make it quick. Hey. Ain't you the one on the desk when we checked in just now? I place your soprano. And my advice to you is to get yourself a new wig, not carrot-colored so you look like you come out of Ringling Brothers, the circus. [*He slams the phone down. Vieux is shaking his head, aghast.*]

VIEUX: —You can take the boy off the streets but not the streets off the boy. Do you realize how you talked?

BEAU: Fuck it. This Essex-on-the-Park's a refugee camp for fags, what it is. 'Sno wonder you come here.

VIEUX: —That Quaalude you took with your straight double rums on the plane has made you as crazy as Tyler before West Virginia. . . . [*With a dramatically prolonged sigh, Vieux automatically sits down. He rises slowly, and turns on invisible TV, switching channels till he comes to a late movie.*] My God! That's Jimmy Dean with Rock Hudson in *Giant*!

[*The invisible set is soundless. Beau goes to a window and opens it, staring out.*]

VIEUX: —What do you see out the window so fascinating at midnight? —Why don't you take a warm shower to cool you off?

BEAU: I won't be cool till I get a separate room.

VIEUX [*rising and approaching the youth at the deep purple window*]: Now, Beau, I told you in San Francisco I have to have somebody near me at night.

BEAU: A trained nurse would do better.

[*Vieux grabs Beau's shoulders.*]

BEAU: PAWS OFF ME!

[*There is a knock at the door.*]

VIEUX: Shh. —Room-service, I hope, come in.

[*A discreetly dead-pan waiter pushes a rolling-table into the room and sets two straight chairs at it. Vieux produces a bill from his pocket, tosses it onto the table as he signs his check. The waiter nods dreamily and retires from lighted area. Vieux pours himself a bit of wine and tastes it tolerantly. He then fills his glass to overflowing. A siren is heard on the street below and Vieux's face turns somber.*]

VIEUX: —Ambulance rushing, so many emergency nights. — Always a terror when alone in a city, why I must have with me a sympathetic young traveling companion everywhere that I go. Sit down and have some wine.

[*Beau ignores the invitation and remains at the window.*]

VIEUX: Beau? Are you a jumper?

BEAU [*in a drugged drawl*]: What's a jumper?

[*The guitar is heard: lyrical, sad.*]

VIEUX: "Jumpers" is what they are called in San Francisco. Jump out of windows at night or off the Golden Gate bridge. Usually young, but on drugs. The rate's as high as ten jumpers a week now. Look, Beau. I'm fully aware of the difference in our ages and attractions. [*He lifts his hands.*] All that I still desire is the finger touch, fingertips on the bare skin, light and caressing, that only: the Bangkok massage which I learned there. Come away from that window, sit down and drink wine, the cold roast beef is rare with horseradish, the salmon is fresh with capers, delicious, ahhh.

[*There is a knock at door. The porter brings in portable Valpack, is tipped, and grins as he goes out.*]

BEAU: I wouldn't have took this job if I'd known what you want.

VIEUX: Young companionship, privilege of light caresses, I told you, you said okay.

BEAU: In your morbid imagination. Anyway, must fly back to meet Paul.

VIEUX: Paul. Oh, yes, Paul. But you said that Paul's on a fishing boat in Alaska.

BEAU: Was once but is now in San Francisco, arrived there to-night and Paul can't hack it without me.

[*Beau goes to the table and sits on bottom of bed. He drinks wine from the bottle; some of it trickles down his throat.*]

VIEUX: In that case, why did you leave?

BEAU: No money, no room except at—Escort Service. . . .

VIEUX: My God, that's an alarming confession. You come out of Escort Service?

BEAU: Naw, naw, done with it, they cheat you, would rather hustle the bars. But Paul's got that as my address and is hooked on horse. Terrible situation.

VIEUX: —Yes . . . not enviable.

BEAU: We quit high school together six years ago and been on the road ever since. [*Picks meat off platter with hands and stuffs it in his mouth.*] —Long attachments between ush. So. Now I done the job I was hired for, delivered you here. All I ask now is severance pay and return ticket back, so don't irritate me, I can be difficult too.

VIEUX [*seizing bottle as Beau reaches for it*]: —There's cutlery and wine glasses on the table, and as for your plane ticket back to San Francisco, I travel on credit cards only and midnight's too late to use it.

BEAU: Just gimme the cash an' I'll get it myself. You break my balls.

VIEUX [*smiling a little sadly*]: *Tu rompe me balle* is an Italian expression.

BEAU: I know, I known Italians.

VIEUX: Then I would say you have lived.

BEAU: So would I say so. —More wine.

VIEUX [*pouring him a glass*]: —Is that another Quaalude you took from your pocket?

BEAU: What if it is to you?

VIEUX: How about splitting it with me?

BEAU [*washing the Quaalude down with wine*]: —Too late. 'Slife for you, Vieux.

[*Beau stumbles over to the bedside phone and lifts it from the cradle.*]

VIEUX: Calling someone?

BEAU: Yeh. Paul.

VIEUX: To call long-distance you have to dial eight first and then the number.

BEAU: —Operator? —Gotta call San Francisco. Dial? No, can't dial but can give you the number. Hold on a minute, I'll find it.

VIEUX: Want me to make the call for you?

[*Ignoring the offer, Beau removes several slips from his pockets before he finds the right one. Vieux shakes his head in sorrow and bewilderment.*]

BEAU: Operator, I got it, the San Francisco number is Escort Service. —Sorry. No. I mean it's area code four-one-five and number is eight-one-six-four-two-one-nine. —Number of room here?

VIEUX: Room number is twelve-o-six.

BEAU: Twelve-o-shix. —What time's it in San Francisco?

VIEUX: Three hours difference.

BEAU: Later?

VIEUX: Earlier, being West Coast.

BEAU: —Ringing. —'Sthat you, Hank? —Me, Beau. —Awright, awright, jush wanta know if my buddy Paul's arrived there or not. Had to give him your address. —Yeah, that's him, that's Paul, can you get him to the phone? —Unconscious where? —Aw, your room, huh? I know what that means, Hank, God damn you, you don't like me no more than I do you, but LEAVE MY BUDDY ALONE! I—listen! —take advantage of Paul and I'll expose you and your disgusting house there, everything, all, am in position to do! —Don't talk about syndicate to me, I'm traveling with a writer, can give him all facts to write up for national exposure. SYNDICATE—IS NOT—GOD! —Shun of bitch hung up! — Gahhh! —Can't leave Paul alone in a strange place with jumpers. My age, same age, but I got to protect him. Here is picture of Paul, Polaroid in color, taken Palm Springs las' summer.

VIEUX [*looking at photo*]: Ah, yes, lovely—looks blind. . . .

BEAU: Drugged.

VIEUX: But sometimes travels without you, you said to Alaska?

BEAU: Was took there some way by someone and put on this fishing boat and molested by the skipper an' others in crew. Managed— escape to San Francisco. Waitin' at Escort Service , unconscious in Hank's room. Now look. Turn off that TV—sound of it. —All this has worn me out. Gotta sleep till separate—single's—ready. . . .

[*Beau falls back onto the bed, draws a snoring breath. Vieux looks at him, then sadly into space. The stage is dimmed out.*]

Slightly later.

VIEUX: In China they used to give an old man an opium pipe. —I suppose now they just shoot him. [*With a soft, mirthless laugh, he looks down again at the apparently sleeping youth; says dreamily to himself.*] "Cypress woods are demon dark—boys are fox-teeth in the heart." Pathetic fallacy, that . . . [*After a moment, he slowly and warily sits down on the bottom edge of the bed and takes off him shoes, stealthily, as if the act would incriminate him. Looks again at the youth, who makes soft snoring sounds. Suddenly jumps up to remove the bedside phone from its cradle. Returns stealthily to his seated position at the foot of the bed. Removes socks and sniffs them with dissatisfaction.*] A good traveling companion sends the laundry out at nine A.M. for one-day service or says "You'd better buy a new pair of socks in a shop at the airport." New traveling companions reflect the indifferent times we live in, neglect everything but themselves and their own concerns. Got the "give-me's." Give me, give me, give me. But the give-me's don't always get. Unquestionably there is some intellectual as well as moral delinquency in your new type of traveling companion. You can bet your life that the next conscious remark is a request for something, whether direct or implied. [*He looks a bit resentfully at the youth on his bed.*]

BEAU: —I left my guitar in San Francisco.

[*Soft guitar music is resumed.*]

VIEUX: I didn't know you had a guitar.

BEAU: Don't now anymore.

VIEUX: What happened to your guitar?

BEAU: Nothing happened to it except it moved into a hock shop and last week was being displayed in the hock shop window and maybe it's now disappeared from the window having been bought by some poor sucker like me.

VIEUX: If you'd mentioned this before we left San Francisco I would have been happy to redeem your guitar.

BEAU: You woulda redeemed it for me?

VIEUX: Why, yes, of course I would have.

BEAU: But you didn't's the point.

VIEUX: How could I since I didn't know of its existence?

BEAU: I guess it's slipped your mind that you insisted on flying out at ten o'clock in the morning, which meant getting up at eight and catchin' a cab to the airport before the hock shop opened.

VIEUX: A traveling schedule has to be followed strictly. [*He lies down slowly.*]

BEAU: Now what're you doing for Chrissake?

VIEUX: I have to get some rest, too, after a long plane flight. Rest is more important as you get older. Young people require it less than older ones do.

BEAU: What I require is that separate single. They ain't called back about it?

VIEUX: You would've heard the phone if they'd called back.

BEAU: I can sleep through a phone call, but nobody on a bed with me.

VIEUX [*extinguishing bedside lamp*]: There was not any phone call about your separate single or double with twins or about anything else, nothing at all.

BEAU: Then call the desk and remind 'em.

[*There is a pause. The room remains lighted—yellow now turned to blue.*]

BEAU: Didja hear me or have you gone deaf?

VIEUX: Don't you raise your voice at me, Beau, I have some dignity left and I am your employer and do not accept orders from you.

BEAU: Just get your ass off the bed or I'll phone downstairs to the house dick and say I'm bein' molested by an old pervert.

VIEUX: I suspect you were brought up badly to address an older gentleman in a course manner like that.

BEAU: Jesus, what a laugh.

VIEUX: Apparently, Jesus is not amused, nor am I.

BEAU: Jesus.

VIEUX [*sitting up*]: You're speaking to the wrong party. I'm afraid that Jesus is oblivious to you as I am not. Repeat, I am *not*. I delivered you from the lion's den of that bar in San Francisco. You know, when I noticed you there was a disgusting old middle-aged queen beside you with his hand on your ass.

BEAU: I'd told him twice to remove it or pay me one hundred in cash with which I'd redeem my guitar.

VIEUX: One hundred dollars for a guitar? It must have been an electric.

BEAU: Can't play electric guitars in Union Square, San Francisco.

VIEUX: Then there must be a great inflation in string guitars as in traveling companions.

BEAU: Christ.

VIEUX: Still no response from the alleged Redeemer, Son.

BEAU: Fucking atheist, are you? I was brung up a believer.

VIEUX: In what beside yourself and your hocked guitar and your Paul?

BEAU: In Jesus and his mother, and the Ghost, in all Three.

VIEUX: I hope they were "brung up" to believe in you, too.

BEAU: Don't get wise-ass with me. You got mistaken ideas. You think you can just walk into another person's life. I am another person. You see I'm another person. What I'm saying. I'm saying you can't just walk in a place and take over another person's life and take him away like you bought something at a market.

VIEUX: Please stop talking a moment so I can think. You've presented a problem that I've got to think out. I thought it was all understood, but you tell me it wasn't, it isn't, so this presents me with a dilemma. Being unable to go on alone and having no way to go back to—where would I go back to? To me as difficult as reversing the way the earth turns, if that's—more wine—whew! —comprehensible to you.

BEAU: All right, now you stop talking. I stopped talking to let you talk and you said nothing but words and I got something to say so let me talk now you be still.

VIEUX: Please. —Do. —Talk. —Intelligibly if able.

[*There is a knock at door.*]

VIEUX: Come in, come in, not locked!

[*Two hotel employees carry in a cot and set it downstage from the room service table. Automatically Vieux produces a bill: one of them takes it and they leave. The walls begin to become transparent and the light dims out on Vieux and his traveling companion. A distant and cold-hearted moon become visible through mist.*]

BEAU [*finally and softly*]: —If you got me a new guitar tomorrow, I might stay on a while longer. . . .

CURTAIN

SOURCES AND NOTES
ON THE TEXT

The Chalky White Substance
The Chalky White Substance was originally published in issue 66
of *Antaeus* in 1991. The typescript published here is from Williams' then agent, International Creative Management [ICM],
dated 1982; however, in Donald Spoto's biography of Williams,
The Kindness of Strangers (New York: Ballantine Books, 1986), a
script titled *The Chalky White Substances* is mentioned as appearing as early as 1980, and there are drafts in the Harvard Theatre
Collection, one dated "summer 1980."

The Day on Which a Man Dies
The text is from a script in the UCLA Library Department of Special Collections, dated 1960. Although Williams indicated on the
manuscript in his own handwriting that the play was finished in
1960, scholar Allean Hale believes that while he may have up-
dated the play a bit in 1960, it was likely to have been written in
1959. She cites the fact that in his manuscript Williams carefully
changed the "ten year relationship" between Mark and Miriam

to "eleven years," which she sees as echoing the relationship between Williams and his lover Frank Merlo, whom he met in 1947. Merlo died in 1963, and while some sources document their relationship as lasting for fourteen years, others indicate that they were together for closer to eleven or twelve years. The character of Mark, however, may also have been inspired by Jackson Pollack, whom Williams knew in Provincetown, and who was married to Lee Krasner for eleven years, from 1945 until Pollack's death in 1956. Hale surmises that when Williams recovered the manuscript from the warehouse in 1970, he might have recalled it as written in 1960 rather than 1959. Either way, since Williams dated the play 1960, that is the date I chose to honor here.

As Hale also points out, the "God and Mama" speech that occurs in *The Day on Which a Man Dies* is similar to a speech that occurs in *The Night of the Iguana* (1961).

In a later draft of *The Day on Which a Man Dies,* Williams refers to a "plastic theater" as he did in the Production Notes to *The Glass Menagerie*. This later draft contains a collage of cultural and political images from the early 1970s.

A *Cavalier for Milady*

A *Cavalier for Milady* was the center play of a trilogy titled *Three Plays for the Lyric Theatre* (including *The Youthfully Departed* and *Now the Cats with Jewelled Claws*) that Williams was working on in the mid-1970s. He submitted the plays through ICM to New Directions in August 1980, and a copy exists in Columbia University's Williams Archives at the Butler Library. In the Harvard Theatre Collection there is a draft of the play titled *Magic is the Habit of Our Existence*.

This play mentions the television show *Cannon*, starring William Conrad, which was a crime drama series that aired Tuesday nights on CBS from 9:30-10:30 and ran from Sept 14, 1971 to March 3, 1976.

An interesting aspect of this play is that the desire of the women—the Mother and Mrs. Aid especially—is depicted in terms of stereotypically gay male desire, although they are clearly women. The women are predatory and pay "escorts" to satisfy them, even going so far as to have their rendezvous in "The Ramble," a section in Central Park where gay men infamously go "cruising." Moreover, Nance seems to be a composite of Williams, whose father even called him "Miss Nancy," and his sister Rose, who was chastised by her mother for her "inappropriate" expression of desire.

The Pronoun 'I'

The text published here comes from a manuscript found in the files of New Directions. One of the absurdities of *The Pronoun 'I'* is Williams' playful license with the royal lineage of England; of course, there was never a "Queen May," and Williams' invention serves to highlight the play's anti-realism.

The Remarkable Rooming-House of Mme. Le Monde

In 1984 the Albondocani Press of New York published *The Remarkable Rooming-House of Mme. Le Monde* in a limited edition of 176 copies. The probable composition of the play is 1982. According to George Bixby, publisher of Albondocani Press, in 1982 he requested permission of Williams' agent, Luis Sanjuro, to publish a limited edition of *The Traveling Companion*. Sanjuro conveyed to him Williams' feeling that if Bixby wanted to publish something in a limited edition, it might as well be something new and previously unpublished. Williams instructed Sanjuro to send Bixby *The Remarkable Rooming-House of Mme. Le Monde*.

An earlier fragment of the play, titled *A Rectangle with Hooks, or Mint and Hall (a one-act play)* exists in the collections of Columbia University's Butler Library. Other full-length drafts include one titled *A Rectangle with Hooks, or The Remarkable Rooming-house of Mme. Le Monde* from the Harvard University Theatre Collection, and one titled *A Rectangle with Hooks* from the Williams Research Center in New Orleans. In Williams' 1975 novel, *Moise and the World of Reason*, the young writer calls the room that he shares with his lover in the abandoned warehouse "the rectangle with hooks."

Kirche, Küche, Kinder (An Outrage for the Stage)
The text published here is from a manuscript titled *Kirche, Kutchen, und Kinder* given to New Directions by Eve Adamson, who directed the play at the Bouwerie Lane Theatre in New York City in 1979. An earlier draft exists in the New Directions Historical Collection, which contains the alternative title, *Two Organists and Others*.

The Strategic Arms Limitation Talks (SALT) mentioned in the play were negotiations between the United States and the Soviet Union to agree to place restraints and limitations on their central armaments. SALT I, the first round of negotiations between President Nixon and General Secretary Brezhnev that took place from November 1969 to May 1972, resulted in an interim agreement. SALT II, which began in November 1972, led to a long-term agreement and a treaty that was signed by President Carter and General Secretary Brezhnev in June 1979. ". . . a little cyanide with Kool Aid à la Jonesville" refers to the Jonestown Massacre of November 18, 1978, where over 900 members of the "Jonestown Community" in Guyana—a cult from California known as "The People's Temple" and led by the Reverend Jim Jones—took their own lives by drinking Kool Aid laced with cyanide and sedatives.

The way that the Man's revives his unconscious Wife through the "quick Christening" of pouring sour mash into her mouth is reminiscent of the Irish ballad of "Finnegan's Wake," where the deceased Finnegan is resurrected after whiskey is poured into his mouth. The ballad forms the basis for James Joyce's *Finnegans Wake*.

A parallel can be made between the Wife and the Fräulein in *The Gnädiges Fräulein*—another comic German character—in the Wife's attempt at speech, which fails as she "only opens and closes her mouth like a goldfish." In *The Gnädiges Fräulein*, the Fräulein interrupts herself while performing one of her musical numbers, and initiates a non-sequitur gesture of opening and closing her mouth like a goldfish, which Molly explains as "demonstrating." Ultimately, the Fräulein's expression of "the inexpressible regret of all her regrets" occurs outside of language, through the cry of "AHHHHHHHHHHH!" This image occurs again in *The Frosted Glass Coffin* (1980), which ends as Kelsey "opens his jaws like a fish out of water. After a few moments, a sound comes from his mouth which takes the full measure of his grief." A similar moment occurred in Helene Weigel's performance of Bertolt Brecht's *Mother Courage*, during the scene in which Mother Courage is forced to identity the corpse of her son. After her questioners left, Mother Courage opened her mouth, extended fully, and silently mimed a cathartic scream that expressed the grief that could only be expressed outside of language.

The Man's statement that he had written "a number of epic dramas . . . not all of which closed in Boston if opened" is Williams' reference to his first professionally produced play, *Battle of Angels*, which closed during it's Boston tryout after only thirteen days in 1940.

The Man's statement that "Something is impending" recalls Clov's statement in Samuel Beckett's *Endgame* that "Something is taking its course."

A Lovely Sunday for Creve Coeur, which premiered earlier in 1979, also contained a grotesquely comic German character and German references.

Throughout the play, actual German words or phrases are italicized, while faux or phoneticized English meant to sound German is left in roman type.

The lyrics to "Danny Boy" were written to the tune "Londonderry Air" by Frederic Edward Weatherly in 1913. The lyrics and music to "My Wild Irish Rose" were written by Chauncey Olcott in 1899.

Green Eyes

The text published here is based on the script sent to New Directions by Audrey Wood at ICM, along with *The Demolition*

Downtown and *The Reading*, on Sept 17, 1971, and incorporates changes from the revised version that exists in the archives at UCLA titled *No Sight Would be Worth Seeing*.

The Parade

Williams wrote the original draft of *The Parade* in 1940 and gave it to Joe Hazen, who gave it to Andreas Brown of the Gothic Book Mart. In 1962 when Brown was compiling and documenting Williams' oeuvre, he retyped Williams' handwritten draft and sent both to Williams who then rewrote the play. Both manuscripts are in the archive at the Harry Ransom Humanities Research Center. We know that Williams worked on it after 1962, and ICM sent it to New Directions in 1979 in a folder of various odds and ends called *Pieces of My Youth*; this version is the one published here. Even though Williams may have made some minor final changes to the script between 1962 and 1979, the date of composition is 1962.

The first lines of his poetry that Don recites to Miriam come from Williams's early poem, *Sanctuary*, originally published under the name "Thomas Lanier Williams" and reproduced on page 200 of *The Collected Poems of Tennessee Williams*:

> *Let down your hair, dream-dark at night . . .*
> *I shall forget that fear was bright,*
> *I shall evade whatever doom*
> *Was waiting in this narrow room!*
>
> *I am secure locked in this tower . . .*
> *No peril looms beyond this hour,*
> *No foot shall scale this final stair*
> *When you let down your dream-dark hair!*

We have also seen the image of "the parade" as a metaphor in Williams' work before, but used differently. In *The Parade* it's a metaphor for love, but in the 1959 play, *Sweet Bird of Youth*, Chance uses it as a metaphor for ambition: "I'm talking about the parade. THE parade! The parade! the boys that go places that's the parade I'm talking about, not a parade of swabbies on a wet deck."

In both *The Parade* and in *Suddenly Last Summer*, soliciting lovers for someone else is interestingly referred to as "procuring."

The One Exception

The One Exception was originally edited by Robert Bray and published in *The Tennessee Williams Annual Review*, Volume 3, in 2000. The text published here is from the Harvard University Theatre Collection.

Viola describes Kyra's "agonized" moaning as "Just a long "Ahhh. A long agonized "Ahhh." This is strikingly similar to *The Gnädiges Fräulein*, where the Fräulein's expression of "the inexpressible regret of all her regrets" occurs through the cry of "AH-HHHHHHHHH!" (see note for *Kirche, Küche, Kinder*).

Kyra's attempt to avoid emerging from her room with the excuse: "Please, please, I—forgot something . . ." echoes Blanche's desperate attempt to delay her institutionalization in *A Streetcar Named Desire* with the cry "Yes! Yes, I forgot something!" as she rushed back into the bedroom.

Sunburst

The text published here was given to New Directions by John Uecker. In the Harvard Theatre Collection there are fragments of a longer version of the play called *The Sailing Away of Miss Sails* that is clearly an unfinished draft. In the version published here, Giuseppe refers to Miss Sails as "Miss Sail Away" at the beginning of Scene Two.

In both *Sunburst* and *The Traveling Companion* there is a reference to the "Bangkok massage." In *Sunburst*, Luigi complains that Mr. Peterson "rolls over slowly and starts the Bangkok massage mitt with me." In *The Traveling Companion*, Vieux refers to "the finger touch, fingertips on the bare skin, light and caressing, that only: the Bangkok massage which I learned there." Similarly, in *The Pronoun 'I'*, Queen May refers to being a "skin freak": "I have in my fingertips, this sensual stroking compulsion—would classify me as a 'skin freak'?"

Miss Sails' dreamy recitation that "The rabbit—is pounding—the medicine in the moon . . ." may refer to a 12th-century story, *The Rabbit in the Moon*, written during the time when Buddhism was beginning to spread among the masses. The story comes from a collection titled *Konjaku Monogatari*, a series of stories based on Buddhism and morality. It explains why people see a shadow of a rabbit when they look up at the moon.

Miss Sails lives in a hotel suite "in the East Fifties or Sixties of Manhattan," and Williams himself often stayed in the "Sunset Suite" at the Hotel Elysée on East 54th Street in Manhattan, where he died in 1983.

Will Mr. Merriwether Return from Memphis?
Will Mr. Merriwether Return from Memphis? was originally published in *The Missouri Review*, Volume XX, Number 2, 1997. The typescript published here is a copy of the script used for the 1980 production in Key West, provided by ICM. This typescript originally came from the Harry Ransom Humanities Research Center collection and clearly matches the one used in the Key West production in every way, except that the Prologue was left out of the performance script. I restored the Prologue, since Williams clearly intended it to be a part of the script and it does in fact support the anti-realistic style of the play.

Nora's late husband, who appears as an apparition at the end of the play, is named Cornelius, the name of Williams' father. In *A House Not Meant to Stand* the main character is likewise named Cornelius, and in *Something Unspoken*, the main character is named Cornelia. There is also a phone call from a "Mrs. C.C. Bright"; Cornelius Coffin Williams was often referred to as "C.C."

The "plastic space" referred to in the play is also mentioned in Williams' novel *Moise and thr World of Reason* (1975).

The Traveling Companion

The Traveling Companion was originally published in 1981 in *Christopher Street* magazine. An early draft in the Harvard Theatre Collection, which contains pages both typed and handwritten on the stationary of The Berkeley Hotel in London, is titled *Travelling Companions*, and opens on the airplane flight to New York rather than with the arrival at the hotel room.

Abby Mann
Judgment at Nuremberg

Michael McClure
Gorf

Carson McCullers
The Member of the Wedding,
     Introduction by Dorothy Allison

Henry Miller
Just Wild About Harry

Ezra Pound
The Classic Noh Theatre of Japan
Elektra
Women of Trachis

Kenneth Rexroth
Beyond the Mountains (four plays in verse)

Andrew Sinclair
Adventures in the Skin Trade
(based on the novel by Dylan Thomas)

Dylan Thomas
The Doctor and the Devils (film and radio scripts)
Under Milk Wood

Tennessee Williams
Baby Doll & Tiger Tail
Battle of Angels
Camino Real
Candles to the Sun
Cat on a Hot Tin Roof, Introduction by Edward Albee
Clothes for a Summer Hotel
Dragon Country (short plays)
The Eccentricities of a Nightingale
Fugitive Kind

The Glass Menagerie
A House Not Meant to Stand
*Kingdom of Earth
A Lovely Sunday for Creve Coeur
*The Milk Train Doesn't Stop Here Anymore
Mister Paradise and Other One Act Plays,
    Preface by Eli Wallach & Anne Jackson
*The Night of the Iguana
Not About Nightingales
The Notebook of Trigorin
*Orpheus Descending
*Period of Adjustment
The Red Devil Battery Sign
*The Rose Tattoo
Small Craft Warnings
Something Cloudy, Something Clear
Spring Storm
Stairs to the Roof
Stopped Rocking & Other Screenplays
A Streetcar Named Desire, Introduction by Arthur Miller
*Suddenly Last Summer
*Summer and Smoke
Sweet Birth of Youth
The Traveling Companion and Other Plays
27 Wagons Full of Cotton and Other Plays (one-act plays)
The Two-Character Play
Vieux Carré

*available in *Volumes 1* through *8* of
  The Theatre of Tennessee Williams

William Carlos Williams
  Many Loves and Other Plays